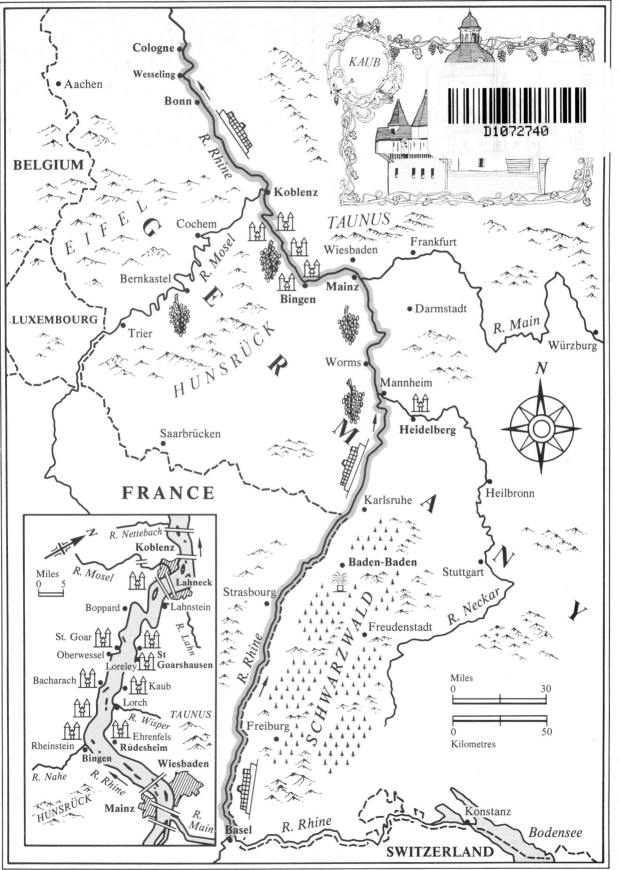

KAUB

BELGIUM

Cologne
Wesseling
Bonn

Aachen

EIFEL

LUXEMBOURG

Trier

FRANCE

Koblenz

Cochem

Bernkastel

HUNSRÜCK

Saarbrücken

R. Mosel

G E R M A N Y

TAUNUS

Wiesbaden

Mainz

Bingen

Worms

Mannheim

Heidelberg

Karlsruhe

Baden-Baden

SCHWARZWALD

Strasbourg

Freiburg

Basel

Frankfurt

Darmstadt

R. Main

Würzburg

Heilbronn

Stuttgart

R. Neckar

Freudenstadt

R. Rhine

Konstanz

Bodensee

SWITZERLAND

N

Miles
0        30

Kilometres
0        50

R. Rhine

**Inset map:**

N

R. Nettebach
Koblenz
R. Mosel

Miles
0    5

Boppard

St. Goar
Oberwessel
Loreley
Bacharach
Rheinstein
Bingen
R. Nahe
HUNSRÜCK

Lahneck
Lahnstein
R. Lahn

St
Goarshausen
Kaub
Lorch
R. Wisper
TAUNUS
Ehrenfels
Rüdesheim

Wiesbaden

R. Rhine

Mainz

R. Main

# THE GRAND TOUR

VENICE SIMPLON
ORIENT-EXPRESS

FOLD BACK AND PEEL

# THE GRAND TOUR

## Hunter Davies

Hamish Hamilton · London

First published in Great Britain 1986
by Hamish Hamilton Ltd
27 Wrights Lane London W8 5TZ

Copyright © 1986 by Hunter Davies

Book design by Craig Dodd
Endpaper maps designed by The Kirkham Studios

British Library Cataloguing in Publication Data

Davies, Hunter
  Grand tour.
  1. Europe – Description and travel – 1971–
  I. Title
  914'.04558      D967

  ISBN 0-241-11907-3

Typeset by Rowland Phototypesetting Ltd, Bury St Edmunds, Suffolk
Printed and bound in Great Britain
by R. J. Acford Ltd, Chichester, West Sussex

# CONTENTS

# ACKNOWLEDGEMENTS

The illustrations are reproduced by kind permission of the following: Sir Harold Acton CBE/Alexander Zielcke, pages 81, 69; Jerry Bauer, page 82; The BBC Hulton Picture Library, page 131 (top); The Mary Evans Picture Library, pages 72, 78; Italian State Tourist Office (E.N.I.T.), London, page 131 (bottom); Mansell Collection, pages 20, 171 (left), 185; Scala Istituto Fotografico Editoriale s.p.a. pages 63, 92, 94, 114, 115 (also by kind permission of Monte Dei Paschi Di Siena); Sporting Pictures U.K. Ltd, pages 122, 123; Venice Simplon Orient-Express, pages 1, 7 (left), 22, 27, 29, 38, 46.

# I
# VICTORIA TO VENICE

The Orient Express
(Paris-Constantinople) in Salzburg Station.

VICTORIA STATION · LONDON

VENICE SIMPLON
ORIENT-EXPRESS
LONDON · PARIS · MILAN · VENICE

# ~ Chapter One ~
# Victoria Station
*On leaving London;*
*M. Nagelmackers' wonderful creation;*
*some interesting passengers;*
*Mr Sherwood's re-creation.*

I arrived early at Victoria Station, heading for Venice. I was about to take a ride on the world's most luxurious train, to savour the delights of a unique artistic re-creation, to experience a phenomenon of the present and re-live the wonders of the past. Unquote. But all the time I was refusing to believe any of it. How could I be about to do anything so exciting on such a dull, dreary day in such a blank, bleary station?

It was mid morning and Victoria's 80,000 early morning commuters had long departed to be busy elsewhere, leaving the station flat and forlorn, except for a few stray souls, hunched and haunted, standing and staring, examining their tickets, looking into their lives, lost in their reveries. Could any of these Lowry figures be going on the Journey of a Lifetime? Could I? I was forty minutes too early. Time for refreshment.

I sat, or at least stood, as the modern method is to provide six inches of sloping plastic and call it a seat, in Casey Jones Burger Place opposite Platform 8, a nightmare creation with neon light so cruel a brain surgeon would find it too strong for operations. It was totally brutal and totally real, proof indeed that I still living in the 1980s. From its open doorway I could read, by straining my eyes, the Continental Departure Board. For over a hundred years, Victoria has been the Gateway to Europe, the Entrance to foreign lands and exotic experiences, yet surely in the heyday of the Golden Arrow, the Brighton Belle, the Night Train, departure must have been more exciting than this. I might as well have been going to East Grinstead.

The station was opened in 1860, named after Victoria Street, not directly after the Queen, and consisted of two separate stations, side by side, one containing broad gauge track (7 feet ¼ inches), and the other standard gauge (4 feet 8½ inches). What chaos that must have caused. Looking around, there still seemed to be a lot of work going on, mainly to do with a high level terminal being built above platforms 9–17 for Gatwick Airport, due to open in 1986.

I decided against a hamburger and stuck to coffee, lingering near the doorway to avoid if possible the nastiest of the smells, but I could feel myself already becoming contaminated. How could I travel with Europe's Quality if I was smelling like a chip shop? I had on my best brown coat, thick tweed, very long and heavy, rather 1920s, so I always like to think, which I bought one midwinter for a journey to Rumania to write about a football team. The microwaves were shooting through it as if were rice paper, impregnating me with a hamburger pong which I feared would be with me across Europe. I also had on a suede cap, a present from my wife many years ago, back in the Sixties, which I was convincing myself still retained a certain period chic.

For the first stage of my Grand Tour across Europe I was determined to try to look the part, especially as I was doing the first leg in what promised to be absolute luxury. There were of course no rules in the old days for what you wore. M'lords would take whole entourages, carriages and baggages full of clothes and uniforms, ready to stun the various courts they hoped to be invited into, plus trunks filled with vital provisions. One's own knives, forks and sheets, they were considered absolutely essential for wealthy travellers in the 17th century, as you couldn't trust those foreigners to provide such things. And door bolts. Mustn't forget them. Goodness knows who might barge into your room in the middle of the night.

On the other hand, Wordsworth set off on his first Grand Tour of Europe with no more than a handkerchief over his shoulder containing a few belongings and the sum of £20 on which he and a student friend hoped to exist for three months. He was wearing an old coat and carrying an oak stick, as he was going to walk the whole way. It was July 1790, the height of the French Revolution, so all round it was a pretty dopey expedition.

Over the 400 years or so since the notion of a Grand Tour began, the image has been mainly that of an English Gentleman touring abroad, perhaps with his family, usually with a servant or two, certainly a man of means and some culture, but in fact a trip across Europe was enjoyed by a variety of people, rich or poor, scholars and students, lords as well as layabouts. Naturally, the aristocracy in the early centuries found it easier than most people to travel. Sir Philip Sidney, in 1572, took three servants with him on his grand tour, doing it in style, getting himself painted in Venice by Tintoretto and Veronese, and his tour in all cost him £1,700.

The main object was almost always to get to Italy, stay there as long as possible, then slowly return through Switzerland, up the Rhine and home, very often taking two to five years over the trip. Most travellers considered it a once and for all experience, which they would probably never do again. France was usually belted through, if France was touched at all, as for so many decades we were at war with France. A true gentleman or scholar needed the Italian experience to feel himself complete. Even Dr Johnson was jealous of those who had visited Italy and admitted an 'inferiority' because he had never been.

What luck then that a new version of the old Orient Express train should so recently have started from London and was now about to whisk me direct to

Venice, the perfect beginning, and in a manner in which we all would like to accustom ourselves, or so the brochures had led me to believe.

I studied them once again, telling myself that of course it must be false, a public relations trick train, how can any normal travellers look as glamorous as those people in those impossibly beautiful photographs. I've been around. I know these advertising and promotional johnnies.

I finished my awful coffee and bid Casey Jones farewell, for ever and ever. I still had fifteen minutes to spare, but I hoped that would be enough time to dispel the fumes.

✻    ✻    ✻

11.44, Platform 8.
VENICE SIMPLON ORIENT-EXPRESS
via Folkestone–Boulogne
Paris, Milan, Venice

Special Luxury Train.

✻    ✻    ✻

In technical books about trains, written by experts for experts, they often have photographs of notices and timetables, of hieroglyphics found on the sides of rolling stock, names and numbers, marks and insignia, most of it incomprehensible to the lay man. The number 4472, for example, may seem perfectly ordinary, but it can send a shiver down the spine of a real railway enthusiast who know that lurking behind that number must be the Flying Scotsman. The name Shildon belongs to an utterly featureless pit village in County Durham, but to engine experts it is part of railway history, as emotive a place name for rail people as Grasmere or Haworth for lovers of literature.

I am a simple railway romantic, one with very little technical knowledge, but I have to admit I did sense a certain quickening as I gazed at the departure board and took in the words 'Orient-Express' and savoured, very slowly, 'Paris, Milan, Venice.' Such images they still conjure up in most British minds. We remain islanders, locked in with ourselves, and, even in this Common Market age and instant aeroplanes we think of Europe as a distant land, where they do things differently. Then I took hold of my imagination, picked up my bag and collected my thoughts. Just another journey. What's so special about going on a train across Europe. My own children would hardly be excited, having done most things except orbit.

Every adult I had talked to during the previous week had certainly *heard* of the Orient-Express, had seen articles or television programmes about it, knew about its incredible luxury, and every one definitely wanted to go on it. I met only one person who did not envy me. My wife. She was totally mystified.

'You are proposing to sit on a train for twenty-five hours? You must be out of your mind.'

It's not just a train, dear, it's a cultural experience, a piece of social history, an artistic event, a unique resurrection.

'Better you than me,' she said as I left home. 'I can't think of anything I'd like less. It sounds like murder, on the Orient-Express . . .'

*　　　*　　　*

It was exactly one hundred years ago that the Orient-Express made its inaugural journey, but its creation was the culmination of several decades of development as various railway companies, inventors and private entrepreneurs competed to offer travellers luxury transport and the sort of amenities traditionally provided by the grand hotels.

In America, the enormous distance encouraged all the companies to introduce as many advances and developments as they possibly could. But it was not until the arrival of George Mortimer Pullman that the quality and *style* of railway travelling dramatically changed.

In 1864 he built what he called the Pioneer, a carriage with its seats covered in embroidered cloth, walls panelled with inlaid mahogany, gold mirrors, brass lamps and deep carpets – a style of interior decor which was echoed in every luxury train coach for the next hundred years. At the time, however, Pullman feared that Pioneer would be a one-off, the end not the beginning of a dream. His prospective customer, the Chicago and Alton Railroad, decided they did not after all want it. They considered it too heavy for the track and too wide for the bridges. So it sat for many months outside Pullman's workshop, unused and deemed unusable.

On 14 April 1865, Abraham Lincoln, while sitting in Ford's Theatre in Washington, was shot in the brain by John Wilkes Booth. Pullman read the horrific news in his newspaper, as did the whole American nation, and later he followed the reports about the funeral arrangements. The President's body was to be taken from Washington to his hometown of Springfield, Illinois. Naturally, it was to be taken by train, as the journey was a long one and trains were an accepted way of American life. Pullman immediately offered his new luxury car as the only fitting and suitable coach for such a train. Through contacts, he managed to see Mrs Lincoln herself who accepted his offer gratefully. Gangs of workmen quickly altered bridges and tunnels and the funeral train set off, proceeding at walking pace, enabling the tens of thousands of people who lined the route to pay their respects. The name 'Pioneer' was prominently displayed and long reports and descriptions of the train appeared in newspapers throughout the United States and all over the world. Can any publicity ever have cost so little and been so effective?

One of the many people who subsequently asked to view over Pioneer was a young Belgian called Georges Nagelmackers, then aged 23, a young European gentleman, doing a Grand Tour in reverse, a year's tour which had begun after an unhappy love affair. He had been rejected, fallen ill and depressed, and his father, a wealthy banker, had suggested a long holiday. Young Georges chose one as far away as possible.

Nagelmackers returned to Belgium and told his father all the details of the Pullman cars. Father and son eventually financed a new company to build luxury sleeping cars, calling it La Compagnie Internationale des Wagons-Lits. As with Pullman, all the Wagons-Lits company ever provided were the coaches. Each individual railway company still owned all the locomotives, stations and all the other bits of rolling stock. A railway company would be offered the use of a Wagons-Lits, or Pullman coach, for free. Passengers paid their normal train fare, plus an extra supplement for using the luxury coaches. That was how the Wagons-Lits company made its money.

Georges Nagelmackers' major ambition, right from his earliest years in railways, was to run his coaches direct from country to country, which of course meant discussions and arrangements with all the various railways and national authorities and other vested interests. Most of all, he wanted to run right through Europe, and out the other end, reaching the Black Sea and thence to Constantinople and the Orient.

He achieved his ambition in 1883 when, on the evening of October 4, the inaugural journey of the Orient-Express began, setting out across Europe for Constantinople. It was the end of several decades of complications and disappointments in the struggle to set up trans-continental luxury express trains and the beginning of a new romantic age of railway travel.

* * *

There was quite a queue for the 1980s' Orient-Express. All the passengers looked smartly dressed with a sprinkling of fur coats, camel hair and some discreet Italian and American accents. Platform 8 at Victoria Station has no atmosphere, little of architectural interest, and it could well do with some careful re-painting and refurbishing, but the officials of the Venice Simplon Orient-Express, to give the present day company its full name, had set up a tasteful little brown and gold desk on the platform. It looked so bright and incongruous plonked down amidst the usual British Rail greyness, as if some film company, trying to create the reception area of a grand hotel, had left behind one of its props.

I checked in, handed over my luggage, which consisted of one small leather hold-all, the sort I normally carry as hand luggage on planes, and processed through a brick archway – and there was the train. It was as if the sun had suddenly come out on a very dull day. It gleamed and dazzled so much that at first I had trouble focussing my eyes. There were eight coaches lined up, each painted in chocolate brown and cream, the traditional colours of the Pullman coaches in England, known and loved by all those who used the Golden Arrow or the Brighton Belle in the great days of train travel.

I have seen some interesting old railway stock over the years, from the wonderfully preserved coaches and locos at the York Railway Museum to the handsome specimens which were trotted out for the cavalcade at Rainhill in 1980 to commemorate 150 years of the Liverpool – Manchester. That was a fine sight. For once, the old engines and coaches were actually moving, or at least being made to move. But here, on the mundane reaches of platform 8, was a real train, with vintage carriages and genuine period furnishings, yet full of real people about to go on a real journey, a museum on wheels yet one which had been recreated to do a proper job.

As in the old days, it was going to be pulled along by somebody else's locomotive, one of those boring BR electrics which we need not dwell too long on, fitting in with an existing BR timetable and using existing BR facilities. Only the coaches and contents belong to the new company.

This new version of the Orient-Express began steaming, I mean 'electricing', out of Victoria in May, 1982. It had taken lengthy arrangements and negotiations to fit it into Victoria, the second busiest London station, and all the continental schedules, just as it had caused Nagelmackers so much trouble one hundred years ago. It was scheduled to leave Victoria just before midday in order to avoid either of the rush hours, something Georges did not have to worry about in 1883.

I found my seat, which was on *Phoenix* – every coach has a name, apart from the baggage coach – a first class parlour car which was built by the Metropolitan Cammell Carriage and Wagon Company at Saltley, Birmingham, in 1927. In 1953 it brought foreign dignitaries from Dover to London for the Coronation and it was also used frequently by the Royal Family and by visiting heads of state such as General de Gaulle. From 1952 to 1972 it was part of the Golden Arrow, until it was put out to grass in 1972. It was left in storage for a while in Brighton, then it was turned into a stationary restaurant in Lyons. It was bought back from France by the new Venice Simplon Orient-Express Company (or VSOE from now on) in 1980 and restored.

In the next seat to mine was a Japanese gentleman, arrayed with cameras and photographic equipment. A typical Japanese gentleman, so I thought. Opposite him was another Japanese gentleman, with even more photographic equipment. More type casting. The first gentleman said he was Osamu Kumasegawa, a professional photographer, based in Paris, who was working on a project about the new Orient-Express. He was to be my companion all the way to Venice. The other Japanese gentleman was a Professor of Social Welfare, Shigehiro Takahashi of Komazawa University. They were strangers to each other, and I to them, but we soon exchanged names, cards and politeness. I was pleased to see all their photographic equipment, having myself come only with a pen and notebook.

I listened to them comparing notes in Japanese, then they suddenly started smiling. It turned out that the Professor of Social Welfare had got cameras which were twice as expensive as the professional photographer's. Well, Osamu *seemed* to be amused, but he was already having difficulties with one of his cameras. The Professor laughed heartily. He was wearing an English tweed jacket and an expensive woollen polo neck.

I looked around at the other occupants of *Phoenix*, wondering who everyone was and where they all had come from. My Japanese friends were the only Orientals in sight. At a rough estimate, listening hard to catch the accents, trying to place clothes and faces, about half were English speakers of some sort, British, American or Australian, while the other half were Europeans of

Latin extraction. There were two black ladies, both with white men, one very old lady, all in black, who could be French, and one family with two young children who appeared to be speaking Spanish.

I could see a lot of expensive hand luggage and jewellery, then well cut suits and costumes as they each took off their coats and settled down. Many were like children on Christmas morning, discovering the goodies around them. There was a young suntanned man with a much older, middle aged, heavily made-up lady. They did not appear to be speaking to each other. Would I get to know them all by the time we got to Venice? Would none of them turn out to be as they appeared?

'I just *hated* the Dorchester,' so an American lady with blonde hair and a leopard skin coat was announcing rather loudly. She was aged about forty and wearing a short skirt which well displayed some rather muscular but well formed legs. 'It was dirty, dirty, dirty! We could have stayed anywhere, the Connaught anywhere. Even the ice box didn't work. It looked good from the hall, but my God, our room! I've already got a description for it. Wanna hear? "It was like a beautiful woman who has gorgeous clothes and accessories, then you discover she has body odour." Charlie, wasn't that true?'

She had in her wake a much older American gentleman, tall and distinguished, who smiled and nodded, watching her every moment, admiring her every word.

'In Venice, we're staying at the Danieli, that's supposed to be kinda good, huh. Then we're going to Milan. We've got tickets for La Scala.'

She was telling all this to an official from VSOE, a young lady called Josephine, who was to travel with all the passengers to Venice. It was Josephine who had put a discreet little note on everyone's table saying that a Japanese photographer was on board, a member of the Japan Photographers' Society, but that he would not cause any inconvenience and passengers would not have their photographs taken without their prior permission.

'I have my own column back in the States,' so the American lady was now explaining, asking if she could get some of the Japanese photographs for her own use. 'I appear on television. I can do you a *lot* of good. I get syndicated all over the place. Health and Fitness is my speciality. Here, have my card.'

I had been waiting to get down the gangway and as I moved forward I managed to get a card myself, just to add to my collection. Two Japanese and one American so far. And we hadn't left Victoria.

The card announced that she was called Mary-Lou Anderson followed by a whole alphabet of her qualifications. 'Health Promotion. Counsellor. Consultant. Physical Fitness. Relaxation. Weight Control. Behaviour Modification.' I could see no reference to her column, or her TV programme, but perhaps there was not enough space on a little visiting card.

'Gee, I'm so looking forward to this trip. I can't think of anything more wonderful or romantic than the Orient-Express. It all looks so marvellous.'

I returned to my seat, just as we set off, and immediately champagne was served. I had meant to keep an eye on our progress, but Brixton had slipped by just as smoothly as the champagne, transported inside a time machine, cut off from all reality. I didn't see much of Kent either, though I had wanted to look out for Tonbridge, home of a famous school and some high quality cricket balls, but the champagne led into lunch, all the while chattering away to my two Japanese friends.

It was a fairly simple lunch, but then this first stage of the journey lasts only 90 minutes. We started with leek and potato soup, followed by cold roast veal, smoked turkey and cranberry tartlets, accompanied by a red cabbage and stilton salad. It finished with caramel tangerines and brandy snaps, then coffee.

All the waiters and attendants were dressed in uniforms, buttons and coat tails gleaming, and they worked quietly and exceedingly smoothly. After lunch, I managed a few words with the chief steward, Michael Rennie, a young man of thirty with a large period moustache. He said he had been in the Army Parachute Regiment before joining BR as a dining car steward. All the staff on the English train are technically still employed by BR, who pay their wages, but they work full time for the Orient-Express company, between Victoria and Folkestone.

'There wasn't a big rush when the job was first advertised. People didn't know what it all meant, what the train was supposed to do. Some stewards didn't think it would last. Now that the whole world knows about the new Orient-Express, *everyone* wants to work on it. Yes, I do very comfortably, thank you, sir. With all the overtime, I probably earn more than many people on this train.

'I had Prince and Princess Michael of Kent on board last week, and had my photograph taken with them. Not that they are any different to me. Everyone who comes on this train is a VIP, as far as I'm concerned.'

*Minerva* was his favourite coach, and I must go down and examine that, but he loved the furnishings in all the coaches. Had anything perhaps disappeared since it all began, a few VIPs possibly becoming forgetful? Every single item on the table did look so beautiful and valuable.

'Four flower vases, a dozen sets of cutlery. That's about all. Very little else has gone. Nothing really, compared with some places I've worked.

'It's the best job I've ever had. People on this train are on holiday. This *is* part of their holiday and they aim to enjoy themselves. On ordinary trains, most people are going to work and if they get on with the hump, or things go wrong, they take it out on you. People come on this train jolly – and stay that way.'

He was pleased that they never have to handle money, as the lunch and the unlimited champagne are free, included in the ticket, at least as far as Folkestone. He and his stewards only go that far, returning straight back to Victoria, either with return passengers from Venice or with special excursions.

It was only then, in talking to the steward, that I began to fully realise that today's Orient-Express consists of *two* entire trains, one which takes passengers to Folkestone and the other which takes over at Boulogne. Not just two vintage trains, but two sets of staff and two sets of furnishings. So whoever thought of re-creating the Orient-Express had to do it all twice. He must have been mad. Or a millionaire.

*      *      *

It was an American, a modern Pullman called James Blair Sherwood, who decided to bring style and quality back into European travelling, but it all happened by chance, a sudden inspiration, not connected with anything he had done before, either in his business or his personal life.

Mr Sherwood, a fresh faced, boyish looking American, was born in Newcastle, Pennsylvania in 1933, the son of a lawyer. He was educated at Yale, where he read economics, then he served in the Navy for three years, ending as a full lieutenant. He was considering going back to college, to do a course in Business Studies, when a friend from the Navy, a retired Admiral, offered him a job in a shipping company he was now working with, United States Line.

During the next four years, Sherwood realised that the future of shipping lay in containers. The old fashioned system of handling cargo manually, by lifting the goods in and out of the holds, was being replaced by special containers, large steel boxes which could be automatically transferred from shore to ship.

'I knew a company which had a large supply of small steel containers which were all standing idle. He had about 40,000, doing nothing. I had no capital, but I knew the sort of people who might want to rent them, so I offered him a small rental, per day. I said I planned to rent them out at a higher rent. He let me try it with 2,000 of his containers, which I successfully rented. Then with two partners I set up my own business, managing to raise about 100,000 dollars between us.'

This was in 1964 and he called the firm Sea Containers, naturally enough, which he was soon running on his own, as the two partners stepped down. In 1965 he decided to move to London knowing that 75% of the world's shipping is controlled through London, or at least within a reasonable radius of London.

'There was tremendous growth in the late Sixties and Seventies as British lines all went over to containers. I decided very early on to build the first container ship, specially made to take the new containers.'

The rest is shipping history. Sea Containers today (1986) owns eleven container ships, 300,000 container units, has offices and agents in 62 countries, employs a world wide staff of 15,000 and is currently worth 1.6 billion dollars. In 1984, they bought Sealink UK from British Rail for £66m. It is now a public company and Mr Sherwood is President owning about 15% of the shares.

They have some of the most luxurious office accommodation in London, a three-acre site on the South Bank, backing on to the River. Container leasing is still their main activity but in their associated company, SeaCo Inc., they own the Orient-Express and several hotels including the Cipriani in Venice and the Villa San Michele in Florence.

'We bought the Cipriani in 1976. I had always wanted a little pad for myself in Venice, then this hotel suddenly came on the market. It was being sold by three Guinness sisters and it had made a loss for eight years running. There was a political crisis in Italy at the time, and it looked as if the Government might go Communist, and I think they wanted to get out.'

Having established himself in London and then in Venice, Mr Sherwood fell to thinking how to connect the two of them. He was at this stage working on plans to expand the company's Leisure Division, possibly by buying or building a hotel in London, to complement his Venice hotel. That was the initial thought in his mind.

One day in May, 1977, just a year after he had bought the Cipriani, he read a newspaper report about the final run of the Orient-Express. It had become by then a shabby shadow of its former self, a once great train now reduced to a few ordinary passenger coaches, not even with a dining car. What interested him most was the enormous public interest being shown all over the world in the death of a famous train.

In the autumn of 1977 he heard that Sotheby's was auctioning off five vintage carriages from the Orient-Express, ones which had been used for the film *Murder on the Orient-Express*. He decided to go to the sale, along with two English friends who were both keen railway enthusiasts. One was Lord Garnoch, who as a young man worked on American railroads and is a Director of two British preserved railway companies, the Severn Valley and the Festiniog. The other friend was Bill McAlpine, of the building family, who has his own railway in his back garden.

Mr Sherwood had, until that time, no interest in railways. Even as a child, he had never collected numbers nor wanted to be an engine driver. The sale was to be in Monte Carlo, on 8 October, 1977, and he went there with an idea only half forming in his mind, not quite sure what exactly he would do, should he buy anything at the sale. The main fascination was still the world attention which the sale was attracting.

'I have never seen such scenes in my whole life. There were between 300 and 400 press, radio and TV people there. Every US TV station was represented. It was incredible. Yet there were only five bidders. I said to myself if there is such enormous media attention in the death of a company, what must happen if it is born again.'

He was rather alarmed to find that the first of the five bidders was the King of Morocco. Even Mr Sherwood realised that if it came to a fight, the King's coffers would be deeper than his. The King turned out to be interested in only two items, a Pullman parlour car and a sleeping car, which he bought for his own Royal Train. He is a railway buff and he wanted to restore them for his own private use when driving around his Kingdom. The King then retired and Mr Sherwood managed to buy the two coaches he fancied, two sleeping cars, numbered 3489 and 3543, which cost £10,000 each. He sent them to Bordeaux, then spent a year thinking about what he would have to do next.

It was one thing having the idea of re-creating a train, but another thing to actually go ahead and do it, even if you have a large sum of money at your disposal. There are always various authorities who can obstruct you and enough experts who will say it can't, or should not be done.

So began two years of feasibility studies, talks with railway experts and discussions with the nationalised railway companies of the countries concerned, Britain, France, Switzerland and Italy. 'They know how to run railways. I knew nothing.' In theory, it could have been possible to transport the same train from London to Venice, putting it on a boat across the Channel, as this had happened at times in the past, but because of different European regulations, rolling stock, different styles of bogies and other complications he was told the English train could not possibly go all the way. So the hunt began to track down *two* sets of period coaches and carriages.

The original two coaches grew to thirty five as they dug out suitable period stock from all over Europe. Many had been originally the property of Wagons-Lits, Nagelmackers' company, though they were no longer working. Several had been left in sidings to rot in different parts of Europe, especially in Spain and Portugal. Railway regulations had not been as strict in the Iberian peninsula and as old Wagons-Lits coaches had become run down and no longer serviceable in France or Germany they had been shunted to Spain or Portugal to get a final few years of work out of them.

The work of stripping down all the coaches, then rebuilding and re-creating them, was a colossal undertaking. In Europe, the job was relatively simple, though expensive, as there already existed privately owned railway workshops, more than willing to take in outside work.

In Britain there are very few private passenger coaches or workshops. BR were not able to do any of the repair work, and for a while the British end of the renovation presented a major problem. The solution sounds rather out of proportion, but they could see no other alternative. They decided they would have to *build* their own factory to do the work, thus entering another new industry, one several stages removed from the ultimate object of the exercise. They bought some land at Carnforth, in Lancashire, through the help of Bill McAlpine, built new workshops and hired sixty men, many of them out of work craftsmen, and for two years they worked full time on the English Pullman coaches.

It meant a new lease of life for many french polishers and cabinet makers, some of whom had worked on the Pullman coaches in the old days, as well as state apartments on the old *Queen Elizabeth* and *Queen Mary*. Waring and Gillow, who had provided most of the soft furnishings pre-war, managed to find some of the original drawings in their archives.

The total cost came to £11 million, not the £5 million which Sherwood had originally imagined. But within three months of the new launch in 1982, it was running at a profit. 'If a product is right, then you can sell it. I started by hoping to recreate some history. Now I think we have gone on to *create* some history.'

# ~ *Chapter Two* ~
# Crossing The Channel
*An encounter with Japanese;*
*Folkestone to Boulogne*
*and some Cross Channel memoirs;*
*on the Captain's deck.*

My two Japanese friends were talking away in Japanese, but now and again I could pick out occasional words, such as 'Sim-sons' and several times they mentioned 'Hay-rods'. When they paused I admired the Professor's tweed jacket and he smiled and said of course, he had bought it in Simpson's, Piccadilly, London. That was what most Japanese people did when they came to London. He had had little time for clothes on this trip and had been in London only one day. His sole purpose was to catch the Orient-Express back to Paris.

'I saw the film *Murder on the Orient-Express*, and from then I always was very interested in the train. When I heard in Japan that it was running again, I had to come. It is very beautiful.'

He had visited London several times over the years on academic business, as Britain, so he said, is a model of social welfare, an example to all civilised countries. 'The British have a lot to teach us.' He was on his way to East Germany in connection with some meetings being organised for International Youth Year in 1985.

The Japanese photographer had got all his cameras working and was concentrating on getting a picture of a butter pat, a little circle of butter, about the size of a ten pence piece, which had the VSOE letters embellished on it. Over lunch, he had photographed every dish as it had appeared. Now he was doing the accessories, from the plates and forks to the bread rolls.

I asked if they could place each other by their accents. Had the Professor, for example, a more educated Japanese accent than the Photographer? Perhaps it was a typically British question, indicating our own prejudices, rather than theirs, and it took me some time to explain my question. I'd begun to wish I hadn't started it. Then they smiled and said the Photographer had a very Tokyo accent, as that was where he had worked most of his life. The Professor had more of a country accent.

'In Japan, this would be only for the Emperor,' said the Professor, beaming round at all the intricate marquetry work on the walls of our carriage. 'I have seen one like this in a museum. It belonged to the Meiji Emperor.'

I went to the lavatory at the end of our coach, after all that champagne, and discovered to my surprise that it too was as ornate and decorated as the coach interiors. The floor was a mosaic, which appeared to show some heraldic device, possibly a bird arising from the ashes, to symbolise Phoenix. All the lavatories on the English train, or rake, as it should technically be known, have a mosaic floor, done specially for the new Orient-Express, each one in keeping with the name of the coach, usually depicting some classical or mythological scene.

I felt the train stop while I was in the lavatory. I didn't want to be stuck inside, despite all the classical grandeur, while everyone else staggered off the train, so I hurried back to my seat.

We had arrived in Folkestone, exactly on time, but the train had stopped for some reason just outside the station. Eventually, several VSOE officials came round and explained that the Channel was rough and that our boat was not yet in. I exchanged glances with my Japanese friends. Their faces betrayed nothing.

Two further officials appeared, as we all sat talking, taking advantage of the champagne which was still flowing freely. There were two ladies in smart brown uniforms, neither of whom I had noticed before. They walked amongst the passengers handing out envelopes.

I examined my envelope carefully, admiring the quality of the paper and the Orient-Express logo, all nicely designed with neat typography. Inside I found two pills. 'A sea is running in the Channel today,' so I read. 'Our ferry has stabilisers, but if you are unaccustomed to motion, you may wish to take the Kwell tablet in this envelope.'

I asked the lady if she *really* recommended it. Her accent was German and she said she was called Rita. 'Oh yes, it is very good.' Had she taken one herself? 'Oh no. I have done the crossing eleven times, and never been sick. I don't take pills. Perhaps that's why I've never been sick. . . .'

My Japanese friends were taking theirs. As a nation, they are far ahead of us these days in most technical knowledge, so I followed their example, but I decided not to drink any more champagne. Around me I could see one or two worried faces. I could also see one rather blotchy one. It was a boisterous Englishman who had already taken on too much champagne.

'We should have set off twenty minutes earlier from Victoria,' said one lady, 'and gone more slowly. I found it a bit bumpy at times when I was eating.'

It had been slightly bumpy, as we changed tracks and changed speed, but I had not found it too unpleasant. I had noticed only one glass of champagne being spilt. But I would have enjoyed a slower ride. We had rather bashed on at times, no doubt because of timetable problems.

The delay, however, was proving a pleasant interlude. Everybody seemed suddenly to become much more friendly, having something to talk about, such as the possibility of a nasty crossing ahead. I decided I would work my way down the train, talking to as many people as possible until we had to get off, taking advantage of a captive audience.

I spoke first to an elderly and very dignified Italian couple who had sat behind me in silence most of the way so far, not joining in any of the jollity. She turned out to be an Italian Countess and he was a Doctor of Law. They were getting off at Milan, their home town. I told them how much I was looking forward to seeing Milan Station.

'As a little boy,' he said, 'I used to go and watch it being built.'

There was a very well dressed and well spoken couple nearby, travelling with a sensitive younger man who looked like a 1920s' poet. 'I would like to stay on this train for ever,' said the lady. 'I really could live on it, travelling for ever round the world, stopping only when I wanted to, getting off perhaps for a few days, then back on board, staying on the train till I grew dusty and died. . . .'

The couple said they were called Audrey and Jack from Melbourne, Australia. I had to be sure to talk to them again before Venice. The young man said nothing. He was a luxury train freak. He went round the world looking for luxury trains to travel on. He had recently been to South America. I don't think I heard him talk during the whole journey. He just stared and stared.

I came to two rather noisy English couples and assumed they were in a party, but they had only met on the train. One couple was from Yorkshire and he gave me his card at once, Clifford Wood, chairman of a yarn firm in Bradford. Then his wife gave me her card as well, Ritva Wood, managing director of a travel agency in Ilkley. They were purely on holiday, though being in the travel business, she was looking forward to finding out all about the train. 'I've read so much about it. It is so fascinating. The uniforms are marvellous. But I don't expect many people from Ilkley will be likely to ever go on it.' Her husband said he too had enjoyed it so far. But he had one complaint. 'The ash trays. Look, they haven't been emptied yet.'

The other English couple were from Cranbrook in Kent. He was the proprietor of a golf club. 'We've come for a dirty weekend in Paris,' he said, shaking me by the hand. 'Just a joke. This is the wife.'

'We read about it in the *Sunday Times*,' she said, 'and thought we'd treat ourselves. I didn't think much of the meal, but the champagne was good.'

The second black lady on the train, whom I had taken to be Asian, was from Malaya. Her husband, who looked Arabic, was originally from London. Both of them now lived and worked in Saudi Arabia. 'It was my idea,' she said. 'I got the brochure and said to my husband, here you are, this is what I want for my birthday.'

I came to three German speaking couples, travelling together in a party, all tall and well dressed with a lot of furs. I got very little out of them, except that one couple was from Hamburg and the others from Copenhagen. The men were all in shipping, which was how they were connected. They were very pleased. 'So far.'

MENU

AFTERNOON TEA

Selection of Finger Sandwiches

Country Scones, Clotted Cream and
Strawberry Jam
Norfolk Fruit Cake
Bakewell Tartlet

Ceylon Tea (China Tea available on request)

†Drawing from original menu 1884.

Gratuities at passengers discretion

A sea is running in the Channel today. Our ferry has stabilizers, but if you are unaccustomed to motion, you may wish to take the 'Kwell' tablet in this envelope. The Channel crossing will take approximately 1 hour 30 minutes.

VENICE SIMPLON ORIENT-EXPRESS

A Naval looking man with a beard was sitting alone, but he was friendly and open. He said he was called Kevin Wilcher, a publican from Broadstairs. 'This is the only civilised way to travel. I hate driving and I hate planes. Boats and trains, they're the only way to go.

'My wife would hate this sort of holiday. She likes sitting on a beach in the sun. I hate all that. So every year we take a holiday on our own. She's going to Tenerife when I get back. I'm going all the way to Venice on the train. Then I'm turning right round and coming back on it again. My wife thinks I'm mad.'

He had on his lap a book called *The World's Greatest Cranks and Crackpots*. One of his pub customers had given it to him that morning on his departure.

So far, people had turned out to be much as I had imagined. All of them were on holiday, as opposed to a business trip, and had paid for themselves. Four people in all had mentioned it as being a birthday present. There was a high number of people in the restaurant or hotel business, but that was to be expected in January. The emigré element was less expected. There seemed to be a lot of British-born people who had come back to England on holiday, especially to go off on the train and relive life in the good old days. I had heard no serious complaints. Perhaps the boat would sort them out, bring out a few hidden personalities.

On the way back to my seat I met Mary-Lou, the American Health Expert, and she too said it had all been very good, not bad at all. 'Did I tell you we've got tickets for La Scala in Milan? Some show I've never heard of, but it's supposed to be very good. We did *Noises Off* last night in London. It was excellent. The Michael Frayn play. He's very good.'

'Which part was he?' asked Charlie, her companion.

I said it was a nice little play, but they should really have tried to get tickets for something more unusual and exciting, something that they could really have boasted they had seen, such as *Starlight Express*.

'*Noises Off* was *very* highly recommended,' continued Mary Lou. 'Very much indeed. And Charlie loved it. Especially the L. and A.'

I asked what that meant and she explained it stood for Legs and Asses.

It didn't sound like the performance of *Noises Off* which I saw. Who anyway had recommended it?

'The concierge at the Dorchester. He was very knowledgeable but the *hotel*, did I tell you what the bedroom was like . . . ?'

There was a sudden flurry further down the train. It was time to get off and board the boat for France, all of us wondering what the trip ahead would be like.

*       *       *

Almost all diaries and accounts of travelling to Europe are full of being seasick, from the sixteenth century to the Victorian era. And beyond. It was an expected hazard of the journey in the days of sail, just as you expected to have endless delays if the tides and the weather were not in your favour, despite what some timetable might have led you to believe. When Wordsworth went on his second trip to France he had to wait a whole four days at Brighton, putting in time till the winds changed.

Addison, the early eighteenth century writer, had a nasty experience when he crossed the Channel at the beginning of his Grand Tour. He had managed to get a £200 grant out of the Treasury, as he had persuaded them that his travels were a necessary preparation for a diplomatic career. He took with him presentation copies of his books, which was a smart move, to impress likely people on his journeys. (I planned to do the same, though it had proved rather difficult, not having any impressive books to give out to people. I realised not many Europeans would be exactly thrilled by a copy of my wonderful book about the Lake District, or even Tottenham Hotspurs, but I had brought with me, just in case, a few copies of the Beatles biography, in Italian, German and French. What lucky people, I wondered, would end up receiving them?)

Anyway, Addison got to Calais in 1699 in reasonable order, without too much discomfort, but on getting off the boat he fell into the sea. Even worse, his cries for help didn't do much good as he couldn't speak any French.

Horace Walpole and Thomas Gray did the same trip in 1739 when they were beginning their Grand Tour. (Isn't it interesting to think of writers going off together. They were both young men of twenty-two at the time. They'd met at Eton.) The crossing to Calais took them five hours – and for the whole five hours, Gray was sea sick.

Dickens had an interesting experience while coming home on the boat train in 1863. On the French quayside he recognized a once very familiar face, hidden amongst the crowd who were watching the boat depart. It was George Hudson, a vital figure from his past, the draper's assistant from York who had built up a railway empire worth £30 million. At the height of his national power in 1846, Hudson had been one of the backers of the *Daily News*, the paper which had appointed Dickens as its first editor. Four years later, Hudson had collapsed, his method of bribing politicians and fiddling the books exposed, and he had exiled himself to France where he was now living as a pauper. Dickens had not recognized him at first, yet thirteen years earlier the Railway King had been the best known and most caricatured commoner in the country.

Dickens that day had been travelling on a paddle steamer, the normal method of crossing the Channel until 1903, when the first cross Channel turbine steamer was introduced. The trains themselves, which connected with the boats, always offered much more comfort than the steamers, if you were prepared to pay the extra charges. The first Pullman train was introduced in 1882, the Dover Continental Pullman Car Boat Express, but this particular service stopped after only two years as passengers were not keen to pay the large surcharge.

It was not until 1936 that you could actually cross the Channel on the train itself. Twenty sleepers were constructed by the Wagons-Lits company which could be transferred straight on to custom built train ferries. This route became known as the Night Ferry and was very popular with the Duke of Windsor and other well known people, trying not to be too well known, slipping quietly into Victoria and hoping to make a discreet arrival next morning in France. The Night Ferry came to an end in 1980.

By that time, the great days of luxury train riding to the Channel ports had gone. In 1964, the Pullman Car Company itself disappeared, being merged with British Rail, and in 1972 the Golden Arrow made its last journey. Included in the rake that day, on October 30, 1972, were *Phoenix*, *Perseus* and *Cygnus*, part of the present day Orient Express.

*    *    *

The walk to our boat was not far but it was not very pleasant. We proceeded in a straggling single file along a draughty dock side and I could hear quite a few people behind me complaining, or perhaps they were becoming more worried at the journey ahead, now that we could see the rough sea and feel the strong winds.

On board, we were shown into a specially reserved lounge for Orient-Express passengers. It turned out to be decidedly ordinary, after the luxury of the train. It was the first time I had been disappointed, having led myself to believe from the company's brochure that the surroundings would be in keeping with the train. 'Enjoy coffee or a drink in the Verandah Deck Saloon which is reserved exclusively. . . . the sea is normally calm and the large ferry affords a comfortable passage.' They can't of course control the weather, but they should perhaps keep tighter control on some of the purple prose.

The bench seats did have purple coverings and an attempts had been made to decorate the walls with a few artistic Orient-Express posters, the new ones designed by the old 1930s master, Fix-Masseau, but even so, it was all very functional. At least anyone being seasick would not spoil any antique marquetry or a Lalique tulip lamp.

Tea, coffee and biscuits were served by our two stewardesses in brown, who came with us on the boat, but few passengers seemed very keen to eat or drink anything. I saw the Train Manager talking to a gentleman in naval uniform whom I took to be the ship's captain, so I hurried across, just in time to join a small party of passengers invited up on the Captain's Deck. It seemed an ideal way to spend what I could see was going to be a far from pleasant one and a half hours on a very rough sea. The last time I had stood on a Captain's Deck had been on the QE2. I thought I'd mentioned this rather quietly, not wanting to show off in front of the other passengers, but the Captain himself had heard. 'We have more full Masters than the QE2,' he said loudly. 'Everyone wants this job. After a lifetime on deep sea ships, can you imagine a better job than crossing the Channel each day, getting home most nights.'

The Japanese photographer asked if it would be all right for him to shoot. There was a line of very impressive looking computerised radar machines, ticking and pinging away, showing little pictures and funny symbols, just like those dreadful space invader machines. The Captain said go ahead, none of them was secret, in fact they could cross the Channel without most of them.

I peered into one of them, to see what was on television and an officer kindly explained how it worked. It was being tested out for the firm which made them, Racal Decca. I could see circles of lights bouncing off an object ahead. He said it was the Varne Lightship, which he pointed out through the long window in front of us. He got out some maps and showed how we were taking a course to avoid some sand banks called the Varne Banks. They stretch for miles, right down the middle of the English Channel, and at places the water is only 13 feet deep. Even quite small boats could do themselves a nasty injury, if they hit a sand bank. 'Local knowledge of course is quite sufficient. We know where they all are.'

The weather was becoming slightly better, so the Captain announced, though it seemed just as bad to me. The strongest wind he had ever known in the Channel was a Gale Force 10. On the way back from France that day it had been a Force 9. Now, it was around Force 8 which meant the winds were howling at about fifty-five knots. The sea ahead loomed like huge slabs of bright green marble. At times we seemed to be underneath it. I could feel my body and the whole ship climbing slowly up, and then slowly down again. It was not frightening. Just unreal and rather eerie.

In front of the Captain was a large notice saying FINS OUT, meaning that the stabilisers were in position, doing their work. Beside it was a little tin of boiled sweets, Smith Kendo Mixed Fruit Flavoured Tablets.

'Those are my bad weather sweets,' said the Captain. He ate sweets in bad weather because he was unable to smoke his normal cigar. In bad weather, all the doors on deck were always closed, and his fellow officers complained about his horrible cigar smoke. So, he had been forced to turn to sweets instead.

He took me out of one of the side doors, pushing hard to open it, onto a small uncovered deck, and we looked back at the white cliffs of Dover on the far horizon. 'I wish they'd get rid of that red,' he said. I thought there must be some building at Folkestone or Dover which my eyes were not capable of seeing, so I nodded wisely.

'Sealink is no longer part of British Rail,' he continued. 'You'd have thought they would re-paint our funnel.'

I altered my eyes, with difficulty, and focussed instead on the ship's enormous funnel which was just above our heads, noting on its side BR's familiar white on red rail symbol.

The *Horsa*, when full, can carry 1,400 passengers. That day there were only 110 on board, almost all from the train. It was of course January, not exactly the nicest time for a Channel crossing. He considered this and said that you could get bad weather at any time, fog and mist. In bad fog, the radar could take the boat within 300 yards of the quayside, but after that, you were on your own, hoping by luck and local knowledge to gently ease the *Horsa*'s 5,500 tons into the right position, without knocking off too much paint.

'My legs are a bit tired,' he suddenly said. 'Do you think anyone would like some tea in my cabin?' We all jumped, the ones still capable of jumping. Josephine from VSOE, despite umpteen trips to Venice, looked as if her jumping days were over and was obviously feeling very seasick.

On the way down, I asked the Captain if his legs really had been tired. Varicose veins and backache, he said, were a professional hazard for all seafaring types. 'I suppose without realising it you are permanently balancing your legs. I've never been seasick, not once in 25 years at sea, but my legs and back do get very sore.'

His cabin was large and neatly furnished, almost as big as the QE2 Captain's cabin, though not as expensively decorated. On his television set was a fluffy toy which had hanging from its neck the name Horsa. It was named after the Viking hero, sister ship to *Hengist* and *Vortigern*, other Sealink ferry boats.

'The summers are very hectic,' he said, as he poured us out a cup of tea and handed round biscuits. 'The football crowds are terrible, but the rugby supporters can be just as noisy. We had a big gang of French crossing this morning for tomorrow's rugger match at Twickenham. They played the Marseillaise on a bugle the whole way across. When they got off, I found our Red Ensign had disappeared.'

Orient-Express passengers, in their exclusive verandah deck, would naturally never be expected to do such a thing.

# ~ Chapter Three ~

# The Continental Train

*A very elegant Australian lady;*
*observations regarding 1883;*
*our hero dances on the train through France.*

Somewhere in front of me I could hear what sounded like little screams. I was not seasick, but my body felt as if it was still going up and down and I was very glad to step off the good ship *Horsa* as quickly as possible. I was concentrating more on getting safely across the gang plank than wondering what was ahead in the gloom of Boulogne, so it was only when I looked up that I realised that the noises ahead were screams of delight. There, right in front of us, just a few yards away from the boat, was the French Connection.

I had already seen photographs of the Continental train in the Orient-Express brochures and accepted that the beautiful young ladies in twenties' clothes, posing artfully against the Art Deco interiors or lounging seductively in their cabins in Janet Reger silk underwear, must obviously be models, paid to pose. We all understand that convention. They had made the backgrounds look posed as well, as if the train was a theatrical set, moved into position for the photograph, held together at the back with safety pins, so I was prepared to be disappointed. But my first glimpse of that dazzlingly blue train, with its gleaming coats of arms and those famous gold letters, *Compagnie Internationale des Wagons-Lits*, convinced me straight away. As man-made sights go, it was as impressive as anything I have ever seen, almost as magical as that first view of the New York skyline when you sail under the Verrazano Narrows Bridge.

Lined up on the platform was a whole host of brightly uniformed porters and officials, all looking French and exotic, ready to welcome us aboard. I was loath to get on, wanting to take it in slowly, to walk up and down the length of the train. It would have taken some time. The Continental train is normally a quarter of a mile long and consists of seventeen carriages in all, twice the length of the English train. Tonight, we were only fourteen coaches, still more than enough to spend several hours exploring. I had a train ride of over 800 miles to come. I was bound to see most of it during the journey ahead, and get to know better our English passengers and meet all the new ones joining us at Boulogne and Paris.

The re-creating of the Continental rake was an even bigger job than the English one. The work was divided between the Wagons-Lits workshops in

Ostend in Belgium and the Bremer Waggonbau workshops at Bremen in Germany. More than a hundred extra staff were taken on for the renovating work in Ostend.

I was welcomed aboard my sleeping car, which was lettered S, not nearly as romantic as being named *Phoenix* or *Ibis*, by Olivier, the car's steward, in his bright blue uniform, who showed me to my cabin, numbered nine. As on the English train, there was highly polished wooden panelling everywhere. Even the corridors were decorated with inlaid designs, little brass fittings and Lalique lamps.

Olivier took my passport and said he would look after everything. I would not be bothered by any customs or frontiers either in France, Switzerland or Italy. Just like the old days. That was one of the many attractions for travellers on the original Orient-Express, especially for those who might not want their business, their identity or their travelling companions to be on public view.

My cabin was very small, being a single, and probably measured no more than six feet by four. I immediately stretched out my arms from side to side in order to estimate. Thanks to clever lighting, the ingenious use of mirrors and by having little shelves and objects at different heights and at different corners, it seemed very much bigger. It contained the sort of facilities and the sense of style and period you would find in a high class hotel bedroom, such as the Ritz in London or the George V in Paris, only on a miniature scale. It was like a doll's house, but a very luxurious one, the sort our dear Queen used to play with when she was a Little Princess.

In the next cabin was my friend the Japanese photographer. I could hear him exclaiming as he too examined his little room. Beyond him was a family with two children I had noticed at Victoria. I could hear them rushing up and down, shouting with delight. I went along the corridor to see them and found the parents and an elderly lady, their grandmother, sitting in their cabins with the doors open, all rather bemused. This was the first trip that their children had ever had on a train. The father gave me his card which said his name was E. Miguel Astudillo from Lima in Peru. He was in shipping. The two children, Miguel, eight and Anna Marie, fourteen, eventually returned to their cabin and sat down. 'It's wonderful,' they both said with one voice.

I went back into my cabin to explore it properly. The main item, dominating the cabin, was a very comfortable sofa, richly upholstered, with a lot of thick cushions. Opposite at the window end, was a little mahogany writing table with a brass lamp. On top of the table was a folder of Orient-Express note-paper, envelopes and post cards; a bottle of Yves St Laurent toilet water, some other smelly thing labelled Vianni Versere toilet atomiser; and finally a half bottle of champagne, with the Orient-Express logo on the label. Well, I thought, no need for me to buy any presents in Venice for my family back home.

There were two heavy brocade blinds on the windows, a small radiator, several little cupboards and five brass light switches which controlled hidden lights and lamps all over the little room. Even the normal railway sign 'Do not lean out of the window', written in four languages, English, French, German and Italian, was in gleaming brass. Where was the sink?

I looked on a shelf and found soap, neatly packed in a little box, and five sparkling white towels, of all sizes, though on closer inspection I realised one was a face cloth and one was a bedside mat. They were all monogrammed with the VSOE logo. Above my head, on an ornate gilt rack, I noticed some cushions, a blanket and my travelling bag which had somehow been whisked off the English train, on and off the boat and put in my cabin without me noticing. I decided the sink must be one of those clever folding ones, so I pulled a knob and found myself falling into the next door cabin where my Japanese friend was undressing. We made elaborate apologies, him more than me, yet it was my fault. He said he was to blame for not closing his door. I said no, no, I should not have opened it. Then, with great ceremony, and more apologies, we each locked the connecting door from our own side.

I removed some of the goodies from the little table, lifted it to see what would happen, and there below, voila, was a marble sink. Damn clever, these French. Then I walked down the corridor, to explore the rest of the train, and discovered that my coach had in fact been made in Birmingham. Damn clever, these Brummies.

Sleeping Car 3425, which was how it was referred to in the records of the Wagons-Lits Company, was built in Birmingham in 1929. It was decorated by René Prou and sent direct to Italy to form part of the Rome Express. It joined the Simplon Orient-Express in 1934, then the Sud Express, finally ending its Wagons-Lits working life in 1971.

At the end of each coach they have a special plaque telling its history, which was where I got the above information. All the coaches have a long history of work with the various forms of the old Orient-Express, and with the other great luxury Express trains, dating from the 1920s to the 1950s. Their track records read like a roll call of all the grand European trains. Horses have pedigrees, paintings have a provenance, humans have ancestry, what do old railway coaches have? Raillery would sound like an insult so perhaps pedigree is the best word. From reading all the train pedigrees, I found that *Enterprises Industrielles Charentaises Aytre, La Rochelle* appeared to be the French equivalent of the Birmingham carriage works.

In the last War, several of the coaches were commandeered by the Germans. Some were used as stationary restaurants and others were stored at Lourdes. Sleeping Car 3544, another of those built in 1929 and decorated by René Prou, was used as a brothel in Limoges during the War. Afterwards, it returned to normal service, acting as the Dutch Royal Train from 1946 to 1947.

I worked my way down to the Bar Car, having arranged to have a drink with the two Japanese. It was laid out like a bar in a smart hotel, with uniformed flunkies hovering around, lots of plants and flowers, little alcoves and sitting areas, all tastefully lit, and a long polished bar with high stools and barmen shaking complicated drinks. At the end of the bar, to my amazement, was a grand piano. In a moving train. I could hardly believe it. The train had seemed slightly higher than the English version, though no wider than a normal train, yet the grand piano fitted perfectly. Nothing seemed cramped.

I finally had to concede that the glossy photographs were not a fiddle, taken by a wide angle lens with the photographer hanging upside down outside. I could clearly see that almost anyone could take photographs of the Bar Car and make it look sensational.

I had a beer with my Japanese friends, which seemed the cheapest thing to drink, and they taught me how to say *Kampai*, the Japanese for 'cheers'. I learned quite a bit of Japanese during that journey across Europe.

Osamu, the photographer, was immediately at work, clicking away at every item and ornament in the bar, while I sat and talked to Shigehiro, the Professor, who was feeling rather sad. He was due to leave the train at Paris, on the way to his conference.

On our second beer, he started to tell me about his special subject, back at his Japanese University. It was as bizarre as our surroundings. He turned out to be an expert on Parent-Child Double Suicides, apparently a very common event in Japan these days, the numbers having doubled in the last few years.

In Japan, so he explained, the relationship between the mother and father is nowhere as strong or as emotional as it is in the Western world. The father is out all day and has little time for his family or his wife. The bond between the mother and the child can therefore become very intense. When things go radically wrong, with the child or the mother, the mother can often be driven into killing the child, then committing suicide.

The fact that it is called a 'double suicide' in the Japanese press indicates a strong degree of sympathy for the mother. In the West, it would be classed as child murder. In Japan, there is some acceptance for the murder, the way there is for a 'love suicide' when two lovers commit suicide together, hoping to live more happily in the next world. In a recent three month spell, so the Professor said, as we sipped our beer and slipped luxuriantly through the French countryside, fifty-nine of these double deaths had occurred in Tokyo.

He has written a book on the subject and promised to give me a copy of an abstract published in English. It didn't sound the sort of light reading I had planned for my sleeping cabin, but I promised I would study it back home in London.

'Darling, isn't it all marvellous. Do have a drink.' It was Audrey, the ultra smart Australian lady. 'It's all just perfect. On an ordinary train today one gets treated like cattle. On a plane, you are not even treated like animals. You are simply cargo. But here, I feel like Royalty.'

She described in detail what she was planning to wear for dinner. Just a simple little black dress, in sheer black net, which she had bought in London in 1960 for £200 long *before* it was fashionable to buy 1920s' dresses. Must be worth a fortune now, so she said. Then she would probably put on her turban, the one studded with diamonds.

'I don't care if no one else does dress up. At least I will look good in *their* photographs, posing in the background. But I *hope* people do. I think they should be *made* to, don't you?'

She had already changed into a large and floppy hat, just for the Bar Car, bought especially for the trip from Harrods. The Professor and I both admired it.'

'Did I tell you I once travelled on the old Orient-Express, back in the 1960s? It was *completely* run down, my dear.

'Going through Italy we were gassed and robbed. I was with my son and we were put into this large compartment for the night with no lock on it. We must have dozed off. During the night, some robbers put their heads in, fired a gas gun at us, and we were out cold. My son half remembered waking up and seeing two men in the compartment, but he thought it was a dream and went back to sleep again. When we did wake up, all our bags had gone.

'I didn't *know* at the time we'd been gassed. It was the police who told us later. I think the conductors were in on it. One of them arrived later with my handbag, which was empty of all money of course, saying he'd found it in a lavatory. It contained our passports and tickets, so we could carry on with our journey. We'd set out on that trip so smart and so well dressed. We were absolute sights when we arrived, filthy and utterly fed up.'

I said that today's Orient-Express must be a huge improvement on the old ones in the sixties and seventies. I bet *they* never got free bottles in their compartments. There was silence from my Australian friend. 'What sort of bottles? Do you mean the toilet water?' No, no, I said, the champagne.

'I never got champagne,' she said.

I quickly tried to explain it away, saying it was only a little bottle, a half, perhaps even a third, really, just a miniature.

'You must be a VIP,' she said, flouncing away. 'I see. It's like that, is it.'

She then retired to her cabin to change for dinner.

We were due to eat about the time the train got into Paris. I decided I should at least put on a clean shirt, after all these fashion discussions. What a shame I hadn't brought an evening suit. Or would none of the men have such things. Would Audrey from Melbourne be the only fashion plate?

When the original train first left Paris, back in 1883, *all* the men and *all* the ladies dressed up. But then, that was a very auspicious occasion, followed with interest by almost everyone who was anyone in Europe.

*    *    *

Nagelmackers was a master of public relations, like Pullman before him, and he hand picked his passengers for that first trip in 1883, choosing the foremost political journalist of the day and also a leading novelist. The result was that two books appeared telling the story of that one trip. Few train journeys in history can have been so well documented.

The precise route was being kept secret, as Nagelmackers did not want to scare his passengers, knowing that there were many problems and obstacles to overcome on the 1,900 mile journey he had planned for them, but he assured everyone that they would travel in the utmost comfort, promising them a 'grand hotel on wheels'.

As his passengers arrived at the Gare de l'Est (then called the Gare de Strasbourg), they saw on the opposite platform a very dirty and run down coach belonging to a rival company. It was alleged later, but never proved, that Nagelmackers had arranged for it to be there, so that his train should look even more magnificent by comparison. There was a large crowd of sightseers and a farewell party was held on the platform. The Paris papers next day called it The Magic Carpet to the Orient.

The train was indeed magnificent, but comparatively small, just 200 feet long, consisting of only five coaches – two sleeping cars, one restaurant car and two fourgon wagons for baggage. The two sleeping cars and the restaurant car were brand new, fitted with bogies for the first time to give a smoother ride. The station was lit by the latest breakthrough in technology, electricity, thanks to Mr Edison, and the train itself was hung with gas lamps, another leap for mankind.

There were forty passengers on board, all guests or officials, including Nagelmackers himself and several other railway dignitaries, all in top hats and tails. Almost all the passengers were either French or Belgian, plus three Germans, one Dutchman and one Turk. (An Austrian party of three joined the train later at Vienna.)

The two star writers were Edmond About, a best selling French novelist of the day, and Henri Blowitz, the Paris correspondent of the *London Times*. M. About was tall and handsome with a grey beard and apparently had taken some persuading to come on the trip. He was worried about travel sickness and whether the smell of the new paint would upset his stomach. Blowitz was very small and ugly with an enormous head, terribly self-important and very voluble. The two writers handled each other cautiously for most of the journey. About appears to have disliked Blowitz at first for dominating every conversation, showing off his knowledge and boasting of his important friends, but grew fonder of him as the journey progressed. (Two of the three Germans on board were also apparently journalists, but nobody talked to them and they kept themselves to themselves.)

Blowitz was the big catch, one of the most remarkable journalists of all time. His biography was written in 1962 by Frank Giles, later Editor of the *Sunday Times*, who called his book *A Prince of Journalists* which was how the world referred to Blowitz. He had amazed everyone in 1878 by printing in *The Times* the details of the Treaty of Berlin, including all its secret clauses, *before* it had been signed. His *Times* reports were usually reprinted in the *New York Herald* where the editor, James Gordon Bennett (the originator of a gentle expletive which has gone into the English language) paid him large sums of money. Nagelmackers knew that anything Blowitz wrote about the train would be read in all the right places.

Blowitz had lined up, or so he hoped, two world exclusive interviews along the route, though he was keeping this fact to himself, not wishing any of his rivals to know about it. He was a personal friend of the Rothschilds, for whom he had intrigued on many occasions, and knew both Gladstone and Disraeli and probably did secret agent work for them. He had tipped off Disraeli about the Suez Canal venture, before it had been built, and helped Disraeli buy half the shares for the British Government. He always boasted that he was French, born a Roman Catholic, but in fact he was the son of a Jewish shopkeeper from Bohemia.

M. About explored the train and marvelled at all the fine marquetry in the coaches, the silk sheets on the beds, the damask draperies, gold tasselled blinds. Part of the dining room had deep leather armchairs and was furnished like the library of an English gentleman's club. Best of all was the dining room proper, sumptuously decorated and hung with enormous gas-lit chandeliers. Between the windows hung watercolours and engravings by contemporary artists, Delacroix, Decamps and Seymour.

Blowitz, who considered himself a gastronomic expert, went to inspect the kitchen and discussed the cooking arrangements with the chef de cuisine, a huge Burgundian in a coal black beard. He looked in every corner of the tiny kitchen, most of which was taken up with a large gas fired cooking stove.

For dinner that night they had ten courses, each item on the menu being written in gold letters. It started with soup, then hors d'oeuvres which contained lobster, oysters and caviar. Then came fish, a gigot of game, capon, fresh vegetables and salad, decorated cakes, sorbets, a selection from a dozen cheeses and then fresh fruit. The ride was so smooth, so About wrote, that 'not a drop of the champagne or the wines was spilt.'

Next morning, Blowitz noted that he was able to complete his toilet in complete comfort. This was not a reference to the excesses of the night before, as such banquets were quite normal for the upper classes in those days, but to the fact that he had expected the shaking of the train to cause difficulties. He wrote that he was able to shave 'without my hands trembling in the least.'

The dinner was served by waiters in powdered wigs which was thought to suit the Louis XV style of the furnishings and drapes. Later on, the powdered wigs were abandoned. Passengers complained that they were getting powder in their soup.

Blowitz got the first of his major interviews when they stopped at Bucharest. Most of the party got off and set out with him to visit King Carol of Rumania in his Palace of Peles. They were taken by coach to this brand new Ruritanian folly of a castle, perched high on a cliff, then ended up walking for several miles in the rain, arriving wet and dishevelled. To the amazement of both Blowitz and About, the walls of the castle were hung with paintings by Titian, Rembrandt and other masters, most of which they recognized. All of them turned out to be copies, rather crudely done.

Blowitz eventually received his private audience, and lectured the King on the state of Europe, told him stories about his famous friends and contacts, advised him how to run his country and patiently heard his complaints about the Treaty of Berlin and his problems with the Russians.

The Orient-Express party was then entertained to tea and music, during which the Queen played the piano. 'A rather unfortunate decision,' so M. About noted, rather cattily.

It was not just the speed and comfort and the incredible luxury of the 1883 journey which impressed these and later passengers, but the simple culture shock, zooming as if in a time capsule from their sophisticated Parisian life straight into primitive, or at least very strange and sometimes frightening, foreign lands, right at the far ends of Europe.

They finally arrived in Constantinople eighty-two travelling hours after leaving Paris. That was at least thirty hours less than the normal time. They had actually spent eleven days on the journey, counting all the stops and local receptions and visits. Almost all the passengers turned round fairly quickly, and their return trip to Paris was relatively uneventful.

The intrepid Blowitz, however, stayed on. He had been promised the first interview which the Shah of Turkey had ever granted. There were many delays and he had to hang around for two weeks before it all came to pass, after various secret meetings, mysterious messages and complicated signals. The Shah was being vilified throughout Europe at the time, and caricatured in *Punch* and most newspapers, for his massacre of Armenians and the execution of his enemies, even those in his own family. He rarely slept two nights in the same room and kept a pistol under his pillow.

The Shah, according to Blowitz's report of the meeting, was very interested to hear Blowitz's inside views on what the European powers proposed to do about the Ottoman Empire and their attitudes to Egypt and the Sudan and whether they might help his troubles with some financial loans. It was a magnificent scoop, read with interest around the world, as not even the diplomats or spies of the European nations knew how the Shah's mind was working.

After the audience, Blowitz was presented with the Order of Medjidieh, Third Class, pinned on him personally by the Shah. He had actually hoped for a higher award. The Shah's Royal Guard presented arms and saluted him as he left, wearing his new honour. 'I hope we don't meet any European cartoonists on our way back,' said Blowitz to an official.

In the 1980s, there are not many world scoops to be picked up on train rides, certainly nothing on the scale of the ones Blowitz managed. How could I possibly compete? I did, however, have one person in Venice in mind, highly recommended by Lord Norwich who had given me her phone number and described her as The Queen of Venice. That sounded quite promising.

As for those ten course meals, those receptions and real live dancing, no modern train could hope to match any of that ever again. Or could it?

✳     ✳     ✳

I was putting on my clean shirt for dinner, not wanting to be left out of any possible fashion parade, when I sensed that I was being watched. I was alone in my cabin, and the door was now firmly locked between me and my Japanese friend, and I had had only two drinks in the bar before dinner, having seen the prices, but I turned round slowly and there, through the window, were at least fifty pairs of eyes, all studying me getting changed, unable to resist the free show. We were standing in Amiens station and I had forgotten to pull down either of the two blinds.

Since leaving Boulogne, I had not looked out of the windows once. I had been so absorbed by the internal excitement, the furnishings and all the passengers. Both Monsieur About and Mr Blowitz rarely describe the scenery they were passing through back in 1883, so obsessed were they by the inside action.

I had meant to look out for Abbeville as we started our journey across France, the scene of my first foreign holiday, back in the 1950s when I had been in the fifth form at school. Our school party had stayed at the Station Hotel in Abbeville and I had spent almost the whole week wracked with asthma. We had had a day out in Amiens, to look at the largest Cathedral in France, and I was ill all day. Thirty years later, here I was, back in Amiens, giving the evening commuters some simple amusement as they waited for their trains home. I quickly pulled the blinds to hide my Marks and Spencer labels.

It used to be one of the sights of the old Orient Express, in the days when its route went over the River Vardar near Salonika, to look out of the windows in the summer months and watch the local girls bathing naked in the river. When this happened, the train conductors were instructed to pull the blinds down in second and third class compartments. First class passengers were allowed to watch.

I made my way to the Bar Car where I was greeted fondly by my Australian friend, dressed as if she was going to a Royal Garden Party. We seemed to have been chums for eight years, not just the eight hours that had passed since we left Victoria. Throughout the journey, it was like one large cocktail party to which we had all been invited by someone we all knew individually, but this unseen host never appeared and no one was quite sure what the party was for or how it had all begun.

'Did I tell you about the Ritz?' she said. 'We had a terrific room there this time. Quite fabulous.

'On our early trips to Europe I was always finding we were being given the worst room. They would see from our address that we're Aussies, so they think oh yes, Aussies, put them in the worst rooms, over the car park or beside the lift.

'But nowadays, I always write personally beforehand to the general manager. I admit straight away that I'm Australian, but I promise not to light a barbecue in the middle of the carpet or spray the walls with Fosters. People all over the world have these *awful* images of Australians. Most of them true.'

I noticed an old lady sitting at a little table on her own and went across to talk to her. I asked where she was from and she said Cumbria. That happens to be my homeland, so I sat down beside her. From a distance, she had looked rather forlorn. She was aged eighty-two, the oldest passenger by far, and seemed rather out of all the smart cocktail chat, but she said she had not missed one thing. Her professional eye had analysed every woman who had got on that train.

'I've counted twenty furs, dear,' she said, 'but only one has been any good. That was a Persian lamb. It was an American woman, fifty-ish, blonde hair, good teeth. Most of the rest have been fake. That one over there. Look, in the corner. Don't stare. That's *quite* good. Squirrel, but it's made up of very small pieces. *Not* very expensive.'

She was on the trip with her niece who runs a small hotel in Sedbergh, near the boys' public school. But as she spoke, I realised her accent wasn't at all Cumbrian. 'I'm an Aussie, dear, then we moved to London, then I retired to Cumbria. I spent fifty years in the fur trade. We've saved for this holiday for a long time. Put away all the twenty pee pieces.'

Osamu, the Japanese photographer, appeared, in a very smart suit, and asked her if he could take her photograph. 'Not till I've put my best teeth in, dear.' Then the two of us went in for dinner.

The first course on the set menu was *La Fricassée d'Ecrevisses et de Langoustines au Caviar servie dans son Marmiton*. Which was what it said it was. I counted them out and I counted them in, identifying shrimps, lobster and caviar, but the whole was even better than the sum of its parts, a piping hot mixture in a succulent but delicate sauce, served in a small glazed pot.

I asked Osamu what he ate at home and he thought hard and said that in ordinary Japanese homes they eat a lot of noodle soup. That was very popular with every family. Wasn't that a Chinese dish? Of course. Then curry, everyone liked curry. That's Indian, I said. What about some native dishes? He thought again and said spaghetti. I had to tell him this was Italian. Do try harder, Osamu. Then he had a brain wave and said that *all* children loved hamburgers. I don't think he managed to mention a single Japanese dish.

'Japanese men have one hour for lunch, but they only spend five minutes eating. Then they rest, or walk, or play a game, or go back to work early. Japanese men are not very interested in eating.'

Our second course was *L'Elegante Saint-Jacques cuite dans sa Coquille aux Herbes Fines*. It proved quite a challenge for both of us. Having been rather superior about his 'Japanese' cuisine, I failed to gain entry to this common or garden French dish. The shell was closed and seemed absolutely secured. Round the rim was a thin layer of pastry, so I ate that, worrying at first if it was edible. It was delicious. But was that all? Osamu followed suit, then he too paused, waiting for me to decide whether that was the end of the course or not.

There had been so little of it to eat, even by cuisine minceur standards. I picked up the whole shell for a final inspection, poked it with a knife, and suddenly I had managed to prise it open. Inside was the fish, or the scallop I suppose it would be called in England, all fresh and steaming, in a light, herby sauce. It was sensational, so pure and fresh, with none of those nasty mashed potatoes which so often muck up any trace of fish in the English versions.

The main course was *Les Noisettes de Chevreuil Renaissance Nappées de leur Sauce poivrade aux Baies de Genièvre*. I had to ask what this was. 'Fillets of deer,' said the waiter.

It looked strange when it arrived, a small roll of almost black meat, garnished with flowers. Every plate so far had arrived decorated with flowers or shrubbery. This had amused Osamu and I told him that in the Lake District, at a place called Sharrow Bay, everything comes decorated with flowers, even the porridge. I took a small slice of the venison, which was very nice, but it was lukewarm. I waited for Osamu to try his, and he agreed that his meat was only slightly warm, though everything else on the plate was hot. That's it, I said, I'm sending mine back. He looked worried, confused by the etiquette. Dinner was obviously the highlight of our evening, possibly of the whole trip. We were in no hurry. We were going nowhere, even if the train was. Let's get it to our satisfaction, I said, and called the waiter.

'No problem,' said the waiter.

How quickly 'no problem' has become an international phrase, second only to 'OK' as being understood by almost every human being on the planet.

'I have a love marriage,' Osamu was telling me, so I nodded. That's what they all say. He explained that he had married for love, unlike fifty per cent of the Japanese who still have arranged marriages. It is the godparents who make these arrangements, so he explained, working out a suitable partner of the same age, class and background.

'There are more divorces amongst love marriages than amongst arranged marriages,' he said. We had now come to little cake things, *Les Mignardises*, so I was not quite concentrating.

'When a love marriage goes wrong, they say that's it, no more, and they leave each other without telling anyone else. When an arranged marriage is going wrong, the godparents arrive at once and say you can't do it, it is bad for the family, bad for your career, bad for the children, you must not, you must keep trying, so people in arranged marriages are stopped from getting divorced.'

The latest fashion, so he said, was to have photographically arranged weddings. Many professional photographers had turned to this. Business was excellent, but he would never do it. He was a real photographer, an artist, who did books and photo-reportage. What happens, apparently, is that godparents arrange for their likely girls to get into their kimono and have their photograph taken by the best portrait photographer they can afford, someone who can cleverly brush out all blemishes. In the old days with an arranged marriage, you often never met your partner till the wedding day. Now, in the age of the photograph, you can at least have an advance image of what has been arranged for you.

And what about the geisha girls, I asked, all those places where tired businessmen go, according to the stories we're always reading about the Orient. Or was I thinking of Hong Kong. It was getting rather late by now.

'Japanese wives do exactly what men say. If a husband say that this white plate is a black plate, the wife will agree. That is her duty. If a husband comes home in the middle of the night with a business friend, the wife has to get up, be very welcoming, make a meal, smile and be nice till the friend decide to go. She must then say please, you're welcome, please stay longer. Husbands are king.'

His marriage, he added quickly, was not like that, being a love marriage and being one which had been exposed to Western values and ideas.

'In Japan, men come home to do two things – to eat and to sleep. They don't come home for sex. They have no time. A man comes home at around nine or ten. He has worked late or had a drink in a bar. When he gets home, the women ask for it, but the men are too tired. That is a joke, but a true joke about Japanese men.

'The trouble now is that in the afternoon television we are having a lot of sex series. The women watch all these, waiting for their men to come home. It goes through their heads. Very difficult. Many problems. So it happens with men who come to the door, to mend the television set . . .'

I rose with difficulty. It had been a terrific meal. Only six courses, if you count all the bits and pieces, but more than enough. How ever did they manage a hundred years ago?

*     *     *

After dinner, I set off back through the train towards the Bar Car. On the way, I could hear my American friend, Mary-Lou, having some altercation with one of the waiters, complaining about something or other, or perhaps exclaiming about something or other. There were three dining cars, each decorated in a different style, one of them in Chinoiserie, and by now all of them were rather noisy and boisterous.

Sitting at the bar were six French people I had noticed getting on at Boulogne, three couples in furs and dark suits. They had obviously been first out of dinner and had bagged the best seats, nearest the pianist. They were now very jolly and looked completely different from the very sombre people I had observed earlier. One of them was celebrating a birthday and they got the pianist to play 'Happy Birthday to You.' They sang the song in English, to my surprise, and then proceeded to take photographs of each other. The birthday woman made them gather round a couple of armchairs and told them to say 'cheese'. This was also in English. I thought at least the French would have their own pet phrase for taking photographs. Apart from that, their English was non-existent. I got talking to one of them, in my O level French, and discovered that the men were all notaries, partners and associates in the same legal firm. They were off to Venice for a few days.

The pianist was French, so I gathered from the way they were shouting requests at him. He was small and suave with crinkly eyes, the sort of ageless face which has spent a lifetime in night work yet still manages to look tanned and boyish. He was called Luc Harvet. It was a bit of a handicap being French, so he said, as the French have not given the world many popular classics.

'There's only about fifteen French songs which the world knows, but hundreds of Anglo Saxon tunes. Once you've played 'Ça c'est Bon' and 'La Vie en Rose', that's about it.'

I asked him for his five most requested songs, the songs which he knows, month after month, go down best, apart from 'Happy Birthday to You' and 'Jingle Bells' and other seasonal offerings. The number one, he said, must be 'New York, New York.' Second was 'Memories' from the musical *Cats*. Then 'As Time Goes By', the tune from the film *Casablanca*. Then came 'Don't Cry for me Argentina' from *Evita*. Finally, at Number Five, was a French tune, 'La Vie en Rose'. In nationalist order, that made two American tunes, two English and one French.

Yes, he thought that would also be a fair division of the train's passengers. From his observations, the majority were either English or American. On my particular trip, there would appear to have been more French and Italians than normal, while the Australians were just as prevalent as the English, but perhaps he was classing all Australians as English.

The bar was very crowded by now, though thanks to the discreet lighting it was very hard to make out exactly how many people were in the rest of the car. In the height of the summer, when the train has its full complement of coaches and passengers, it must become very crowded. I was pleased, though, that it was not smokey, which was what I had feared. Perhaps I was lucky.

The French lawyers were still going strong, as were their lady wives, and were now requesting Scott Joplin and rag time tunes. Suddenly they were all on their feet, moving back the armchairs. The bar car was arranged like a real bar, not a coach, with little polished tables, armchairs and sofas, more like a lounge in a gentleman's club than a train. When they had cleared a space near the bar, helped by one of the waiters, they all then started dancing. It was a most surprising sight, six sedate, rather ample, middle aged, bourgeois French couples, all jiving as they used to do, back in the 1950s, before the world went decadent and the scandalous sixties arrived.

I had never expected dancing, thinking that belonged to history, and the 1883 inaugural journey, but why not? On long journeys, passengers even on ordinary trains should be given a lot more facilities. I can never understand why British Rail don't have a book stall on their trains, with magazines and paperbacks. And why no telephones or television or radio? Individual ear phones could be provided, as on planes, so that other passengers would not be inconvenienced. I hate piped music, but the whole world seems to like it, so it's strange you don't come across Muzak on trains.

Almost everything has been done before of course, somewhere or at some time. Nagelmackers himself made sure that on his long three-day Trans-

Siberian expresses that the dining car saloons contained a library as well as games such as chess and dominoes. Secretaries, or dictating machines, would be a help on modern trains. Or little gyms or saunas for relaxing. As for more personal services, most of them have been tried at some time, if unofficially.

As my mind was wandering off onto rather more fanciful ideas, I found that my hand was being taken by one of the French ladies, a very attractive blonde lady, who was asking me to do something. I was a bit flustered at first, wondering what was going on, then I realised she wanted me to dance. I immediately got up. They were doing a sort of jive, bee-bop step. Just my style of dancing.

Osamu immediately appeared, as if from nowhere, with his camera. I had thought he had given up working for the night. He spoke to the lady in French, asking which was her husband, so he could go and get permission to take her photograph dancing with me. She laughed at his oriental politeness and said there was no need to ask *his* permission. Photograph as much as he liked. I wonder if any of them ever came out.

As we danced, I asked her if she came here often, ho ho, then we discussed children. She had three, about the same ages as my three, so we compared notes about awful teenagers.

I sat out the next dance, near the piano, and asked the pianist if dancing broke out on every trip. He said no, but regularly enough to be accepted. Every trip was different. On some trips hardly anyone dressed up and sometimes the bar would be half empty for most of the journey. You just couldn't tell from the way people looked when they got on how they would behave during the journey. Sounds very much like real life. Only quicker.

I went to bed just after twelve o'clock, telling myself that it did not matter whether I slept or not. I had never tried sleeping on a train before and was prepared for it to be a failure. I can never sleep in hotels, or anywhere except my own bed, so what chance had I in a toy bed on a train hurtling through the night.

I was right. I did not sleep, not that I was aware of, but I was perfectly happy not sleeping. I lay listening to the train noises, the tracks being crossed, the different speeds, the rushing through stations and under bridges, whistles in the distance, murmurings in the dark, then the whoosh of other trains suddenly hurtling past, wondering where we were, thinking about all the real people out there, living their normal lives, asleep in their normal beds, while we were flying past them in our fantasy world.

# ~ Chapter Four ~
# The End of the Train
*Breakfast in Italy;*
*the unfortunate demise of the Orient-Express;*
*Morning in Milan.*

There was a flash of whiteness as if the dark slate which had been the night had been miraculously wiped clean. I looked up and out at a slice of bright blue sky through the top of my cabin window. In the foreground, was a snow clad Alp, double decked with pine trees covered in snow, and beyond a little frozen stream running down a valley. It was broad daylight after all. I must have awakened in the Simplon Tunnel, catapulted into reality. We were now emerging from the bowels of Switzerland, zooming down into the belly of Italy.

A knock at the door and in came Olivier the steward with fresh coffee in a black Thermos pot, a fresh croissant, two rolls, butter, three pots of jam, marmalade and honey. Beside the tray, was that morning's newspaper. In English. It was not the London *Times*, as even the new Orient-Express is not yet that clever, but the *International Herald Tribune*. How had they got it on board? And where had the fresh croissants come from? They must have stopped somewhere in the night, without me realising. That proved I must have slept.

I moved my breakfast tray aside, carefully observing every item, in case anything should have accidentally slipped into my luggage, and got out of bed. The *International Herald Tribune* did not delay me long. Having got over the initial delight of finding that day's English speaking newspaper, I soon discovered it was full of American news, most of it several days old, though I did enjoy the American football and baseball reports and the detailed analysis of superstars I had never heard of.

I shaved and agreed with Henry Blowitz that it was an operation completed with ease and comfort, despite the moving train, though I did have trouble finding out how to put the plug in the sink. In the end, I let the tap run while I shaved, wasting the Orient-Express's valuable supply of water.

The train stopped at a place called Domodossola in Northern Italy, a rest after the exertion of the Alps, a rather nondescript looking town, where we changed locomotives. On the platform I could see several of our stewards in full uniform, walking slowly up and down. I hoped none of them got left behind. Domodossola did not look the nicest place in Italy to be stuck in.

It was in Italy in the 1930s, on the Rome Express, that the worst possible leaving-behind happened. In those days, this luxury express had a bath car and just before Florence the steward told one of the lady passengers, who had requested a bath, that he had run the water for her and she should now get in. She was a regular traveller, and thought she knew the train's timetable well, but for some reason she put off getting into the bath for half an hour. After she had finally had her bath, she got out to return to her sleeping cabin. But she was too late. The train had gone on and stretching ahead of her was the empty track. Her bath car had been left behind in a siding and so had she, with no clothes, passport or money.

It would be a great convenience today to be able to have a bath or even a shower on the Orient-Express. Many Americans are always asking if there is such a thing, but it would obviously create great complications. Storage space is limited and they could never carry enough water to give all 170 passengers a bath. You have to be the Royal Family these days to have a bath on a train, preferably an Arab or a Moroccan Royal family, as they are the ones with their own luxury private trains.

The British Royal Family had bathrooms on their trains, complete with silver taps, from 1914 when George V and Queen Mary lived on the royal coach for many days at a time, touring munition factories. As he was working, a bathroom was considered as much a necessity as a luxury.

I had tried to talk to Olivier the previous day, but with getting passengers settled, he had had no time for idle chats. Now, as he took my tray away, he managed to pause for a few questions. From Bordeaux, he said, aged twenty-six, trained at a hotel school and worked at the London Hilton for a while, as chief waiter and then Maître d'Hôtel. He was back in France, and temporarily unemployed, when he saw the advert for the Orient-Express job in the French catering magazine, *Hôtellerie*.

He found the movement of the train not too difficult for working, but the hours and the shift system very tiring. Almost all the staff are young and unmarried, otherwise they probably could not stand it for long. 'I get only three hours sleep a night. When I do sleep, I have to make sure another steward is covering my coach in case I am needed.' On his coach, S1, he had eight single rooms like mine, plus four doubles, which meant sixteen people to deal with. He does not clean the cabins as that is done by a contract cleaning firm in Boulogne, but he makes up all the beds, prepares and serves continental breakfast and provides constant room service. All the sorts of services one would expect in a grand hotel. He also looks after the fire. The fire?

I had missed the fire completely. So he took me along to the end of the coach and there, behind the beautifully panelled door, was a live stove, glowing away, with fresh coke about to be put on. This heats the water for the central heating in each cabin.

He loved the train, and found it very intimate, but he could not imagine working on it for ever. 'Another couple of years perhaps. But it will do me good. It will be like a certificate, having worked on here. Very good when I go for another job. And it has been fun.'

What sort of fun? Well, he had looked after Catherine Deneuve, Liza Minnelli and Sidney Poitier when they had recently been on the train. That was fun.

'Oh, this is very funny,' he said. 'This will amuse you, being English. On the last trip we had two Englishmen in next door cabins – one was called Mr Holmes and one was called Mr Watson.'

I went down the train and peered into the kitchen where all was quietness and calm. The previous evening, when they had been preparing dinner, from seven-thirty till two in the morning, it had been pandemonium. They were now working away on the midday meal, our final meal on the train before Venice, a cold buffet, known rather unattractively as Brunch, which gave little clue to its scale and richness.

There were five chefs, all very young, silently working in their full uniform with very tall white hats. Like all train kitchens, there seemed hardly enough space for them to stand up, never mind cook for 140 people. They were in a line, side by side, like bishops engaged in some silent religious ritual, anointing vegetables, blessing fish, saving the souls of artichokes. It bore no comparison with the kitchens on British Rail I have glimpsed when the sweat and steam and the squalor make them look like a penitentiary for chefs not a place of work, never mind worship. The whole kitchen area seemed to be garlanded with flowers and leaves, as if by mistake I had stumbled into one of the glass houses at Kew Gardens. As each chef finished preparing a dish, he stretched out and decorated it with leaves or flowers.

I doubt if those two writers on the 1883 Orient-Express, who made it their business to inspect the kitchen, could have been any more surprised than I was. It seemed inconceivable that so many beautiful things could be created in such a confined space.

Through a glass door at the end I could see two men washing up, the *plongeurs*. They were in blue checked uniform with red scarves round their necks, working equally silently and intently. They stared at me through the glass, their eyes far away, then returned to the soapy suds.

I did not dare speak to any of the chefs, for fear of ruining their concentration, but watched them for a while as they made shapes out of smoked salmon, filled avocados with shrimps, removed mussels from their shells and then returned them, transformed and decorated into new creations. The image of those five young chefs, so completely occupied by their artistry, stayed in my mind long after that journey was over.

\*　　　\*　　　\*

The heyday of the old Orient-Express was between the wars. That was when Grand People took the Grand Trains and lived a Grand Life which disappeared for ever when the last war began. Or so it was thought.

Royalty had travelled on it from the beginning, thanks to King Leopold of the Belgians, the Company's first patron. Later Royals often travelled with it, rather than on it, attaching their own private luxurious coaches, as in the case of the Emperor Haile Selassie. Others sometimes travelled as humbly as possible, such as the Emperor Charles of the Austro-Hungarian Empire who on his return from exile disguised himself as a gardener. King Ferdinand of Bulgaria once travelled on the train locked in the lavatory, trying to avoid assassins.

Ferdinand was a great railway enthusiast. In 1912, just before the first Balkan War, he was travelling on the Orient-Express from a conference in Paris when he pulled the emergency cord, just as the train crossed the frontier into Bulgaria. He then demanded to take over the controls of the train. Now that they were travelling through *his* country, he maintained he had the right to be the engine driver. He made a mess of this first attempt, jamming the brakes so that the train was delayed for four hours, but he improved on subsequent attempts. It was eventually agreed with the company that he could drive the train in Bulgaria if he wanted, but only between scheduled stops.

One of the strangest episodes on the Orient-Express involved a President of France, Paul Deschanel. In 1920, he was on his way from Paris to Lyons to unveil a monument. An early breakfast was ordered on the train for him and his officials, but he didn't turn up. Someone was sent to his sleeping cabin, but found he was not there. He seemed to have completely disappeared. Then it was reported that a body had been seen falling from the train some twenty miles back.

The 64-year-old President was meanwhile staggering along the track, bruised and shivering in his pyjamas. He eventually came to a level crossing where he told a railway worker that he was President of France. 'And I'm the Emperor Napoleon,' so the workman replied.

Had he been pushed or had he opened the wrong door by mistake? Rumours swept France that he had either been drunk or had become mentally deranged. Four months later he resigned.

Royals used the train simply to travel Royally, but many big businessmen, especially the international financiers, used the Orient-Express as a place to do business, moving mysteriously from one country to another, setting up deals as they did so, operating from the train itself. The best known Orient-Express customer of all time was Sir Basil Zaharoff, the world's greatest and most notorious arms dealer. His enemies maintain that during the First World War, by supplying arms to both sides, he amassed £10 for every person killed.

Zaharoff began his deals on wheels on the Orient-Express in 1885, two years after the inaugural trip, selling submarines in Greece and Turkey and other countries along the route. He always booked a complete compartment, number seven, and would sometimes spend weeks on the train.

In 1886, he was in his usual compartment, on his way from Paris to Vienna in the hope of selling guns to the Austro-Hungarian Imperial Army. Also on the train was the Duke of Marchena, a cousin of the King of Spain, and his sixteen-year-old bride. They had just married and it was their honeymoon trip. In the middle of the night, the young Duchess came hammering on Zaharoff's cabin door.

She was half naked and bleeding, her nightdress ripped, and she maintained that her husband had gone berserk and attacked her. She pleaded to be let in, saying that her husband was going to kill her. Down the corridor came the Duke, carrying a dagger. Zaharoff let the frightened young Duchess into his compartment and called a steward who finally managed to disarm the Duke.

Zaharoff was approaching forty at the time but this brief encounter with the sixteen-year-old Duchess resulted in love at first sight – a secret love which lasted forty years. They were ultimately able to marry on the death of the Duke, who had long since been put in an asylum.

The marriage took place in 1924 and Zaharoff bought his bride the Monte Carlo Casino as a wedding present. He paid one million pounds for it, using some spare funds from his London bank account.

His wife died not long afterwards, in 1926, and for the last ten years of his life, Zaharoff became a recluse, living a Howard Hughes existence. He died in a hotel suite in Monte Carlo in 1936. A faithful servant then set out to execute Zaharoff's last wish, booking compartment seven on the Orient Express. At the exact spot on the line where Zaharoff had first heard the screams of the sixteen year old girl, some fifty years earlier, and at exactly the same time, 2.32 in the morning, the servant tore up her photograph, one that Zaharoff had always kept in his wallet, and threw the pieces out of the window. Beat that, Agatha Christie.

The other great financier associated with dealings on the Orient-Express was Calouste Gulbenkian. He and his wife escaped from Constantinople in 1896, during Turkish persecutions of Armenians, with his baby son Nubar wrapped up in a carpet. The Orient-Express stewards were not very keen on having a refugee family in the restaurant, dressed in ragged clothes and carrying so many bundles of what looked like rags, till out of one bundle Gulbenkian produced enough money and jewellery to pay their way.

It was many years later on the Orient-Express, this time in a dining car, that he did his most famous deal. He had brought together several oil companies, including Royal Dutch Shell, and the representatives of the Middle Eastern oil fields, and did a deal whereby he got 2½% of all future oil revenues. It was to be from both sides, hence the name by which he became known from then on, Mr Five Per Cent. The original deal was written out on the back of an Orient-Express menu.

The Orient-Express was never a hard and fast route, fixed in time and place, and over the years after 1883 its routes and termini changed several times, spawning sister Orient-Expresses, often going at the same time but taking different directions to get roughly to the same places. The basic Paris –Constantinople Orient-Express service remained an exclusive luxury train until 1970, give or take a few world wars, changes in national frontiers and various other acts of God and man which interrupted or temporarily changed its history.

During the First World War, Germany would not allow 'foreign' trains to travel through its country and many were confiscated or destroyed. The great express trains were looked upon as instruments of war, services on vital routes which had to be controlled or destroyed, and on occasions they became part of international power politics.

At the end of the war, Wagons-Lits provided what became the best known railway coach in history, car no 2419. It was ordered for Marshal Foch, commander of the Allied Forces, and conversion work was done by the Company at great speed, turning it into a conference salon. It was in this coach that the German surrender was signed, on 11 November 1918, and the First World War came to an end.

The historic car was then put on show at Les Invalides in Paris and over the subsequent years tens of thousands of visitors came to see it. It became a symbol of the defeat of Germany, not just to the Allied countries but to Adolf Hitler, who had been a young corporal in the German Army and could not forgive his leaders.

In June 1940, when Hitler had successfully invaded France, he ordered Wagons-Lits number 2419 to be taken from its exhibition site. It had by now been removed from Les Invalides and put inside a special hall near the spot outside Paris where the German Armistice had been signed in 1918. They had had some difficulty in building the hall round the coach, but the German panzer soldiers, sent to retrieve it, did not bother with any engineering niceties. They simply blew up the walls of the exhibition hall and hauled the car to the *precise* spot where the German humiliation had taken place.

Two weeks later, Hitler, along with Goering and other high-ranking Nazis, arrived to dictate terms to the French delegation. The French were made to sign their surrender inside the coach and afterwards Hitler apparently did a brief dance of joy, a sight which was captured on film. 'The historic German car,' so Hitler proclaimed, 'and the monument to French triumph will be brought to Berlin. The rail on which it had stood in 1918 will be destroyed so that no trace of Germany's defeat in 1918 shall remain.'

The historic coach was then exhibited in Berlin, this time becoming a focus for German pride and aspirations, a symbol of their achievements.

However, as the war progressed and the Allies advanced, the coach became a prime target and bombers were directed to try to destroy it, but they failed to find it. Intelligence sources reported back to London that Hitler had changed its location. De Gaulle personally requested its site to be discovered and the coach blown up, but Hitler managed to keep its new position secret.

By 1944, he knew the end was coming. When General Patton's troops were marching on Berlin, Hitler finally gave the order that Number 2419 should be destroyed. 'It must never become a triumph of the Allies once more.' The SS then blew it up. A piece of railway and world history had gone for ever.

So why, with all that history behind it, did the Orient-Express come to an end? The aeroplane killed it off. It was not an instant death, however, as the early planes could cover ground no more quickly than the train. The first scheduled Air France and Imperial Airways flights to Athens and Turkey took longer than the Orient-Express because of the need for overnight stops. But by the 1960s, the jet set went by jet planes, businessmen went on business flights and holiday makers started going on all-in package flights. Even the Royals gave up the train for the plane.

The train got slower and tattier and passengers who wanted to do the entire 1,900 miles journey from Paris to Constantinople had to change endlessly, rarely getting restaurant accommodation or sleeping cars. Local engines would be used and even cattle trucks would be hitched on from time to time.

But even if Sherwood had not resurrected it, the train would have lived on for ever, if only in fiction. It has regularly appeared in books and plays for at least eighty years, though not always by the correct name. It is hard to find the first reference, but Oscar Wilde in *Lady Windermere's Fan*, first produced in 1892, hints at it when he has his mysterious Mrs Erlynne depart for Paris on the 'Club Train'.

In *Lady Chatterley's Lover*, which appeared in 1928, D. H. Lawrence does spell out the name of the train correctly, managing to get in a sneer at the same time, when he is describing Lady Chatterley going off to Venice on the train with her father. 'The old artist always did himself well. He took berths on the Orient-Express, in spite of Connie's dislike of trains de luxe, the atmosphere of vulgar depravity there is aboard them nowadays.'

Auden and Christopher Isherwood went East on an express train in the 1930s and wrote about it in *Journey to War*. They recalled that the cars had samovars and that Chinese car boys brought round hot towels as well as teas, but they were not very complimentary about the wagon lit accommodation which would have upset old Nagelmackers. They described it as a 'shabby old Belgian sleeping berth.'

The most sensational book about the Orient-Express, and the one which started the whole mystique about the train, was *The Madonna of the Sleeping Cars* by Maurice Dekobra, first published in France in 1925. It was quickly translated into twenty-seven languages and became a play and a film. The novel was thought rather scandalous at the time, involving seduction on the train, Communist plots, violence and intrigue, all the sort of stuff which later Ian Fleming did so well. The heroine was a Scottish aristocrat, daughter of the Duke of Inverness, which no doubt gave it that extra exotic air, as far as French readers were concerned.

Graham Greene produced a rather classier thriller, *Stamboul Train*, which appeared in 1932 and combined excitement with psychological insight. It was the book which established him as a writer. He had left his job on *The Times* to finish it, hoping it would enable him to live full time on his novels. The route in the story covers most of the original Orient-Express route, going all the way to Istanbul, but Greene starts it in Ostend rather than Paris. The atmosphere, and the descriptions of the Orient-Express train, were all authentic.

The novel which most people think of, when they think of the Orient-Express, is Agatha Christie's *Murder on the Orient-Express*. In fact, Miss Christie never wrote such a book. She called it *Murder in the Calais Coach* which was its title in the first few editions when it came out in 1934. She was a regular traveller on the Orient-Express, accompanying her first husband, Colonel Christie, on his trips to the Middle East and then her second husband, Sir Max Mallowan, on his archaelogical expeditions to Greece.

Ian Fleming's *From Russia with Love*, published in 1957, is thought to be the most accurate description of life on the post-war Orient-Express. The climax of the novel happens on the train, as Bond is trying to unravel some Smersh plot, going from the Balkans to France, via Venice and the Simplon tunnel.

The final run of the real train, by then called the Direct Orient-Express, was on 19 May, 1977. And much to the amazement of the Turkish migrant workers, and to the amusement of Balkan villages along the route, those television and newspapers from around the world arrived to cover the last trip. It was but a shadow of the old days, with only four shabby coaches, no restaurant, which meant passengers had to bring their own food, and they were five hours late reaching Istanbul. Oh, such ignominy.

*          *          *

There was no sign of snow by the time we got to Milan so I got off the train to stretch my legs, careful not to wander too far, much as I wanted to. It was the first time I had left the train since Boulogne. To my surprise, I had never felt the need of it. I had imagined, before setting out, that I would miss the fresh air and exercise, sitting on a train for twenty-five hours, but I felt remarkably fresh. I had walked up and down the train so often, and talked to so many people, that I had not had time to read any of the books I had brought with me, nor time to look out of the windows. I had missed the Rhone Valley, the Matterhorn, Lake Maggiore, though of course it had been dark when we had gone through those places.

I had also not felt cramped or claustrophobic, which had been another fear. Apart from sitting in the bar before and after dinner, there had seemed ample space and privacy, if I had wanted it.

Several other passengers were on the platform, most of them taking photographs of each other. I posed for Osamu once again, having become his tame model, getting on and off each coach at his request. Back in Japan, who will they think this funny Englishman is, the one in the long coat and silly hat? Perhaps they will assume I am the eccentric millionaire who owns the train.

An English couple were in high excitement. They had discovered that their sleeping compartment was right over the Wagons-Lits coat of arms, a massive heraldic device in gold on the side of each coach which displays the original wording of the company, *Cie Internationale des Wagons-Lits et Des Grands Express Européens*. It made a splendid photograph, him and then her, sitting in their own cabin at their little polished desk beside the Lalique lamp, cleverly glimpsed through their own window, with below the coat of arms framing perfectly the shot. Very arty.

It is only off the train that you get the full impact of the vestibules at either end of most coaches, little enclosed platforms with their own glass doors, set at an angle, havens of fresh air when the train gets too hot where gentlemen could take their cigars in the old days, before air conditioning was invented. I think a lot of people had still not explored the train properly, either inside or outside, which was a shame. If you are travelling in a museum, and paying for that privilege, it is a waste not to see all the exhibits.

It is always claimed about Mussolini that at least he made the trains run on time, which was something of an exaggeration, though he did greatly improve all train services. Under his Fascist regime, from 1922–43, a distinctive form of architecture emerged, especially in the public buildings. Milan Station was begun in 1906, the year the Simplon Tunnel opened, and was completed in 1932, Milan's answer to Rome's Colosseum. It is still the biggest station in Europe. Above my head, the vast dome of the roof seemed to stretch for miles, but I was too scared to explore the station. I remembered that lady in her bath who had been left behind.

Back on the train, I went into the Bar Car and sat drinking coffee with a group of passengers. They were all discussing Mary-Lou, our American lady friend. Apparently there had been some incident the previous night at dinner and she had been heard shouting at some of the waiters. I asked the train manager, but he held his lips tightly together, looking very serious and sombre, giving nothing away. Someone else suggested that she had perhaps become tired and emotional. But where was she now? No one had seen her all morning. Surely she would appear for brunch, an all American title for a meal which was reportedly going to be a visual feast. Osamu was already taking photographs of the buffet table being set. Had Mary-Lou walked out of the train or just slept in? A mystery at last.

We then discussed Cynthia, a much younger and very attractive American girl, and we all remarked on the change in her personality during the journey. After leaving Victoria, where everyone had seen her kissing her boy friend, she had been quiet, keeping herself to herself, but last night at dinner she had suddenly blossomed, becoming the life and soul, the one everyone had wanted to dance with.

Cynthia was also nowhere to be seen. No one had bumped into her all morning. Having exhausted any gossip about personalities on the train, we then turned to generalisations.

'I think most people on this train fall into two categories,' said John, an English lawyer. 'They are either very wealthy and have no idea what it is all costing, or they are in a high cash-flow job. They have quite a bit of money coming in, and are quite glad to get rid of it, before the tax man takes it.'

We then discussed the prices, and whether the whole journey had been worth it. The single fare on my journey, from London to Venice, had been £250, without meals. (In 1986, the price had jumped to £520, with meals, for a slightly longer journey.) As the company pointed out, this was no more than a single first class plane fare to Venice, plus the cost of an overnight stay in a good hotel. After all, you are getting twenty-five hours on board, including your own bedroom and morning breakfast.

'I don't think it was expensive,' said an art dealer. 'The food was excellent.'

'I didn't like the French waiters,' said the lawyer. 'I think they are disdainful of the English.'

'I thought they put on a much better show than the English,' said another. 'I thought the French outclassed us.'

'I thought it was *all* wonderful,' said Audrey, the well dressed Australian lady. 'It did cost us £100 for our dinner last night, which was pretty strong, but it was terribly good.'

'If I come again,' said the lawyer. 'I'll fly to Paris and join the train there. I don't think I'd like to do that Channel trip again.'

Listening to the chat round the tables in the bar, I would say nobody I met had disliked the journey. Nobody thought it a waste of money or regretted having come. There were, of course, minor complaints. Some had felt it very hot. Many people thought the bar was too expensive and the bar service not very friendly or efficient. The dinner had been enjoyed by everyone, though most people had been amazed by the price.

Brunch was served in one of the restaurant cars. My eyes could hardly take in all the many displays and I chose something from about a dozen items, ranging from shell fish, smoked salmon, stuffed vegetables to various meats. All in small quantities, of course. We were now not far from Venice. I did not want to get off the train at the end of the journey and be sick.

There was still no sign of Mary-Lou. Surely she would emerge before we got to Venice. Could the Orient-Express turn out to be as disappointing for her as the Dorchester Hotel had been?

On the way back to my cabin, to start packing for our arrival in Venice, I met Mary-Lou, coming out of her sleeping cabin. She looked a bit bleary, but soon came to life when I asked her how she was feeling. She had missed Brunch. On Principle.

'That dinner was supposed to be the "*pièce de résistance*" ' she said. 'Forget it.'

I said I'd heard there had been some argument over dinner. What exactly had happened?

'They just couldn't get it together. Charlie ordered the set menu, but I decided to choose from the other side. We always do that. That way you get to sample everything. I got my first course, and Charlie got nothing. Then after an hour, I got my second course. And he still got nothing. Then they came and cleared away Charlie's silver! Gee, what a performance.

'Eventually they brought back his silver, laid it all out and served his dessert! That was when I shouted at them. We got into this big conference, this big scene with the Staff. So we started all over again and Charlie at last got his coquille.

'What I had was fine, just fine. So was all Charlie's food, when he got it. The salad, well that was a bit salty, and you know salt is very bad for you. Salt creates high tension.

'Looking back, I would say Act One was best. I wanted to be treated really graciously on this train, and I was when we were in England. That champagne, wow. Their Pullmans were much nicer than anything I had expected.

'Act Two, well they didn't get it together, not for me. I don't like saying it, as I am a warm hearted person, but they just gotta tighten up Act Two.

'I want them to succeed, oh my, I really do. It's a lovely idea. This world needs the Orient-Express.

'I'm told the Danieli in Venice has *very* good food. Oh boy, I just can't wait for the Danieli . . .'

# ~ Chapter Five ~

# Venice

*Grand Tours to Italy;*
*a meeting with a Contessa;*
*a short walk round Venice;*
*a small person at the door about double*
*glazing.*

The new Venice Simplon Orient-Express company has gracefully turned the clock back and resurrected one of the original pleasures in making a journey, when to travel was more important than to arrive, confounding at last the age of the plane which has successfully taken all the fun out of travelling, making the arrival its sole justification. All the same, if the new Orient-Express was *not* going to Venice, would it be anywhere as attractive as it undoubtedly is? Would it be as enjoyable to end up in Birmingham?

Venice is one of the wonders of the world, preserved in water and aspic for humanity, a place which everyone on the planet should visit. I'm not sure then why I took so long to visit it. It was only in the previous year that I had ever been, on a brief holiday with my wife. I think all those people raving about it had put me off. They seem so elitist and superior, those Venice lovers, like people running a terribly worthwhile charity who will admit no weakness or criticism and in the process become unbearably self-righteous.

For twenty years, I had never fancied a town holiday anyway, preferring the sun and the sea, beaches and swimming, rather than walking around streets or looking at galleries and buildings. With age, of course, we all change, especially when you no longer have young children to drag round. Now I positively like exploring new cities.

For my own Grand Tour, though, the main Italian city I had lined up to visit for the first time was Florence. I had got it into my mind that Tuscany is the area which no truly civilised person should miss, so that was my particular aim, on the Italian section of my Tour.

At one time, in the seventeenth century, Naples was the main attraction. Rome was in and out of fashion, though it was always there, on most itineraries. By the 19th century, Florence had taken over as the number one goal.

The Elizabethans started this craze for Italy and were responsible for the whole notion of a Grand Tour, though the phrase itself did not appear in print until 1679. Shakespeare rather mocks this passion in *The Merchant of Venice* (written about 1596) when he has Portia teasing the Englishman who 'bought his doublet in Italy, his round hose in France, his bonnet in Germany, and his behaviour everywhere.'

Why did they all go to Italy? Well, it was educational for a start, a part of one's learning. As neither Oxford nor Cambridge taught languages or the arts, anyone with any ambition or cultural pretensions had to go to Italy in order to round off his education. It could be considered an education purely for its own sake, as the young man would then return to settle down on his estates, or it could be used as an aid to a future career, as a diplomat or in some public position.

So many young gentlemen were crossing the Channel by the late 16th century that in certain quarters it was felt they could be picking up bad habits. One of the reasons why Trinity College, Dublin was founded in 1592 was as a rival attraction to the Continent, hoping to offer young Englishmen the chance of travel, but to somewhere relatively safe and traditional.

Milton made sure he picked up no bad habits when he toured Italy in 1638. 'I never once deviated from the paths of integrity and virtue, and perpetually reflected that, though my conduct escaped the notice of men, it could not elude the inspection of God.' What a prig. Most other young men were hoping for a bit of fun along the way, such as Thomas Coryat, a well born young man from Somerset, fresh out of Oxford, who did his Tour in 1608. 'Of all the pleasures in the world,' he wrote, 'travel is in my opinion the sweetest and most delightful.' He exudes about all the new and exciting things he came across in Italy. He saw forks being used for the first time, and fans and umbrellas, things he had never heard of before, and he also tasted dried frogs.

Coryat had read all the latest guide books to Italy – and the first one, written in English, was produced by William Thomas in 1549 – but he noted in his diary one thing which none of the guide books had mentioned – brothels. He was told there were at least 20,000 'courtesans' in Venice. 'Many of them esteemed so loose that they are said to open their quivers to every arrow.' What a neat description.

He was surprised that brothels were tolerated by Venice, but was told that the citizens thought it helped to protect the chastity of their own wives because of these places of 'evacuation'. He discovered that a foundling hospital was provided, for any children of the courtesans, but noted that in fact they had very few babies. 'According to the old proverb, the best carpenters make the fewest chips.'

*    *    *

Out of season, I didn't expect to see many brothels in Venice, or very much at all, because the weather on my arrival was appalling. I might as well have been anywhere. Early in the year is obviously not the best time to see Venice and Venice was not to be seen, however much I strained my eyes as the train crawled over that long causeway, one and a half miles long, built in 1933, which takes the railway line over the lagoon to the main island of Venice. The mist had completely taken over. Normally, a train arrival in Venice is an experience, almost as exciting as arriving by taxi boat across the sea from Marco Polo airport, which is probably the nicest way of all to arrive.

A railway arrival is nonetheless exciting as the train brings you right to the very entrance of Venice itself. Santa Lucia Station guards one end of the Grand Canal, the magnificent waterway which curves in a giant S bend right through the heart of Venice, dwarfing all the other canals in size and grandeur. It is the city's main street, stretching for two miles, and is never less than forty yards across, in some places over seventy, with 200 palaces lining its banks. At the far end of the Grand Canal stands St Mark's Square, the largest and most magnificent square in Venice containing the two most splendid buildings, the Basilica of San Marco and the Doge's Palace. The train brings you right to the edge of all these treasures, thus avoiding the nastier elements of modern urban life on the mainland coast. There are no cars from now on, no lorries or vans, no carbon monoxide fumes or traffic noise. Nothing to choke on. Except, on that particular day, the terrible mist.

There is a school of thought which maintains that mist enhances Venice, bringing out the Turneresque shapes and the eerie silence, heightening the mysterious alleys and the empty squares. Perhaps a *slight* mist does some of that, but I prefer a clear Spring sun. Venice is magical anyway and does not need any further aids to improve it. I want to see it in *all* its glories, with nothing obscured.

I went down the train to say farewell, to cast my eye for the last time on some other things lovely. Osamu was busy taking his final photographs of every coach and every item on them. I walked along the corridors with him, realising that our sleeping car was one of the more restrained, not as highly decorated as most of the others. Some of the upholstery was peacock bright. The panelling around many of the washbasins created a *trompe l'oeil* effect, with disappearing mirrors and hidden cabinets.

I was so busy examining the other sleeping compartments, which of course I had been unable to do when the train was occupied, that I was nearly drowned. I hadn't noticed that a massive automatic washing machine, like a mobile car wash, was slowly and stealthily sliding itself down the platform, clinging to the side of the train like a giant watery limpet. I had my head out of a coach at the time, but drew it in with only seconds to spare. Next came a polishing machine. I was ready for that, though I came off the train smelling like a hospital corridor.

I left the station at last, hoping the mist had cleared. Peering across the Grand Canal, I could hardly see the other side. As for the public water buses, the highly efficient and very cheap vaporettos, I could see none at all. They seemed to have given up the ghost, swallowed for ever by the mist. So I shared a taxi boat with a young English couple who had been on the train, so they said, but I had never noticed them. They were Sue and Geoff Harper from

Shropshire, where they run a small hotel, on their first holiday for five years, the first since they got married. They had never even had the time or the money for a honeymoon. The train had lived up to all their expectations. 'Superb but expensive. We paid £2 for some Perrier, which we gave away. So we never went back to the bar again.' So that was why I had never seen them.

I had booked into the Gritti Palace Hotel as the Cipriani, where I had stayed on my only other visit to Venice, was closed. The Gritti has a superb position, right on the Grand Canal, with a magnificent terrace, though of course this would not be much use in winter. In that mist it would have been dangerous just to step out on it.

The important person's name I had been given was Countess Anna Maria Cicogna. She had been personally recommended to me by John Julius Norwich, and also by two other experts on Venice I had spoken to. They all said she was the most knowledgable lady in Venice.

I decided to ring her as soon as I had checked in. The hotel was almost empty and it was like starring in my own film, walking through enormous reception rooms, full of fine furnishings and paintings, with silent staff lurking somewhere in the background. I rang the Countess's number from my bedroom on an ultra modern press button phone. A maid said she was 'in repose'. I thought for a moment that was it, I had arrived too late. Then she said ring back at five o'clock. The Contessa would be awake then.

So I walked round Venice in the mist, watching the scurrying figures bend forward, long coats tightly fastened, moving quickly across the grey squares like pinball men, going home from work in a trance, their minds elsewhere. From time to time, I could hear echoing down the alleyways the sounds of students, arms interlinked, laughing loudly, then a moment later they and their voices had disappeared, over a little arched bridge, into another lane, lost in the mist. It was eerie but not frightening, mysterious yet not mystifying.

Those films and novels about Venice which have played up the element of menace do it a disservice. Perhaps if it had been my first visit I would have been more alarmed, concerned that I might get lost, or stumble into something or someone dangerous. I soon did lose my exact bearings, but I knew the general direction in which I was walking, what square or bridge I should soon come to, and I felt safe and happy, almost at home, cheered by a familiar church or a recognisable square. There were few tourists around, which was a relief. Once the locals had finished their short journeys home, the city itself seemed to go to sleep completely, floating off into its own dream-like sea.

I rang from a café at five o'clock precisely. A lady with perfect English said fine, certainly come at once, just across the Accademia Bridge and turn left, heading for the Salute Church.

For most of the way, I was on my own, unable to believe that down those narrow, darkened, silent alleyways any life could possibly be going on, suppers being cooked, televisions being switched on. Her front door, when I eventually found it, looked far too humble to enclose a Countess, but once inside, a butler took my coat and I could see some very large rooms and beyond a galleried sitting room lined with books and paintings. The Countess was sitting on a long settee talking to and petting a chihuahua. She looked about sixty, but could have been older, or younger, as she was so perfectly dressed and made up.

Her father was Count Volpi, in many ways the maker of modern Venice. He was Governor of Libya from 1921 to 1925, having reconquered Tripolitania for the Italians, which was when he was given his title. He came back to Venice and was instrumental in establishing the film and theatre festivals and in bringing various industries to the mainland. He was also part owner at one time of the CIGA hotels, which own the Gritti, Danieli and several other top European hotels.

'I spent my early years between Rome and Libya. I never went to school. We always had an English Nanny and then an English Governess. In 1936, after my marriage, we moved to London for a year, and lived in Hill Street, Mayfair. My husband was an anti-Fascist and life in Italy had become difficult.'

Countess Cicogna was born in Venice though her title, which comes from her husband, is Milanese, and she has been active for many years in the struggle to save Venice. From sinking, I said. No, no she replied. That is the common misapprehension. The danger to Venice is from the *rising* waters which every winter erode the City.

'The problem is all man made. In the first place it was caused by the creation of three great dykes and the dredging and deepening of the canals by the Austrians, so that bigger ships could arrive. Now when high water comes, the City is flooded.

'The first real killer flood was on 6 November, 1966. That day St Mark's Square was covered to a depth of one metre. This year it has also been bad. Every day before Christmas we were flooded. It is all a tragedy. I fear now that the only way to save the City will be moveable dykes, the sort you have built for the Thames Barrier, but that will cost billions. The major countries of the world have already given great help, such as the United States, Germany, England, France, but we need more. It is a crisis the world should share. Or Venice will be lost.'

She misses the emigrée communities, artists and writers and aristocrats from America and England, the sort who once took over the grand palaces in the summer. They have all gone. She remembers that the finest balls of all were given by the Cole Porters to which her parents were invited.

'Venice at one time only had elite tourists, the English baronets and German princesses, painters, writers, cultured American millionaires. It was a centre of culture and elegance. Now Venice is flooded with *rucksacks*. These young people, these hippies, fill the vaporetti with their enormous *rucksacks* and all they bring with them to Venice is their smell.'

She emphasised rucksacks several times, pronouncing it 'rooksacks', the only flaw in her otherwise perfect English.

'When Venice was an elite city it had excellent shops and people from the provincial towns, like Padua, Verona, Treviso, Vicenza, used to come here to buy their wedding trousseau. Venice was a small capital. Now they don't come any more. They have their own shops.

'The young people are all leaving. There are no houses for them in Venice, so they go to the mainland to work and live in those terrible modern blocks. Venice is now a City of old people. When a City becomes old, it loses its momentum.

'The revival of the Carnival, that has been one good thing. It was nothing five years ago. Now it is an international attraction and rather important. It brings people in the winter (it takes place in February) who otherwise would not come.'

I asked her for the *best* things in Venice for a visitor to do and see – and her answers took hardly a moment's thought. Usually, when you ask someone such an inane question, to name the best paintings, or the best hotels, they dither and dother, wanting to know what is meant by *best*, and at what time of the year are we talking about, for what sort of people, in what sort of mood, then finally they dismiss the question as utterly ridiculous and impossible to answer. All true. But ask a real aristocrat, one of a certain age, and you will find they have few doubts, just as they have few doubts about their place in the world.

'There are only *two* painters to see in Venice and just two places in which to see the best of their work. Come here. I will write the words down for you so you get the right spelling.'

I obediently moved beside her and her dog. Before writing anything, she got out her make-up case and gave herself a brief inspection, then applied a quick dab of powder.

'There is no point in searching for the Canalettos. No point at all. Yes, there are two fine ones here, but the Queen of England has some of the best ones. The same with Titian. Titians and Canalettos can be seen better elsewhere in the world.

'So you come to Venice to see Tintoretto, and the best place for him is San Rocco. Secondly, you come to see Carpaccio, and the best place for him is San Giorgio degli Schiavoni. These are both Schools. You know what Schools are?'

I did know that. Schools in Venice look like Churches, but they're not, being more akin to the medieval guildhalls in England, places where people in the same profession grouped themselves together to perform good works or instruct their members.

'Naturally, you will have to *suffer* the Doge's Palace, which is not at all agreeable and the crowds can be horrible, and as a visitor you will also want to see San Marco, which is full of treasures but also full of crowds. Try to see them, but quickly and early.

'Now, let me see, two islands. Yes, firstly, Murano. The glass blowing is fascinating, a miracle of ability and cleverness, and the Cathedral of San Donato is a marvel. Look for the mosaic floor which has just been restored. The other island to see is Torcello for its cathedral, which is also being restored.

'The Lido? Certainly not. No one visits the Lido. On a short holiday or a long holiday, my advice is the same – don't go.

'Right, hotels. Well that's easy. In town, the best is the Gritti which is a very special place, then the Cipriani for out of town. In the summer particularly, during the height of the season, the Cipriani is the place to be. No, I am not mentioning the Danieli, even though my father used to own it. You asked for two, and those are my two.

'Restaurants, that is rather more difficult because they change so quickly, but I will choose firstly Harry's Bar. It is horribly expensive, but reliable and always the same and people do still go there. The Do Forni is very good, but not cheap. For a cheaper place, with very good fish, try the Madonna. It is very Venetian.

'The best guide books, well, I think I will mention the James Morris because it is very amusing, but the truly complete book is an Italian book by Lorenzetti.

'The best time to come to Venice is either in June or between late September and early October. Anything else?'

The new Orient-Express, I blurted out, as it was still in my mind. Had that entered her consciousness?

'Certainly, I have looked over it and found it delightful. It has been like restoring a work of art, and they have done it with good taste and high quality. I have not yet been on it, and I am told it can be rather wobbly.

'I went on the original Orient-Express in 1926 with my mother, on the way to Athens. We left Paris in such style, all spick and span, everything beautiful, but little by little, bit by bit, as we got to the Balkans, things got worse and worse. We could see our local conductors becoming dishevelled and the train getting filthier. In the Balkans we were shunted on to a side line while some cattle trucks went past us. By the time we arrived we were like refugees. Yet we had set off feeling so chic.

'Everyone in Venice is pleased about the new train. I met Mr and Mrs Sherwood when they first came here. I was half expecting some terrible American millionaire, but they were both so cultured. Mrs Sherwood has such simplicity.

'The Orient-Express is putting Venice on the map again, amongst the right sort of people. It can only do good. We have had far too many rooksacks for far too long.'

I took my leave, thanking her for her time and words of wisdom, and returned to the Gritti Palace where I had a bath in my marble bathroom. I changed and went down into the bar. And there were Mary-Lou and Charlie, my American friends from the Train.

'The Danieli! Forget it. All it is is a hall. That's all it's got. The bedroom was lousy. I changed rooms right away, and made them give us another, but I'm not happy with that either. It makes the Orient-Express look like a Palace. I don't think I'll even stay there one night. What's this place like?'

Full, I said. All the bedrooms are taken.

*     *     *

The next day, the mist had gone and the morning was quite bright so I set out for a walk round Venice, bearing in mind all the tips my Countess (or should it be Contessa?) had given me. She had said St Mark's Square *had* to be seen, but done when it's quiet. Is there such a time? I doubt it. There were thousands of school children, plus what seemed like millions of pigeons. I don't know which was noisier. They all seemed to be Italian school children, presumably from the mainland, as it was still not the foreign tourist season, and it was interesting to see them having not the slightest interest in their own heritage, mucking around, pushing each other, guzzling, sitting around bored, carrying boogie boxes and Walkmen, just like their counterparts in most countries, preferring 1980s' junk music to the Renaissance masterpieces.

I think I disliked the waiters most of all. The famous St Mark's Square cafés, such as Florian's, are architecturally interesting, with fascinating decor, but the service was unfriendly and the prices ridiculous.

I stood in the middle of the square, and tried to ignore the birds and the school children, but the big red tower annoyed me. It seemed ugly and out of scale, in the wrong place in the wrong design. It was the Campanile, so my guide book told me. Why dismiss it without proper inspection, I'll take a lift to the top. An attendant in the lift took my ticket, an elderly chap in unmatching suit trousers and jacket, wearing a trilby. Funny clothes, for an indoor job, yet it was obviously not a uniform, just his own choice of working wear. He tore my ticket in half and I asked him if I could keep it, as on my Grand Tour I was keeping all ephemera, and he said no, against regulations.

The view from the top was terrific and I could see over all Venice and the surrounding islands, but such was the angle that I couldn't see the Grand Canal, which was what I most wanted to see. I watched a tower on a church nearby with two figures, hitting each other. I noticed that almost all the roofs in Venice had red tiles. I had never thought of roofs before, as in Venice you seem to be trapped down inside the alleys or beside narrow canals, surrounded by sheer buildings which appear to have no roofs at all. If asked, I would have imagined that all Venetian roofs must be flat, in some sort of grey stone. The red was a pleasant surprise.

On the way down, the lift man gave me my ticket back. It seemed somehow typically Italian. There are regulations to be followed, but having done that, you can bend them.

I went into St Mark's Basilica, to do the proper tourist bit, where the Italian school children were even rowdier and I wondered if I was becoming old. It was so dark inside that I could hardly see anything, except miles of mosaic on all the walls and ceilings. Perhaps I was going blind as well as decrepit. Upstairs, walking round the roof area, it was much lighter and more attractive. The balustrades were crumbling, and it seemed so dangerous to be allowed to walk freely around, yet there were no guards or safety instructions.

The Ducal Palace was more attractive, not as crowded and with more atmosphere. There were lots of parties being conducted by guides carrying umbrellas or a flag as their signal and rallying point and I learned quite a lot from following them. I never realised that inside the Bridge of Sighs there used to be dungeons. Hence all the people inside who were sighing.

As with the Basilica, the Doge's Palace was covered in graffiti, both Italian and English. 'George' 'Sandra' and 'Ian Thompson' had all been there. Outside again, in the fresh air and proper light at last, there were two Italian school boys in the square, throwing a dead pigeon at each other.

That evening, I had dinner at the Madonna restaurant near the Rialto, as recommended, which was excellent. It was full of locals, always a good sign. I had my photograph taken by a strolling photographer, which most Venice restaurants appear to allow, who was working his way round the tables. Venice is such a superior place, so it seemed strange that this sort of Butlins-Blackpool habit should be so prevalent. At the next table was an American couple. The man was very bossy and self important while the girl just gazed at him with adoration. He was not only wolfing back his own meal, but taking forkfulls of her meal as well, until he had finished both. She talked non stop, while he just nodded his fat head and dribbled over his meal as he stuffed his face. I left while they were still there, no doubt about to order two puddings, which he would eat, and I noticed that she had her hand up the inside of his trouser leg, fondling him somewhere in the region of his knee. Ugh. Am I getting puritan as well as old and blind.

Next day, I went out to Torcello, as the good lady had suggested. The boat trip took about thirty-five minutes and I enjoyed the ride, though I got stuck beside a very fashionably dressed young couple who never spoke to each other. They were both wearing designer boiler suits and knee high leather boots. All they did was stroke each other's hands and admire each other's rings.

There was not much to see on the island, considering that every guide book to Venice raves about Torcello. The ruined Cathedral was interesting enough, but it was surrounded by mud flats and scrawny fields full of litter. I wished I had stayed in Venice, especially when the meal I had, good though it was, came to £37 for the set lunch, about three times the cost of set meals in Venice itself. Yet they had framed letters to prove that the Queen and Giscard d'Estaing had eaten there.

Back in Venice, I decided to do a few more cultural sights, though I was happiest really just wandering about. Away from St Mark's Square, I enjoyed absolutely everything in Venice, the places and the people, particularly the young boatmen arguing at the boat piers, or the elderly and rather stately gondoliers in their purple ribbon hats, looking sad and underemployed. I thought about hiring one, just to give them some business, but their highly polished gondolas looked so sinister, black and polished like shrines, as if by taking one I would be on the way to my own funeral.

I cursed the street maps all the time, as every alley I was in never seemed to be listed, but that is one of the pleasures of Venice. There are just so many side turnings and secret courts and little squares that it would spoil the fun to name them and pin them down. I saw few priests, which is unusual in Italian cities, and even fewer policemen. Is Venice a museum after all? I also cursed the guide books. James Morris is good fun, but it's a bedside read. The more conventional guide books, the sort you are supposed to take round with you which describes each square and area, never give real judgments or true opinions. They're so busy pouring in all the history, especially boring church history.

However, my Contessa had recommended the San Rocco for the Tintorettos. Once again, the Church was too dark to see them, though I was beginning to think anyway that religious paintings were not for me. They're too much of a chocolate box, beautifully executed and polished, but empty and emotionless. I then went into the Accademia Gallery, thinking a proper gallery is bound to display its wares properly, whereas an ordinary church cannot afford modern lighting and proper exhibition techniques. Once again, the paintings were ill lit, hanging on bare concrete walls. There were massive Tintorettos and Bellinis – but to me, alas, they all looked much the same.

I decided to take a boat trip, up the Grand Canal, and admire the architecture from the outside. I'm obviously not an inside person. I could wander round Venice for weeks, just looking at the fronts of all the buildings.

In my mind, I had always imagined Venice would be quite small, an oasis of niceness, with pretty canals and a few old palaces, but surrounded by a bigger, more modern city, a sort of bijou, pedestrian, water-y Covent Garden, with horrible Oxford Streets leering not far away. Venice is in fact a sizeable city all on its own, completely unspoiled, with so many different areas and countless squares and alleys hidden away, all waiting to be found. A pity about the word canal. Sounds so prosaic and industrial and gives entirely the wrong impression.

On the boat, I stood outside to watch the views, and was joined by a very pukka young English couple. He was rather serious and dopey looking in tweeds, perhaps on the way back to Oxford, whereas she was an archetypal Sloane, studying at some potty language school in Venice. She was bumptious and loud, lecturing him on Venice and showing off and I didn't like her at all.

That night, I decided not to try a smart restaurant, as I had eaten too well at lunch, so I went across to the Giudecca, and explored a more working class district of Venice, the island where the boatmen are supposed to live, though it's also the site of the smart Cipriani hotel. I stopped in a bar and had a glass of wine for 100 lire, which I worked out at about 10p. The walls of the bar were lined with AC Milan photographs and posters. I noticed a pennant saying 'Milan 1973', which was the year I went to Milan to watch Spurs play AC Milan in the San Siro stadium. I wished my Italian had been up to explaining this, or would it have been considered not done for a visiting tourist to come into a locals' bar and show off.

I heard some music at the rear so I worked my way through. There were about twenty men gathered round the bar, some were tough looking sailors and boatmen, but others were clerk types, in suits and carrying brief cases, on their way home from work. They were all listening to a boy in dark glasses playing an accordion while alongside him a one-armed man wearing a trilby was singing light operatic arias. He was hamming every gesture, putting on the sad face, or joyous face, overdoing every grimace, pretending to cry one moment, then laughing unbelievably the next as he went through each soppy ballad. At the end, there was an enormous cheer. Most people left when the music finished, going home to their wives or families, but I sat down and had another glass of wine and pizza. The pizza was revolting. The ice cream is always good in Italy, far better than so-called Italian ice cream in Britain, but I don't think I ever had a good pizza in Italy. The USA, that's the best place I know for really good Italian pizzas.

I returned to Venice on the Cipriani boat, pretending I was a guest. The mist was coming up again. As I walked across a little bridge over one of the canals, on the way back to my hotel, I came face to face with the Sloane I had stood beside earlier on the boat. She was now all alone and looked very forlorn. I didn't think she would recognise me, as on the boat she had been so engrossed with her boyfriend, but as we passed each other, she gave me a quick smile. Then I liked her.

I decided to have a late night cappucino in a café near the Gritti Palace. I sat up at the bar on a stool and got talking to a young couple beside me, both in their mid thirties, from Maidstone in Kent, smart, rather chirpy, very out-going. It was their first visit to Italy and so far, they said, it had been trific. They had been to Monza, then a chauffeur driven car had brought them from Como to Venice. The next day they were catching the Orient-Express back from Venice to London. A week of great luxury. And all of it for free.

Free? I couldn't believe it. I had hardly been concentrating at first on their itinerary. When you meet fellow Brits or Americans abroad, that's the first topic of conversation. They reel off the places they have been to and unless you have actually seen the same sites, in which case you chip in quickly with your experiences, then otherwise you wait for a pause and trot out your itinerary, where you have been, where you are going. After listing places, you then go through the hotels, good or bad, the food, good or bad, the things that went wrong, then finally how are you managing with the currency. I should think tourists, grand or otherwise, have always done this.

But a free holiday? They didn't somehow look as if they had come into a legacy or had inherited wealth. Nor did they look like bank robbers, whatever bank robbers look like, getting rid of their loot. A newspaper Bingo prize perhaps, or a pools winner? I was getting close, said the man. His name was Jeffrey and his wife Veronica Anne, though I could call her Anne. It turned out he worked for Marley, the firm best known for its tiles, but they are also apparently very big in double glazing. Jeffrey had won a competition for the best double glazing salesman of the year. I was suitably impressed. Not often you get to meet a star of the suburban streets when sitting in a café sur le continent.

In a ten week period, he had sold £60,000 worth of double glazing, so beating another eighty Marley reps in the South of England and winning the number one incentive bonus which the firm had provided. He had tried especially hard because he didn't want to win the number two prize. This had been a week in Holland. Nothing wrong with a week in Holland, but the week in question would have coincided with his own holiday week.

In one miraculous week on the knocker, he had sold £18,000 worth of double glazing.

'It was all to do with VAT. It was known they were putting VAT on double glazing on June 1st, so in May I made a huge effort to contact as many people as I could, going round the doors and I also did a mail shot to all my old customers. They get £25 if they bring me in new customers. I pointed out that as long as you *paid* for your double glazing by June 1st, you didn't have to pay VAT. Well, in the last week of May, it all happened. The orders came piling in. It was trific.'

'I don't know how he does it,' said Veronica Anne. 'I don't know how he has the nerve. It would just need one person to say no to me, and I'd cry.'

'I have a re-inforced steel toe cap,' said Jeffrey. 'If they slam the door on me, it takes off the bottom of their door frame . . .'

Jeffrey used to be a gas fitter, but was made redundant and could find no other job, except door to door salesman on commission. He thinks his years as a gas fitter equipped him for the cut and thrust of house to house encounters.

'They did make me a manager a few years ago,' he said. 'That meant I had to organise a little group of other salesmen. I was still working on commission, not a salary, as we all do, but I didn't like it. Too much aggravation, looking after other people. I look at it this way, you're only here once, I'd rather be responsible for myself, to be an individual. So I went back on the knocker.

'I've done the double glazing for four years now, but I still get nervous when I knock at every new door. I suppose it's like a stage actor, or a singer, you're all worked up. But once that door opens, then I forget it.

'When I'm working, I don't dress like this you know,' he said. He was wearing light weight trousers, short sleeve shirt and a neat leather zip-up jacket. Smart and presentable enough for anywhere, I should have thought, not just a Venice café.

'Oh no, I wear a suit. I dress up smart.'

'He's got a lot of style,' said Veronica Anne. 'When I first moved in with him, he cooked me liver and bacon for breakfast, with champagne.'

'I don't think I'll do it when I get to forty-five. I'll take it easy after that. I fancy a nice little salt beef sandwich bar. I could buy it now, I suppose, but I'll give it a few more years.'

'He endears himself,' said Veronica Anne. 'That's what does it. They love him because he's little and got blue eyes.'

'I do feel I could sell anything now,' he said. 'I've got a very good presentation.'

'But it's mainly cheek,' she added. 'Cockney cheek.'

I asked about their Italian trip so far. They hadn't thought much of Monza but had loved the chauffeur driven black Mercedes which took them to Venice.

'He was a real chauffeur, peaked cap, the lot. He got behind cars doing 100 mph and just peeped them till they got out of the way. It was great.'

'The nearest I've been to Italy till now,' she said, 'was when I was a little girl and I got a letter from the Pope. I don't know how I got it. I must have done something daft, like send a letter to him.

'I've felt like a millionairess on this trip. I changed £500 today – and they gave me one million lire.'

'We're at the Gabrielli, do you know it? I've worked out it would be costing us £120 a day each, if we were paying.'

'I'm looking forward to the Orient-Express trip most of all,' she said. 'Have you seen today's *Daily Express*?'

I said I had not yet had that pleasure. The cost of buying English newspapers abroad is pretty steep.

She got out her folded copy and pointed to a story about the Orient-Express suddenly being brought to a halt miles from nowhere. Someone had pulled the emergency brakes and stopped the train. It was traced to a couple making love in one of the compartments. The woman had accidentally, without realising, put her foot on the brake.

'That's what I'm looking forward to,' she laughed. 'Getting my foot caught on the Orient-Express . . .'

I could still hear them shrieking and laughing as I went off down the street to my hotel, the noise echoing in the Venetian mist.

SAN GIOVANNI E PAOLO
WITH THE MUNICIPAL HOSPITAL.

# II
# TUSCANY

# ~ *Chapter Six* ~
# Florence
*Some worrying thoughts about Florence;*
*Bobbie and Chuck and a great deal of Pasta.*

At first sight, Florence was such a disappointment. We walked over the Trinita bridge, which all the guide books had raved about, and looked towards the old part of the city, and then stared at each other, not wanting to be the first to start rubbishing a world famous city. I had been joined, some time later, by my wife and daughter Flora, eleven years old, who had begged to be allowed to explore Tuscany with me, none of us ever having been there before. On the old Grand Tours, this was quite common, meeting up with friends and relations, joining with them for a while, then moving on. We had booked into a hotel about a mile to the south of the Arno, within walking distance of the town.

Flora is named after Flora McDonald, as my wife was writing a biography of Bonnie Prince Charlie at the time she was born. It's not short for Florence. I wonder how many Victorian girls, named after Florence Nightingale, realised that she got her name from the town of Florence. Mr and Mrs Nightingale were on a Grand Tour to Italy in 1820 when their second daughter was born. They named her after her birthplace. Their first daughter had been born two years earlier in Naples. They hadn't fancied Naples as a girl's name and instead christened her Parthenope, the Greek for Naples, though she was always known as Parthe. Those were the days, of course, when Grand Tours often lasted from two to five years.

Flora my daughter and Florence the town do have a floral connection. Firenze, which is what the Italians call Florence, is so named because it was built on a flowery meadow. I've never discovered at what stage the English speaking world decided to call Firenze Florence. I used to think they were two different places. You never have any trouble with Paris and Paris, or even Lisbon and Lisboa, and London is obviously the same place as Londres and Edinburgh must be Edimbourg, but Firenze and Florence could be two separate cities. Even after a week in Tuscany, every time I saw it on street signs I had to think twice.

But this first view was worrying, compared with Venice, though few cities in the world can possibly compete with Venice. Before coming to Tuscany, I had talked to friends who had done both, and the whole civilised world has done both, and I asked them to compare Florence with Venice. The reactions were much the same, a sort of troubled look of pleasure, contorted smiles of recollection, adoring both, yet unable to think in terms of which was 'better'. One just does not think of them that way, as if they were in a race. Both are such marvels. The best comment I got, now that I have seen both and can understand the normal tourist's reaction, is that Florence is a Museum while Venice is a Fairy Tale. Not bad. But it still doesn't give the flavour of Florence, which was what I was hoping to discover.

The famous Trinita bridge seemed so utterly ordinary. In fact we had walked along the Arno for some time, looking at several bridges, unable to work out which might be the Trinita bridge. It was clear which was the Ponte Vecchio, as that was further along and had buildings on it and stood out on the skyline, but we were leaving that for later. We had decided that the Ponte Santa Trinita would be the best way to enter the old city. It was finished in 1569 and is supposed to have been based on sketches done by Michelangelo. There were doubts about its strength, as the arches appeared so thin and delicate, but by the 18th century it was treated as a minor miracle with endless essays about its magnificent engineering and its aesthetic subtleties. During the First World War, the French army sent heavy artillery across it, without any apparent damage.

In the Second World War, the Germans did much the same, when they were retreating from the City, but in 1944 Hitler had it blown up. He is said to have given orders for all the Florence bridges over the Arno to be blown up, except 'the one with shops on.'

The rebuilding of the Trinita bridge galvanised the City after the war and it became a symbol of Florence's re-birth as all sections of the community came together to work for its reconstruction. It was decided to use original stones, stick to the original plans, and use where possible the methods of the 16th Century. The river was dredged for any original stones and sculpture and the bridge was opened again in 1957 – but without the head of the Primavera, which could not be found. The Parker Pen company offered a reward, a nice example of American–Italian co-operation, and finally in 1961 a dredging crew dug up the head. It was ceremonially placed in position and the famous bridge was once more complete.

We stood on it, looking into the murky, mucky water. I don't hold the colour of a town's river against it. Look at the Tiber in Rome. What a dump. The Seine usually has rubbish floating in it and the Thames at Westminster is rarely a pretty colour, though at least it is no longer noxious the way it used to be when Thomas Hardy, as a young architect, worked beside it and was physically ill with the fumes all summer. But the River Arno does look particularly dismal, a deep shitty colour, which even a perfect sun cannot illuminate.

We hit the traffic, once we had crossed the bridge, although it was early evening and the shops and offices had closed for the day. I knew that Florence, unlike Venice, is full of cars, but I had not expected so many or that they would be allowed down almost every narrow street and alleyway. And what a noise.

In Italy, the Florentines are considered quiet, dignified people, compared with the Romans and Neapolitans, but their exhausts are just as ear shattering. Those small cars and the under-powered motor scooters make a sound out of all proportion to their size. In America, the cars are enormous, and so are their engines, but paradoxically they go much more slowly than their power would allow them. Nasty little Italian engines eat into the soul, reverberate round the head and body, following you round otherwise silent and empty alleys, delighting in coming up quickly from behind, frightening you out of the way. It was at least interesting to see so many young girls riding little motor bikes, especially the bike size one called a Ciao, but worrying to see that none of them wore helmets.

We hurried down some side streets, to avoid the worst of the traffic and litter, and eventually found a quiet spot to stand and stare. Looking carefully at the buildings, I could see they were not built as one, like a massive terraced block, but as separate units, with pediments on top, designed individually, and when first built each must have looked very grand. Even today, if each building could be isolated and given due prominence, it might still look imposing. But taken all jammed together, the buildings in almost every street gave me the feeling of a prison, grim, forbidding and fortress like. They seemed somehow gritty and Northern, like Newcastle or Aberdeen, when I had expected an Italian Bath or Brighton. I suppose an outsider thinks of everything in Italy as being of the warm South, the exotic Mediterranean, and forgets that in a large country there are large variations. The stone was dirty and dull, the windows severe and prim, the decoration minimal and the whole effect is not helped by the fact that almost all the windows in Florence, especially on the lower floors, have iron bars over them.

What have we done? We had booked in for five days at our hotel, the Hotel Villa Belvedere. Should we have made another base for our tour of Tuscany? What was all the excitement about, why for hundreds of years had all tourists raved about Florence?

There is a slight feeling of pride, of independence of spirit when confronted by a Famous Place, a Famous Play, a Famous Face, a Famous Painting, and finding it wanting, but then follows a feeling of some doubt. Have I missed something? Have I no taste, no education, no real feeling for culture? Coleridge used to say that you had to have your taste educated to truly appreciate Wordsworth. Was I perhaps just being bolshie, deliberately turning against Florence to go against the herd. I had gone with an open mind to both Venice and Florence, almost feeling I knew both already, having seen so much, as we all have, in paintings, films and television. Venice looked familiar – yet much, much better. Florence looked familiar – yet so ordinary.

*      *      *

On the map, I could see the Uffizi Palace, the town's best known museum, but I had not yet got to grips with understanding the scale of the map we were using. Maps, like people, have to be experienced, so that in time you know the signs, understand the codes, and are able to read the symbols. It was closed. Florence might be a museum, but they do have the most peculiar opening hours.

We cut left, heading in the direction of the Duomo. That seemed the next most important thing to gape at, in our quick run through the main sights. I smiled when I saw it. It was like a huge ice cream cake, made up of slabs of different coloured icing, mainly white, pink and green, amazing in its vulgarity, but a delight to see after all those dull, dark brown gritty streets. Florence might be fun after all.

It too was closed, of course, but I went round licking it, just to make sure it was real. Well, I ran my hand along its marble slabs and felt its coolness. The different coloured marble came from different parts of Italy – white from Carrara, green from Prato, pink from Maremma. Ecumenical architecture. It is virtually isolated by the traffic which sweeps round it on all sides, a cathedral locked up in a traffic island. One English visitor in 1831, Dr James Johnson, likened it to a 'huge architectural zebra and its keeper' and did not think much of this 'gothic and tasteless idea'. I suppose by the keeper he meant the little building beside it, the Baptistery, a small chunk of icing which has fallen off the big cake. As I led my eyes upwards I could see that all the clever stuff and fancy decorations finished in a simple red tile roof. Perhaps they had tired by then.

By now, Flora was fed up. She hates looking at buildings, either inside or out. On a corner of the Duomo square we came to several stalls selling postcards, one of which had a little fountain playing water over a pool which contained slices of fresh coconut. I examined the fountain, and the pipe behind it, and could see that it appeared to be simply re-cycling the same old water, over and over again, no doubt full of dirt and traffic fumes, probably been there all year, perhaps even since the Duomo was begun in 1296.

I bought her a slice, only 300 lire, then I went into a nearby café to have a beer. My wife refused to join me, saying it looked horrid and anyway it would spoil our dinner, to start eating now. I drank my beer standing up. The guide books had warned me that they charge you double to sit down.

My wife had decided we would try a restaurant called Acqua al Due, which had not strained her tired brain too much as it was the first one, alphabetically, in a list of recommended restaurants in the American Express pocket guide to Florence and Tuscany. (A very good one, by the way.) But it took us a long time to find it as the street maps in the book don't give all the little places. I asked the way from a very charming lady, wearing a lot of make-up, who was standing waiting and smiling in a dark doorway, just as ladies have done for centuries, hoping that some young gentleman on his Grand Tour might want a break from all that culture. Her directions were useless. Twenty minutes later we ended up back at her front door. No doubt that was the plot.

We eventually got to the restaurant, but found it closed. I could see movement inside so I banged on the door and a bored waiter opened up, only to tell us they didn't open till 7.30. You expect in tourist towns that tourist eating places will never close, but it was the same in Venice. They have their strict times and stick to them. Very sensible. Why let tourists and their selfish demands dominate your life?

We pressed our noses against the window, hoping for clues to its goodness. If a restaurant is crowded, then that is some mark of success, but an un-open place, one you have never been to before, gives nothing away. On the front door someone had stuck a fresh looking scribbled message in felt pen. 'Bob and Chuck – see you here at 7.30.'

Perhaps we should book. It could be a very popular place, being the first recommended restaurant in the guide book. I banged on the door again but the waiter ignored me this time. Just that half witted English bloke again, in his silly Marks and Spencer shorts, Green Flash shoes, clutching his guide book, with his long suffering wife and v. bored looking daughter.

We wandered through a few streets, looking for a cool place to sit down, and came to a large square, the Piazza Santa Croce, a real local square, not a tourist trap, with children in the middle playing on bikes and old men feeding pigeons. We sat on a stone seat, silently watching the sunset play tricks on the cobbles, following disappearing darts of light and receding shadows, all at odd angles, as the sun bid its farewell over the towers and roof tops, then it decided to pop back to take another bow through the gaps, while going backwards off stage, unwilling to leave us, then finally returning to say sorry, really have to go, back tomorrow, all being well, have a nice evening.

My wife and Flora were too tired to move, but when at last the sun did go in I took a turn round the Square. I tried and failed to get into the church of Santa Croce, which dominates the square, as it was closed. I had wanted to see the graves of Michelangelo and Galileo and the other famous Florentines buried inside. Sante Croce has become the Westminster Abbey of Florence, though not without some struggles over the centuries. Rival churches have squabbled in the past over the bones of famous Florentines. Dante was born in Florence, but his bones were never returned from Ravenna where he died in 1321, though there is a statue of him outside the church.

Michelangelo was born in the Sante Croce neighbourhood, and started, as most young artists did, by copying the works of the great masters, but his genius was recognised from an early age and commissions flooded in. In his old age, he used to work with a candle fixed to his cap to help his hands see and feel. He died in Rome in 1564, but his body was brought back secretly to Florence where a magnificent funeral was organised by the Medici court.

I wondered if he ever played football as a boy in this square, or some early form of football, because there are records of ball games being played here in the 16th Century. England likes to think she gave football to the world, which she did in its modern version, but in many countries football games have been played since medieval times. The Santa Croce square must have made a perfect setting for local matches, being nicely rectangular, not big and awkward like the Signoria. It also proved an ideal place to burn heretics, which is what happened in the 15th Century, during the wave of religious hysteria whipped up by Savonarola. He was a Florentine friar who accused the church of vice and corruption in high places, even attacking the Pope. He ended up being burned as well, though in the Piazza della Signoria.

I came across a little group of American tourists in a corner of the square, being lectured to by an Italian woman in halting English. They were all looking very bored, probably wondering how long to go till the restaurants opened.

'Excuse me,' said one of the Americans, interrupting the set lecture. 'Excuse me, you remind me of my mother.'

It took the guide some time to work out this sudden observation, or its relevance to the wonders of the Santa Croce square, then she started smiling. 'Thank you,' she said.

'Wait till I get home, I'll tell my mother you looked like her.'

'Thank you.'

*     *     *

At seven thirty exactly we returned to the restaurant to find that several people had already got inside, the cheek, and were already sitting down. The waiter took some time to attend to us and then had difficulty finding a place not reserved, but finally he put us on the end of a table set for eight people.

At the next table were three young American girls, all overweight, dressed in baggy Bermuda shorts with bulging thighs and bulging wallets tied round their waists. All of them were smoking heavily. I can never understand why smokers smoke during a meal. It seems far worse these days in Europe than in England. Why can't they take one sensation at a time. The tastes must be utterly confused, eating, drinking and smoking simultaneously. The girls were having difficulty with their drinks. They asked three times for Coca-Cola, but were refused. The restaurant did not stock it. Well done restaurant, but Flora was also disappointed.

We let the waiter recommend a meal for us which turned out to be five pasta dishes, one after the other, and they were all delicious, delicate little plates of pasta, each a different shape and texture, served with different sauces and fillings.

We were joined at the end of the table by two young Italians, both bearded, who talked non stop, but not to us, then a young American couple arrived and were put down right beside us, filling up the gaps. They immediately said Hi. Flora was at that moment rather worried about the latest pasta dish, number four, which was fishy and appeared to her to have bits of caviare in it.

'Yuck, I hate caviare,' she moaned.

As far as I know, Flora has never had caviare in her life, so how could she hate it. And anyway, a cheap, student type restaurant would not be serving up caviare in its pasta.

'I *do* know what it's like. It's fishes' eggs. That's why I hate it.'

The American girl beside us assured her it was not caviare. She had eaten here lots of times. Then she asked us if we were Australian. Australian?

'Yeh, you sure sound like it, especially your daughter.'

I've never been taken for Australian before and I was quite charmed. Italian, yes, or Spanish or French, as I do have dark hair, what's left of it. I like to think I look Celtic rather than Anglo Saxon, though Flora and my wife are both fair skinned. Flora does have a cockney sounding accent, being born and bred in London, whereas we are both Northerners. I suppose there *might* be a connection between her accent and some parts of Australia, amongst those descended from cockney convicts perhaps, but it's unlikely. Not that we minded being thought Australian. We were British, though.

'I would be pleased *not* to be taken for American,' said the girl, 'more than you are not to be taken for English. This whole goddam town is full of Americans.'

She said she was called Bobbie and came from Wisconsin and was in Florence for a year studying Fine Art, along with a million other young Americans. 'I'm at an English speaking college and the block I live in is full of English or American girls, so I hardly ever speak Italian. I was worried I might be wasting my parents' money, but they came to see me a week ago and were thrilled to hear me saying 'ciao'. Really, they were most impressed.'

She warned me not to order a salad, as they were lousy, but to try the mixed pudding. This consisted of a plate with about six dollops of different puddings, from ice cream to gateaux. Some were better than others. Flora enjoyed them all.

'Chuck, you want any pudding?' asked Bobbie.

So that's who they were – the Bob and Chuck who had exchanged notes on the front door. I had half thought it might be a complicated joke by the waiters, or the patron, to make it seem an even more popular place than it obviously was.

Chuck had just come from the station, carrying a forty-five pound rucksack, as he was backpacking round Europe. The best thing about Europe so far was the desserts.

'I never eat desserts at home, but that's all I've been eating. In every town I go to, I just eat ice cream or desserts. They're all wonderful.'

He thought his best so far was a creamy cake called a Napoleon which he had bought from a stall near the Eiffel Tower in Paris. Switzerland was also pretty good.

I told Bobbie that I'd been rather disappointed by the physical look of Florence so far, and she agreed it could appear depressing, compared with Venice, but it was best to see Florence in the dark. That's when it came into its own.

It was true. As we walked back through the city, the buildings did seem much more colourful. The major ones were well illuminated, highlighting the stone work and decorations. The Piazza della Signoria had a completely different atmosphere, prettier and friendlier, even romantic, whereas earlier it had seemed cold and totalitarian. There was a large crowd listening to an Italian folk group playing songs on what looked like medieval instruments. The people at the front were mainly Italian, singing or clapping along with the songs. It gave the tourists two things to observe, the musicians and the Italians enjoying the music.

In amongst the musicians was an old man, dressed in scruffy jeans and worn sandals, who was dancing between them while they played, trying to take girls out of the crowd to dance with him. They all refused, so he danced with himself, badly, awkwardly, perhaps even drunkenly, but harmlessly. He reminded me of an almost identical old man who does the same thing in the Covent Garden Piazza in London on Saturday mornings. The world is full of them. Probably always has been. The atmosphere was like a community street party. Were we going to enjoy Florence after all?

# ~ Chapter Seven ~

# Harold Acton

*A morning with the gracious Sir Harold;*
*some tales from his past;*
*a tour around his enchanting garden.*

Next morning, I went to present my compliments to one of the grand old men of Florence, possibly the grandest old man in all Italy, as far as visiting Anglo-Americans are concerned, the sort with the right connections and the right background, a gentleman whom all modern gentlemen travellers to Italy like to say they have seen. How can anyone of taste and culture boast they have been to Florence, if they have not inspected that living monument, Sir Harold Acton.

I had written in advance from London, not knowing if he would be fit and well and at home and able to receive yet another passing stranger, then I telephoned him from my hotel, just to be sure, and he was utterly charming. Come at ten-thirty. I live at number 120, Via Bolognese, on the right as you come out of Florence on the old road to Bologna. I look forward to meeting you. Goodbye.

I knew without knowing it that a simple street number, given out as matter of factly as one might give out an address in Acacia Avenue or Laburnum Grove, would turn out to be magnificent. His home, after all, was said to be a palace, amongst the last of the grand residences, lived in by possibly the last of the grand collector-artists. Throughout the 18th and 19th century, Florence had many such homes, lived in by the nobility. You sent your cards up, hoping to be granted an audience, or at least you sent your servant with it, skulking in the via outside, hoping it would do the trick.

Even Milton, on his rather desiccated Grand Tour, went out of his way to secure invitations to well known writers of the time. On his journey from Naples to Rome he met up with someone he called a mysterious hermit who was persuaded to take him to see Manso, the writer and poet.

Perhaps the pushiest literary rubber neck of all was James Boswell, going to enormous lengths to track down the celebrities, invited or not. In Germany in 1763, at the beginning of his Grand Tour, he started by making one terrible mistake. He sent his card to the local Princeling's court by way of a maid from the inn where he was staying. No reply. He hadn't realised that this suggested that the visitor did not have a servant of his own.

By the time he got to Switzerland, he was an expert at getting into places. It was masterly the way he tracked down Rousseau, then a very sick old man, who had deliberately cut himself off in a mountain refuge in the Alps and clearly did not want to see anyone, least of all this inquisitive stranger. Boswell sent round a long letter, which he considered a masterpiece, (so he kept a copy) and informed Rousseau he was a distinguished Scots gentleman. Boswell was at that time aged twenty-four. Rousseau replied that he was ill, in pain, in no state to receive visitors. Boswell persisted and Rousseau was either daft or weak enough to say oh well, if it could be made a *short* visit. And Boswell was in. In the end, he managed five visits with Rousseau.

Boswell next went after Voltaire, Rousseau's formidable rival, then living near Geneva. He wangled an invitation to dinner, met the great man, but was not invited to further meetings. In Italy, when he got there (for Boswell was doing a Grand Tour route in reverse) he seems to have concentrated as much on chasing the ladies as chasing fame.

Thackeray was equally bold when he was determined to have a chat with Goethe, which he did manage to fix. He had discovered, at the beginning of his German journey, that a uniform was essential for their courts. Any sort of uniform, the more splendid the better, so he wrote back to his mother to send him one.

I don't suppose Harold Acton would consider himself in the same class as Voltaire or Goethe, but I was equally keen to meet him. I was also eager to catch a glimpse of a grand house and a grand garden, a way of life which will soon be gone for ever. Today, most of these private palaces have vanished, or are being used as posh headquarter offices by Italian industrial conglomerates or by American educational establishments.

I got lost coming out of Florence, driving myself in a rented car. The Via Bolognese didn't seem to have a street sign anywhere, nor did it begin at the roundabout I thought it would. I seemed to circle the outskirts of the town several times before I picked up the right directions.

La Pietra, to give the house its correct name, has its own gatehouse, with large gates on the main road. They were locked, so I got out of the car and pulled an ancient bell on the wall. Through the gates I could see a long, straight drive, lined with cypress trees, stretching into the distance. Sir Harold had added on the phone that if I got a taxi, be sure not to let them leave me at the gates. I would still have half a mile to walk to reach the house. An old retainer eventually opened up and I drove myself slowly up the drive, passing fields of olives and vines on either side, the grand house at the end becoming bigger and bigger as I got nearer.

It's not quite the size of Blenheim, but almost as impressive, a Renaissance Palace of stuccoed stone, built in the 15th century, then added to over the next 200 years.

Harold Acton was born here, eighty years ago, and I thought how rare these days to live in the house where one was born. They're an Anglo-Italian family, the Actons, with branches back to the historian Lord Acton (who said all power corrupts) and forebears who have been ministers of the Kingdom of

Naples. His own father, Arthur, lived in the house and devoted himself to the arts, and to the gardens, helped by the fact that he had married a wealthy American lady, daughter of a Chicago banker.

I tried to park my cheap little hired car as artistically as possible, on the gravel in a corner, not wanting to spoil the picture. It contains some sixty-four rooms, but like all grand houses, estimates change as even the owners are never quite sure. In this house, Sir Harold Acton lives alone. He remains an impenitent bachelor.

A butler in a white jacket had the front door open as soon as I parked and smiled me in, down a corridor, through a large circular hallway, with a staircase winding up above me, and then down another corridor into a large drawing room. I had to re-adjust my eyes as the shutters were down and there were no lights on. It seemed almost a museum, with paintings and sculptures everywhere, except for little piles of obviously used magazines and personal ornaments on tables. The butler indicated that I should sit beside a small rather formal looking two seater couch in front of a shuttered window, which I did. The butler then went off into another room to announce my arrival.

Sir Harold Acton *bounded* in. I had images of a decaying octogenarian, possibly even in a bath chair, living a left-over life, a remnant from Henry

James, too removed from this world to give me much of his time or attention. He was tall, erect and well built, dressed in an immaculate suit, sparkling white shirt and tie, highly polished black shoes, and his complexion looked fresh and smooth. I did have a suit on, if only just, a light weight flimsy thing, but no tie. I felt under dressed and far too casual. He sat down on the rather stiff looking double sofa and gave me his rapt attention for the next two hours.

I don't think I have met a more courteous person, interested, concerned, amused, lively, without a hint of it being a performance or a chore, yet over the decades he must have greeted scores of visitors into his house, from Royalty to passing hacks, treating them all the same, with utter politeness.

He apologised for the dark room, saying he had to restrict strong sunlight to stop everything fading and to keep cool. He had had a cataract operation on his right eye, a miracle performed in Switzerland, so he said, but was now in blooming health again. He poured out china tea and asked about my hotel, my comforts, and my impressions of Florence. I blurted out my feelings about the prison-like streets.

'Ah, you sound just like Dickens and Ruskin. On their first visit they came out with almost identical remarks. Dickens found it gloomy and austere and Ruskin said it reminded him of Newgate prison.'

Had he actually *talked* to these people? I had to think for a moment, then realised it was preposterous. He's not that old, though he does appear to have met every literary and artistic person of the 20th century, from Picasso to Diaghilev, T. S. Eliot to Maugham. Not that he boasts or drags them in. Only when asked.

'Florentine Society was very English when I was born here in 1904. I can remember all the English tea rooms, the English shops, English hotels and pensions, English baker, English chemist, and most of the villas were lived in

by English people, Lady Enniskillen, Lady Sybil Scott, Mrs Keppel, Mrs Janet Ross, and Miss Violet Paget. She wrote books under the name of Vernon Lee.

'A lot of them were Anglo-Indians, realising that England was not Victorian enough for them to adapt to. My first school was Miss Penrose's, for boys and girls, when I was about six. There was an English newspaper, an English bank, and everyone's travel arrangements were made through Thomas Cook. English tourists were met at the railway station by the man from Cook's in uniform, a jolly fat fellow. Now Thomas Cook doesn't exist in Florence any more.

'Florence had been strikingly English for at least 200 years before that. English people on the Grand Tour in its grand-ducal days, like Samuel Rogers, used to leave their letters in the Uffizi, in front of the Medici Venus, in the Tribuna. That room became their social club. They were mainly Protestants, those wealthy gentlemen who did the Grand Tour, so they tended to ignore churches in favour of antiquities, museums, classical monuments, Etruscan and Roman remains.'

Today, according to the latest figures, there are only 2,000 permanent English residents in Florence, that's the number at least who have bothered to register with the British Consulate. The true number might possibly be double that, as many English people who come to teach at the language schools, for a year or so, don't always bother to register.

But in 1914, which was the period Sir Harold was remembering clearly, there were 13,000 registered British residents. An amazing number. Probably in the 19th century, though no figures exist, there were even more. And at that time, Florence was a much smaller City. No wonder it did seem to the visiting French that Florence was a 'ville toute Anglaise'.

Sir Harold puts the change down to several things. The older English residents did not in fact have a surplus of money and the cost of living was relatively cheap. When they were pushed out, during the fascist era, they could seldom afford to come back.

'During the Abyssinian crisis, there was a lot of anti-British feeling stirred up. Hotels with English names, such as the Eden and the Bristol, changed them. Italian families who had English governesses, as all the best ones did, got rid of them.'

He went to England for his own secondary education, to Eton, where he felt a fish out of water, though he made many good friends whom he has kept through life. 'It was the compulsory games I hated, the football, oh such a waste of time, but athletes were deified at Eton. I suppose it impelled me to devote myself to art, especially poetry. That was what I loved – and still do.

'By the time I got to Oxford, I was publishing my first book of poems and naturally I regarded myself as a 'poet', so I proceeded to behave like one.'

According to reports, in the memoirs and books later written by his contemporaries, Harold Acton was about the Brightest of the Bright Young Things. He dressed outrageously and made flamboyant gestures, such as reciting Eliot's *The Waste Land* through a megaphone at an Oxford garden party, just as Waugh described it in *Brideshead Revisited*. He was said to keep a harmonium and an elephant's foot in his rooms, ate plovers' eggs, drank pink champagne, produced magazines and wrote poems, dressed in a cloak and popularised Oxford bags. He was looked upon as a leader of style, an exotic, who entertained in his rooms, while still an undergraduate, Gertrude Stein and the Sitwells. He was rich, handsome, well connected, talented. He did most things to excess, all in the name of art. Oh, every memoir of that period has its Acton story.

I studied this old man in his formal suit and white shirt and neat black shoes, his smooth features, his old fashioned manners, and looked hard for the 1920s exotic. Was it all true?

'Exuberance, dear boy, that's all it was, the exuberance of youth. We were all so full of hope and adventurous expectations. At eighty, I do myself find it hard to believe, as if it had happened to another person. It was definitely juvenile, like my verses.

'When I look at the clothes worn today, no one would pay the slightest attention if they saw us now. You just have to walk down the King's Road to see far more flamboyant costumes than we ever wore. All we did was introduce a little colour into a life which seemed too conventional. Clothes in those days were sober lounge suits, so things like fancy waistcoats were frowned upon as theatrical. I remember wearing a high necked sweater which was considered eccentric. It all boils down to fashion, fleeting fashion.'

After Oxford, he went to Paris for a year, still determined to spend his life as a poet, or perhaps a novelist. Gertrude Stein introduced him to Hemingway, Scott Fitzgerald and her devoted Alice B. Toklas. Nancy Cunard lived round the corner with Aragon and ran the Hours Press. His parents were not very keen on his Paris jaunt, considering it all too bohemian.

He came back to London with a novel which was published the same day as Evelyn Waugh's first novel, *Decline and Fall*. Cyril Connolly, who had been with Acton at Eton, though they had never been friends, reviewed them both together.

'He said I "wrote like a Chinaman who knew English through reading *Punch.*" My novel was called *Humdrum*, and I'm afraid it was. I persevered with fiction for a while, but I realised I lacked the creative talent. So I turned to history.'

But his friend Evelyn Waugh flourished. He was best man at Waugh's first marriage and *Decline and Fall* was dedicated to him.

'He had given it to me to read, wanting my opinion. I had referred him to Duckworth, who had published my first book, the book of poems, *Aquarium*, in 1923, but they objected to the character of Captain Grimes, and in the end he found another publisher – his father's publishing firm, Chapman and Hall in fact.

'I suppose my opinion was noticed in those days. I did seem cosmopolitan, adult and experienced. Perhaps through having come from abroad, from Italy. When I spoke at the Union, I had a responsive audience. Maybe I had what today you would call "charisma". I wasn't the sort of aesthete who reclines on a couch and smokes opium. I was very energetic and gregarious, writing and organising and talking.'

Being born to affluence, it naturally helped him follow what he most wanted to do in life, and devote himself to the arts. Looking back, had it ever struck him that he'd missed the satisfaction of having to struggle for a living? He smiled at the very thought. 'No, I don't think so. I have been perfectly content *not* to have to struggle.'

But there was one period in his life when he did do a proper job, and managed to live on a stipend, and this was the seven years he spent in China before the Second World War, working as lecturer. The chance came out of the blue, when an uncle offered him a trip round the world. He looks back on his seven years in China, collecting Chinese art, living with the Chinese people, translating their vernacular poetry (some of which has recently been reprinted) as the happiest years of his life. It was the Second World War which brought him back to England.

In 1962, he inherited La Pietra and returned to Florence as his permanent home. By then he was established as a writer, mainly on Italian subjects, such as his classic study of *The Last Medici* and *The Bourbons of Naples*. He has published almost thirty books, including his autobiographical work, *Memoirs of an Aesthete.*

His chief aim has been to preserve his father's art collection, and add to it, and care for the enormous garden which his father created. Staff these days is a constant problem, but he manages to make do with four internal staff (two men and two maids) and five gardeners outside. His father usually had a total staff of ten, rather than his eight, but that included two chauffeurs.

'People don't care to be in domestic service these days. I don't know why. My butler and his wife have an apartment of their own, their keep paid for, their food and essential comforts, yet most people would sooner *not* do it. They imagine it is somehow demeaning, to be in service. What rot! There is nothing demeaning about it. It's a position of responsibility. I even pay for all their endless telephone calls. I had a man who ran up a bill of 1½ million lire while he was courting. His girl lived in Ancona and I think he rang her on the hour. Most Italians are apt to be garrulous.'

Did you sack him because of his huge phone bill?

'Certainly not. He was a very decent sort, an invaluable handyman. I was more than willing to pay his phone bills just to keep him on. He left me. I think he runs a restaurant now. And he has married again.'

The house was burgled about ten years ago and a dozen Old Masters were stolen. He had had no security measures until then, leaving doors and windows open, especially in summer, without anyone ever taking anything.

'They were obviously experts, knowing exactly what to choose. One of the thieves was tracked down later and they found in his flat a copy of my book, *Tuscan Villas.* The Italians have recently become more consciously involved, in their own culture. I saw that as a sign of the trend.

'The craze for Michelangelo's David is much the same. There are continual queues these days, of Italians and foreigners, yet at one time David got little more attention than many other masterpieces. It is a work of genius, Michelangelo at his peak, but I suspect the excitement about it, judging by the number of reproductions you see everywhere, is due to fashion, or that film about the artist.

'The other day I was asked by some Americans if I could use my influence to arrange a loan of David for Chicago. I have helped to organise such things in the past, and the Vatican has recently allowed its treasures to cross the Atlantic on tour, but David! The Florentines would never tolerate that.

'I think this revival of popular interest in their own culture, at least in Florence, started after 1966. That was the year of terrible floods when enormous damage was done. The whole world offered sympathy and practical help and that bucked them up. We all did as much as we could, the American and the English community, and appeals were launched. The V. and A. sent specialists over. Plane loads full of Japanese paper were flown in which could be used to absorb the mud on the paintings. The Italians had a term for the strenuous volunteers, *Angeli del Fango*, Angels of the Mud.

'But fundamentally, there has not been a significant change to the heart of Florence in my lifetime here. The centre is very much as it always was. Only the suburbs have spread out more. We did manage to stop a Hilton being built on a spectacular hill. That would have ruined a wonderful panorama. *Firenze Viva* fought hard against that. We are hoping to stop a new airport. Oh, they make such a fuss about wanting a big modern airport for Florence. [At present, Pisa is the nearest, after Peretola.] The shop keepers want it, thinking it will bring more custom, just as they wanted the Hilton. If you once get a big new airport here, you'll just get more bureaucracy and noise. Rome and Milan airports are appalling, but both are far from the city. I like that little airport at Pisa. It's rather cosy, convenient and informal and one can enjoy the drive from Florence to Pisa.'

My back was becoming sore, sitting at an angle on a hard chair, though Sir Harold seemed ready for several more hours of conversation, so I asked if we could go out into the garden, before it became too hot. He opened some shutters and we stepped out, pointing to some horrid burglar alarm contraptions, which he said I should ignore.

I had to re-adjust my vision again, this time to the intense mid day sun, and also to the garden. It was pure Marienbad, endless lawns, squares, terraces, colonnades and avenues, stretching as far as the eye could see, all of them empty, with not even a gardener in sight. (They were all at luncheon, he said.) It reminded me of a smaller Versailles, except there you can't escape people for very long. This was a private fantasy garden.

At every corner, along every path, there were statues, over a hundred in all, some of them enormous, and all of them valuable, collected by his father from different parts of Italy in the days of so-called 'English gardens' when you could buy such unwanted statuary relatively cheaply. Today, said Sir Harold, not even he could afford such artefacts.

While going round, I noticed that many of the fine sculptured figures, some of them as large and muscular as David, were missing their organs of manhood. What had happened?

'Oh that was the last War. My parents fled to Switzerland and I was in the RAF in the Far East. The Germans took over the house. They treated it rather well and there was no damage inside, but they knocked off most of the private parts of statues. I've never discovered why. It could have been a puritanical commander, who disapproved of nudity, or perhaps they were taken as souvenirs. I have never bothered to put them on again, except on Apollo.'

It was clear from all the garden, the walls and the flights of steps, the paths and statuary, the arches and colonnades, that a fortune is being spent to keep everything in prime condition. I did point to one bit of masonry which I thought was crumbling, but my eyes, or the artist, had deceived me. I thought lumps had fallen off, but it was deliberate, to age it, just as elsewhere he showed me some false stalactites and a bogus wasps' nest, all done in elaborate plaster work.

The garden is on a hillside, so you are endlessly going down steep steps, yet he was always ahead, trotting round the different levels, never faltering once, even on some sloping pebbled steps, disappearing behind enormous hedges, some up to thirty feet high, which separate the various formal parterres. On one terrace there was an unusual two tier hedge, with cypress below and ilex above, but alas some of his cypress have been attacked by a disease. He has treated it with copper sulphate and other chemicals, but with no success so far. 'The whole of Tuscany is under threat, and the cypress is the Tuscan tree *par excellence.*'

We came down further steps and into a sort of sylvan grove, his own private out-door theatre, with a neat row of box at one end, under which stage lights can be hidden.

'Brigitte Bardot played here. She was doing a film with Roger Vadim and they wanted a scene set in a large garden. In French it was called *Le Repos du Guerrier* – Warrior's Rest. I don't know what the English version was called. It was from a popular novel, and had nothing at all to do with Florence. They just wanted a Tuscan scene for the sake of variety. Brigitte Bardot was very pleased with herself, I remember, but not very pleased with anything else. I think she was going through an unhappy love affair at the time.

'More recently Lattuada's film crew came here, doing a Mastroianni film. He plays a middle-aged man who falls in love with a young girl played by Nastassia Kinski. I gather she was superb in *Tess*. Mastroianni then discovers that the young girl is his own daughter. Rather typical of the D'Annunzio tradition, don't you think. That streak of perversity.

'No, I don't mind film people using my garden, or photographers or art students, as long as they behave themelves and don't leave Coca-Cola bottles or cigarette ends behind.'

As we left his theatre, he pointed out eight statues by Bonazza, an 18th Century Venetian, which particularly appeal to his taste. They were mostly little groups of people doing things, such as a girl with a rake, a man punishing a dog, a girl with some chocolates, a couple of musicians, all very lively and realistic. He likes them because he feels they animate his theatre in the absence of actors. The biggest statue in his garden, a thirty feet giant of a man, very much in the David style, by the late 16th century sculptor Orazio Marinali, has deliberately been put in a far grove, on its own, so not to dwarf the rest.

Back in the house, we had drinks and he explained where the name *Punt e Mes* comes from, but I can't quite remember his explanation, except that it is not true Tuscan. Some king, apparently, had first tried the drink and said, in his dialect, yes, that's enough. Well, I think that was it.

'The famous Russell Harty came to film me here a couple of years ago. What an unusual type. Many of his questions were embarrassingly personal, with a sexual undercurrent, as if anyone would talk on television about such matters. Were Chinese women hairy, that sort of thing. All very rum.'

He was going to London soon, and would be attending a birthday party given in his honour by Princess Margaret at Kensington Palace. He had been invited to stay at the Palace, but had declined, deciding that the Ritz Hotel would be more suitable, within walking distance of his clubs. Kensington Palace is a bit remote and he is afraid of inflicting himself. 'I prefer to be quite independent.' He was setting off alone for London, even at the age of eighty, without a companion or a secretary.

He was going for only six days, intending to get back as soon as possible, to his house and garden. He still has various details to tie up about its future, making sure things like death duties would not upset his plans for its preservation.

Was it a secret, the future of his magnificent house?

Well, you see, he has no children or near relatives to leave it to. He had at one time suggested to Oxford University that they might like to take it over. 'I talked to Maurice Bowra about it, and Roy Harrod, and they both said that Oxford would not be interested in owning anything abroad. They have already got their hands full with college administration.

'I want the property to remain intact, as a memorial to my father, so I have decided to leave it to the University of New York. Americans are so enterprising and New York's Department of Fine Art is one of the best in the world. I see it as a gesture of good will. After all, my mother was American.

'I hope it will be part of their Fine Arts Department, an overseas link. I see the Director and Fellows settling in this part, with a library and paintings, while the students will live in the adjacent villas. There are four other houses on the estate – at present I let them to firms like Olivetti. I want to leave it in apple pie order. No university wants to be saddled with death duties.'

By my calculations, there are already twenty American colleges or similar institutions with establishments in Florence. Bobbie and Chuck are going to be spoilt for choice. When the last of the Grand Old Englishmen goes, they'll inherit the best remaining private palace. By then, English life in Florence in the Grand Old Style will have gone for ever.

# ~ Chapter Eight ~

# Renaissance Man

*On the trail of the Renaissance;
going up at the Uffizi; gazing at David;
a remarkable occurrence while waiting
for the procession.*

What was the Renaissance? I had hoped I would not ask myself that question. All week, I had been surrounded by signs of it, by symbols, what am I saying, by *It* itself. The Renaissance is what brings people to Florence. I had been using it myself in conversation, nodding in wise agreement when other people referred to it, reading the word in every guide book, accepting it from the pens of the scholars, from the mouths of earnest young Americans just out of school, hearing it on the lips of every tourist fresh off the overnight coach.

I had had the same trouble when writing a biography of Wordsworth. How do you define the Romantic Movement? Which words can be used which will make sense to the layman yet not upset the scholars. Defining 'The Renaissance' is even harder. It is a portmanteau concept which varies in time and place, with fashion and feelings, and can be used to describe dozens of disciplines, not all of them in the pure arts. No wonder true scholars now shy away from such definitions. Life does not come along tied with labels. 'Periods' don't suddenly happen, then suddenly end.

Alas, it is now too late. The Renaissance has been grafted on to a period of European history and it will tag along with it for ever. Technically, it means 'rebirth' or 'revival'. Generally, and here we have to take care, it describes a period of roughly 200 years, from about 1300–1500, which began in Italy and then spread throughout Northern Europe, during which there was a rebirth in the arts and sciences. Well, that shouldn't cause too many arguments.

The term 'Renaissance' does not appear to have been used by scholars until much later, after it was all over, and was popularised by 19th Century writers and artists. In turn, just to confuse matters, they wrote and talked about an English Renaissance, a French Renaissance, as well as an Italian one.

The main attraction of the term is that it dismisses and packs off The Dark Ages, an equally omnibus term, but very handy when teaching school children. Once the Renaissance comes along, you can say goodbye to 1,000 years of history, dry old medieval stuff, in which not much happened, just a load of vandals running around, doing not much in particular, except finally wreck what was left of the Roman Empire. The Renaissance was a going back in part to the classical age, to studying and copying and learning from the glories of Greece and Rome, to the world's first great cultural and scientific age. That was the sort of 'birth' they were hoping to see reborn.

The single most remarkable thing to my mind is that it originally centred on one small spot on the globe. How did one city state, during a period of just 200 years, find itself giving birth to so many geniuses? The word genius is over used, just look at any sports report, but nobody is going to argue when it refers to Leonardo di Vinci or Michelangelo. But these are just two of about a hundred great men who were born or brought up or lived around Florence between 1300 and 1500. It also includes Dante, Petrarch, Boccaccio, Cellini, Raphael, Machiavelli, Galileo and of course the Medici family, the richest most powerful Florentine family. And yet Florence is such a comparatively small town. In 1338, its population was just 90,000. Even now, Florence is not big, just over 400,000, about the size of Bradford. Name me twenty world famous folk from Bradford.

*     *     *

The number one place today in Florence to taste the Renaissance is the Uffizi. I don't know how we missed it on our first walk round, but until you've actually been inside, it's not clear from the Signoria square where it begins. I expected something obvious, yet another huge palace with an impressive front, forgetting that the Uffizi was built as an office block. (Uffizi in Italian means offices.) It's not exactly Centre Point, more like a low lying suite of gentlemen's offices, which is what the Medicis wanted when it was built in 1560. It has an Oxbridge feeling, with its long internal quad and some monastic cloisters, though these days the cloister area is usually full of rather scruffy hippies and artists and street salesmen. In 1581, the ruling Medici of the time, Francesco I, had the upper part glazed in to make a museum and it became the treasure trove for all the Medici collections. In 1743, the widow of the last of the Medicis bequeathed it to the people of Florence.

We went up in the lift, the quickest way for all visitors in a hurry, as the galleries are still on the top floor. In the lift there was a graph on the wall, boasting about their success, showing that in the 1970s they had only half a million or so visitors a year but now, in the mid 1980s, there are over 1½ million, making it the most visited gallery in Italy. (In Britain, the British Museum manages 3 million a year, about the same as the Tower of London and Westminster Abbey, while the National Gallery averages about 2½ million. So there.)

We came out in an enormous corridor, lined with sculptures. Most people seemed to be hurrying past, at least there were few standing and admiring, yet at one time it was sculpture which most people came to see. Shelley visited the Uffizi every day during his time in Florence, just to take notes on the sculpture. It is only in the last one hundred years or so that many of the painters have been finally acclaimed as masters, such as Botticelli. (Another Renaissance painter who did most of his work in Florence. I forgot him on my list.) Today, his painting *The Birth of Venus*, is looked upon by many people as the painting which most expresses the spirit of the Renaissance. I therefore moved quickly through the rooms 1–9, rushing the late Gothic and early Renaissance, to get into room 10 and the Medici Botticellis.

*The Birth of Venus* looked very familiar, and somehow modern, as if perhaps Salvador Dali had done it. It does have a surreal rather than a mythological quality. It was at least a pleasant change not to be staring at another religious setting, but although it is well painted, good lines, clear colours, I have to say I found it amusing rather than moving. I asked Flora what she thought. 'Soppy.'

I then took her to look at the Botticelli *Primavera* which portrays, amongst other things, Flora, the Goddess of Spring. I thought she might like that. 'Stupid,' she said. I suppose the educated Renaissance noblemen knew their classical mythology, and could understand what the figures were meant to represent, but I was completely mystified.

The two paintings I would have most liked to have taken home, for my sitting room in North London, were two small portraits by famous Florentines I had never heard of before. (There were scores of those.) I copied their names down, Filippino Lippi and Pollaiuolo, thinking I might go mad at Sotheby's one of these years.

I enjoyed room number 18, the so called Tribune room, where Harold Acton had said the Young Gents on the Grand Tour used to meet and leave notes. We had to queue, as only thirty people are allowed in at a time. It's an octagonal room, with linen wallpaper, more like a private drawing room than the other art gallery style square rooms.

Flora was getting tired by now, but I insisted we went into room 28, to see Titian's Venus of Urbino. We all stood respectfully and stared at it for some time, along with a few hundred other people. It is clear and understandable, which is a help, though doubtless there are allegorical elements I missed. You don't need 'O' levels to appreciate that well known and very sensual lady, lying on a couch, clutching grapes in one hand while with the other hand she lightly caresses her pubic hair. Had she just been pleasured or was she about to be? Every *Sun* reader can speculate. But what is the little girl in the background doing, the one looking in a chest, watched by a maid? And is the dog on the couch beside the lady definitely asleep?

'Her legs aren't very good,' said Flora. 'They're the wrong shape. And her hands are too small.'

Perhaps the Venus in the title is a joke. She's nothing more than a page three girl, the world's first pin up. No wonder she has been loved, and parodied, for so long. Byron thought she was *the* Venus for all time. But then he would.

The room after number 45, just at the end of the West Corridor, is the room no one should miss, especially those who have had a long tiring day, or are just surfeited with richness. This final large room, with a terrace looking over the

roofs to the Signoria square, is the Uffizi's bar and café. What a perfect place, right in amongst the galleries themselves. Too often in British Galleries the bar, or more likely a crummy cafeteria, is hidden away in the basement, unappealing, unappetising. Only the Tate in London has a place where you can actually enjoy eating.

We all flopped and had ice cream and drinks and took them out on the terrace and slowly brought our legs and eyes back to life while we contemplated the next move in our culture fix. We just had to see David. Flora thought she meant her Uncle David, then groaned when she discovered it was another statue.

\*     \*     \*

The statue of David is in the Accademia and there are often long queues, but we were fairly lucky and managed to get to room two without too much difficulty. It used to be outside in the Signoria Square, in front of the Palazzo Vecchio, till it was brought here in 1873. (The one in the Signoria is a copy, though many visitors take it for the original.)

You walk down a sort of long gallery to reach it where it stands in its own tribuna room, dwarfing all the millions of visitors who over the years have come to stare up at him. Having seen the copy in the square, and the millions of post cards, I knew vaguely what to expect – a big naked bloke.

William Hazlitt didn't think much of it. 'Like an awkward overgrown actor at one of our minor theatres, without his clothes.' The copy in the square is rather dusty and grimy these days, while the original is white and clean, except for his curls which, if you look closely, betray the fact that they were once golden.

Flora pointed out that his head and arms are too big for his body, but I said it must be deliberate, to make you realise that the mind is stronger than muscles. Then she said *why* was he so big? Wasn't it Goliath who was supposed to be the giant? Hmm. Daddy's not sure what size David was. I made a note to consult my Bible for clues, but I suggested that he was big because he won, he was the successful one, and a great King, so it probably meant to show the triumph of man.

We both stared for some time at a strange bit on his left shoulder. He appears to be pulling a bit of skin away with his left hand. None of the guide books I could find gave any clue to what he was doing. Perhaps it's supposed to be his catapult, getting ready to sling it at Goliath? But did David have a catapult? Oh no, more things to find out.

Michelangelo completed it in 1504, using a huge chunk of Carrarra marble which had been abandoned, left as being spoiled and useless after another sculptor, Duccio, had had a go at it. It was a technical feat, just to get any sort of figure out of it. (Perhaps that is why the head is so big. The shape or weaknesses in the marble forced those proportions upon him?)

There were some Italian school girls, giggling at David's testicles. They're not particularly huge, considering he's a thirty feet high superman, but it's not often you see such things at close quarters. All the post card stalls, throughout Florence, have detailed close-ups of them, which visitors can send back to the office with suitable cheeky comments. Much more artistic than sending home a Donald McGill.

The David statue is now the symbol of Florence, and the Italian nation as a whole takes great pride in it, but its familiarity had lessened its impact. Harold Acton's garden statue was just as surprising. I was more stunned by the four other Michelangelo figures which line the entrance to the David. These are his four Slaves, meant to decorate Pope Julius II's mausoleum, but left unfinished. The impact is due to the fact that they *are* unfinished, tortured bodies trying to escape from their marble prisons.

*    *    *

We then walked back through Florence, heading for the car which we had parked on the other side of the Arno. We were tired and hungry, but it was too early to find a restaurant, and we didn't want to put in the time by looking at yet another building or museum.

We heard a tremendous roar and for a moment I thought I was walking down Tottenham High Road and that a goal had been scored at White Hart

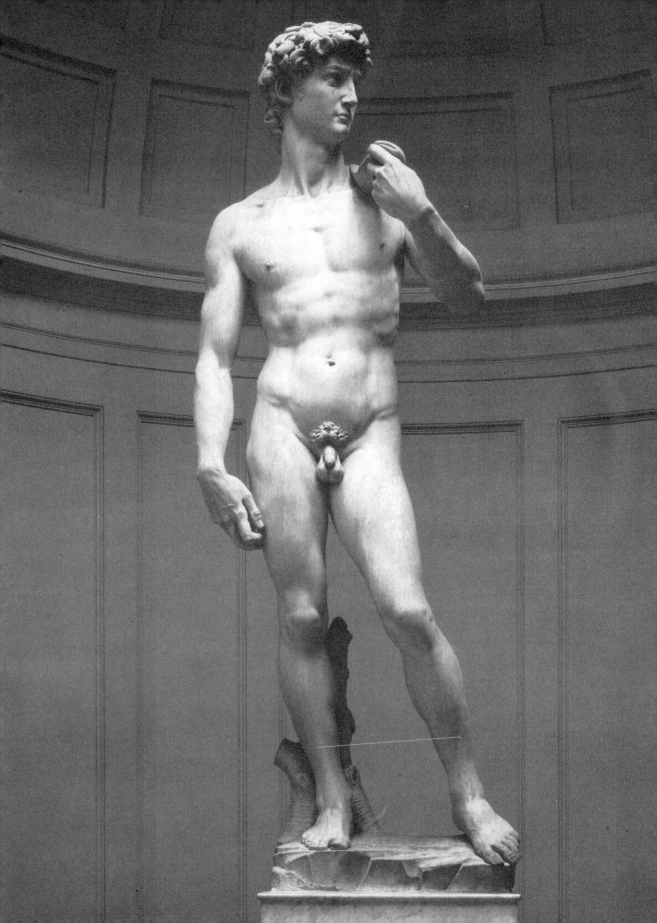

Lane. It seemed to come from the direction of the Piazza del Carmine, so I persuaded Flora and my wife to have a quick look.

The narrow streets became more crowded as we walked towards the noise, till suddenly we came to a road block, manned by police and Carabinieri. Behind them, inside the square itself, seemed to be a huge wooden stadium. There was another tremendous roar from a large, excited crowd – and I realised it *was* a football match.

I asked if we could go in, but no, you needed tickets. All seats were taken. On a wall, I noticed a very colourful poster, advertising a 15th century football match. What a shame we had missed it. However, a policeman said there was going to be a procession, coming this way, very soon, very soon.

Should we wait? I might have misunderstood what he had said. The procession might take hours to arrive, then turn out to be boring, or go another way. We decided to give it half an hour, so we settled down at a street corner and watched another road block which the Carabinieri were now setting up. We were joined by more people, then the shutters above in the narrow street started opening and locals took up positions at windows and doorways. Something good was obviously expected to happen. The twenty Carabinieri manning this little crossroads were loving it, marching back and forward, keeping the crowds back, arranging us one way, then deciding to move the barriers and line us all up another way. They were in full military uniform, with heavy rifles over their shoulder, a pistol at their waist, a white belt, big black boots and black spats. They could have been rather frightening, but looking into their faces, they were obviously so young, so innocent, so callow, hardly old enough to shave, peasant boys conscripted from the South, a comic opera army.

There seemed to be two older NCO's in charge, both with real moustaches. One had a whistle, which he used constantly, and the other had a walkie talkie, which he talked into, crouching down, straining hard to hear whatever instructions were coming through. When he eventually worked out the orders, he sprang up and did some manic shouting and whistling. It seemed clear that the higher you go in the Carabinieri, the more noise you are allowed to make.

The crowd were in great good humour, enjoying the sight of the Carabinieri working themselves into a state of excitement. One or two of the younger Carabinieri did look a bit frightened, worried about doing the wrong thing, standing in the wrong place, misunderstanding whatever it was they were being screamed at to do.

Two very pretty girls on a little motor bike, yet another Ciao, came down a side street, and arrived at the junction. They smiled at one of the youngest Carabinieri, who very nicely moved the barrier to let them down the street they wanted to go into. He was immediately shouted at by a superior, and forced to put the barrier back. The two girls started haranguing the senior Carabinieri, and they were soon all shouting at each other. I thought it was deadly serious at first, but slowly realised it was a mock row, a performance, all playing their street parts. Two of the less callow looking of the Carabinieri, ones old enough to shave, were in fact obviously chatting up the girls. In the end, the girls roared off, giving them all waves, saying *Ciao*, going back the way they had come.

The superior then beckoned the culprit forward, the very young one who had mistakenly let them through. I waited for him to be dressed down, court martialled perhaps, even shot on the spot, as the superior did look very fierce with his weapons and insignia. I couldn't quite catch the conversation, but the result was the young soldier putting his hand in his pocket and handing over a cigarette. They both lit up, smiled, then went back to their places.

The crowd was now about six rows deep, all of them locals, chatting to each other, sending back indoors for other members of their family. I could see few tourists or foreigners. We were joined by several Italian photographers and then a TV cameraman. Something *must* happen soon.

In the distance, there was an awful wailing of an ambulance, and the soldiers, most of whom had been lounging and smoking, burst into action, quickly opening one of the barriers, leaving one way free. Then they quickly closed them again when they realised the ambulance was coming from the other way and would crash into the barrier. The crowd did enjoy that. It was like something from M. Hulot. The ambulance tore across the junction, its siren shrieking, just as they got the right barriers in the right arrangement.

From another side street, coming towards us, I could hear new sounds and about a dozen young teenage boys slowly appeared, some of them skinheads, clapping and shouting in unison. I couldn't make out all the words, but the last bit of their cheering definitely ended in 'Hoo-Ra'. Not only did they look like lads from the Kop end, they were giving old fashioned English cheers. They walked past us, pushing each other and laughing, following the route marked out by the barriers, heading towards the Ponte Vecchio bridge. The match must be over. Surely the procession would be very soon.

At last, we could hear drums in the distance, slowly beating a ceremonial march, and everyone craned forward, while the Carabinieri stiffened their shoulders, straightened their guns, smartened themselves up. I found myself beside one soldier, looking straight into his ear. On the butt of his rifle was stuck a little price tag, the sticky sort from a supermarket, which said £6. In English. Did he know? Was it some joker, one of his friends, or had he picked it up from a gutter while resting.

The Procession arrived so sedately, so grandly, so serenely, that I was rather caught by surprise. I don't know what I had expected, but certainly not to see over 200 Florentines in full Renaissance regalia, walking in formation through these little streets, along with horses, cannon, trumpets and drums, wearing armour and carrying swords and muskets. The velvets and silks were so rich I could almost feel them as they passed, just a few feet in front of me.

In the middle of the procession, a dignitary held high a green ball, a sign that the green team had won. He was closely followed by the green team itself, a dozen very sweaty, very dishevelled young men in knee breeches, medieval tunics, the full 15th century outfits in fact – then I noticed all of them wearing very modern training shoes. Some of them had torn shirts. Others had blood stains on their arms and makeshift bandages. It had obviously been a very physical game of football. But all of them were covered in smiles, shouting and waving to friends in the crowd, several of whom rushed forward to kiss and shake their hands.

Then we had the three defeated teams – Blue, Red and White. I wondered what the Italian phrase was for being as sick as a parrot. They looked worse than that. So dejected you felt it had been a real 15th century battle, that they had been completely humiliated in a pitched fight and were now on their way to the gallows. They were drained and exhausted, all their pride and manhood gone.

The procession finished with further groups of costumed figures, marching in rows, equally brightly coloured, representing the 15th Century burghers and merchants of the various wards of Florence. Flora pointed to their feet. Apart from the footballers, who had been mainly shod by Addidas, every other single figure in the whole procession had been wearing the same style of medieval sandals, in perfect condition, flat heeled, with a sort of open floral leaf pattern at the front. What wonders they must perform each year, not just in getting new bodies into those elaborate old costumes, but in finding the right sandals to fit everyone.

It was not simply the beauty and finery of the Procession which was so startling, but the dignity of all the men and boys taking part. No one looked embarrassed and no one played up to the crowd or showed off. I have seen similar local processions in Britain, though not on this scale, where cat calls or even shouts of affection can ruin everything and turn Medieval Burghers into self conscious, Modern Wallies.

Each face was a study, both the young, earnest boys and the old, dignified gentlemen. Without exception, they looked distinguished, almost aristocratic, wearing their costumes so proudly. The Royal Shakespeare Company could not have done it half so well. I believed completely in all of them. Those sallow, Tuscan faces, those sharp noses and dark eyes staring out through the centuries.

They looked somehow familiar, yet I had chanced upon them, never having seen such a procession before, not knowing what to expect. Then I realised where I had seen these self same costumes, these identical men, their exact expressions.

All week I had been studying them, on the walls of the Uffizi, in the churches, on the frescoes. Renaissance art *was* about real people.

# ~ Chapter Nine ~
# Old English
*Home thoughts from an abroad cemetery;*
*hurrah for the British Institute;*
*a rather trying time with Ms Muriel Spark*

We were standing outside the Cemetery, trying to get in. It was mid afternoon, so there was no reason for it to be closed, though in Florence, anything can happen to any supposedly public place. The English Cemetery, home of so many English speaking exiles, is on the itinerary of most English speaking tourists, though that afternoon, we were the only people knocking at the gates, wondering if there was a Macbeth type porter inside, muttering and moaning about being interrupted.

I had seen snap shots of it, and read references, but nobody had said it was on a roundabout. In fact the cemetery *is* the roundabout. On all sides, the traffic goes hurtling past. At one time this cemetery, being for Protestants only, was just outside the city walls, but in the mid 19th century many of the old walls were destroyed to make way for broad avenues ringing the city, and the cemetery ended up right in the middle of a main road.

Eventually, an old woman appeared at the window of the gatehouse which was behind the locked gates, and waved at us. It wasn't clear if she was telling us something, or just telling us to go away. So I waved back. She kept on waving, rather angrily, so this time I waved a 1,000 lire note in the air. She disappeared, then slowly emerged from out of the gatehouse and limped towards the gates, holding a large set of keys, and stood staring at us.

I looked at my watch, indicating in pidgin sign language that it was far too early to be closed, so why couldn't she let us in. I held up my fingers for ten, meaning ten minutes, that's all we'll need. And other lies. She finally opened up and I gave her the tip for her kind services – admission is supposed to be free – and we started to walk into the cemetery. But she said no, we had to follow her into her little house.

In a dark little hallway I admired a photograph on a faded wall of a young man in football strip and I asked if it was her *figlio*. She said yes, but with no expression. There was another equally ancient photograph, presumably of herself about twenty years ago, wearing spectacles and looking even fiercer than she did today. She opened a visitors book for us all to sign while she sat down heavily on a little wooden chair and sighed. She pulled up her dress to let us see her legs, all swollen with varicose veins, so I looked suitably concerned. It was not exactly what I had come all the way to Florence to see.

At last, her little formalities over, she allowed us to go through the gate house arch and into the Cemetery.

It has always been called the English Cemetery, and appears on Italian maps and guide books as such, but in fact it is owned by the Swiss Evangelical Reformed Church and technically it should be called The Protestant Cemetery of Florence. As Harold Acton described, there was an enormous English community at one time in Florence, so much so that the Florentines naturally imagined that every white, non-Roman Catholic, must be from England.

The land was bought in 1827, for use as Protestant graves, much to the annoyance of the more reactionary local clergy, and many of the early graves were destroyed by vandals. Things settled down and from 1838 to 1877, 1409 Protestant men, women and children were buried there. It was officially closed in 1878, there being no space left, so for over 100 years it has been a dead cemetery, visited by tourists and students, rather than mourners or relations, a pilgrimage place for those interested in 19th century English Literature, Tuscan Division.

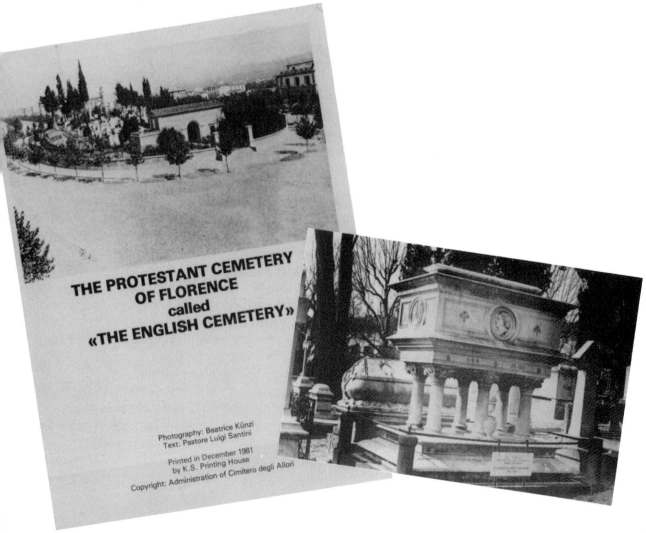

THE PROTESTANT CEMETERY
OF FLORENCE
called
«THE ENGLISH CEMETERY»

Photography: Beatrice Künzi
Text: Pastore Luigi Santini

Printed in December 1981
by K.S. Printing House
Copyright: Administration of Cimitero degli Allori

Of those 1418 graves, 760 are British, so you can see why it has always been called English. Next come the Swiss with 433, Americans with 87, Italians 84 and 54 Russians. This was the final resting place for many on their Grand Tour, especially the young. Families passing through on Grand Tours, staying for up to two years, often moved on without one of their children. I counted 164 graves containing children under two years of age. There is also a large number who died in their prime, without reaching the age of thirty, some 345 in all. Now they all lie in a foreign field, which is forever England.

What made them all come to Florence? The Grand Tour, in some shape or form, would explain the English, but it's not the whole story. The Swiss who bought the plot came to Florence and Tuscany to work. They were mainly tradesmen or craftsmen, emigrating for economic or religious reasons, settling down for good in a new country. It's hard to say what all those Russians came for. They were mystery men, passing through for a few years, eccentric princes with strange habits who kept the foreign community in gossip, then just as suddenly left.

The English and then later the American gentlefolk never worked, not in the economic sense. Many bought old palazzi and renovated them, much to the amusement of the locals. Others just bought up all the Italian culture they could find, objects as well as ideas and fashions. Inigo Jones on his Italian travels sketched ruins and buildings. William Kent picked up a lot of his gardening ideas from Naples. These and other artists and designers influenced several centuries of English landscape and architecture. As for the artefacts, they were being sent back in shiploads from as early as the 17th century. Two brothers called Nicholas and Henry Stone did an Italian Grand Tour from 1639 to 1642 and crated up boxes of statues, of Venus and Apollo and whatever else they could get their hands on. They despatched them by land from Rome to Leghorn where an English merchant shipped them home to Daddy in England.

Thomas Coke of Norfolk had around £10,000 a year in spending money in 1712 and he lavished a great deal of it on Italian treasures, enough to stock his famous home, Holkham Hall. Hundreds of our stately homes today are still crammed with Italian objects, sent home or brought back on Grand Tours, paintings by the acre, libraries by the yard, sculpture by the ton. Was it gentlemanly looting or cultural collecting? Some Italians today would like some of the stuff returned to the homeland. It is noticeable that in recent years there have been public exhibitions in Britain of Grand Tour 'souvenirs', so at least we can now all have a gape. Some of the souvenirs, like the water colours by Ducros, were done for the Grand Tourist trade, made especially for them to take home.

Dr Johnson's great friend Mrs Thrale, who changed her name to Piozzi when she startled London by marrying her children's Italian music teacher, did an account of her tour round Italy in 1784 with her new husband. In Florence, she booked into a hotel and found to her surprise that she was amongst her own country folk.

'Eating, sleeping, etc, all in the English way! Accordingly, here are small beds again, soft and clean, and down pillows; here are currant tarts which the Italians scorn to touch, but which we are happy and delighted to pay not ten but twenty times their value, because a currant tart is so much in the English way; and here are beans and bacon in a climate where it is impossible that bacon should be either wholesome or agreeable; but that makes it still more completely in the English way.'

English currant tarts in Florence in 1784? It makes English beer in Benidorm sound absolutely natural.

By the 19th century, English writers were flocking to Tuscany, to write, not to eat English food. Shelley died in 1822, off the coast near Viareggio. Byron visited Italy and so did Keats and Wordsworth. Lawrence wrote *Lady Chatterley's Lover* sitting on the grass outside his Tuscan villa. George Eliot set her novel *Romola* in Tuscany and so did E. M. Forster with *Where Angels Fear to Tread* and *A Room with a View*.

Many Americans also did a lot of writing in Tuscany, such as Mark Twain, who said he had managed more in four months than he could have written in two years at home. Henry James's *Aspern Papers*, though set in Venice, was based on his Tuscan experiences. Nathaniel Hawthorne, Fenimore Cooper, Longfellow all had profitable stays in Tuscany.

The English Cemetery, then, is the easiest place to commune today with the memories of those literary folk and literary circles now gone. As we went through the archway and into the main drive, my wife spotted a grave which said Arthur Clough, and she gave a little yelp of recognition. You have to know a little bit about Eng. Lit. to know much about him. He was Thackeray's friend and they travelled together round Europe. My wife, despite having done a biography of Thackeray, never knew that Clough had ended his life here.

We admired the grave of Fanny Hunt, the wife of Holman Hunt, who died on December 20, 1866, after just one year of marriage. There was a grave for the Crawfords, a very aristocratic English family of the 1840s who built a beautiful garden in their palace at Fiesole and entertained Queen Victoria. I followed a sign leading visitors to the grave of Walter Savage Landor, in English and Italian. On his tombstone were some lines by Swinburne. His own poems and prose are hardly read today, yet he was such an influential figure of the Romantic Movement. He left London for Florence in 1821 and was buried here in 1864. Landor was a great republican and supporter of the Risorgimento movement in Italy, as many of the English literary exiles were, spurred on by the romantic ideals and the personality of Garibaldi. It is one of the things which made the English, to this day, popular in Tuscany.

I noticed the name Trollope on a gravestone, but it was Frances Trollope-Milton, a fine literary name, who was part of the Trollope family. She was a focal point of Anglo-Florentine life and both Dickens and Thackeray came to visit her on their Grand Tours.

The vast majority of the graves are, of course, of unknown English and Scots, who came out and never returned, but their names will live on as long as the cemetery has visitors. I stood and wondered about 'Sir George Baillie Hamilton, Her Britannic Majesty's minister plenipontentiary at the court of Tuscany, September 1850, aged fifty-one.' What a grand mouthful to have on your gravestone, safely hidden amongst the sad cypress, away from the sight if not the sounds of the thundering traffic.

The most visited grave in the English Cemetery is of course that of Elizabeth Barrett Browning, the most romantic of all the Florentine exiles. Until she eloped with Robert Browning, when she was aged forty, she had been a semi invalid and recluse. Her secret passion for the younger Robert Browning finally got her out of her bed, out of the house, and they secretly fled to Italy. They ended up in Florence in April, 1847 where they lived happily together, until her death in 1861. The new life, the new conditions, transformed her, and it was in Florence that they wrote some of their finest works. Elizabeth wrote her poem *Casa Guidi Windows* from the window of their Florentine house. Robert wrote *The Ring and the Book* while in the same house.

Elizabeth's tomb is one of the biggest in the cemetery, raised on six short columns, designed by Lord Leighton. Underneath, my wife pointed to two small red candles, unlit. We wished we had brought matches. It would have been nice to have lit them, not just for EEB but for all those English writers who passed this way.

\* \* \*

After the English Cemetery, the other main pilgrimage place for English speaking visitors or residents in Florence is the British Institute. It celebrated 65 years of service in 1983 and claims to be the oldest overseas British cultural institute in the world. When it opened in 1918, the idea was to try to build up Anglo-Italian relations after the anti-British propaganda of the War years. It went slightly too far in the twenties and thirties, when the Director of the time became rather enamoured of Mussolini, much to the concern of the Foreign Office back home. D. H. Lawrence went into the British Institute one day, upset by the Director's fascist leanings, and shouted 'This is the *Anti*-British Institute.' He was forcibly ejected.

I was told this story by the present Director, David Rundle, an energetic and affable gentleman who took over the job in 1981, charged with gingering up the Institute. He comes from Devon and after an English degree at Cambridge, spent the next twenty years working for the British Council in various postings round the world.

He has a large and gracious office in the Palazzo Lanfredini, a building let to them by Sir Harold Acton. (Which they will eventually inherit.) I recognised Virginia Woolf on the wall which he said he had personally put up, taking down the Oscar Wilde as it set the wrong tone, but I didn't know who the 1920s gent in rimless specs was, guessing either H. G. Wells or Albert Finney dressed as Poirot. Turned out to be Arthur Acton, Sir Harold's father.

Firstly, they are a teaching institute. They teach English to Italians and have about 1,000 students every year. They also teach Italian to English people, and they have about 500, mostly Brits and Americans. I took a brochure for my eighteen-year-old son as it looked so good. Then they organise cultural events, lectures, films, exhibitions, showing some of the cultural wonders of the British way of life. Thirdly, they are a library, with the biggest collection of English language books in Italy, 60,000 in all.

One of Mr Rundle's minor jobs is to put flowers on Arthur Clough's grave every Easter. Rugby School sends £10 for the purpose. He usually manages to spin it out to buy flowers for Elizabeth Barrett Browning's grave as well.

They obviously do a great job in the community, waving the cultural flags. In the old days, it was also much more of a social position, going to endless cocktail parties with the exiles. 'I am trying to shift the emphasis from being an expatriates' club to a place for young people, but trying to keep the balance.'

Mr Rundle presented me with a British Institute Tie and a British Institute key ring. Should I spoil him with a Beatles book? Didn't seem the sort. Luckily, I had also brought with me a tin of Earl Grey tea and some bars of Kendal Mint Cake, knowing how these exiles can feel deprived. He apologised for not being able to offer me a drink, as he had just come back to his office that day from leave – all overseas chaps have leave, never a holiday – but invited me round to his flat, with my family, to meet his girl friend and have a drink.

His apartment, just a street away, turned out to be sensational. The Acton mansion is semi-rural and famous and I knew roughly what to expect, but this was the first time I had got inside an ordinary looking Florentine building where people live, right in the middle of the town, the ones which look so austere on the outside. It had a massive inner courtyard, so full of greenery and trees it was like Regent's Park, yet totally hidden from anyone passing in the drab little street outside. The views from his windows looked South over the city, towards the Boboli Gardens. There seemed to be so many rooms, and all exquisitely furnished. Perhaps a lifetime with the British Council is no bad thing. No wonder they never want to come home.

The flat goes with the job, a wise investment by a previous Director, and is now worth about £250,000 on the open market. His American girl friend Teresa arrived home from work, and we chatted about this and that, and it came out that she had just become the new curator of Casa Guidi, the Browning home. She said it was within walking distance. As my wife was very keen to see it, we all set off. Flora was not best pleased.

\*       \*       \*

Robert Browning left their rooms in the Casa Guidi after his wife's death in 1861, never to return. It had only been a rented apartment, but when it later came up for sale, their only son Pen Browning bought it, planning to move in his parents' furniture and mementoes. But Pen died without taking it over. A representative from Sotheby's in London came out to Florence in 1913 and the whole lot was sold at auction.

It remained in private hands till 1969, though a memorial plaque was erected over the front door by Browning lovers in Florence. The Browning

Institute Inc. of New York was founded in 1971 to acquire the apartment, and they launched a campaign which received coverage in the *New York Times* and other papers. They raised 82,000 dollars, receiving contributions from fifty states and ten foreign countries, enough to take over the apartment. :

Renovating work is still taking place, and it was only open afternoons, but Teresa was pleased that things had started so well. In a month, she had had forty visitors. Didn't seem a lot to me, when you think little old Dove Cottage averages 6,000 a month, but I did not say anything. After all, she was going to open it up, especially for us to see. Jolly kind of her.

We came to the main front door of a large, boring looking house, and some strange looking men came down the stairs, residents of other flats no doubt, but very suspicious. She said it can get a bit weird sometimes, especially if no one has been to see the Browning rooms for a good few hours.

'I had a doctor in the other day who got me in a corner and said he was very interested in sex.'

The Browning apartment, on the first floor, was a surprise. Not exactly a delightful surprise. I suppose I have been spoiled over the years by seeing literary shrines, such as Shaw's house at Ayot St Lawrence, or Hardy's in Dorset. At first glance, there appeared to be nothing to see, just three or four large empty rooms. Teresa did her best and chattered away, but it was more like being taken round an empty apartment for sale by an estate agent. There was nothing on most of the walls or the floors. You would have to be a *real* Browning enthusiast to imagine what the atmosphere was like in the old days.

Teresa opened up the big shutters and took us out on to the terrace where Mrs Browning was inspired to write one of her best known poems. Well, she *called* it a terrace, but it was simply a little balcony, only about three feet wide, above a very busy, narrow street. Opposite was a church, but all you see from the window is its side wall, grey and dull. How had that inspired her to write such a good poem? She had heard below a procession, going into the church, and a child singing, and that had been enough.

'She never had a job, you know,' said Teresa. 'I think the hardest work she did was pour out the coffee.'

There was one display case in the apartment which I found interesting, but then I love memorabilia. It contained visiting cards, one of them handed in from 'Mr Charles Dickens, Gads Hill Place, Higham, by Rochester,' with a handwritten addition, giving his Florence address. There were also cards left by Hallam Tennyson, Alfred Tennyson, Sir Charles Dilke. What Flora enjoyed seeing best was the christening robe in which Pen had been draped.

Teresa then brought out from a cupboard a collection of hair, not normally on show, given by a local lady. There were locks of hair from Florence Nightingale, Leigh Hunt and Shelley, all of them with Florentine connections, though it wasn't clear if the hair had been snipped off in the city. Leigh Hunt was a great hair collector, as were so many Victorians, and his best hair collection is now in Austin, Texas.

'Right, are you ready,' said Teresa. 'Now you won't believe it. This is it!'

She made a clicking noise with her teeth, getting us ready for the next excitement. It has to be said that she had not a lot to show us in any of the Browning rooms, but, as a curator, no one can accuse her of not trying.

'Look at this! Edward IV's hair!'

I had to stop and think. Who? When on earth was he king? I always get the Edwards wrong as they have been so spread out over the last 1,000 years. Edward IV. Hmm. He must have been 15th Century at least.

'How do you *know*?' I asked Teresa, 'not that I'm doubting you, my dear.'

She picked up some notes and read out that the hair had been taken from Edward IV's head while lying in his tomb at Windsor. 'But I don't believe it,' she said. 'Do you believe it, huh? Isn't it amazing? If it is true.'

We all then went for dinner, very grateful to Teresa for opening up and showing us such exotica. She comes from South Dakota, which in itself is pretty exotic.

'Every New Yorker I meet says the same thing. "Well, you sure are the first person I've ever met from South Dakota." I've now developed a remark I always use. "Have you ever been to South Dakota?" They always say no. Then I say, "Well, why not? I've been to New York."'

We were half way through our dinner, in a restaurant in the Piazza Carmine, the square in which I had failed to see the ancient football match, when suddenly a huge swarm of motor scooters arrived, right beside us. The noise was incredible and we couldn't hear ourselves talking. The riders were all young, smartly dressed, not yobboes or hooligans, but they sat there just revving up, going nowhere. There must have been fifty, a veritable invasion, a plague of petrol driven locusts. At last the patron went out and remonstrated with them. A lot of good humoured arm waving took place, then they roared off, as suddenly as they had arrived. As they did so, I realised from their accents that several of them had been English, Sloanes at that, the sort sent by Daddy to study for a few months at places like the British Institute. After all these centuries, the English are still here, even if they're not all writers.

*     *     *

I had seen Harold Acton and he had been easy; utterly welcoming and accessible. The other writer I wanted to meet before leaving Tuscany was Muriel Spark, the best known of all the present day British or American writers who have emigrated to Italy in recent years. In the old days there were scores of them, now there are only a handful who live permanently in Italy. Germaine Greer has little more than a holiday home. Jan Morris has long left.

Mrs Spark lives in Rome, but I had heard she spends the summers in Tuscany, so I had written to her, saying that I was Grand Touring and would like to chat to her about life in Italy, and also do an interview for BBC Radio's Bookshelf programme about her latest book. I thought that would do the trick. More impressive than sending my servant up with my visiting card. Through her publisher in London, I was told to ring when I got to Florence. Then I might be lucky.

I rang from our hotel and she agreed she could see me at eleven-thirty, but only for an hour. One hour, no more, was that clear? She had so much to do.

I got on to the autostrada, the main Bologna–Rome highway, the A1, which does a big loop to the South of Florence, and even managed to get on it so I was going the right way. Previously, coming from Venice, I had somehow ended up going South at a great speed before I realised I should be going North at a great speed.

I hate all driving, and motorway driving most of all, but in a strange country there are at least different sights, smells and sensations to contemplate. How small Italian cars are, yet how quickly they go. How small Italians are, yet how fierce they can become behind a wheel.

I felt fortunate not be in the South, or near Naples anyway, as they are reputed to be the worst drivers in Italy.

*'The people have made of this paradise a hell, in particular a motorist's hell. If Naples be distasteful to the railway tourist, how much more so to the traveller by automobile.'*

Three guesses *when* that was written? The answer is 1907. I bet you were nowhere near it. It appeared in a book called *Through Italy with Car and Camera* written by a wealthy American called Dan Fellows Platt. He was actually in a chauffeur driven Fiat and it was the state of the roads round Naples which upset him, plus 'miles of pavement filled with loitering beings, deaf to all sounds of warning.'

I sounded my warning, in the Italian fashion, as I came to several long tunnels, carved out of the landscape. Each time they caught me by surprise, and I failed to find my lights. It was a Fiesta and I still hadn't got to grips with how everything worked.

I was heading in the direction of Arezzo, about an hour south, a Tuscan town hardly visited by the tourist industry, being considered not as attractive as Siena or Pisa, but it was the birthplace of Petrarch, and has a fine square and Duomo. But then most Tuscan towns have that.

I had to leave the autostrada just past Arezzo, then strike West into the interior, so I was keeping my eyes open for the right junction, but also thinking about the Muriel Spark book I had just read, *The Only Problem*. It contains a vital scene set on an Italian autostrada. A couple stop at a service station and the wife, when they are back in the car, boasts that she has just stolen some chocolate. They are all capitalist pigs, she says, they deserve to be stolen from, when so many people in the world are poor and starving. The husband is so horrified by this that he stops the car, there and then, gets out and leaves her, completely disappears, and the marriage is over.

Naturally, there is more wrong with the marriage than just a stolen bar of chocolate, but I completely believed in this incident, the sort of triviality which starts up a storm. I was looking forward to discussing it with the author.

I had to make for a hill village called Civitella, then go four kilometres down a dirt track. The house appeared to be deserted, locked up or even abandoned, with the shutters closed, but I noticed a car round the side with a Roma number plate. It was a small, detached, Tuscan farm villa, with faded red shutters, nothing of any architectural interest.

Muriel Spark and her friend Penelope Jardine came out, apologising for the mess, saying they had builders. Mrs Spark was small and neat, rather fragile looking. Her friend was younger and plumper, but scurried away when I tried to talk to her. All I had asked was if she might spare me some time later for a chat, about her life in Italy. She is a sculptor, a close friend of Mrs Spark's, though Mrs Spark, taking me through the house, went to great pains to explain that it was Penelope's house and she had just taken part of it for the summer. For whatever reasons, it was obviously not wise to ask further personal questions, not if I wanted my hour's chat.

'I do dislike autobiographical things,' said Mrs Spark, leading me up the open stairs to a top floor room, large and bare, an attic room, with a couch, an expensive looking stereo, some drinks on a shelf, and that was about all. In a corner, a small staircase led to what I took to be a bedroom.

'Don't forget, we have to go in an hour,' said Penelope to Mrs Spark, closing the door behind us. A warning to me, so I thought.

Mrs Spark was married, but a long time ago in another country, to a Mr Spark in 1937, and they lived together in Africa for a while before the war, then the marriage was dissolved and she came to work and live in London and eventually started her writing career, though she did not become a professional novelist till she was almost forty, a late start as writers go.

I could detect a pronounced Edinburgh accent, like the one Miss Jean Brodie must have had. Apart from that book, she has not used her Scottish background in any novel, which is strange, considering she spent the first nineteen years of her life in Edinburgh.

'People are always asking me to write about Edinburgh again, but I don't think so.'

She won an *Observer* short story competition in 1951, her first attempt at fiction. She had written non-fiction stuff before, about Emily Bronte and Wordsworth, plus some poems. Her job in London was working for the Poetry Society.

'I remember the competition well. I remember the telephone ringing and I thought it was a dentist who was bothering me for his bill and I wasn't going to answer and it was Philip Toynbee, saying we've just opened the envelope. It was all done under a pseudonym and you put your real name in an envelope. He said they thought it was a man who'd written this story, but anyway it's you, and you've won. My pseudonym was Aquarius.'

It was Graham Greene who encouraged her to do a novel, in fact he even paid for her to do so. He gave her £20 a month because he had liked some of her short stories. 'A friend of mine told him I needed money and needed a patron and he applied for the job.'

Did you pay him back?

She looked surprised. 'It never struck me. It would not have seemed proper. I don't think I want to talk about that.'

That first novel, *The Comforters*, came out in 1957 and Evelyn Waugh was one of the many people who praised her wit and style.

It was Jean Brodie, some five novels later, which made her name and brought in a bit of money. Over the years, it has been made into a film, stage play, and TV series, with well known actresses such as Vanessa Redgrave and Maggie Smith playing the lead role.

In Edinburgh, she had a Protestant upbringing, despite having a Jewish father, but in 1954, she converted to Catholicism. (Very like the girl in *The Mandelbaum Gate*.) That gave her the confidence, she said, to go on and be a novelist, clearing her mind, letting her see things.

I asked if she had felt an exile, while living at home in Edinburgh. A terribly good question, or so I thought. It had come to me while driving down the autostrada. But like so many good questions, it was better than the answer. She mumbled something on the lines that she had always been a bit of a dreamer, not really attached to any one place. 'I suppose a state of exile is something one carries around with one. I always feel exiled from wherever I am in a sense.'

She became a real exile in the 1960s, when she moved first to New York, and then to Italy, taking a place in Rome.

'Oh, I wanted to leave England because I was too well known. It was very distracting.'

Many writers have managed fame and success, yet still survived with a normal life in England. I searched in my mind for some example to throw at her, a lady novelist of a similar age and importance, and said what about Iris Murdoch, she has managed to carry on her own life in England.

There was a pause and I realised I had again said something wrong, though without intent. She asked me why I had brought in Iris Murdoch. Was I trying to compare them? What was I trying to do? This conversation was supposed to be about her books. She didn't want any mention of Iris Murdoch in the broadcast.

'All I was trying to suggest was that it was probably not your *real* reason for coming abroad. I'm sure there was something else, perhaps . . .'

'There was,' she said, after a long pause. 'Family pressure, a certain amount of family pressure I wanted to get away from.'

'You mean your family, your parents, were getting you down?'

She nodded and I waited, but she would not discuss the matter further. I would like to have heard more as it might change the normal impression about her flight to Italy and the way she cut herself off. After all, people have suggested it was a tax exile, which I don't believe.

Her novels have changed a lot since she came and settled in Italy, the realistic settings of her earlier books have gone, such as Jean Brodie in Edinburgh, or *Memento Mori*, *Girls of Slender Means*, and *The Bachelors*, which were rooted in London, usually bed-sitter land in Kensington just after the war.

Very often, when writers become exiles, they end up far from home – writing about home. They have to get away, in order to realise and remember their roots, as D. H. Lawrence did in Florence, or James Joyce did in Paris. Mrs Spark has not done this. Many of her novels since coming to Italy have had indistinct settings, European, vaguely Italy, nowhere really that mattered to the subject. She appears now to be more concerned with style and form, technique and atmosphere, rather than place or subject matter, as if she is *thinking* her books, now she is an exile, rather than experiencing them. She is also, though I did not dare suggest it, not as witty.

I asked, carefully, if *she* felt any changes in her writing, since coming to Italy. Well, for example in the use of less realistic locations?

'I don't write about foreign countries from the point of view of the natives. I always do it from the point of view of an English person, or someone like that. It wouldn't be possible for me to enter really very much into their minds. I did it with an Arab in *Mandelbaum Gate*, but how successfully I don't know.'

As for her work methods, she didn't think they had changed much. An idea would come, usually based on a philosophical observation. She would think about it, then start, putting her name on the blank exercise book, the title, then away she would go. She still uses the same school exercise books she used as a girl in Edinburgh, when she was writing poetry to amuse herself. She gets James Thin of Edinburgh to send them out to her.

*The Only Problem* had been inspired by the Book of Job in the Bible, a topic she has been thinking about for about twenty years. She wanted the main character in the book to be a scholar, obsessed by the Book of Job. Scholars do exist, that is how they are, so they deserve to be the subject of a novel.

Some readers have doubtless taken the book at a more obvious level, reading it is a sort of thriller. The wife who is left by the scholar on the autostrada, having stolen the chocolate, comes back into his life as a terrorist, shooting up the local community, and he gets the blame for being part of her gang, so the local police think. He is made to suffer for something he has not done, just as Job did.

It is always interesting to find out what a novelist's original inspiration was, as so often a reader can never see it. Jane Austen always said that *Mansfield Park* was sparked off by wanting to write about curates, yet the curate in the book is about the last character the public can remember.

'I am an English writer. I write in English. My next book, the one I've just started on, is set in London. I suppose one day I will end up in England, but not for the moment. I like it here. I like the voices I hear.'

I asked if she meant the local Italian voices, or the voices in her head, but she didn't answer.

'I did think of moving to England this time, and I might if the right house came up. Then I thought about France, but owning property in France is so complicated.'

It then came out that she was planning to leave Rome, not for any particular reason I could gather, and had made a bid for a house near Lake Como, all rather art deco inside, she said. She hoped she got it, but was waiting to hear from the estate agent.

'I just want a change. I am very mobile. I don't have a feeling for a nest. I don't need much space, just enough to dump my books, records, my archives. All I really need is a base, so I am free to go off when I need to.

'I still find Italy very good for a writer. They don't bother you. Tuscany is very democratic. People sometimes try to rope you in, but not much.

'Italy is beautiful, full of antiquity and I find it conducive to good writing. I like the climate and the Italian food.

'There's a general atmosphere of positiveness and of well being. But there's also, I must say, the bureaucracy's a bit of a bore. It's worse than England. It's very bureaucratic. I also have a job here, you know. I'm a *New Yorker* correspondent. I write. I've got a contract.'

I suggested it wasn't a real job, just a secondary thing, as her real job is surely writing novels, but she insisted it was a proper occupation. She needed the money. Things like Jean Brodie had not made her the fortune some people thought.

She poured me out a glass of wine, the audience obviously nearing an end, and I proceeded to spill it slightly, as I was trying to balance a book in my other hand.

I said Italian food was terrific, except for the bread. Didn't she find that disappointing, after the lovely bread and baps in Edinburgh?

'What you must do with Italian bread is put salt on it, then dip it in oil, then it's much better.'

It looked as if we might be getting on to lighter, more personal things about life in Italy, but very soon Penelope Jardine came in, exactly on the hour, and said abruptly time to go, we have to be off.

I have done this myself over the years, arranging a sign with my wife so that visitors can be brought to an agreed halt, but always leaving the option of extending the time, if things are going well, or if they seem amusing or interesting. But Mrs Spark immediately got up. That was it.

I admired the house on the way down, thanked them both profusely for the lovely time and hospitality, wished her luck with the publication of the new book, then found myself back on the autostrada, heading for Florence. Ah well, you can't win every time.

Next morning she rang me at my hotel, saying not to bring in any comparison with Iris Murdoch in any broadcast, nor go on about her being a tax exile. Heh ho.

# ~ Chapter Ten ~
# Siena and Jimmy Jimmy

*A most wondrous sight greets our travellers;*
*a frightful mistake but a memorable meal.*

We set off for Siena on the back roads, determined to have a last leisurely look at rural Tuscany, instead of the rude rear end of Fiats on the Florence freeways. It was July 2 and everyone in the hotel warned us not to go to Siena that day. That is the day of the annual Palio and the whole world and his wife goes to Siena. We were not sure what the Palio was, except some sort of horse race, but everyone warned it would be impossible to get in, to see anything, or even park anywhere near the town. It was pure chance we had chosen July 2. It fitted in with our plans, to take in Siena on a gentle Tuscan tour, so why change it, just because for hundreds of years something else also happens that day?

We headed South to Grassina, carefully getting across the autostrada, without making any mistakes, such as joining it and ending up at Rome, and we were soon in gently rolling hill country, with terraced vineyards on the hills on all sides. This is pure Chianti country and the road was empty, except for regular signposts telling us which particular Chianti house we were passing. They didn't look as grand as the French wine chateaux look, at least on their bottles, but they were exceedingly handsome. I told Flora to keep an eye out for any wine tastings, invitations to have a free drink, but she saw nothing. It was July. Rather early in the year for the new vintage.

As we neared Siena, we got ourselves ready, all prepared to gasp in wonder. The guide books had said it was a magical city, standing on three hills, a beauty on her pedestal. We strained and strained our eyes as we entered the outskirts of the town but could see nothing, except boring suburbia and increasingly busy roads. Perhaps you have to approach it from the South or West to see it at its best.

I thought about parking at once, as already I could see police hauling cars away, but I decided to bash on. My theory is always to reach where you want, then work back. If we got near the centre, and it was impossible, we would just go elsewhere for the day. We came at last to some ancient City Walls, and I realised this must be the famous part, and I managed to park, squeezing in on a pavement under a tree, hoping it wasn't illegal. Once inside the old walls, walking down some narrow lanes, it was so much cooler and quieter. The heat in the car, now it was approaching midday, had become unbearable.

We came to two big squares, with lots of greenery, much more attractive than the Florence squares. The crowds were growing denser the nearer we got to the centre and the pavements were overflowing, but there was a relaxed, festival air about the place. Lots of young Italians were wearing different coloured rosettes and sashes across their chest.

Siena is a much smaller town than Florence, only 65,000, but architecturally I was beginning to think it was more attractive, warmer and friendlier, not just because of the red tinted 'Siena' colour bricks, but the lines were more flowing, more feminine, not as austere and hard as the masculine public face of Florence. It also seemed cleaner, less litter, fewer tourist stalls around, and the shops seemed real, selling real things.

We were heading for the Campo, the main square, taking what seemed like a subterranean back route, going under and behind buildings, through arches, round pillars, into dark alleys. It felt medieval, yet at various intersections we could see down narrow passages towards a main street where hordes of tourists were sweeping past like a torrent, then we lost sight of them again.

I was beginning to think we were heading in the wrong direction, as the lane we were following grew even darker, and then it petered out. Ahead seemed to be a gap in a little courtyard, so hesitantly we moved forward, and the sight which met us silenced us all completely. We had stumbled without realising right into the Campo, straight from the dark of the lanes into an incredible scene, as if we had parachuted, or been expelled from a gun. The impact was stunning. It was the best single image, the most memorable sight we'd seen so far in Tuscany.

The Campo on an ordinary day must be remarkable. It is not so much a square as a circle, with buildings all the way round, so once inside, you are completely enclosed, a perfect amphitheatre. That's the first surprise. Then there's the buildings themselves. The main one is the Palazzo Pubblico, one of the greatest Gothic buildings in Italy, but all are equally wonderful, different and individual, yet making up one marvellous whole. You need a 180 degree eye to take it all in. No camera or film could ever do it justice. The nearest is an aerial shot, and there have been many, but even that doesn't give the exact multi dimensional effect of being there, right in the middle, part of a miracle.

But this day, this chance day, the day of the Palio, the Campo had been transformed and was looking absolutely spectacular. There were banners and decorations and flags draped from all the surrounding palaces and buildings. The balconies on each of the buildings had been specially set out to provide the best seats for the spectacle to come. Lower down, completely obliterating the normal shop and restaurant fronts, tiers of wooden grand-stand seats were being erected. In front, going all round the Campo, turning it into a complete circle, was a race track, about twenty feet wide, strewn with a darkly golden sand, Siena sand. A wooden fence had been erected with padded stretches at the corners to stop the horses from crashing. The main crowds would be standing in the middle of the square, with the race being run around them. This again needed careful studying because on second viewing I realised the Campo wasn't flat, like a normal square, but bowl shaped, like a conch shell, sinking gently towards the middle.

Thousands of people were pouring into the square, just as we had done, from about a dozen narrow entrances, spilling out of the side streets and lanes, catapulted into the arena. Most of them did what we did – standing back, rubbing their eyes, getting out their cameras.

I suggested we should sit down, in one of the pavement cafés which were still doing business, before they all shut for the race and turned into grandstands. To hell with the cost, I said. These famous places always are a rip off, with rude waiters charging you £2 for a cup of coffee, listen, I've been to St Mark's Square in Venice, I know what happens, but let's lash out all the same.

The waiter came singing, full of old chat, terribly friendly, and talked to Flora about the horse race to come. I would have excused poor service on such a hectic day, but his good humour was remarkable. I could have sat there all day, watching the preparations for the race, looking round at the shapes and styles of all the five and six storied 14th Century buildings behind and around us, some with castellated tops, some elaborately arched windows, balconies and little towers. It all blended together so well, unlike the Signoria Square in Florence, but I really must stop comparing things. This is the vice of all tourists, all critics, all people who have seen more than one place. Enjoy it for itself.

A little truck stopped in front of us and two workmen got out with old fashioned, long handled wooden spades and took a few spadefuls of fresh sand from the back of their little wagon and threw it gently on the race track, against a fence, for extra security. Three ladies dashed forward, said something to the workmen, and each took a handful of sand, wrapped it carefully in a handkerchief, then put it safely in their handbag. As the truck moved on, working its way slowly round the circle, I could see other people doing the same. A handful of the Palio sand, a memento for ever. No dafter than locks of hair.

Palio means banner, which is all the winner gets for winning the horse race, but the honour is what matters. Ten of the city's twelve districts are chosen by lot to compete in the race, and each has a different colour and symbol. The locals cheer on their respective district, but so does the whole of Italy as it is shown live on television. The race is bare back, beginning at the drop of a rope, and it can be very tough and brutal. There are no laws against pushing or obstructing or even whipping each other.

The first Palio, on the modern lines, took place on July 2, 1660, and it is now one of Italy's greatest sporting events. Practice races go on for several days beforehand, and they can attract tens of thousands of spectators, just watching the free show. But tonight at six, for the big race, three times round the track, there would be almost 200,000 people crammed into the Campo.

I asked the waiter about tickets and he laughed and shrugged his shoulders.

Gone, years ago. The good seats cost £50. All gone. We could stand in the middle, which would mean taking up a position now, but it would be very rough, too dangerous for children. The crowds go wild, he said, as unruly as the riders, and there are always accidents. So that was it. No Palio for this year.

Slowly, we got up and walked round the entire square, examining the exotic fountain in the middle, then going into the Palazzo Pubblico to have a quick look at a few of the state apartments. In an inner courtyard I admired a statue of Romulus and Remus, being suckled by the wolf. Siena is said to have been founded by Senius, son of Remus, and the wolf appears on many of the City's

decorations. Then we sat on the steps of the Duomo and ate delicious cherries, as large as plums, as firm as apples.

The crowds were now impossible in the streets and very soon we would be unable to fight our way either in or out, so we returned to the car, to continue our little Tuscan tour.

*     *     *

Jimmy, Jimmy, let's go there. Look, it's not far away on the map, and everyone, but everyone, has been telling us that Jimmy, Jimmy is the most beautiful village in Tuscany, if not the whole of Italy. So we all agreed.

We had been referring to San Gimignano as Jimmy Jimmy all week, partly because we had still not quite come to grips with Italian pronunciations, but also as a family joke. Flora has this phrase she says when she catches people out, such as elderly Wrinklies, when they have lied or exaggerated or just made a genuine mistake. 'Jimmy, Jimmy,' she says, rubbing her chin. Don't ask me the derivation.

So we set off for Jimmy Jimmy about midday, leaving the Siena hordes, estimating that it could only be twenty-five kilometres away so we would be there in under an hour, just in time for lunch. Visiting the famous Tuscan sights with Flora consisted of finding a place for lunch, having a quick look at the outside of yet another utterly magnificent and marvellous Renaissance thingy, then rushing for the nearest and best ice cream place. Flora's record so far was five ice creams in one day.

My wife was navigating and she did very well, getting us safely off the bit of autostrada from Siena, and we were soon following the signs to San Gimignano. We saw it first in the distance, an amazing walled town, on a hill with towers and battlements, the sort of skyline travellers must have seen all over Italy, back in the 14th century.

We climbed up and round a narrow road and eventually got through the town wall and into the old quarter and by an amazing bit of luck we managed to park. Well, it wasn't really so much luck. The place was deserted. Every Italian, not just the tourists, must obviously be in Siena for the day. At this rate, we might be back in our hotel in Florence in time to watch the race on the tele.

We had parked near a street called Via 20 Settembre. Flora asked why it was called that, so I told her to ask her brother Jake, next time we meet him. He's the expert on Italian history. I found it on the San Jimmy map, though the next stretch we came to wasn't on. Typical. All week we had been struggling with the Michelin guide, never finding on their town maps the actual street we happened to be standing in. But I worked out the general direction and eventually we reached the Duomo. Next to it, just as the map said, was the Museum of Sacred Art. It looked quite cool inside. After lunch I might give it a few seconds.

We felt we were in medieval times. The old town was so atmospheric, cut off from all modern life, with no nasty modern buildings and hardly any cars. Walking round the ancient streets we realised we were the only tourists in the old town. Clever old us, choosing the Palio day.

We stood in the central square, wondering where the restaurants might be, which place we should give our custom to. My wife got out the American Express Florence and Tuscany guide, in case they suggested any little places to eat, and she happened to see them refer to the main square as being *triangular*. Now, we happened to be standing in a main square which was *rectangular*. Even I know the difference, though it's centuries since I did geometry. Stupid guide books. As the author of several, I know how untrustworthy we can all be at times. But the Duomo was in the right place on the map. So was the little museum. Perhaps this wasn't the main square after all, but some minor square. The place was deserted. It was siesta time. All the locals still at home must be inside, asleep or watching children's television. The rest of the world was in Siena. I eventually caught a glimpse of an old woman, flitting from one dark alleyway to another, and I raced after her and in my fluent English I asked her where the Piazza della Cisterna was. This is what they call their main square in San Gimignano.

She tried to escape, but I got in front of her and repeated my question, enunciating my English more clearly this time. Some of these remote Italians can be a bit slow. She shook her head, so I got out the guide book and showed her the name I was looking for on the map. Now this is always a mistake, so naturally my wife started muttering, don't be stupid, how cretinous, she won't understand a map, locals never do. This is true. My father-in-law knows Cumberland backwards, every secret road and route, but show him a map and he's lost. He has his own map in his head, one which Mercator could never reproduce, and he will have it there for ever, but it bears no relation to those coloured squiggles created by the Ordnance Survey chaps.

Suddenly, the old woman burst out laughing and broke into very fluent Italian, forgetting for a moment I was a visiting idiot in my Marks and Spencer shorts. She pointed over the town walls into the distance, then pointed back at the map, and it slowly began to strike us what had happened. We were not in San Gimignano. We were in some place called Colle di Val d'Elsa, an equally ancient medieval walled town on a hill with a Duomo, a museum of Sacred Art, and even a 20th September street. Oh no.

Colle is mentioned briefly in both guides, the Michelin and the American Express, as it is quite a famous place, but in neither did they recommend any eating places. No wonder the whole town had no tourists. But how on earth had we got here? We had carefully followed all the San Gimignano signs.

It was your stupid fault, you were supposed to be navigating, oh no it wasn't, you parked the car and you said that's the Duomo and that's the main square, you half wit, you have buggered up the whole day now. Shush, said Flora, it doesn't matter, let's just have an ice cream and forget lunch.

'I'm not staying here,' said my wife. And I'm not leaving now, so I said. It's another eight kilometres to the right place, and I'm shattered and starving and anyway I've got a good parking place, so hard cheese, we're staying here. But there's no place to eat, and *you* can't go without eating, she said, I know you.

To the right of the Duomo I noticed a sort of hardboard hut, a shack set up in a passageway, and on the pavement in front a handwritten scrawl said 'Oasis for Tourists'. I went across and found a little sort of tent selling trinkets, cheap glass ornaments, the sort of mementoes you win on fairgrounds. It seemed to be run by a local peasant looking family. There was a mum in black and two daughters beside the souvenirs, while a dad with brawny arms and two sons were sitting in the shade at a table eating what looked like a half a cow. He waved his half cow at me, like Desperate Dan, and kissed his fingers and went yum yum, or whatever is the Tuscan for yum yum.

'Do you do food?' I asked, in pidgin Italian. One of the girls, aged about sixteen, produced a simple, handwritten menu. She was doing English at school and was quite good, if hesitant, though she wasn't helped by her Dad who continued to shout in Italian at her and at me, shaking his cow, and encouraging me to sit down at once and tuck in.

My wife was still in the square, doing her Greta Garbo act, I want to be alone and have nothing to do with this tom foolery. Flora was looking miserable, wishing we would stop arguing. I said I had discovered this terrific little place, look just over there, beside the cathedral.

I persuaded them to come nearer and look, but my wife quickly stopped. 'I am not eating *there*. You two can go. I'll wait.' 'Oh God, this is supposed to be a family Grand Tour,' I said, 'a cultural experience, one which little Flora will never forget, now you're being silly.' 'No I'm not,' she said. 'Anyway, I'm no longer hungry.'

I went back to the shack and cross examined the teenage girl on her menu, then I rushed back to announce success. You can just have bread and salami and wine, honest, it looks lovely, very clean, you'll love it, very cool, please, oh come on Flora, they've also got icecream.

At long last we all three sat down, watched with great glee by the triumphant father.

We were there for almost three hours, their only customers, and it was the most enjoyable meal we had in Tuscany. My wife admitted her salami was delicious, and such a generous amount. Flora and I had the same, plus spaghetti bolognese. The bread was great, and the best we had so far. The wine was excellent. The father made us join him in sharing his own chianti, when our bottle had finished, then he sent his daughters off to get us fresh apricots. He forced brandy upon me and then made his wife go to their own home to make me real coffee.

For an hour I discussed football with the father, especially Graeme Souness's chances at Sampdoria, for whom he had just signed. He knew all the Liverpool stars and we agreed we preferred Dalglish to Rush. I asked about Rossi and he made a face and put his thumbs down. You forget, of course, that one country's national hero is not necessarily a local hero, not if he happens to play for a team you don't support. I told him about the time I went with Tottenham Hotspur when they played AC Milan in Milan.

When the bill came, for this incredible meal, it was only 8,400 lire. I have it in front of me. Even I could work out that it was amazingly cheap. We had guzzled and drunk for almost three hours, yet the bill was only £3. Things in Italy are about the same as here, even in the countryside, so it should have been more like £30. I queried it, but the father waved and shouted some football slogan at me. He sent a daughter off somewhere and she returned with some huge peaches, twenty in all, and presented them to us in a plastic bag. I made his whole family line up while I took their photograph, hoping it would come out, promising I would send him a copy.

That evening, I had another drink with David Rundle at the British Institute, and told him what had happened. He said that Colle was one of his favourite places, so we had had a lucky mistake, but the price of the meal, he just couldn't understand it. The father must just have charged me for the bottle of wine, and let me off everything else. Why? Was he so in love with Grand Tourists?

My wife thinks it was because of a misunderstanding between my pidgin English and his pidgin Italian and that he thought I actually *played* for Spurs. Don't you remember, he asked for your autograph after he had given you the bill? Hmmm. Perhaps.

I like to think it was simply because we are part of that wonderful world wide brotherhood of Fathers.

# III
# GENOA TO
# THE RHINE

Köln-Düsseldorfer Weinkelle

Qualitätswein mit Prädikat
1982er
FORSTER UNGEHEUER K
RIESLING — trocken —
*Rheinpfalz*

Erzeugerabfüllung Weingut Reichsrat von Buhl, Deid
A.P.Nr. 5 106 044 0        021 83

0,75 l

## 150 Years of Rail in Germany

# Chapter Eleven

# Playing in Genoa
*Mr Souness and Mr Francis kindly*
*give an audience and explain to our hero*
*what exactly they are doing in Italy*

On a Modern Grand Tour, there are not many princes to visit, famous personages who have their own courts, people with faces which are recognised throughout their own area, who are worshipped and revered by the local inhabitants. Yet I was on my way to Genoa to visit two of them. Even more surprising, they are both British born. I'm sure James Boswell would certainly have gone out of his way to meet them, hoping his visiting card would gain entrance.

First of all I went to Pisa, dropping off my wife and Flora at the little airport, and yes we did all climb the Leaning Tower. I was prepared for it not really to be leaning, well just a little bit, and I never expected you could actually climb up inside it. It was a marvellous sight, better than I expected, and exquisitely set amongst green lawns, not all jam packed like the usual Italian architectural gems. We all climbed to the top, counting 294 steps, though I didn't make the very top. I'm not going out there, I said, on that dodgy looking balustrade, with no safety rails and all open, you must be joking, but they took their shoes off and climbed another twenty steps or so in their bare feet. I waited below, my eyes closed.

Once they'd left for London, I set off alone to meet the two emigrés. I hoped they would form a contrast to the two writers I had met in Tuscany and would give a different insight into the country. Writers, anyway, tend to take their own lives with them, creating their own environment, much as it was at home. But salaried workers, forced to work day by day, shoulder to shoulder with the natives, see their new country at ground level. In this case, they also happen to be rather well paid for what they do.

Could they be perhaps something naval? After all, Genoa's claim to Italian, and European fame, is based upon its magnificent harbour. From the 12th to the 15th century, its sailors and explorers and administrators created their own empire, with colonies as far away as Corsica, Sardinia, Cyprus and North Africa. They manipulated the Crusades in order to hire out their own shipping and built up even more power and wealth. By 1300, Genoa was one of the largest cities in all Europe with a population of almost 100,000. As a City

State, it rivalled Florence in power, and it was as successful overseas as Venice, although not quite as disciplined.

Christopher Columbus was born in Genoa, the world's best known sailoring gentleman, though it was the Spanish court which gave him backing when he went off and discovered America in 1492, not the Genoese. By that time, Genoa was beginning to crumble, and in turn the French got control, then Spain, then France again, then the Austrians.

As a port, however, Genoa is still Italy's greatest, although I'd met an Italian engineer in Florence who warned me I would be disappointed by the harbour. Strikes and economic problems had disrupted the docks and I would be lucky to see any shops in the harbour. The opening of the great tunnels through the Alps had originally been of enormous help to Genoa, expanding its hinterland, but now many importers find it easier and more reliable to land their goods at Rotterdam, over 1,000 miles away, and send them by boat and train down the Rhine valley to Italy. It sounded very strange, but my engineering friend, head of a business in Milan employing over 1,000 people, said it was now true. Genoa harbour had been in real trouble. It would need some engineering or marketing miracle to put things right.

My two friends, alas, are not up to such maritime problems, although they do work for an organisation which takes part of its name from Admiral Doria, one of the greatest sailors and legislators in Genoese history. You see the Doria family name everywhere in Genoa, in streets and palaces.

Could they then be academics? Genoa was very active in the Risorgimento and has a long radical tradition. Mazzini was born in Genoa and it was from Genoa that Garibaldi sailed for Sicily with his army of liberation. Anybody interested in Italian political history might well come to Genoa. The local University is rather eminent, although in Italy there is not the pecking order amongst universities, the way it happens in Britain or the United States, with certain places being considered smarter than the rest. Bologna is the oldest University in Europe, founded in 425, and is good for science, but it's not thought of as the 'best'. In Italy there is no number one. It tends to be individual departments which are looked upon as being particularly excellent, rather than a university as a whole. For example, Milan is considered good for engineering, Florence for agriculture, Pavia for physics, Milan and Florence for medicine, Florence and Rome for the Fine Arts. Genoa is thought rather good for mining and engineering.

Genoa, then, might well attract visiting academics. Perhaps someone working on a special research project? Clever though my friends are, it would be hard to call them academic, though they have both written books. Or should I say books have been written about them, with their names on the cover.

Perhaps artists? Rubens came to Genoa, and so did Van Dyck, to paint the Genoese nobility and there are some fine paintings to be seen in the city's galleries and palaces.

I would certainly call my two friends artists, though they tend not to perform their artistry with their hands, not unless it's a mistake. They perform with their feet. You've obviously guessed by now. Yes, I was on the way to talk to two footballers.

Graeme Souness was the one I was most looking forward to meeting again. He'd arrived in Italy only two months previously, trailing clouds of glory with him. And a host of medals. As the captain of the European Champions Liverpool, who had recently had the cheek to beat Roma in the finals, he was already a household name in Italy, at least in homes where football is followed. That means almost every home. You may think there are football daft folk in Britain, but in Italy it is a national mania.

In Florence, I had met an Italian journalist who kept on talking about the 'Italian miracle'. I thought at first he was talking about the economy, but it turned out to be football. How their top league clubs, while bankrupt or with enormous debts, can pay out up to £5 million for a foreign footballer, that is the miracle which no one can understand. The faithful demand it, which is why at present Italy has acquired the cream of the world's footballers.

Souness is playing for Sampdoria, not a glamorous club in Italian terms, in fact they were in the second division only four seasons ago, but they still managed to hand over £650,000 to Liverpool for his services, despite the fact that he is thirty-one. For the next two years, he will be on a salary of at least £150,000 a year.

I first met Graeme Souness in 1972 when he was a young player at Tottenham Hotspur. At the time, I was doing a book about the club. (*The Glory Game*. No need to hurry, hurry. It's just been reprinted.) He was in the reserves, and never got a first team match, a rather moody young man, I always thought, sullen, yet aggressive, with enormous chips on his shoulder, convinced the world was against him. He had been brought up in a prefab in Edinburgh and was feeling homesick, unable somehow to fit in. All the other players used to tell me how good he was, then they'd shake their heads. He appeared to be his own worst enemy, for ever arguing with the management. He ran away once. Then he was suspended. Eventually, they let him go, probably with some relief, for a relatively small sum, just £30,000, to Middlesbrough.

In six years at Middlesbrough, and then seven years at Liverpool, the duckling turned into a swan, if rather a stocky, tough, extremely beligerent swan. Opposing crowds have always enjoyed booing Souness for his aggressive style. But he matured enormously as a footballer, becoming polished and dominant, with an excellent football brain, an inspiring leader who never gives up, becoming captain of the Scottish team.

Off the pitch, he also became known for his style, his clothes, his girl friends and his social life. He appeared in a TV series, *Boys from the Blackstuff*. Souness is the sort of footballer you could stick in a TV programme. He is known to be intelligent, with great panache, and won't let you down.

When Bob Paisley, as manager, made him captain of Liverpool, he suggested that they wouldn't need a 10p coin any more to toss up with before the match. Graeme would probably insist on doing it with an American Express gold card.

He married rather late in life, as footballers go, when he was twenty-seven, and as footballers go, his wife is rather unusual. They often go for young hair stylists, from a similar working class background to their own.

He married Danielle Wilson in July, 1980, a divorcee with one daughter. That was unusual for a start. Footballers are terribly conventional. But more surprising is the fact that she comes from a wealthy background. Her father, now retired and living in Majorca, built up a chain of over 100 shops in the Merseyside area. There is a family trust, in which Danielle shares, said to be worth £750,000.

'It worked both ways,' she said. 'No one could say I married Graeme because he was rich and famous. Nor could they say that was why Graeme married me. We married because we were sure of each other.'

She had more recently arrived in Genoa, as Graeme had gone ahead for pre-season training, along with her eight-year-old daughter Chantelle by her first marriage, and their son, four-year-old Fraser. That day, she'd discovered that another is on the way, due in March. 'I haven't found a gynaecologist yet. They've all been on holiday in August. The whole of Italy seems to pack up in August. I'm still waiting for the furniture I've bought.'

The club had put them into a luxury flat, rent free, in a villa in the affluent suburb of Nervi, just outside Genoa. Trevor Francis, the English international player, who has been at the club two years, has the flat next door. That has proved a great advantage.

Trevor Francis, unlike Souness, was a star almost from his first professional game. At fifteen he played for Plymouth schoolboys, his home town, and a whole host of top clubs were after him. He chose Birmingham City and was playing in the first team at the age of sixteen. In 1979, he became Britain's first million pound player when he was transferred to Nottingham Forest for £1,150,000, paying some of it back when he scored the goal which won Forest the European Cup.

In the two years since he moved to Italy, he has adapted well and picked up a lot of Italian. Graeme was going to ask permission for me to watch training the next day, but wasn't sure how he would do it. 'The manager doesn't speak English. I don't speak Italian. I'll have to get Trevor to do the translating for me.'

The entrance to the villa and its extensive grounds are through a high gate which is electronically controlled. No strangers can get in, or out, which means that it is perfectly safe for their children and friends to play all day on their bikes, rushing round the villa and the paths. Danielle can therefore get on with her sun bathing. She seemed very fond of sun bathing, like all new arrivals to a hot country.

'When we got married, Graeme said I must be prepared for a move at some time, probably abroad, so it wasn't too much of a surprise. I am pleased for him. It's a short life as a footballer. You should take all the chances you can.'

She had already got Chantelle into the American School and Fraser into a playgroup, but she wouldn't feel she had properly established herself till the flat was fully furnished in the way she wants it. After that, she'll attempt the language.

'When I've been in Europe before, I suppose I've always been a tourist, in tourist places, so when you go into a shop, there's always someone who can speak English. I went into a local shop today for sugar, and I asked for it in English, but they didn't understand. I tried to look for it on the shelves, which is what I usually do, but I couldn't see it. So I came out without it.'

What about a dictionary, wouldn't that have helped? She shrugged. When things are settled in the flat, then she'll buy a dictionary, not that it will help her to buy some of the minor things she already misses, such as Oxo and Paxo stuffing.

Graeme, meanwhile, had suffered more severe culture shocks in his eight weeks so far. While his wife had been busy with her young family all day, much as she would be in England, doing bits of shopping and talking to other mums, in this case Helen Francis next door, Graeme had entered a new environment with new sets of rules.

For much of the eight weeks, he had been miles away, up in the mountains, for two long spells, of three weeks and ten days, living a spartan, monastic life. They called this, in Italian, the *Rituro*, and it is like a retreat, keeping the players away from the flesh pots, or even family pleasures, confined to their remote training camp. The very thought horrifies every British player.

'We were up at seven in the morning and did some early training, then we had breakfast, if you can call it breakfast. Just a cappucino. Then it was morning training. After lunch, we slept till four, then more training from five till seven. Dinner was at eight to nine, then we had free time from nine to ten. We all had to be in bed by ten. One of the coaches did catch a young player talking to a girl in a bar, just talking to her, and he was told off.

'We've had a long talk on what to do about sex generally. Our League matches are on Sundays, so we're allowed to have sex on Monday, Tuesday or Wednesday. But not after that.'

In Britain, training, even pre-season training, normally ends at lunch time every day, then the players go home. And no one would ever dare interfere with their love life.

'The other thing that has amazed me is that Italian players don't drink. After training in England, or after a match, all players have a few beers. They don't here. Perhaps a glass of water, that's all. And they don't "go out" for a drink, the way we do. It's so strange. Italians never think of going out in the evening for a couple of hours drinking in a bar. They only drink when they have a meal, and then of course it's wine.'

As for the football, he has had to get used to different methods. Not better, or worse, just different. 'After all, I played for the best team in Europe for seven years, so I didn't come here expecting the football to be better. I've never hidden the fact that money was the prime motivation.

'I'm having to adjust my play. I can't expect them to adjust to me. They play man for man here, so before each match there are lots of tactics to understand. In all my seven years with Liverpool, we never once played man for man. Oh no, Sammy Lee once had to mark Breitner in a European match, but that was all. At Liverpool, we never worried about the other team. We let them worry about us.'

So far, he had been a success. The Italian League season had yet to get into its stride, but in friendly and in cup matches the team had won their games, with Francis scoring several goals, many supplied by Souness from midfield.

On his arrival, 2,000 fans gathered outside the club to greet him. Up in the mountains, he had been amazed one day to find two boys outside their remote training camp, asking if they could take his photograph. He had assumed they were local village lads. 'It turned out they had ridden hundreds of miles from Genoa – on a scooter.'

Football in Italy has an enormous following, yet he had heard little about crowd violence, even though in Genoa there are two rival teams, traditional enemies, Genoa and Sampdoria. 'The worst that has happened to me so far is that when I came out of a restaurant one night, a Genoa fan had put a notice on my windscreen which said "Souness, you are a shit." If that's the worst I'll have to put up with, I'll survive. But one of the lads in the team had his dog poisoned last season by a rival fan.'

It does seem to be the case that in Italy it's the players, and the referees, who get the abuse, rather than the opposing crowd.

'Perhaps in England they should turn their attention on the players, if it would mean less violence. It would be worth the price. The crowds here do behave like human beings, not freaks. But I do miss the singing and chanting from Liverpool. There's none of that. Italians watch a lot of English football on TV and they can't get over all the noises.'

He had also been surprised so far by the lack of perks. In Liverpool, his wife hardly ever had to pay for her groceries or fish, as local people insisted on supplying them free. Most First Division stars in England can manage to get free meals, free furniture, even free cars.

Even more amazing to Graeme, and he knew every home based Brit player will be appalled at the very thought, Italian newspapers and TV don't pay for interviews. In England, the leading players are paid highly for their ghosted opinions which appear in the popular dailies. They get paid if they do a column for Roy of the Rovers.

This has made some of them very greedy, so the British press think, demanding huge amounts just to say I'm over the moon, but the press has only itself to blame for having started the system. (Famous authors or actors never charge for interviews.) In England, most footballers therefore have agents, to do all the negotiations for them.

In Italy, of course, being paid three times as much as in England, it rather makes up for any losses. The previous day Graeme had asked what the fee might be when Italian *Vogue* had contacted him and Trevor to model some pullovers. At home, this could have commanded a rather fat sum.

'I just wanted to see what would happen. I asked the manager to enquire. He said there would be none, and was surprised I'd asked, but I said go on, just see. I've just heard the answer. No fee at all, but we might be able to keep a pullover each. Big deal.'

All the same, he and Trevor think they'll do it, just for the amusement.

That night we all went out for dinner, Graeme Souness, his wife and children, plus Trevor and Helen Francis and their son and friend, to a local restaurant in Nervi, where of course they were treated like the Second Coming.

Over dinner, Trevor explained that there was very little commercialisation of footballers in Italy. In a normal year in England, he would expect to attend up to 200 functions, around four a week of some sort, purely in his capacity as a famous footballer. It might be charity appearances, because the club wants you to turn up at a local hospital, or for your own financial advantage, because there's a fee to open a shop or please some sponsor.

'In two years here, I haven't done more than six or seven engagements in a year. The whole system is different.'

He then reassured Graeme that the worst was now over. You don't go to training camps when the League gets into its stride. They play fewer matches in Italy and there are no mid week games.

'You'll have much more time at home. I see more of Helen than I ever did in England.'

Danielle was very pleased. Back in England, with Liverpool every season involved in so many competitions and for ever travelling to Europe, she hardly saw him during the season.

The ladies and the children were sitting at the far end of the table. We men were at the other end. Feminism has not yet struck the football world. But being Italy, the wives and children were at least out with the men folk, even though it was quite late at night. In Italy, of course, children are welcomed in restaurants. The men don't go off to the pub on their own.

It was interesting to watch Trevor and his wife Helen speaking Italian so confidently, to waiters, to other people in the restaurant, to fans coming up to them, all with great exuberance and appropriate gestures. I could sense Graeme and Danielle wondering if they would ever get to that stage.

In two years, the Francises have both done well, though not as spectacularly well as their four-year-old son Mathew. He is now bi-lingual. It had been fascinating to watch him at the villa, playing and shouting with the other children, going from Italian to English, almost without realising. When I first met him, and asked him his name, he replied 'Matteo'.

Trevor and Helen did have a few lessons when they arrived, but gave up quickly. Luckily, they had another footballer, the Irishman Liam Brady, and his family, living in the flat the Sounesses now have, to ease them in. (Brady then moved to Milan.)

'I did four lessons, but they weren't teaching me what I want. It was just like school, and I hated school,' said Trevor. 'In the end, I just picked it up from the players.'

'I've learned from friends,' said Helen. 'I've made so many since I came here. There's one girl in particular in the villa I'm very close to, and she helped me a lot.'

'I do feel out of it in the dressing room,' said Graeme, rather wistfully. 'At Liverpool, we used to have such good laughs. Footballers are the same the world over – you get the joker, the moaner, the one who gets picked on. I come in in the morning here and have to sit very quiet while they're chatting away, which is not like me. I feel a bit of a dummy. But och well, I suppose I'll start picking it up soon.'

'He'll have to do it more quickly than me,' said Trevor. 'In his position, he has to shout and be dominant. It's not so necessary for a forward. I know the coach wants him to take control of things. I can sense him getting frustrated when he can't make himself understood. He has to ask me the words at half time or after the match.'

However, he was absolutely confident that Graeme would soon master enough of the language, and then he would love Italy, just as much as he and Helen do. *Love* Italy? Was it as strong as that?

'Listen,' said Trevor, 'if someone was to offer me the same money to go back to England now, I wouldn't go. Why should I? I'm happy here.

'I enjoy the football. It suits me better than England. There's an image in England that Italian football is defensive. It is, but not so much as it was. It's true that many teams will be happy with a draw and play for that. The Italian League is vitally important and it's taken very seriously, whereas the cup hardly matters.

'When I played for Birmingham City, we struggled almost every season to survive, but we began each game thinking we were going to win. Even if it was Liverpool, we went out convinced we could beat them. Here, if you're playing Juventus or Roma, the big teams, most other teams start off feeling that a draw will be good. And if you do get a 0-0, the players and the crowd go away happy.

'But technically, the Italian players are superior. I would say this is a better league than the English league. Standards have diminished so much in England in the last few years. In England, it is still all blood and guts. Here, we are encouraged to put our foot on the ball, slow it down, try something different. It's only now, seeing it from the outside, that I see what has happened in England.

'What England has got is the never-say-die spirit. There is such a will to win, with great running power and competitiveness. It means that English league matches can be exciting to watch. Liverpool versus Man. Utd. is a great spectacle, as they go at it hammer and tongs. In Italy, the League matches are more like international matches, the sort England now plays, where it's so vital to get a good result and there is a lot of tension.

'I much prefer this more technical sort of game. It's my style. If I was six foot two and a brilliant header of the ball, I'd probably prefer the English game.

'Italian football is also not as dirty as British people think. If you go past them, they hate it, but they don't go out seriously to injure you. It's much pettier, shirt pulling, little niggling fouls, spitting at you, but not really nasty. Ask Helen what I used to look like after a normal English game. I'd be a mass of bruises. I can get infuriated here though by the petty fouls. I often think to myself, why don't you give me a good kick and get it over with?

'But on the whole, there is no question in my mind. The football is better. I have recovered the excitement I used to have as a youngster at Birmingham City. I was only seventeen when I got in the first team and when we played the big teams, I was knocked out. If it was Man. Utd., I'd ask Charlton or Best for their autographs after the game.

'I now have similar feelings all the time here. Every game there is some player I have always admired or wanted to meet and play against – Maradona, Zico, Rummenigge, Falcao. In England, after twelve years, I knew every English defender I played against, because I'd played them so many times before.

'I consider Platini the world's greatest player at the moment, and it's a thrill for me to play against him. Can you imagine Platini surviving in the hustle of the English First Division. No chance. Yet he's brilliant here.'

Outside football, Trevor and his wife also have no regrets. They have made good friends, fitted in to Italian life, and they even like Italian TV. Both Danielle and Graeme were upset on their arrival to find that when English programmes do appear, they are dubbed into Italian.

'The sport on TV is superb. Every First Division match is shown and every day if there's no soccer on, there's boxing and something else good. They even show Brazilian matches here.

'The weather of course is terrific. Here on the coast, unlike Milan, you're not aware of the winter. There's no snow or ice. You *feel* healthier when the weather is so good. It's nice to know it's a wonderful place for my little boy to grow up in.

'I only miss one thing – the cricket. That's all.'

Graeme nodded his head. In his two months, he had found a few things confusing, but he had no real complaints.

'I *expect* to have complaints. I know that I will have problems some time. It's inevitable, but so far, I have nothing to moan about. The weather, that's been a bit hot for training, that's all.'

What about the other players? Wasn't there some jealousy perhaps, two foreign players swanning in and getting all that attention and much bigger wages than the home grown players?

When I went to visit Kevin Keegan in Hamburg a few years ago, at precisely the same stage Souness is at, he was very aware of political tensions in the clubs and felt some people were out to get him. But Trevor says he has felt none of this. Graeme agreed. All the Italian players (each club is allowed only two foreigners) know how much more the two of them are getting, but there is no emnity.

'They know if I do well and score goals,' said Trevor, 'they will all gain from it. This whole thing about money and success is so different here. People don't hold it against you that you earn a lot, the way many English people do, especially the press. Here and in America, where I've played a few times, they *admire* success.'

'Yeh, I've noticed that already,' said Graeme. 'In England, you often get attacked for being a greedy bugger, getting all that money, just to kick a ball around. The British press have built up this image of greedy footballers. But why shouldn't we earn as much as we can?

'In Liverpool, they did try to make me feel embarrassed or ashamed somehow. Earning all that money, while all around there was terrible unemployment and depression. You saw it everywhere you went in Liverpool. I didn't personally feel ashamed about my wage, but I felt uncomfortable.

'In England, I think people don't like you to be successful. It's as if it's a crime to do well. That's another reason why I think I'm going to enjoy it here . . .'

Most of the reasons why Graeme moved to Italy are pretty obvious. There's his enormous salary for a start. Then there's all that sun and warm sea for his family to enjoy. But after dinner, as we were walking round the garden of their large villa, he was struck by another, more minor advantage about living in Italy.

It was almost one o'clock in the morning and he had decided to give his dogs some exercise before bed. The night was soft, the stars bright, and we strolled in short sleeves round his garden, in amongst the palm trees and cacti which stretch straight down to the Mediterranean.

'Cuddles,' he suddenly shouted. 'Come here, you little bugger. Where are you. Cuddles!'

The Sounesses have an Alsation called Jock and three Yorkshire terriers called Churchill, Oscar and Cuddles, all of which have gone to Italy with them. Next week, the pony was due to arrive.

In Liverpool, this was always a bit of a problem, taking the dogs round the block before bed. He didn't mind shouting for Jock or Churchill. Even Oscar. But Cuddles. What would his Liverpool neighbours think. Now, in Italy, there was no embarrassment.

'It's very hard in England to keep up the macho footballer image, if you have to go around the streets shouting "Cuddles". . . .'

## ~ Chapter Twelve ~

# Genoa to Basle

*The local train to Genoa;
a near escape in Milan;
lunch with a mysterious family;
what, pray, can these West Indian ladies be
adoing of?*

*I*went into downtown Genoa to book an overnight train from Genoa to
Basle. The town was much more attractive than I had anticipated, with
many fine cream coloured buildings, and the harbour was magnificent, a
huge bowl with the hills coming straight down into it, beautifully sheltered, yet
broad and deep. It was true there were few large boats around, as my Milan
engineer had warned, and all the cranes and docks looked idle, but there was
no feeling of decay or depression as on Tyneside or Clydeside, more a sense of
a public holiday, as if the dockers were away for the week and would be back
soon.

The booking office in the station was all computerised and my request for a
sleeper to Basle was fed into a flashing machine. There were lots of bangs and
screeches and then various symbols started coming up on the screen. After
some time, the answer was flashed back. There were no sleepers to Basle. They
didn't exist. A printed timetable could have told the booking clerk this in a
tenth of the time.

There was a queue forming behind me, but I thought what the hell, I'll ask
the clerk to try to get me a couchette. The film show started again, with a lot
more bumping and grinding, and I was told there were no couchettes left. All
had been booked. It was early evening. Should I just take the first train to
Milan, spend the night there, then set off tomorrow to Basle? Or should I stay
another night in Genoa, then set off at the crack of dawn? Decisions, decisions.
At least I had only myself to please, not a wife and family.

I wanted to get to Switzerland as quickly as possible, which was why I had
planned on an overnight train. I didn't really want to spend a whole of one day,
sitting on a train. On the other hand, I had seen hardly anything from the
Orient-Express coming down across Europe, as I had been so busy with the
passengers and the meals. Perhaps after all it would be an experience, to sit still
for a day on an ordinary train, staring out, or staring in at myself.

I set off at eight o'clock the next morning from Nervi, booking out of my hotel, the Astor, just round the corner from the Souness–Francis villa, and only a moment's walk from the station. It was such a lovely bright September morning and the pretty pink station looked so attractive that I hardly wanted to leave Italy and the palm trees and move North to colder climes. The station itself was practically in the sea. When I got on the train, I looked straight down from my carriage window and beneath me, there was the blue water, breaking on the rocks.

There were some early morning commuters and students reading newspapers, going the seven miles into Genoa. It was obviously a local, suburban train, with wooden seats and not much comfort, but pleasant and artistic, the polished wood so elegant and clean. There was no sign anywhere of graffiti or vandalism. I thought sadly of my local North London line, the Broad Street line, with its equally simple wooden compartments – and its desecration by persons unknown and the filth which never seems to be removed.

I got into Genoa's Principe Station with twenty minutes to spare before my connection, so I went for a coffee, something I never like doing a British station. Have you tasted their coffee? I could hear and smell the coffee machines hissing away, while the young staff, mostly in white aprons, quick and efficient, were cleaning up as they went along, polishing the counter between orders. I waited my turn, then asked for a cappucino. The boy on the coffee machine pointed behind me, rather abruptly, then attended to someone else. Had I dropped something? I was clutching my two bags safely, one with my clothes in, the other over my shoulder which contained books, paper, camera, notes, maps, money, passport. They were both intact. So I queued up again.

'Ticket, ticket,' he said this time, again pointing behind, rather irritably.

What a dope. I had not realised the system. Well, it was early in the morning. You have to queue up first at a little desk, pay for a ticket for what you want, then take it to the serving counter. Many places in Europe have this annoying system, especially airports.

I looked for a seat, to rest my bags and my bones, and was just about to settle down when the same boy waiter gave me another warning look, putting his hand up. What had I done wrong now? Europe these days is hardly foreign, as we all look alike and work alike and all clerks have computers to play with and the same television programmes to enjoy, but now and again you can be brought up short by little things. Then you realise you are not after all in Kentish Town.

You have to pay extra to sit down, said a helpful woman. What a con. I remember as a boy on that first school trip to France and being amazed at this, just as we were all amazed by the old dears sitting in lavatories to take money off you.

There was a mad rush when the train came in, but I was ready, elbows flying, and got the last seat in a pleasant compartment, without any rucksackers. It's one thing to admire them from afar, going round Europe on the cheap, but one doesn't necessarily always want to travel with them. Their rucksacks can take over a carriage so you can hardly move. And I have been on trains where they took their shoes off.

I found myself opposite three middle aged, well dressed people. They were studying a familiar looking map, which I knew I'd seen somewhere before. It was the London Underground. I wondered for a moment if perhaps they thought they already were on the Tube. We can all make daft mistakes, when travelling abroad. So I offered to help. Despite being in Italy, they were trying to work out the nearest tube to the Bloomsbury Hotel, so I suggested Russell Square.

They were all from Chile. They had done Europe and were now heading for London to spend five days in England, before returning to Santiago. I told them what to see, and what not to see in London, and one of them gave me his address in Santiago. He insisted I had a free meal at his expense, next time I'm in Santiago. He runs a restaurant at the airport. Could come in handy one day, but how do I get there? I have vowed never to fly long distance ever again.

It was just two hours to Milan, and the train, of course, was on time. I suppose you grow to expect that in Europe.

*     *     *

I had booked a first class seat for the main stage of my journey, Milan to Basle, thinking that for the long journey ahead I needed some comfort. It was still very cheap, only about £30. By my reckoning, a similar ticket in Britain would cost four times that.

Changing trains in Milan was easy, and I didn't have long to put in, but I decided to get on the Basle train early, when it was still almost empty, and bag myself a good seat in the corner.

I was idly studying the timetable and looking out of the window, wondering if I should go back down the platform and buy a beer and sandwiches for the journey. The timetable said a refreshment car would join the train at Chiasso, wherever that might be, but could I trust it? On Brit. Rail timetables, all those stupid symbols signifying dining cars or even buffet are often a nonsense. You can rely on none of them. I think it's just the typesetters, trying to prettify the lay-out. Let's throw a few crossed knives and forks in here, lads, there seems to be a gap. And what about a few cups in the margins.

The carriage door opened, as I was still thinking about timetables, and two gypsy looking kids came in, a girl of about fourteen and a boy of ten. They rushed towards me in my corner and the boy put his hand flat out against my nose and went 'Money, money, money'. They were quite a handsome couple, if ragged and dirty. I was half thinking of giving them something, but knowing one should not, and at the same time thinking no, I'll need any left-over lire if I buy a beer.

The boy was pushing me harder, very aggressively, and was practically on top of me, which was why I was completely unaware for some time that the girl behind him had put her hand inside my bag. The cheeky buggers. I'd been abstracted when they had come in, and then confused by what they wanted, but I jumped up and shouted at them. They turned and fled with the girl showing me her open hand, trying to convince me she had stolen nothing. They dashed down the corridor with me chasing them, but we ran into a load of hefty German businessmen getting on and I lost them as they disappeared onto the platform.

I spent the first hour of my journey trying to work out if anything had been stolen. In my bag, which I'd stupidly put on the seat beside me, was all my money. That was intact. I think. I checked Jake's camera, which I had borrowed from him, and that was still there. What an idiot to be caught like that.

*       *       *

Chiasso turned out to be simply a little railway town, right on the border between Italy and Switzerland, just after we had passed the edge of Lake Como. We stopped for a few moments and some self important customs officials got on the train, but no passports were requested and no one came into our compartment. European officials always look more official than British officials, perhaps because they wear more official looking uniforms, often rather threatening looking uniforms, at least to British eyes, like actors from war time films. In European literature, self important, petty officials have a long history, from Kafka to Dostoyevsky, yet it's hard to think of many English novels where they have played a major part. Perhaps they have never been taken seriously enough in Britain.

The restaurant car was put on at Chiasso, so not long afterwards I went to investigate, asking the Germans to keep an eye on my bag, though I took my money and documents with me, just in case. The dining car was large and airy, much bigger than British versions, but then European trains are higher anyway. That's why you always have to step up into them. Young blonde waitresses in neat uniforms were busy serving lunch, so I sat down and picked up a menu. It was ten pages long, with an enormous range of snacks, light refreshments, as well as proper meals. Every day of the week appeared to have a different set lunch. I couldn't quite make out what it was for that day, Saturday, some sort of meat by the look of it, but I pointed and said I would take it.

The dining car was German run, judging by the small print on the menu, an Intercity Restaurant belonging to Deutsche Schlafwagen. All the prices were given in five languages and currencies. It was just a simple dining car, not one of your super de luxe ones, which the highspeed express trains across Europe provide, but to me, it suddenly seemed very abroad. For once, I didn't feel like a tourist. Suddenly I was a traveller.

The main course was delicious. It was beef olives, at least that's what I've always called it – strips of meat rolled and stuffed with herbs. A salad came with it, which was crisp and excellent, and it had a French dressing. What bliss to get away from British Rail salads – and British salad cream. I must stop running down British Rail. Perhaps they should ban us all from venturing off the island, then we might remain more contented.

An old man sat opposite me for a while, drinking a large beer and eating an enormous baguette, filled with salamis and hams, but he was too busy stuffing himself to talk or catch my eye.

We were bending in and out amongst the Alps and I could see high up the snow capped mountains while nestling among them were some immaculate little villages with picture book churches. Outside one church I watched an old priest in flowing robes sweeping up some leaves, lost in his own world, then slowly lost from mine as he disappeared into the distance. It was all so neat and tidy and affluent, even in the remotest village. Beside the rail track, crossing over and under it, were several grand highways, expensively landscaped, elaborately engineered to cut through whole mountains, take in fierce rivers, cross waterfalls without disturbing their beauty or their power. Millions of pounds must have been spent, and millions of tons of rock removed, but nature had been put back in its place, well laundered, well packaged, well cared for. Britain *is* run down, I caught myself thinking, but just in time I rejected such an idle thought and threw it out of the window.

The ticket collector came round. I wasn't sure of his nationality, but with both German and Italian passengers, he answered every query in English. And they in turn replied in English. Yes, we do have something to give the world.

I put on my spectacles, the better to improve the view. I find I do need them these days for long distances, such is my age, but the light outside was so strong and so bright that I hardly needed them.

When I took them off again, I found that the old man had been replaced by a peasant looking girl. She was sitting opposite, at my table, and she was carrying a babe in arms, and dragging a toddler of about three.

She looked at me rather worriedly, her huge dark eyes staring at me, as if I might say she was trespassing, get off, this is my table, my dining car, my train, my world. Her baby also stared at me, a huge madonna like baby with an enormous bald head and fleshy cheeks so smooth and strong they might have been sculptured. The three-year-old had his eyes on my basket of bread and was slowly manoevring his hands across the table towards it, a street urchin, going for the kill. The girl-mother appeared not to realise, but then suddenly, without taking her enormous eyes off me, she gave him such a slap, right across his face, with the back of her hand. It was a masterpiece of striking. Trevor Francis could not have scored better.

He didn't yell or cry or show any sign of pain, but he did stop, immediately. He watched his mother carefully for the next few miles, then slowly he started to look around the rest of the table, for some devilment, for some sport, giving me a sly smile.

I said ok, ok, ok, to the mother, knowing that everyone understands ok, signalling that it was fine by me. He could finish off my bread. I had had enough. She thought for a while and eventually gave a quick, furtive smile and then a nod, but her main demeanour was still one of fear and suspicion.

The waitress came round and the mother pointed to something on the menu. It took some time to come, whatever it was she had ordered, by which time the baby was getting bolder and had started arching its back, leaning over, trying to get free, while the urchin was into the last of my bread rolls and was now opening packets of my sugar. From time to time, she gave him another vicious slap, almost abstractedly. She even gave the baby a slap, when he started moaning, then immediately started cuddling him, still watching me, waiting for my disapproval I smiled and smiled. We parents. We have all given them a slap at times, especially in public dining places when they won't bee-have. I decided she must be Italian, from the few words of admonition she gave the urchin, but in a very strong regional dialect.

They were untidily dressed, especially the urchin, and the first impression had been one of raggedness, but as I examined them I could see their clothes were perfectly clean, if well worn and rather too big. The girl had a long black dress with on top a grey woollen pullover, slightly too big for her, though she kept pulling it down, as if it were tight.

We stopped at a little Alpine station with red geraniums hanging from baskets along the platform, near a large churchyard filled with gravestones. I wondered how many foreign travellers were buried there, collapsed or just faded away on some long forgotten journey across Europe, their bones resting thousands of miles from home.

The waitress brought two enormous bowls of chicken broth, massive tureens with ladles in each, enough to serve a regiment. The smell was so enticing I wanted to start eating all over again.

The mother ladled out a bowl for the urchin and one for herself from which she also fed the baby. They polished off between them three bowls of the soup, before giving up, though still without emptying the two tureens. I examined the menu, wondering what it was she had ordered.

She produced a large purse, which she had been clutching under her long black dress, and paid for the meal and left, still watching me intently. We were nowhere near a station, but I never saw them again on the train.

*         *         *

We entered the St Gotthard tunnel and the train became rather eerie, the sound and the light and the atmosphere changing. I remembered a story about a man who had disappeared when going through an Alpine tunnel, an ordinary passenger, sitting on his seat, who wasn't there when they cleared the tunnel. Had the gypsy girl been spirited away?

The St Gotthard tunnel, like the Simplon, completely revolutionised traffic between Italy and Central Europe when it was opened in 1882. It took eight years to build and they encountered endless difficulties as two teams bored from different directions to complete the ten miles. As a result of all the accidents and illnesses, 300 lives were lost. The engineer in charge, Louis Favre of Geneva, collapsed under the strain and died of a heart attack.

In the old days, Grand Tourists had to go this way by road, such as it was.

Richard Lassels, who is credited with first using the term 'Grand Tour' in any book, in *An Italian Voyage, or a Compleat Journey through Italy*, published in 1679, recommended it as the best route from Milan when returning home. (Wordsworth chose the Simplon Pass route in 1791 – and got lost.) The tunnel itself cuts through the pass lower down, but this is still almost 4,000 feet high. So I was riding a train which was higher than any mountain in England.

Lake Lucerne was magnificent. I hadn't realised how large the Alpine lakes are, as grand as oceans, ice green and clinically sharp. When we stopped at a little station near Lucerne, I was beginning to doze off, still recovering from lunch, though vaguely keeping an eye on the empty seats in the compartment for a party of Germans who had now gone to the dining room.

The corridors were suddenly filled with great shouts and screams and about thirty large West Indian ladies collapsed onto the train. They were carrying piles of luggage and cheap plastic carrier bags full of cheap looking trinkets, bought as souvenirs on their journey. It appeared they had been on the wrong train, going the wrong way, and had suddenly changed platforms at this little station and thrown themselves into my train, realising it was the one they should have been on in the first place. Hence all the noise and pandemonium.

About five of them burst into my compartment, dumping their mountains of luggage, and sank with enormous sighs into the seats. I pointed out, ever so gently, that the seats were, actually, sorry to say it, taken. Germans, I said, they'll be back from lunch very soon.

'I am very com-for-table here,' said the largest of the ladies. 'I am not moving at the moment.'

What were thirty West Indian ladies doing on this train anyway, right in the middle of Europe? What was the connection between them? Were they members of the Barry Manilow Appreciation Society going to a concert? Were they cricket groupies, celebrating their team's latest successes? Unless they had told me, I don't think I would ever have guessed.

They were members of the Sacred Heart Church choir from Trinidad. And they had been to see the Pope. Really, they showed me photographs to prove it, all of them wearing very snazzy maroon blazers and neat black skirts. They had been the first West Indian choir, so they said, to sing at a High Mass in St Peter's in Rome – in Latin. They'd also thrown in the Banana Boat Song, Island in the Sun, and a few calypsos for good measure.

Once they got their breath back, from their mad dash between trains, they were great company and took me through all their adventures and excitements. I told them about the gypsy kids who had tried to rob me in Milan – and they told me about one of their members who had had *everything* stolen by a gypsy in Rome.

The trip had cost them 5,000 TT dollars each, so they said. I wasn't sure how much Trinidad Tobago dollars were, but by translating into US dollars, and then into sterling, it sounded well over £1,000 each. They had managed it by having barbecue parties, flea markets, tea parties and in the end they had only to pay half the money each.

They had also been to Lourdes, which they thought had been marvellous. 'It was so nice to see sick people looking so contented.' But the highlight had been singing to the Pope.

When the Germans eventually came back from the dining car, the ladies who had taken their seats graciously gave them up. By that time, after further running up and down corridors, shouting and laughing, they had managed to find some empty compartments together further down the train.

One of the ladies decided to stay in our compartment, as her seat had in fact been vacant. She was the largest of them all, carrying so many plastic carrier bags that at first I'd hardly seen her face. I wanted to know what she did back home in Trinidad, if she was married with children, though it seemed a rather rude question. So I asked her what she thought about coming to Europe, assuming it must be her first trip.

'Just the same as usual. Wonderful.'

'Oh, you've been here before?'

'Oh yes, many times.'

'It must be pretty expensive, coming all that way.'

'Well I do have a job.'

'Oh yes. Eh, what do you do?'

'I'm an accountant.'

I got off the train at Basle smiling to myself. I'd caught myself out betraying so many subconscious prejudices – racist, sexist, ageist. Just because she was black, a woman and middle aged, I had presumed she must have no occupation.

The arrival of the ladies had been the highlight of the train journey, beautifully orchestrated, coming on as top of the bill, the perfect diversion, just when I was about to doze off, which I knew I would have regretted and ended up feeling rotten.

The whole journey, from eight in the morning till five o'clock, had been fascinating. I had never been bored once. That's the thing about travelling by train, as opposed to those boring tubes of metal which fly in the air where you get pinned down and your ear drums take a battering and you can't move around, stretch or relax, because you're trapped. How can a plane trip ever be stimulating. You experience nothing.

But on a train, it's Pure Theatre, especially going between different countries. At every stop, in every country, humanity rushes across the stage, right at you, images and sights, people and places, are paraded before your eyes and your imagination.

Now, at last, I was about to take to the water for the first time. The boats in Venice had been enjoyable, but they were no more than ferries, local buses, getting you quickly between short stops. This time I was going on a *real* boat, a proper passenger steamer, sleeping and eating and talking, or so I hoped, as we sailed down the Rhine, following the precise route which travellers have traditionally taken for centuries, working their way slowly back from Italy.

Could the boat possibly beat the train?

## ~ *Chapter Thirteen* ~

# Basle

*Some Switzifying stories and encounters;*
*some good luck at the Regatta*

I had been quite looking forward to Basle. It's not a big town, just 200,000, the second City of Switzerland in population, and I thought in three hours I might pick up something of its feeling. That was all I had, as I had to be on the boat by eight o'clock if I wanted to have dinner. Can you do a town in three hours? We travellers, we do bigger places in smaller times.

In idle moments on my journey so far I'd been reading some of Thackeray's collected letters, notes to his mum and friends which he wrote back from his various Grand Tours. He did one up the Rhine to Italy in 1830 when he was a young student, having just failed at Cambridge, giving himself a year off while he decided what to do with his life. Then twenty-one years later, in 1851, he did almost the same trip, this time rich and famous, taking with him his two young daughters, Annie and Minnie. The differences between his attitudes, doing one trip on the cheap, then his later trip in style, were most revealing. Each time, as we all do, he was summing up places visited in a couple of hours, or seen from a boat or through a train window, but he also added drawings and sketches, which do help to make his impressions sound more authentic.

He arrived at Basle station in July 1851, having travelled first class with his daughters. 'the most delightful Journey through the deliciousest landscape of plain and mountains which seemed to Switzify themselves as we came towards here.' I liked his use of 'deliciousest' and Switzify'. Thackeray is always so witty and colloquial in his letters, completely undated in his style.

They had a terrific time in Switzerland, and fell in love with Berne and Lucerne particularly, but then the Victorians were all very fond of Switzerland. The 'discovery' of the Alps and the development of skiing as a sport was very much an English creation. In Berne, Thackeray even fantasised about living there for good. 'O Lord how much better it is than riding in the Park and going to dinner at eight o'clock. I wonder whether a residence in this quiet would ennoble one's thoughts permanently? And get them away from mean quarrels, intrigues, pleasures? Make me write good books, turn poet perhaps or painter, and get out of that baseness of London.'

All nonsense of course. He loved dinner at eight in London, and absolutely thrived on the intrigues and base pleasures, but like all travellers through the ages, even those on packaged tours to Spain, there comes a moment when we think yes, wouldn't this be nice, to leave the rat race and settle down here and do good things. It hadn't happened to me yet. And I certainly didn't see it striking me in Switzerland. Those Alps had been magnificent, but like Wordsworth, I still prefer our own little Lake District.

Today, I think British people are divided about Switzerland, if and when they think about it all. A lot consider it totally boring and sterile and lifeless and would never want to go back. But a great many adore the landscape, love the people, admire the neatness and cleanliness, particularly the cleanliness.

John Evelyn, the Diarist, wasn't so thrilled by the cleanliness of Switzerland in 1644. He arrived at an inn, which was practically full, but the landlord kindly gave him up one of his own family rooms. His daughter was 'removed out of her bed and I went immediately into it whilst it was yet warm.' Evelyn was so tired and exhausted he didn't even wait for the sheets to be changed and, alas for him, he picked up smallpox. Leeches were applied and he was bled but he still had to spend sixteen days in bed and didn't leave his room for five weeks. He was lucky to survive.

Evelyn had been doing much the same sort of route as I had taken. Down through France as quickly as possible, belting from town to town. Many people believe that it is only in recent times that travellers, especially packaged travellers, have moved at such a speed, hardly knowing where they are. If it's Tuesday, it's Belgium. But 17th and 18th century travellers by coach or horseback went at great speed to get to the next town before the gates closed, then they were up at the crack of dawn next day, hardly aware of where they had been, confused by the currencies, all the local regulations and customs.

Once Evelyn got to Italy, he then took his time, doing Florence, Rome, Pisa. He even went to Genoa, which not many do today, which he thought beautiful, but 'stained with horrid acts'. After Switzerland, once he had recovered, he then went on by boat, as I was about to do, but on the Rhône, not the Rhine. In the meantime, I had three hours of Switzerland to fill in. What to do?

The last time I was in Switzerland was in 1969 when I was sent by the *Sunday Times* to interview Noël Coward on his seventieth birthday. I booked into the Palace Hotel in Montreux which was an event in itself as it was out of season and it felt like being in a ghost hotel, with enormous reception rooms, all of them empty, and corridors leading as far as the eye could see, all equally empty.

I spent the day hanging around the hotel, getting ready to go up to Les Avants, where Coward lived, to join him for dinner, but he cancelled at the last moment, putting it back for the next day. That always seemed to happen to me on foreign jobs, and I used to moan like hell. In those days, I always hated going abroad and schemed to be kept at home. I remember once falling out with the late Nicholas Tomalin, who was my boss at one time on the Atticus column, and to get his own back he sent me to France on a job. I was furious. My definition of a good story was one that got me home for tea.

Next morning at breakfast in the hotel, sitting in state in a vast room on my own with endless flunkies hovering around, I said to the waiter oh come on, there must be some other guests in this hotel, apart from me. Well, he said, there are the permanent residents. It turned out there were about half a dozen people who actually lived in the hotel. After a bit of soft soaping, I got him to tell me their names and nationalities. All of them were meaningless, except for a couple called Nabokov.

Could it be Vladimir? Back in my room, I decided to ring him up, on the hotel phone, getting reception to put me through. Nabokov had been one of my all time heroes for many years. I had a whole day to put in. It was worth a try.

I asked if that was *Vladimir Nabokov*, and the voice neither denied nor confirmed it, so I prattled on quickly before he could hang up, giving my name, that I was on the staff of the *Sunday Times* in London, in Montreux on a job, and wondered if he might have time for coffee, a chat, or just to say hello, as I did admire his books. There was a long silence and I waited for him to say no, please go away and stop bothering me.

'Do you know Alan Brien?'

I was rather taken aback by this. Had I misheard? Was it some sort of test, a code for someone else he might have been expecting, or just a Nabokovian tricksy joke.

Certainly, I said, he's one of my friends, in fact we not only work for the same paper (which we both did at the time), but we live practically opposite each other in North London. Our daughters were in the same class. Our sons at the same school.

There was another long pause. Had I passed the test, whatever it was. I hoped I'd got the right Alan Brien. I would sound rather foolish otherwise.

Right, he finally said, I'll see you in one hour. What a stroke of luck. All journalists, like all travellers, long for the unexpected to happen, to pick up something extra on their journey, to achieve more than was planned. If nothing else, it does help to make one's expenses look more respectable.

My only worry was lack of preparation. I had Noël Coward's whole life story in my head, the plots and years of his best known plays, the names of his songs, and could have gone on *Mastermind* to answer questions, all thanks to the library cuttings. In a week, I would forget it all, but I was ready for dinner with Coward as if for an examination. But with Nabokov, although I had indeed read all his books up to that time, I couldn't remember which was his last one. Who was he married to? Had he got children? Why was he in Montreux not America which was where I had always thought he lived. There are certain species of famous people who can walk out of an interview, if you make just one crass mistake. I remember once being at a news conference which Vivien Leigh had grudgingly agreed to hold. One young reporter was daft enough to ask what part she played in *Gone With The Wind*. And that was it. We were all chucked out.

It makes you so confident, if you think you know a lot about a person, and it saves wasting time and being taken in by old stories, which they all trot out, and which you know are ancient because they have appeared endlessly in the press. When doing newspaper interviews, you are always desperate for something new. When doing television interviews, you are continually asking questions to which you already know the answers, willing for them to re-tell the best of the old.

Nabokov met me in the foyer, an hour later as arranged, and he took me on a tour of Montreux. He looked a perfectly ordinary, elderly, rather stocky gentleman in an old, neat suit, but his eyes sparkled and he seemed amused by the idea of this stranger landing in his life. For a whole morning, we walked round and round the town, stopping now and again for a coffee or a drink. All the time, he told me stories about people we had just seen, shopkeepers and waiters, citizens of the town, tit bits about their private life, their problems, though in passing them in the street he had not appeared to give any signs of recognition.

I eventually asked about Alan Brien. How did he know him? He brought out some letters, when we were sitting in some café, and showed them to me. They had been in correspondence over the etymology of some word, I think, in one of his novels. He admired Alan's prose style, as of course we all do.

He didn't talk much about himself, though I tried to steer the conversation round to what he was currently writing. When we eventually parted, saying he had to go back to his wife, he said there was only one condition to our little morning's chat. I was not to write about it in the *Sunday Times*.

I had been planning to rush back to my hotel bedroom and write up as much as possible. It is quite possible, if you can get to a notebook within an hour of an informal conversation, to remember almost everything of note which took place, even the mannerisms, the peculiar phrases, the odd looks and throw-away comments. Otherwise, almost everything goes. I wrote down nothing, as instructed, but the mood and memory of that morning have stayed with me, even though I have forgotten the facts of our conversation.

As for Noël Coward, I did see him next evening, and wrote up our conversation at enormous length for the paper. I don't think he was best pleased with it. I was a bit rude and cheeky, but I was very young and cheeky at the time, especially towards so called legends, determined that I wasn't going to be overawed or sycophantic.

Two things stick out from that Noël Coward chat. It came out by chance over dinner that one of his interests was going to watch hospital operations. He had a surgeon friend who often rang him if he was about to do a particularly interesting operation, and invited him to come and watch. It was the first time in the conversation that I felt I'd got through his mannered, polished, rather bored exterior. But what did it show about the real Coward? A clinical, unemotional mind? I said it seemed a rather gruesome, macabre pastime. He laughed it off, when I tried to cross examine his motives further, saying it was simply a matter of watching a perfectionist at work. He could watch any perfectionist perform.

The other thing I remember I never wrote about, as I knew he would have

considered it the height of bad taste. When I was eventually shown into his dining room, which was very formally set for just the three of us – Coward, me and his personal secretary Cole Lesley – Noël started fussing about the smell. He accused Cole of having farted and sent him out of the room to get a deodorant spray. Cole returned and very fussily went round the room, setting if off in all directions, saying what a good spray it was, a rather expensive perfumed one, made in Paris. 'What are you fucking doing?' barked Coward. 'Now you've made it smell like a fucking brothel in Tangiers.'

Over the years, I have had quite a soft spot for Switzerland.

*    *    *

I walked around Basle station looking for somewhere to dump my bags. I didn't want to carry them round with me for the next three hours. There appeared to be no left luggage department, only lockers, and they needed one Swiss franc to operate them. All I had in my pocket was three tons of Italian coins, plus German notes for the boat. I had hoped not to have to Switzify my currency.

The next problem was getting used to saying Bas-el, even in my head. The British appear to be about the only people in the world who pronounce it 'Baal' as if it hasn't got an 's'. The locals themselves, Italians and Germans and even the Americans I had overheard, all observe the 's'. I had gone through life feeling superior towards any poor uneducated English types who had said Basil. I would now have to mend my ways.

In 1967 the citizens of Basle had a vote, a referendum, to decide whether to buy two well known Picasso paintings for the City. Imagine any British town doing that, (even Ken Livingstone's GLC). It was democratically agreed and the two paintings, *L'Arlequin Assis* and *Les Deux Freres*, were bought. Picasso was so touched by what the citizens had done that he donated a further four of his paintings to the town.

I set off first towards the Kunstmuseum, wanting to see the Picassos, plus the Dürers and Holbeins. The City has the world's largest collection of paintings by Hans Holbein.

All the streets seemed very quiet and empty, which was worrying. Had I stumbled on a Public Holiday by mistake. The museum was closed when I got there. It had closed at five o'clock, so I'd just missed it. But the Cathedral, according to my guide book, was open till six o'clock, so I rushed. It was closed as well, despite a notice on its door saying it opened till six each evening.

I walked to the Marktplatz, the Market Square, thinking that at least I could buy some presents for Flora. Give culture a miss for once. But all the shops were closed. I hammered on a few windows, as I could see people still inside, but they were locking up and waved me away. There was a group of hippies in a little corner, playing guitars and singing, attracting only a handful of watchers. Their hats were on the ground but so far they had very few coins.

Apart from that, Basle seemed completely dead. It was like being in Carlisle on a Saturday evening. Once the shops close, that's it. They all disappear into the ground, yet this was a famous city, right in the heart of Europe, on the border of three countries, and it was only early September, still the tourist season. Thackeray must have been very fortunate when he visited Basle. Imagine wanting to live in Switzerland.

I saw signs directing me to the zoo, but I hadn't come all the way from London, England, to look at zoos, not when I have Regent's Park Zoo almost on my doorstep at home.

I tried to find a street called 'Eleven Thousand Virgins Alley' which a leaflet issued by Basle Tourist office said was near a church called St Martin's, but I could find neither on my map.

The legend of the 11,000 virgins is one of Europe's oldest. I noticed that in 1830, Thackeray had heard about it in Cologne. A waiter told him that '11,000 virgins had been destroyed by the Romans and those unfortunate bones have been used to decorate the church.' The bones of the story are true, though the precise number of virgins has gone up and down with the centuries, ranging from 1,100 to 11,000.

It all dates back to the early centuries when pilgrims from North Europe made enormous expeditions across Europe to get to Rome, most of them using the Rhine Valley. Could these early Christians be in fact the earliest Grand Tourists? No, I think the description would be unfair. A religious pilgrimage is a bit different from a cultural Grand Tour, even if the routes were the same.

In these early centuries, travelling rough, they suffered great hardships. An Archbishop of Canterbury in 950 froze to death in the Alps on his way back from Rome. Archbishop Ealdread of York was robbed by brigands and had to return to Rome to borrow money from the Pope before he could complete his journey home to England.

The famous 11,000 virgins were on their pilgrimage in the fourth century, led by St Ursula. All along the Rhine there are legends and stories about them passing through, which is not surprising. It is rather a lot of virgins. They were finally captured and killed, probably near Cologne, possibly by Huns under Attila, rather than by Romans.

Historians agree that St Ursula, daughter of an English king, did meet her end on her pilgrimage down the Rhine, but that the incredible number of virgins must be a slight exaggeration, though even the British Museum has some 'Relics of the Saints', originally from a Yorkshire Abbey, which refers to the bones of 11,000 virgins. You can't keep a good story down. No wonder it swept Europe in the Middle Ages.

It all started, apparently, by the misreading of a contemporary document which refers to St Ursula and the 'XIMV'. Some bright spark, almost but not quite up on his Latin numerals, took this to mean 11,000. Now it is thought it stands for XI M (meaning Martyrs) and V (meaning Virgins). In other words, only *eleven* martyred virgins. Much more likely. I wish Thackeray was still here, so I could tell him the truth.

I searched in vain for the alley named after them, but could find no sign of it. I did eventually find one interesting street, the Rheinsprung, with some very old and well preserved houses, one of them dated 1438.

In the end, I decided to go down and have a look at the Rhine itself, which was a bit difficult, as the banks of the river are very steep. I kept getting glimpses of it, but couldn't find a way of actually getting down so I could walk along it. I went back to the Cathedral and worked my way through some cloisters to a terrace, where at last I had a magnificent view, right over the river.

This was my first sight of the Rhine and I was amazed. Not by its colour, as I had expected it to look grey and sludgy, knowing how contaminated it is reputed to be, but by its sheer size and enormous speed. I was right in the middle of Europe, miles and miles from the sea, so I'd imagined it might be gently meandering about, but it was in a mad panic, as if trying to throw itself straight into the North Sea at once. I wanted to tell it, hold on old son, there's another 833 kilometres to go, so take it easy.

It was Renos to the Celts, Rhenus to Romans. It's now Reno in Italian, Rhin in French, Rijn in Dutch and the Germans affectionately call it Vater Rhein. The original root of Father Rhine's name is the same in all these languages, coming from the Old German for flow or run. Run, it certainly does.

I had to put my specs on to see properly across the other side, all of 200 metres away. It made the Thames in London look decidedly narrow. Below me, I could see a strange boat, large and long, like an overgrown gondola, in which were eight men, in brightly coloured strips, all rowing like mad, as if the Valkyrie were after them. Their oars were not normal oars, but monster oars, about twelve feet long, which they rowed individually, not in pairs. Also on board was a sort of cox, standing up at the rear with a flat shaped oar which he was using to steer, and a coach who did no steering or rowing, but just stood, shouting and screaming at the eight oarsmen for greater effort.

Despite all their incredible efforts, the boat seemed almost stationary, then I realised it was taking all their muscles just to keep it from being swept away by the tide. As I watched more carefully, I could see they were, very slowly, inching towards a bridge. Finally they reached it, went under, turned round, then whoosh, they were travelling with the current and going like the wind.

I could hear loud shouts and on the far bank I saw that they were being encouraged by a large crowd of people. In fact, now my eyes worked it all out, it was obviously some sort of regatta. There were several other crews, waiting to set off, and a large marquee full of people and stalls. Basle was not completely dead after all. I had at last stumbled upon signs of life.

I had to go back into the main streets and work my way round to a large bridge, the Wettsteinbrucke. Once I was across that, I was able to walk along an embankment and reach the regatta. There was loud pop music being played and stalls offering beer, chips, sausages and some sort of Tombola game. The crews, now I was amongst them, were all wearing different coloured track suits with their boat club names on the back, such as the Wasserfahrverein Nautischer club (founded 1916), who were wearing orange, and the Fischer Club (founded 1884), wearing green. I got their foundation dates from their little club houses which lined the bank of the river. It was a most attractive sight, gay and colourful, all the local crews and their supporters and families having a great time.

I seemed to be the only outsider, but I bought a beer, half expecting to be told it was a private meeting, then sat down amongst them on their benches. Some of the oarsmen were older than I'd imagined from afar, well into their thirties, and many were very fat with large beer bellies. I suppose weight does help with those leviathan oars. Their children and wives and friends were rushing round, drinking and eating, sending up little cheers when the times of the rival boats were announced over a loudspeaker. They were not racing against each other but against the clock.

I liked the idea of this being an ancient sport, which local oarsmen had practised on this part of the Rhine for centuries. I asked one man what it was all called, this special sort of rowing regatta, and he wrote it down for me on my notebook. *Schlagrudermeisterdraff.* It went across a whole page, all on its own and looked very impressive. I then asked about the boats themselves because I now noticed there were two sorts, some with eight rowers, some with four. He did some more writing for me. *Langschiff* was what the long boats were called, while the smaller ones were *Weidling*. Don't say I don't research.

I sat for a long time, enjoying their enjoyment, but I had come rather late and the last races were finishing, though the drinking and merry making was obviously going to continue. One of the supporters, an elderly man, fell over me, staggering around but there was a rush to pick him up and he was put right and everyone apologised to me.

I walked slowly back along the river bank, wishing I had come across the Regatta earlier, rather than wandering the empty streets.

I noticed some neat stacks of little cardboard boxes on low stands as I walked along the road. They were presumably meant for the use of the public, but I couldn't translate the wording on the side – *UMWELTSCHUTZ MITMACHEN!* I thought at first they might be free newspapers, or some sort of advertising gimmick. I picked up one, and then another. The perfect presents to take home to Jake and Flora. They had said they wanted something from Switzerland.

Inside, there was a little cardboard shovel and a neat little bag, all beautifully packaged, just for the sake of picking up dog shit from the pavements. Aren't the Swiss marvellous

# ~ *Chapter Fourteen* ~

# Rhine Boat

*Dinner on board the good ship Europa;*
*the Rhine and some rather famous personages;*
*breakfast with the Purser;*
*a quiet welcome from the Captain.*

I had to board my boat just before eight o'clock, nicely in time for dinner. It was moored only a mile down stream from where I had been watching the little regatta. That was my third surprise about the Rhine. I had not realised that Basle, despite being over 800 kilometres from the sea, is a port. There used to be a rather lame joke about someone whose ambition it was to be an Admiral in the Swiss Navy. I think it amused me in the third form at school. As every school child knew, Switzerland is completely landlocked, an Alpine state, deep in the heart of Europe, so how could it possibly have any sort of Navy? Today, Basle is the home port for over 500 sea going boats, which sail in the North Sea, plus hundreds of Rhine barges which go up and down the river, from Basle to Rotterdam. This merchant navy is a modern development, turning Basle into a harbour town, as a result of some recent and very expensive navigation work on the Upper Rhine. It is now Switzerland's principal gateway for imports and exports and 9 million tons of goods are handled by the port of Basle every year. I wonder if they had to re-write all the school geography text books.

My boat was the *Europa*, one of the KD German Rhine Line's eight ships which cruise the Rhine and the Moselle. I had booked a cabin rather haphazardly, not knowing what sort of boat it was, or what was the KD line, because it happened to fit in perfectly with my arrival day in Basle.

When I took my family on the QE2 to New York, the first and only time so far I have been on a proper liner, the five days seemed like five years. You can't see the boat, because you are on it, and all you can see from the boat is a load of unchanging water. Yes, the food and the comfort and the service were terrific, but after one day I was screaming inside with boredom and my body was turning ectoplasmic with all the guzzling and lack of exercise. Then I got sea sick.

So when I'd left my wife at Pisa, she'd felt rather sorry for me, about to be cooped up on board ship for three days. What a waste of three days, she said.

Well, at least on the Rhine there will be no waves, so I thought, and I should have three peaceful days without feeling ill.

It was getting dark as I boarded, and I could see very little of the boat itself, though naturally it was a lot smaller than the QE2. It looked more like a much bigger version of one of those steamers which goes up and down Windermere, very low and flat, but with three long tiers of decks, all with massive windows and viewing stations.

The *Europa*, so my leaflets told me, is the smallest of the KD's cruise ships, 89 metres long, built in 1960 and it holds a maximum of 138 passengers. The biggest is not much greater, holding just over 200 passengers. It seemed a manageable amount of passengers. After three days I should be able to recognize most of them.

I queued up at the purser's office, first on the left over the gangway, where I had to give in my ticket and get my cabin number. There was a group of American ladies ahead and one of them was complaining loudly about the fact that she had not got a shower in her cabin.

'I'm sorry, madam,' said the purser, 'you did not book a shower.'

'Of course I did,' said the woman. 'I never don't have a shower.'

I liked her use of negatives. The purser, a small man with a beard, whom I took to be Italian from his accent, was looking through his lists. He said there was just one cabin left with a shower, but that would cost her twenty-two dollars extra.

'Extra!' she turned to the queue, looking for help or sympathy.

'I can tell you something. My travel agent is never gonna get my custom again.'

But she took the room, paid the money, and walked off, still grumbling. The purser made a little face, then got on with the next person. When it was my turn, I asked if this was a common problem.

'It's not the customer's fault. Some agents will promise whatever a customer wants, even if it's not possible. But there's been no mistake at this end. I have a copy of the booking on the computer.' What a boon the computer has been to modern life. Blame it, and no human will argue.

He shrugged his shoulders, gave me my cabin key, number 121, and a smartly dressed young girl in a blue dress took my bags and told me to follow her. I had heard her speaking German to another girl in blue, lining up beside the queue to help passengers, so I was rather surprised when she asked me if I had had a good journey – in a broad Scottish accent. I guessed Glasgow but she said no, then she rushed back to the queue again.

My cabin had two beds, one of which was folded flat against the wall, as I was travelling alone, so the space was better than I had expected. There was a large picture window, a table and couch, wardrobe, sink, WC and yes, I found it at last, my very own shower. No complaints. I unpacked a few things, then went to get details about dinner and found people queueing up at the Head Waiter's desk. He was tall and dark haired and worried looking, studying large plans in front of him. The same thing had happened on the QE2. It's vital the minute you get on board any ship, especially if you are in a group, to bag a good table which will be yours for the entire trip.

The head waiter looked serious because he was trying to fit in all sizes of parties and groups, their likes and dislikes, and also sense what sort of people they were, characters and age and nationalities. I was pleased to see he was doing it by sucking his pencil and thinking. Not a computer in sight.

I said he could put me anywhere. As a single person, I would prefer not to have the same table for every meal, but be moved around, fitting in at his convenience. He asked if I would like first or second sitting, and I chose second to start with, thinking I would have a walk round first, possibly a swim, get the lie of the land, I mean the boat.

Things were much more complicated on the QE2. There was a mysterious pecking order I never worked out, with elite guests getting on the captain's table, less elite sat with senior officers, and the remainder sat with each other, though I think we did get a chance to break bread with one of the uniformed heroes at some stage. The QE2 officers took their meals with the passengers, which was smart public relations, but it must have been pretty boring for the officers, being on duty even at meals.

I went up on the top deck, to find the famous swimming pool, as advertised in the KD brochure. It was very cold and blowy and I was absolutely alone, as no one else was mad enough to even think about swimming. It turned out to be a joke pool, hardly bigger than a large dining table. They must have used a very clever photographer to get so many people grouped round it for the brochure. The QE2's outdoor pool is equally laughable, suitable only for little children. The whole notion of a swimming pool on board a moving ship, surrounded by water, is bizarre, but passengers do like it. It's one of the definitions of luxury living.

The dinner was very good, avocado, steak and then mousse, but I was a bit disappointed by the decor of the dining room. It seemed a little bit functional, almost like a Butlin's, not as posh as I had expected from a luxury cruise liner. My fellow diners all thought it was wonderful, and couldn't understand my observations. I discovered later that in fact I had booked on to a second class boat, though they don't use that term, describing it as 'Europa' class. On their first class cruises the big difference is that the service and catering are more elaborate, with five course meals. I was quite glad in the end I wasn't on a First Class boat. The meals were excellent. (For a three day, Europa cruise, the price was £139. The first class version would have been £250.)

The three passengers at the table I had been put at included an elderly English couple who had been on the boat since Rotterdam, now about to do the same trip in reverse. About half the people on board had joined, like me, at Basle, to do the one way trip. The rest were round-trippers. They were eager to see it all over again. He was a retired railway signalman from Victoria station in London. He had his *Daily Express* folded up beside him on his chair.

The other passenger was an Australian lady of about fifty, travelling alone. She had left her husband and three children at home in Melbourne, and was en route to England to see relations. She came to England most years, but this was the first time she had decided to break her journey first. She wished she had thought of it years ago.

'The flight from Australia is so awfully long and horrible. It usually takes me three days to unwind when I do get to England, so I thought this time I would spend the three days on board and relax. It's been pure culture shock so far. We had a stop at Abu Dhabi, which was the pits, then the next place I seemed to wake up in was a 14th century hotel in Zurich.'

Like me, she had spent several hours wandering round Basle, waiting for the boat. She had been in time for the history museum, which she said had been jolly good, but she too had found the town dead with no people around. She had not noticed my regatta, but she had come across a demonstration in a little square. 'They seemed to be Turkish lorry drivers either holding a meeting or a protest. It was awfully sinister.'

She had a strong Australian accent, direct and forthright, bright and sparky, so it was strange to hear old English words coming out of her mouth, such as 'jolly' and 'awfully'. She said she was just putting it on. She always found herself talking Pom when she met Pommies. What an insult. I look upon myself as someone who speaks non-posh, non-county English.

We discussed our children, as we had three of similar ages, and went through the usual teenage litanies, about which one had given the most agonies and sleepless nights. It's the same the whole world over. Then we got on to schools and the scramble for college places. She said there was a class system at work in Australia, despite its wonderful image. In the primary schools, she had noticed that her children would not play with Italians or

Greeks, which had upset her. They in turn maintained it was because the Italians and Greeks were clannish and would not play with them.

I felt too tired after dinner for any more diversions, though most passengers were making arrangements to meet at the bar, so I went straight back to my cabin, planning to read a few of Thackeray's letters, hoping it would get me to sleep. I hate all strange beds, especially hotel beds, but the thought of a moving bed was hanging over me.

\*　　　\*　　　\*

On Thackeray's first Rhine trip, as a poor student, he had been unable to afford any cabin. 'But I managed to sleep snugly on the top of some coals which were placed on the deck.' That's what he told the folks back home in a letter. I wonder what it had really been like.

From his accounts, it sounded as if in 1831 you had to get on a sequence of boats, or use different modes of transport, to get along the Rhine Valley, though it's clear there were regular boats in his day, and even organised parties, all going together to the same destination.

In the 18th century and earlier, you had to work out your own system. It's interesting that John Evelyn in 1644 did exactly what Wordsworth did in 1790. He actually *bought* a little boat, presumably a little rowing boat, and then sold it at his journey's end. Wordsworth bought his in Basle, perhaps a forerunner of those little gondola type rowing boats, and rowed it all the way to Cologne, which was where I was heading. With that fierce tide behind him, it must have been quite exhilarating.

Proper steamers on the Rhine began early in the 19th century, but they were mainly for freight at first, which was probably the sort of boat Thackeray was on. It was towards the middle of the century that passenger steamers developed and various companies then started competing for the excursion market.

The KD line boasts that it is the oldest cruise company using the Rhine. It was founded in 1826 as the Prussian Rhine Steamship Company of Cologne, which is where its headquarters still are. In 1827, it launched two steam ships, the *Concordia* and the *Friedrich Wilhelm*, both made of wood. In 1853, the Cologne based company joined forces with its rival based in Dusseldorf, and this eventually led to the present company, KD, standing for Köln-Dusseldorf.

Queen Victoria was one of KD's earliest distinguished passengers, sailing to Koblenz in 1845 with Prince Albert, the King and Queen of the Belgiums and Frederick William IV of Prussia. In more recent years, their passengers have included President Hindenburg (in 1930, on the steamer *Hindenburg*), Chancellor Adenauer (in 1953 to celebrate KD's 100th anniversary as a joint company), Indian Prime Minister Pandit Nehru in 1956, Queen Elizabeth II in 1965, Emperor Hirohito of Japan in 1971 and President Ford in 1975. It has become almost mandatory for visiting foreign dignitaries to West Germany to be taken down the Rhine, just as they get dragged to the Great Wall in China, or driven out to Stratford-on-Avon when they're doing England.

*     *     *

I awoke next morning very early, startled by the sudden movement of the boat and by the view from the window. The practice on KD ships is to sail during the day, so you get a moving panorama, then moor at night so you have motionless sleep. So that had been the good news. It was what I could see from my window which rather alarmed me. Nothing. Well, not completely nothing. Just a frightening-looking concrete wall, two inches away. The boat seemed to be going up and down and as I was still half asleep, I thought for a moment I'd been spirited away into some Wagnerian Rhinish hell.

I had not been aware how much this part of the Upper Rhine has been changed in order to make it navigable for big ships. In effect, they have canalised it, getting rid of the waterfalls, the marshlands and lagoons, creating a straight, deep channel. But it means the Rhine now has locks, ten in all, which have to be negotiated. Hence the bumping.

The day was going to be a very busy one, according to the events list I had studied on the noticeboard the night before, so I got up quickly and went into breakfast. It's free play at breakfast, so you can sit where you like. I noticed the little bearded Purser eating on his own. I thought about sparing him, as he must be bombarded all the time by passengers and their dopey questions, but I wanted to hear about him and his job.

He was called Giuseppe and he was Italian, from Rome, and had been the assistant purser on the ship for four years. Before that he had worked in hotels. One forgets that on a boat a naval looking uniform doesn't mean a naval man.

He was still in essence in the hotel trade, only this time it happened to be a travelling hotel. He said there were really no differences, except they were on the move. Perhaps he had to do more on the boat, such as ringing restaurants on the shore, confirming numbers going on tours, but apart from that, the job was basically the same. It was however very like a prison. From March to October every year, he was on the *Europa*, day and night, up and down the Rhine, without ever getting off. It was like a six months' sentence. He looked a bit alarmed when he saw me making notes. He worried about his use of the word prison, what his employers might think, but on consideration, he decided it was a fair comment. All boats are like prisons.

On board the *Europa* that trip were 95 people. He knew because he'd just been checking all the passports. There were 47 from the USA, 12 British, 10 Germans, 7 Canadians, 7 French, 4 Australians, 3 from Malaysia, 3 Chile, 1 Brazil, 1 Mexico. The 24 man 'hotel' crew were equally split amongst the various nationalities – from Italy, Holland, Austria, Britain, New Zealand, France, Thailand – though the ten seamen were all German.

'American passengers are the easiest, and the British. They are polite and are very happy people. It's the Germans who complain most. They have minds like this, very narrow, and if anything goes wrong, they get upset.'

*       *       *

We were all invited to meet the Captain and his senior members of the crew, so there was great excitement as everyone gathered in the observation lounge. We were treated to a free glass of German style champagne and a young Austrian lady in a red blazer introduced herself as Ursula, our hostess. She would help with any problems or questions. Then she introduced the captain, a beaming bearded gentleman who nodded and smiled vigorously, but said nothing, neither in German nor English. Then it was the Chief Engineer's turn to take a bow. The Chef got the biggest clap of all. Ursula read out the numbers of people on board from each country and asked them to stand up and we all stared madly around, hoping to answer the questions we had been asking ourselves about the various passengers and their nationalities.

It was all a bit stiff and formal, but nicely amateurish. When the same thing had happened on the QE2, at a meet the captain drinkies party, we all had to queue up for ages, but then we did have our photographs taken, shaking his distinguished hand.

I was sitting with a young Australian couple. When they heard I was British, they told me in enormous detail how they had got married at Gretna Green the previous week. They had actually been married for four years, but they were on a coach trip to Scotland and volunteers had been called for to take part in a ceremony across the anvil.

'I had to wear a top hat and she wore a veil and we were piped in by a bagpiper. They made a big song and dance about it. It was pretty good. We enjoyed it. It didn't cost us anything for the marriage certificate. I'll go and get it for you, if you like . . .'

I said another time, but how fascinating. In Britain there is now a sub-culture of olde worlde re-creations, companies which do mock medieval banquets on a massive scale, Tudor dinners, Roman orgies, all with full scale entertainments and huge meals, yet a world which the native Britons never visit – and would probably not understand, even if they did. I once went to a Tudor feast near the Tower of London in which there was jousting, strong men, strolling musicians, plus Henry VIII and *all* his six wives together, in full costume. Half naked Nell Gwynns gave out oranges and as much mead as you could drink. There was about 500 foreign tourists in this underground cellar, screaming their heads off, thumping the tables, having a terrific time, in what they thought was a typical British evening.

I then got talking to two Chileans, a lawyer and his wife. They were heading for England, where their main object was to visit the Imperial War Museum in London. The best thing so far, in their month's tour of Europe, had been driving from Zurich to Vienna, over the Alps. That had been wonderful. They had hated Italy intensely, especially Rome, for its scruffiness and hippies.

'Thank God we don't live in Europe,' said the lawyer. 'So many young people are on drugs. My children in Chile don't know what drugs are.'

I happened to mention that I did some work for the BBC, presenting a radio programme, and my stock instantly soared. There is one channel in Chile, so they said, the so called University channel, which shows all the BBC classics. (And a lot of classic ITV shows, but they were not to know the difference. Every show from Britain is assumed to be the BBC's.)

'We loved your *Mayor of Casterbridge, Upstairs, Downstairs*. We stay in specially for it,' said his wife. 'Your BBC is an oasis for us. Such a change from *Dallas* and *Kojak*.'

What a small globe we have now become. An American, overhearing our chat, leaned over to tell me that his hero in life was Benny Hill.

One of our sister ships from KD line, the *Britannia*, passed us on the other bank, and a voice over the intercom instructed us to give our sister ship a big wave. Since setting sail, there has been a regular commentary in all the public rooms and corridors, keeping us up to date with the passing scene and sights. It was obviously a recorded commentary, but from time to time, a live voice would come in with special messages.

At once, every member of the crew, waiters at the tables, and sailors outside, started waving frantically at the *Britannia*, while their opposite numbers did the same. It was as if they were on bonuses, extra payments for the crew member doing the best waving. The passengers were a bit slow to react, but most of us dutifully followed. From then on, about twice a day, when we passed a sister ship we were exhorted to wave. Nothing was said if we passed a *rival* ship, but I always waved, nonetheless.

At the stern of the *Britannia*, on the top deck, there was a lone figure sitting on an exercise bike, frantically pedalling away. My lawyer friend said something in Spanish, and he and his wife burst out laughing. When they eventually subsided, I asked them to explain.

'I said he's the man pedalling the ship. He's the engine on the boat.'

It had looked very like that, so I smiled. Not a bad joke. Benny Hill could have used it. Perhaps he has.

I went back to my cabin, to get changed for the day's main excitement, and in the corridor I met our stewardess, the Scottish girl, working away. Her name was Marian. She had been unemployed, living at home in East Kilbride, until three years ago when she met a Swiss boy and got a job as an au pair in Switzerland, just to be near him. When they split up, she decided not to go home but to stay in Europe a bit longer. Someone told her about the KD line and she wrote off for a job, sending a photograph and details. It was very hard work, looking after twelve cabins. There was some free time in the late afternoons, but she was usually too tired and just went to her cabin, which she shared with a French girl, and slept. None of the stewardesses was allowed to take any passengers into her cabin, or to get too friendly.

'You get invited of course, but you can't. There was one Spanish couple, newly married, who were very nice, and always encouraged me to come and do their rooms while they were still in them, saying they didn't mind, which was a help, as I could get ahead. On the last day, they shook my hands and said goodbye and left the ship, then he came back on his own and grabbed me in the corridor and started kissing me. I was just so amazed. I thought dear God, I hope his wife doesn't come back and blame me.

'That's the only time anything like that's happened. The passengers are all awfully good. They're mostly pretty old of course. This lot is quite young, for this time of the year. The most important thing is to have a happy crew, with no conflicts. You have to live so close together, you just have to be friends, or it gets hellish. We're all very happy on this ship.'

She didn't seem terribly well paid, for such a demanding job. She had to work backwards in marks, but she estimated that in her hand she got about £250 a month. 'But I get free digs, food and as many showers as I like.'

Showers? What's so special about showers? At home in East Kilbride, she said, they have to pay for their showers.

'I'd be unemployed if I was at home now, as I've no qualifications. I'd rather be working than unemployed.'

The commentary, which had been waxing lyrical about some quarry on the opposite bank, a producer of a 'particularly good form of gravel', was interrupted to say that all passengers going ashore should get ready to disembark, so I thanked her for the chat and let her get on with her work.

# ~ Chapter Fifteen ~

# Heidelberg

*Hans knows bumps a daisy;*
*a visit to Heidelberg castle;*
*a most enjoyable dinner*
*and a great deal of German beer.*

I had presumed it would be three days completely on the boat when I had booked, but of course the Rhine is not like the Atlantic. You can get off. There are scheduled stops all the way up and down, organised trips to various cities and sights. I had decided to go to Heidelberg. Just for the romance of the name.

About twenty of us left the boat and went on to a coach where a young German guide welcomed us. Over the microphone, he said he was called Hans and he would be our leader on the way to Heidelberg and would take us round and personally entertain us. He was very cocky and confident. I wondered what sort of entertainment he personally would be providing.

I found myself sitting with a gaggle of Americans, all prepared with cameras and British style Burberry raincoats. 'One of the things I like about travelling is the chance to help people. Did I tell you that in London I told this German how to use the Tube?'

There was another conversation behind me about everything 'being all jammed together'. I thought at first they were talking about people on the coach, or perhaps the cabins, but it turned out to be countries. 'Gee, isn't it wonderful the way all the countries of Europe are jammed together. You cross one bridge and it's France, then another it's Germany, and then it's Switzerland again.'

The bits of chatter and stories were brought to a sudden halt by the coach's microphone being picked up and Hans announced in rather loud, bossy tones, that he was going to give us some history. We all sat up to attention, as if we were in school, especially the Americans, eager to learn anything and be good pupils.

He turned out to be an excellent guide and kept up a non stop stream of information for the next couple of hours. It was the first time in my life I had been on a coach tour, but from now on I will look at them with new eyes, whenever I happen to see them lined up on Westminster Bridge or outside Buckingham Palace. Coach trippers always look so dozey from outside, sheep being shoved around, and I've usually felt sorry for them. What can they learn about London, or anywhere, what can they see or experience, stuck in that coach? The answer is quite a lot, if you pay attention and work hard.

Hans also insisted on telling jokes, or at least long complicated stories which you could tell from his beaming face would end amusingly, so he thought.

There was one about a famous Professor of Zoology at Heidelberg University many years ago who gave his students an end of year test which consisted of a row of birds, all with their heads and bodies covered. The students had to tell from their feet what breed they were. All the students did well except one who got everything wrong. The Professor told him he had failed and would now be chucked out of the class. As the student was leaving the room, the Professor said oh, by the way, what is your name, so I can tick you off the list? The student lifted up his trousers. 'Now it is your turn. . . .'

Ho ho. Did we larf. It was Hans's enjoyment of the story which was the best part. But he was very good on local history, and filled us up with lots of suitable facts about the Black Forest and the province of Baden-Würtemmberg, which we were now in. In under an hour, he took us from the Romans right through two World Wars.

'It's taken me a long time to come to Germany,' said a small, rather plump American lady beside me. 'Too many of the boys in our family died here. They got killed in the Black Forest, after peace had been declared. Snipers picked them off. I didn't think I'd ever see it.'

When I'd got on the coach, I'd noticed three single American ladies, all of a certain age, sitting in single seats, as if waiting for customers. I had sat down beside the first and said hello. I had seen each of them vaguely on the boat. One was small and plump, one was large and plump, while the third was thin and academic looking with short cropped hair. It was only on the coach ride I discovered all three were sisters. I had never seen such un-alike sisters. And all three were widows, travelling together for the first time in their adult lives.

'How did that terrible war happen,' said the small sister, looking out of the window at the Black Forest in the distance.

I took it as a rhetorical question, so I said nothing at first, though no doubt Hans, if asked, could have listed twenty explanations, starting with the Romans. Similar thoughts had been striking me since I'd got on the boat. There we were, passengers and crew, drawn from so many different nations, getting on happily together, moving with such ease from country to country, speaking different languages yet feeling part of a whole, like brothers and sisters.

'I don't think the people ever want war,' I said.

'You're right,' she replied. 'It's the politicians who want wars. They begin them, then stand back and let the people do the fighting for them.'

She held my hand and I was too embarrassed to remove it.

'On this trip,' she said, 'I just want to have a good time. I thought I was coming with my husband. We were both booked. He passed away four weeks ago.'

Hans was now back into his commentary as we were getting into the streets of Heidelberg. He explained that Heidelberg was still a famous university town, with 30,000 at the University, out of a total population of only 130,000. It had been founded in 1386, making it Germany's oldest University.

'A lot of drinking has gone on in Heidelberg,' he said, and we waited for another joke, as he was standing beaming, but instead over the loudspeaker came the sound of a drinking song. He had obviously got a tape ready. Clever old Hans.

He explained that the student fraternities were not as strong as they used to be in the old days, but he pointed out various student houses with large, ornate flags hanging outside, the mark of each fraternity. 'About seven per cent are in these fraternities and they have strange customs, rituals and sing old drinking songs.'

He then pressed another tape and this time we hummed along to Gaudeamus Igitur. My American friend pointed out of the window to a shop front which said 'Happy Night Dance Cafe'. That must be American, she said. There are almost 40,000 American servicemen stationed around Heidelberg, so it seemed a reasonable deduction.

When Thackeray did this same trip, in 1830, he was struck by the number of soldiers, all of them Prussians, and he seemed to meet thousands of them in every village. He did some neat sketches of them, but it was the student fraternities and the drinking clubs he was really looking for.

He and some other young English travellers he had met were invited by some German students to watch some duels and later to a student drinking club where everyone had to sing a German drinking song. When it was his turn, Thackeray sang 'God Save The King'. At the end of the evening, he found he was the only sober man in the party, despite having drunk no less than six bottles of wine. Compared with the port wine he had been used to at Cambridge, he said it tasted like water and vinegar. How on earth then had he knocked back *six* bottles in the evening. No wonder he complained later of 'an unpleasant effect on my internals.'

Hans promised us that this evening we would have a real German meal, in a very ancient dining room, and we could drink as much German beer as we liked. All the Americans oohed and ahhed. I worried about my stomach. But first we had culture to attend to.

*    *    *

The most famous thing to see in Heidelberg, after the University, is the Castle, and it did look a fine sight, high up on the banks of the River Neckar, towering over the old Town.

On the way, the coach stopped outside an old half timbered house, for all of us to admire it properly, and the Americans burst into clapping. 'Gee, isn't that gorgeous. Oh Boy, that sure is something.'

I think it's the innocent capacity for enjoyment of Americans abroad which is their single most attractive characteristic. They so *want* to like things, always willing to look on the bright side, to be openly enthusiastic, without any cynicism or sourness. There used to be an image of Americans abroad that they went round the world saying yeh, but we have it bigger back home. It seems to have faded. They don't boast so much these days, and apologise and feel embarrassed if by chance they do so. Has Vietnam knocked some of the bravado out of them?

Our coach had great difficulty climbing the steep and narrow streets to the castle, thanks to all the other tourist coaches creeping down. We decamped outside the main gates and were given ten minutes to stock up on useless souvenirs from a row of little tourist shops. They were already crowded with other trippers, buying tat.

It's easy to be cynical about the way tourist guides always seem to dump their charges right in amongst all the tourist tat. They must be well recompensed, but on listening to my fellow passengers, this is precisely what they want. In every country, at every tourist site, however famous, however historic, however artistic, I suspect that the number one desire of most tourists is a shop. A close second is a café, or some place to get a cup of tea or coffee. Thirdly, it's a lavatory. Then, and only then, are we all prepared to inspect and admire the Famous Sight. And why not? Let's get the outer man settled before we start on inner satisfactions. So many people on the boat, like me, had been moaning because in Basle all the shops had closed so early and they couldn't buy anything.

Once we reassembled, Hans produced a whistle from his pocket and called our little party to attention. It was quite a clever idea. Almost all the other guides were relying on visual aids, such as flowers or large umbrellas, to keep their flock together. The only trouble was the noise of his whistle. It was a piercing bird noise, with several bars of a strangled tune, and he would insist on playing it every ten yards, as loudly as possible. It obviously gave him a great deal of pleasure. 'Oh shut up Hans, please,' said another guide, trying to explain some abstruse historical point to her party.

The wine cellars are the main things inside the castle for the visitors to see, and they are world famous, so the guide books say. How can I have been so ignorant. One of the wine barrels is apparently the biggest in the world, holding over 55,000 gallons. The 'Grosses Fass', or Great Tun, was built in 1751 and is about the size of a three storey house. It was last used in 1886, to celebrate the 500th anniversary of the founding of Heidelberg University when the Kaiser came for the festivities. Now, another hundred years later, there is no Kaiser and no wine in the barrel. It now leaks, thanks to woodworm, but we were invited to climb up some wooden stairs and inspect it. On top, there was a dance floor, big enough to accommodate about twenty couples.

Nearby was a wooden figure of Perkeo, a court fool from the 18th century, who was a famous dwarf. 'He drank fifteen bottles of wine a day,' said Hans, 'and lived till he was eighty. Then, one day, someone gave him a flask of water. And he died.'

Everyone dutifully laughed. I wondered what native-born, educated Germans think of all this potted history and stories which we foreigners get filled up with. No dafter, I suppose than putting on a top hat for a phoney marriage or seeing Henry VIII sitting with all his wives.

We emerged into the daylight, through some passages, and out into a magnificent courtyard at the back of the castle, overlooking the town. Hans pointed to a footprint, embedded in the sandstone slabs, and asked for suggestions about its origins, but hardly waited before he was off telling us some soppy German fairytales about a Princess jumping out of a window to meet her true love. He said it was now used as a test of whether a man had been unfaithful to his wife. If your shoe fitted it exactly, that was the sign. Any

F. Veith fecit. Das grosse Heidelberger Fass, 212422 Ltr. fassend.

volunteers. Several elderly Americans, game for a laguh, came forward, egged on by their elderly wives, and of course their feet fitted exactly. Gosh, what larks.

Back in the town, we were standing in the middle of an old square, with Hans pointing out all the old buildings in view, when someone noticed on the ground floor of one very ancient building a sign saying McDonalds. All the British and other European members of our party burst out laughing, but the Americans were most upset. How gross, one of them said, to ruin such a lovely square. Even worse, when we got round a corner, almost next door to the main Jesuit church, we came to a shop which had a large notice above the door, telling the world about its products. 'SEX SHOP'. The Americans this time tried to avert their eyes. Everyone else sniggered.

We stood in the University square, beside a building which was once the student gaol, and Hans told us to look out for plaques commemorating all the famous people, artists and musicians, who lived or stayed in Heidelberg – Goethe, Weber, Brahms, Schumann. Later, he pointed out a little hotel, the Goldener Hecht, which he said had a notice saying that Goethe 'nearly spent a night here'. We all laughed, but he said it was true. Goethe had booked in, but the hotel had a flood and was unable to put him up.

*     *     *

Our very special, terribly typical, drink as much beer as you like, German dinner was to be held in a very attractive hotel with wooden beams and lots of screens and tapestries. I was a bit disappointed on our arrival to find that at least six other coach loads had already disgorged and the dining room was practically full, with about 200 tourists, all sitting expectantly at little tables. Young girls in traditional clothes were going round with huge glass jugs of foaming beer, filling everyone as they arrived. So that part was true.

I sat down with three Americans from our boat, a man of about fifty called Brad and his wife, plus an older American called Bill. His wife was on another table. He was very laconic and laid back while Brad was more serious.

Brad explained that he had been to college and in fact had a PhD in teaching deaf people, that was his real profession, for which he had been properly educated. Naturally, I asked what in fact he had ended up doing. He managed a condominium in Florida. I wasn't clear if that meant he owned it, but no, it just meant he was a jobbing handyman, part of a team that went round 600 units to keep things ok. The jobs ranged from washing out the pool to changing light bulbs. Did people really pay other people to change their light bulbs?

'Why not? They don't want to do it.'

In his spare time, Brad was very big in a local organisation which runs an annual Medieval Fair in the town of Sarasota. It turned out that Bill, who hadn't been listening so far, went there every year and loved it, though parking was always hell. There were shouts and roars as they compared notes, with the beer flowing very quickly. They gave each other visiting cards and Brad promised, as a huge personal favour, that next year, Bill could park in his drive.

'All the way to Heidelberg to get a car park in Florida,' said Bill.

'Of course you won't recognise me,' said Brad. 'With the beard. I have it on for half of every year, to dress up as a monk in the procession. With my beard, you sure would never recognise me.

'I live in a tourist area, so I know what it's like to be a tourist. I try my best, when I'm a tourist, not to be crude or ugly, no sir.'

Throughout the meal, the beer flowed freely and so did the music. There seemed to be a lot of instruments, but when I went to the lavatory, pushing my way past the crowded tables, I could see that it was just a little man in a white shirt and bow tie playing at an electric keyboard.

When I got to the lavatory, Bill was already there, though he must have set off after me. I got lost, I explained. 'You darned tourists,' said Bill, as we went back together to our table.

At the end of the meal, during which the man in the bow tie played popular German folk tunes, such as 'Tulips from Amsterdam' and 'Yesterday', we were told to expect a special musical event. So we all clapped. Up to the microphone pranced Hans, beaming as ever. The ridiculous whistle he had been shattering our ear drums with all day turned out to be part of what looked like a recorder. To the accompaniment of electric keyboard sound effects, he than played 'Lily Marlene'. Next, for our American friends, so he announced, he would play a famous Elvis number. I waited, wondering how he was going to manage 'Blue Suede Shoes' on his little penny whistle. It was 'Wooden Heart', one of the soppiest tunes Elvis, or anyone, ever sang.

Several people shouted, in pretend German accents, 'Shuttup, pleez, Hans,' the way the lady guide had shouted at him, but all in good humour. He finished with 'Auld Lang Syne', even though it was only September, and just eleven o'clock, but we all appreciated his choice of British music.

On the way back to the coach, Bill was talking about his war time memories. 'I think Presidents should fight other Presidents in the next war.' It was the second time that day I had heard a similar thought.

Brad's wife, meanwhile, was trying to think what Europe reminded her of. All evening, it had been on the tip of her tongue.

Europe's rather a big place, I said, to remind you of one thing.

'I've got it,' she said, as we all climbed wearily onto our coach. 'Europe reminds me of Disneyland.'

I was rather insulted by this. How could she compare all this genuine history, famous universities, ancient castle, with a load of modern, plastic mock-ups.

'I mean walking around Europe,' she explained. 'It reminds me of walking around Disneyland. Disneyland is the only place in America I've ever been to where you walk around and you can hear all these foreign languages. It's the same as Europe. And everyone looks happy in Europe. Just the same as Disneyland.'

## ~ *Chapter Sixteen* ~

# Romantic Rhine

*Legend and lore; Ursula's story;*
*in search of the Naked Lady;*
*a farewell present to the lucky Captain.*

The highlight of any trip up or down the Rhine is the so called Romantic Rhine section, which stretches from about Mainz to Koblenz, a distance of only about 50 miles, but so filled with treasures and legends that my head was already reeling. I was lying in bed reading the Baedeker *Rhine Guide*, which takes you down the river, mile by mile, identifying all the villages and castles, but even reading it was hard as you have to dart the eye from page to page to follow what is happening on either bank.

The ship's commentary was also awake bright and early, droning on about the wonders of the Riesling grape. From the surrounding wine growing districts, so the commentary announced in English, 'come the world's best white wines'. Even with my limited German, I could work out that the same boast was repeated in the German commentary. But when it came to the French translation, I noticed a subtle difference. '*Some* of the world's best white wines.' Very diplomatic. Don't want an international incident on board.

When Queen Victoria was on her Rhine trip, back in 1845, they gave her a new wine to sample. Her German, despite the family connections, was very poor, but she did manage to say that the wine was 'high quality'. However, her pronunciation of the German for high (*hoch*) was all wrong and it came out as Hock. So that was what they named it. And it's been called Hock ever since. Another legend? Well, if you go down the Rhine, you meet such legends at every bend.

I had been trying the Rhine wines on board ship with my meals, and found them rather expensive, considering that the company also owns vineyards. I always find German wines too sweet anyway, so I asked the head waiter, Alberto, for the driest. Even so, it still had a faint perfum-y smell. But I did discover a pleasant red wine which I chose purely for the label – Forster Ungeheuer. As Forster is my wife's maiden name, I took the label off to send home to my father-in-law in Carlisle, asking if he had been keeping his vineyard a secret from us all these years. It is handy to have something to fill up a post card.

During his 1830 trip, Thackeray was moaning all the time about the wine. 'The much lauded Wine of the Rhine is mighty similar to Epsom Salts and

Vinegar in taste and effect.' Then a few days later he was complaining again, this time to his mother. 'I thought I would let you know that I was well in health, save for wine which doth occasionally afflict me, and in good spirits save for fleas which do incessantly torment me. But wine I need not drink, and fleas I must put up withal, shewing thereby an example of resignation and continence worth to be imitated by all travellers.'

For opera lovers, I suppose Romantic Rhine makes them think of Wagner rather than wine. As I have no interest in opera, I had been trying not to think about it, though I realised I would have to face it sometime as we were now deep into *Rheingold* country.

I have this terrible block about legends. I switch off the moment I hear a story is not true, even if it goes back to the Middle Ages, covered in fantasy and folk lore, and must have been based on fact at one time, so the experts say, because there are just so many documents which hint at it, and look at the books and songs which have built up the legend, till in the end there's this great steam roller, thundering down the centuries under the weight of its own myth. King Arthur leaves me completely cold. And as for the Rheingold, oh well, perhaps if I concentrate for five minutes, I might understand something.

It all dates back to a German epic poem, written around 1200. The hero of the poem was Siegfried and his struggles with some big woman called Brünnhilde. Siegfried ends up dead and his family treasure, the gold of the Nibelungs, gets thrown in the Rhine. There's also a dwarf in it somewhere, plus lots of battles and collapses of dynasties. Just another load of medieval twaddle, doing nobody any harm, though probably with a little nugget of history, deep in it somewhere.

(The word Rheingold is interesting. For centuries, gold *was* panned and taken out of the Rhine. Naturally, the ancients must have wondered where all this gold came from, and dreamt up their own stories. But the work of canalising and straightening the Upper Rhine, which began in the 19th century, so speeded up the river that it now travels too rapidly to deposit any gold. All the gold bearing sands are now empty. So where does it go? Search the North Sea, I suppose.)

In the middle of the 19th century, the legends moved into overdrive. During the Romantic revival period, German writers and poets turned for inspiration to their own medieval stories and legends. Richard Wagner produced a four part operatic cycle, the *Ring of the Nibelungen*, which dragged in various other figures from Germanic mythology. One of the four operas is called *Rheingold*, with the others being *The Valkyrie, Siegfried* and *The Twilight of the Gods*.

Over breakfast, I talked to Ursula, our hostess on board, and asked her if I had got the stories straight, or nearly straight, but she didn't seem to know much more than I did. Turned out she came from Austria, not Germany. I suppose they have their own legends to keep them going round the television, late of an evening.

She always enjoyed this bit of the cruise best, as they all did, but she wasn't looking forward to arriving in Cologne as she might have to go into the HQ office. 'That's when they pass on any complaints from passengers.' A common complaint is 'Boring Dancing'. It is her duty to get the dancing going, but sometimes, if people on board are particularly old or doddery, this can be quite difficult. Other times, it just takes off and people have a great time. Tonight, she feared it was going to be an uphill struggle. There did not appear to be many extroverts on board.

'In the office, they don't understand the problems. They see "Boring Dancing", and I get the blame.'

This was her 39th trip. The worst that had happened so far was a German dying of a heart attack in Heidelberg, standing in the University Square. He had insisted on seeing Heidelberg, though his wife had said there would be too much walking for him. I had noticed Ursula on our tour, but keeping in the background, letting the guide do all the talking, ready if any passengers needed urgent help.

Her vividest image of her six months on board ship was going to help an elderly passenger who was unable to switch on his shower. 'He was a Jewish gentleman and as I fixed his shower for him, I noticed on his bare arms his concentration camp number. That sight will stay in my mind for ever.'

She found Americans easiest to deal with. 'If it's a man wearing a Tyrolean hat, then you know he's American. If it's a woman in very bright colours, orange and pink top with green trousers, then you know she's American. They are good fun. Americans know how to express themselves.' She found the Germans the coolest and the British the wittiest.

Her cabin was right in the middle of the ship, opposite the purser's, which meant it was very noisy and she rarely got more than four hours' sleep a night. She showed it to me later, keeping the door open, as passengers are not allowed inside. It was pretty small, but she had made it personal with posters and post cards stuck up, like a student's room. She had had sixteen of the crew inside it once, for a drink. She was hoping one day to squeeze in twenty. That would be an all time, KD record.

The Rhine was getting narrower, the slopes steeper and more rocky, but on almost every available patch of land, however sheer, there were vineyards, stretching over the hilltops, so neat and regular, like West Indian dreadlocks, carefully combed as if by some giant hand.

I went up on deck and spotted my first castle just past Bingen, Ehrenfels Castle, but before I could look it up in the Baedeker, we had come to a more interesting looking one, right in the middle of the river, a yellow tower on a rocky islet. This is called the Mausersturm or Mouse Tower. One legend says it was because of a wicked Archbishop of Mainz who was put into the tower and got eaten to death by mice. Or it could be because the name comes from the word 'Maut' meaning toll. It was a watch tower, rather than a castle, built in the 14th century as a toll collecting post.

The castles started coming thick and fast, so many there hardly seemed space for them all, each trying to upstage, out-grandiose the other in setting

*Am Mäuseturm bei Bingen*

and towers and fancy, fairytale decorations. On the other side I noticed a particularly splendid castle, Rheinstein Castle, so I raced back to my cabin to get my spectacles. I can see why people do the trip both ways. It is so hard to concentrate on both banks at once, especially when you are sailing with the tide. (With the tide, the boat does twenty-five kilometres an hour. Against the stream, only fifteen.)

Rheinstein Castle was perched on a rocky outcrop, about eighty metres above the river, so cleverly balanced, hugging the natural lines of the rocks, that it seemed to be made out of the rock, as if an eruption had shaped it. It too used to be a toll station at one time.

Many of the castles, lining the gorge of the Rhine, were erected to collect tolls, and at one time they had chains and ropes across the river, to stop boats getting past. It must have been like an obstacle race. It was also for protection, as rival lordlings fought out their battles for control of the river. All the castles seemed in excellent condition, far grander and more impressive than I had expected. A lot of them, apparently, were completely rebuilt in the 19th century. Many are still in private hands, owned by descendants of the old Prussian families. Some are council owned and turned into museums. Others are hotels and youth hostels.

I decided to go downstairs, into the observation lounge at the front of the boat. It was becoming windy on top and I was getting cold. There wasn't a seat spare. Everyone was sitting down at the little tables, drinks at the ready, turning over their guide books, trying to find out where we were, exclaiming the while and taking endless photographs. In the middle of the lounge were six American ladies, in baggy slacks and sloppy jumpers, playing cards and

smoking like mad, paying no attention whatsoever to the brilliant views. Having described Americans as enthusiasts for all sights, I had to amend my judgement.

The views were good from the lounge, thanks to the panoramic windows all round, but I decided to return on deck, this time with my camera, not wanting to miss the Star of the Rhine Gorge, the Lorelei Rock. This was coming up at the 554 kilometre mark. All the guide books had been going on about this being the most truly amazing, historic, legendary, wonderful bit on the whole Rhine.

The legend this time is quite a simple one. On this chunk of rock there used to sit a nymph who lured boatmen to their death by singing to them, until she herself was overcome by love and plunged to her death in the river. Ahh. The name comes from the Middle High German, *lure* meaning treacherous and *lei* meaning rock.

It was Heinrich Heine in 1822 who made the legend famous in his poem, the *Loreley*, which was put to music by Silcher, a song which all German school children know. Mark Twain on his trip down the Rhine in 1880, did quite a good English translation, one you can buy on postcards.

As we approached the rock, they played the tune over the ship's loudspeakers. It did sound quite familiar. So far, they had not played the Rhine song which all British children learn at school, in the playground if not the class room. At least they did when I was at primary school. 'Two German Officers crossed the Rhine. Parlay-voo.' I made a note to try and investigate the origin of that song.

I was looking out for a naked maiden, sitting on top, if not literally then some huge statue, commemorating the legend. We passed one rock which had the German flag flying on top, and everyone seemed to be taking pictures, but I could see nothing remarkable about it. What a swiz. I turned to an American, who had been rushing up and down the deck, wildly taking snaps, looking for something dramatic. We both decided we must have missed it, but no, that boring bit of rock had definitely been the Lorelei.

The tourist office in the nearest village, St Goarshausen, did have a competition to find a suitable way of commemorating the legend. There were 900 entries, mostly suggesting a statue of a naked girl. One suggestion wanted *real* naked girls to take it in turns to sit there, posing, giving us all a little happening. Another idea was for a huge eye to be built into the rock face which would wink at the boats going past. That could have been fun. Someone else suggested a huge concrete brassiere on top, one cup containing a souvenir shop, the other a restaurant. The shop and restaurant were built, but nothing else.

On the right, I could see another two castles, this time almost touching, facing each other across a moat, as if squaring up for a fight. These are the so called Feindlichen Brüder, or Hostile Brothers. They are supposed to have been built by two brothers who quarrelled. Yet another legend. I suppose castles attracted castles. Once one lordling had his Rhine castle, others followed suit. In the 19th century, when there was the rush to buy up old ruins and convert them, the Rhine became littered with more castles than ever before in its history.

Lahneck Castle was restored by an Englishman called Moriarty. He was a director of a Rhineland railway company and flew the Union Jack over his castle from 1850–1860. Some time before he started his restoration work, a Miss Idilia Dubb of Edinburgh, on a Grand Tour with her family, arrived at the Castle and decided to do some sketching. She climbed up one of the towers, stepped on an old wooden staircase, which promptly collapsed beneath her. She shouted and shouted, waved her skirts, threw down pages from her sketch book, but nobody saw or heard her. In the end, she died of starvation. When Mr Moriarty's restoration team finally reached this ruined tower, in 1863, the body of Miss Dubb was found, including the remains of her sketch book and a diary she had kept, describing the last four days of her life.

A true story, at last. It would make a good legend, or the basis of a nice Victorian novel.

As I was watching out for each castle, ticking them off in my guide book, reckoning I must already have seen about 200, I realised I was now the only person left on deck. On the bridge, I could see the captain and two of his crew. He suddenly waved at me, beckoning me to come in, which I did, jumping over his little gangway.

He turned out to have a few English words, though at the reception he had been hesitant about trying to use them. I suppose on a cruise ship, surrounded by hotel staff who appear fluent in almost every European language, humble sailors do feel a bit inhibited. His name was Heinz Keller, the replacement captain, as the *Europa*'s regular captain was on leave. I asked if there were particular problems, about navigating on the Rhine, but he said no, it was easy. 'Too little sleep,' that was the only problem.

I wondered if the canals had been a problem or just a bore, back in the Upper Rhine canalised bits, and he said they were easy as well. But what about all the bumping, was that his little German joke, just to waken up the passengers? He got out some paper and drew a diagram showing that the locks were only 12 metres wide, while his boat was just 11.60 wide. On either side, there was therefore only 20 centimetres to spare. The slightest wind, and there usually was a wind round the locks, and you were bound to bump the sides. He certainly did not do it deliberately, oh ho ho, and he laughed and laughed, his great beard quivering like James Robertson Justice's.

He mentioned he had teenage children, so I decided to give him a present, before it was too late, as I didn't want to hump it any further. My Italian Beatles had gone to Graeme Souness, to help him learn the language. I gave the German version to that jolly captain. I wonder what he did with it.

I bid farewell to Giuseppe the purser, who asked again if I thought his remark about prison might rebound on him. Ursula the hostess still looked worried, but managed a quick smile. Four of the Americans asked for my London address, as they were now going to London and would sure like to look me up, but I said I would be away, sorry, still be in Europe, oh for a long time, what a shame. Meeting people on a journey, liking them and sharing the excitements is one thing, but one does not necessarily want to see them again. In only three days, I had glimpsed into the lives of so many people, which is what happens, when you travel alone.

Thackeray noticed this on his 1851 Rhine trip, when he was with his daughters, looking back to his 1830 trip when he had been on his own.

'Travelling as paterfamilias, with a daughter in each hand, I find I don't like to speak to our countryfolks, but give myself airs rather and keep off them. If I were alone I should make up to everybody. You don't see things so well *à trois* as you do alone. You are an English gentleman, you are shy of queer looking or queer speaking people, you are in the coupe, you are an Earl, confound your impertinence.'

I was finishing my last lunch when we passed Bonn, birthplace of Beethoven. It looked pretty boring. Not worth the effort of rushing for my camera. Even worse was an industrial town called Wesseling, further along on the same bank. It's a thriving port and oil terminal, but what a price they pay for its prosperity. It looked surreal from the river, a mass of pipes and cranes blocking the skyline, yet the opposite bank was completely rural, open fields, meadows and trees. I suppose looking *from* Wesseling, the world does not look too grim. But living there. Ugh.

The Upper Rhine, now I look back and think about it, was pretty boring, flat and monotonous on either side, with few interesting sights or towns. The central chunk of the Romantic Rhine, short though it is, was far more dramatic and picturesque than I had imagined, which is why I suppose this industrial section, which most major rivers have, seemed so very ugly. It's not just Wine and Legends and Castles that the Rhine is famous for today. Sewage, that's also pretty big. It takes a fortune to keep it from being completely polluted, but even so, bathing is prohibited on hygienic grounds. Now there is nuclear waste being discharged into it, from various power stations. The Rhine is supposed to have some fish once again, but I never once saw any fishermen.

I got my bags packed and went on deck to await our arrival in Cologne and stood watching all the barges. I had enjoyed the little glimpses of these cart horses of the Rhine, slowly chugging up and down, floating homes which just happen to be hundreds of feet long and full of coal in the middle, with a living room and bedroom stuck all alone at one end. I liked it best when I was sitting early in the morning in my cabin, suddenly finding myself staring almost eyeball to eyeball with a bargeman's wife, in a headscarf, hanging out her clothes along the boat, or putting a child into his brightly painted steel play pen. Many of the barges carried a brand new looking car, slung on at the end, a strange addition to these ancient barges, the family's little run-about for when they reach dry land. Almost every barge has a bike, leaning against a rail, or a dog, mooching about the deck, as if he think's he's going somewhere.

Just past Wesseling I noticed some graffiti, about the first I had noticed anywhere in Europe. 'Heil Hitler' it said, daubed on some concrete slabs facing the river.

I caught my first sight of Cologne after we'd gone under an enormous suspension bridge, the Rodenkirchen, said to be the longest in Europe, according to the indefatigable guide book. I thought the one across the Humber was longer, though that might not be a suspension bridge. 'Longest' and 'bridges' are always a matter of opinion as you can define them so many ways.

The twin spheres of Cologne Cathedral looked most dramatic, but as we got nearer they became less so, rather grim, stuck in a wilderness of modern looking blocks. It was raining when we landed, which didn't help, and the gangways ahead, into the town, seemed to be under construction, with mud and builders' rubble all over the place. It made the memory of the cruise seem brighter than ever.

I left the *Europa* feeling quite nostalgic, having crammed a little lifetime into only three days, and also a lot of food and drink. The Rhine views had been exhilarating, but I looked forward now to some more physical exertions.

# IV
# BADEN, BELGIUM & HOME

Freikarte

67027-S

Herr · Frau HUNTER DAVIES

UK

24. JUNI 1985

Nr. 0122

Nicht übertragbar. Bitte Rückseite beachten und unterschreiben.

F

SPIELBANK
CASINO
BADEN
BADEN

Die Direktion

# ~ Chapter Seventeen ~

# Baden Baden

*Health and efficiency;*
*on arrival at a terribly grand hotel;*
*a very short history of Baden Baden;*
*a small loss in a great place;*
*drinking in the Trinkhalle with*
*Mr Mark Twain.*

A Grand Tourist was after lots of things. He wanted an intake of Culture, and he was hoping Italy would provide most of that. He was hoping to improve his all round Education, about history, languages, and he expected his whole tour would provide that. He was also interested in Nature, to have visual experiences, and he knew in advance that the Alps and the Rhine Valley would be natural wonders he could not miss. Fourthly, he was hoping for a few more basic sorts of experiences. Pleasure in other words, good times, which could range from wine to women, gambling to sports, and very often all of them.

There was also a fifth object – Health. And after too much indulging in some of the others, especially the more basic pleasures, he was more than ready to begin a period of denial, in the hope that it would do his Health some good. A Grand Tour was always considered a healthy activity, and many made it their first priority. But you could also take in Health as part of the optional extras, a peculiarly European experience which must be encountered along the way.

Germany and the Low Countries were where you took your cure, stopping off on the way home to tone up the old and battered body, or get rid of any specific ailments. The idea of a 'cure', in English, sounds something of an exaggeration, as if they could ever possibly guarantee to cure your troubles, though if you read the literature, both then and now, that was and is still what many are promising. It is safer to think of 'cure' in the sense of care, and that was what I was hoping for, heading for Germany's best known resort, intending to get as much cure, I mean care, as I could manage.

There has been an enormous boom in German spas in the last fifteen years or so, and now there are over 200 flourishing spa towns and villages. Do they know something we don't know? Have they actually got *better* natural springs, which contain secret ingredients missing from our British rocks? No, the reason for their success is slightly more mundane. It is true that traditionally the German public, and the German medical profession, have been more slavish in their belief that thermal water can be a cure, but there is one vital factor which exists in Germany and not in Britain: you can get it on the National Health.

Around 1970, the German government introduced a system whereby you were entitled to three weeks a year at a health spa, in addition to normal paid leave, just as long as your doctor prescribed it. Most of them did. The Social Security system paid your medical bills, and most of the residential bills as well, within certain limits.

Immediately, ancient spa resorts all over Germany started doing a roaring business. Doctors wrote out the appropriate prescriptions for almost anyone with a headache, or feeling tired and run down, and at the same time the local state governments poured millions into development grants, helping the spas to build new accommodation and provide new amenities.

One of the resorts which benefited from all this was Baden-Baden, though really, Baden-Baden was doing well anyway. Its position as the smartest spa resort in Europe is pretty secure, and has been for a hundred years, ever since it was known as the summer capital of Europe. It would have taken more than a passing medical fashion, or some temporary economic trend, to affect its position and status.

*     *     *

I had decided to do things in style and I wrote off in advance from London to the town's leading hotel, Brenner's Park Hotel, which the *Good Hotel Guide* described as the last word in opulence and grandeur.

Three weeks went past and I heard nothing. What had happened to the famous German efficiency. I began to assume that my card booking a room had not arrived, so I eventually rang. It took me a while to get through to the relevant reservation department and a female voice, after some searching, said yes, my postcard had arrived, but they were full. Then why had they not informed me? Oh, well, we were hoping a room might come up, please hold on. After a long delay, I was then told a room would be free for the nights I wanted, but just a small one, would that be all right? I said fine, then I hung up and sent off a stinking letter to the manager. British writer, working on a terribly important book, have to make plans well in advance, etc, what on earth was his staff playing at?

It made me feel pretty good. Can't beat being in the right for giving one a sense of self righteousness. It rarely happens to me. I'm usually the one in the wrong when it comes to arrangements.

When I got the hotel's brochure in the post, I began to wonder if perhaps I was stepping out of my class and would in the end be put in my humble place. The lavish colour printing, the heavily embossed paper, the exquisite typography and the words, my God the words, I practically had to lie down and rest as they too were equally rich and overpowering.

'Enter this leafy word. This domain of noble forbears. This globe of dignity and grace. This shelter of the civilised. This habitat of piquant change. This realm of exuberant well-being. This refuge from the common place. This sphere of elegance. This ambient world where joy prevails.'

Oh Gawd. And that was just the introduction. They hadn't yet got on to the yummy photographs, never mind the bedrooms.

'Rest amid the Brenner's comforting folds. Gracious, serene, cloaked in tradition, affectionately watched over by mindful staff, the Brenner's style is the unwavering beacon in a gaudy world.'

Brenner's is said to be the most expensive hotel in Europe, if not the world, with the top suites, according to my 1985 brochure, costing up to 1400 marks. By my reckoning, that's around £350. Well, high class, hand tooled, dripping prose does not come cheaply. There was also a note, in capitals, which warned NO CREDIT CARDS. What had I let myself in for?

There was a long line-up of clipped and handsome blonde reception persons when I arrived to check in, immaculate in full dress uniform, charming for Germany and terribly welcoming. One of them immediately said that someone called von Halem wanted to see me. Oh no. Was I going to be up before the beak already. I should not have sent that cheeky letter of complaint. We impoverished Brits should stick to Butlins, or at a pinch the Club Med, rather than brave the majesty of Brenner's.

Brenner's Park-Hotel in Baden-Baden
AN DER LICHTENTALER ALLEE

A tall, very stately lady arrived, looking very much like Lady Antonia Fraser, and gave me her card which said Margarethe von Halem, Director of Guest Relations. It would be her pleasure and duty to help me in any way, during my stay at Brenner's, to give me any advice and guidance on the hotel and the town and the immediate locality.

Had my complaint resulted in me being given extra special treatment, or at least a high class minder to check the silver when I left? Certainly not, she said. As Director of Guest Relations, it was her job to help *all* visitors to the hotel, a friendly person, someone to turn to. In a big hotel like this, with many many staff, and a very hard working manager, it was found that new guests did like the personal touch, to ease them into all the comforts and delights. I thanked her profusely. I certainly needed all the help I could get. In that case, she said, how about lunch, at my convenience of course. I accepted. It couldn't be a trap, could it, a beautiful spy setting me up for some mysterious purpose? What could she be really after? Oh, if only I hadn't given that German Beatles book to the Captain.

I went upstairs to my room which turned out to be enormous. I had been given a massive suite, not the simple room I'd ordered, with two rooms large and grand enough to hold banquets in, plus a bathroom about the size of our London house. The furniture was all antique, the sort you see in Bond Street showrooms. It reminded me of the last time I was in Buckingham Palace. And the curtains, my dear, the curtains. There was enough material draped round

the four gigantic picture windows to have clothed the Albert Hall, with a bit left over to cover the Memorial.

I wandered round inspecting everything, but hardly daring to touch. I counted six different displays of fresh flowers, a bowl of exotic fruits, chocolates compliments of the management, a selection of stationery, and a bottle of wine. I should be giving a garden party, not just kipping down for the night on my own. I had come to explore the delights of Baden Baden, but it would take me long enough just to explore my own suite. I looked for my notebook, to list all the objects, but I'd already lost it. In wandering round, I had put it down somewhere, on some priceless bureau, some polished table, some chaise longue, but on which one and in which room?

A swim. That would be the thing before lunch. A straightforward few lengths up and down, nothing fancy. Did one take a towel from the bathroom? Could one walk down the corridors in one's cossie? Should I dial extension nine, Guest Relations, and ask for Frau von Halem. What a jerk that would make me sound, as if I'd never been in a posh hotel before. I walked down the corridor of my suite, some twenty yards long, because I measured it, not to be confused with the hotel corridor. I gently opened the front door of my suite and peeked out. There were no signs of other guests, with or without swimming costumes, just glimpses in the distance, down the vast hotel corridor, of silent, starched white staff, going about their business.

The swimming pool was on the ground floor, a picture window at one end, looking out over lush parkland, while the other walls were decorated with marbled decorations. I do like a swimming pool with fresh air and real sky to be seen.

There were only two people swimming, an old lady silently crawling away and a younger, rather tubby, grumpy looking gentleman who was floating vertically in the deep end as if under hypnosis. As I stepped into the pool, having had a shower first like every well brought up municipal swimmer, a young maid all in white stepped out from behind a marble pillar and removed my wet footprints with three, quick efficient sweeps of a large, squelchy rubber brush, leaving no trace or signs that I had ever existed, far less jumped into their precious swimming pool. When I came out, the same happened. In a twinkling, my drops and flops and prints had been wiped away. The moving swimmer swims and having swum, swims on.

I contemplated all the oils of Arabia in my bathroom. Now, what should I stun the good lady with, though she must have smelled them all before. There's probably a Brenner's smell, which every guest takes on, once having helped himself to the toiletry freebies. I shampooed my hair, not that it needed doing, not that I had picked up any nasty municipal chlorine as the hotel pool had felt thermal fresh, but the stuff was there and by golly I was going to use it, whatever my room rates turned out to be. I tried some mysterious looking after shave stuff, but it stung like acid and I screamed, then I worried that the noise would bring forth another unseen maiden in white from behind a pillar who would glide to my assistance. I gently unscrewed the top of some eau de cologne, but that smelled a trifle garish. My skin did feel rather dry, though, after that energetic swim, so I quickly dabbed some bath gel on to the old physog, having read the instructions that it was suitable for bodies. And thus I went downstairs to greet Frau Von Halem. Lucky woman.

I let her advise me on the menu, being an obedient guest, and I now can't quite remember what it was, except there were far more glasses than courses and far more hovering waiters than courses and glasses put together. The dining room was practically empty. It was like being on stage in a competition, a practice guest, picked off the street, as they do in hair dressing contests, so that all the waiters in turn can perfect being obsequious and thoughtful on bodies who are not going to object or react.

For the last two years she had been at Brenner's, which of course, no question, was the most expensive and most luxurious hotel in the whole of Germany. Every civilised German had heard of it. Did I realise it was also the only German hotel which gave no reductions at all. In this age of international companies almost every hotel offers corporate discounts to big companies. But no, not the Brenner's. Hmm, I could see problems ahead with the cost of my suite. Would I have to wash dishes, or mop up after messy swimmers.

Yes, it was true about the German medical profession, willy nilly dishing out prescriptions for every Tom, Dick and Hans to take the cure at the state's expense. 'I find it ridiculous, all this state help, with the state being responsible not just for your wealth but your health. It is bad morality. I have noticed since this system started that the morale of the country has gone down. It is now almost, and I'm sorry to have to say this, as bad as your country. . . .'

She paused, as if wondering whether a well brought up Guest Relations Manager should insult the country of a guest who had barely arrived, but I said no no, go right ahead, speak freely, I am here to get a true feeling of your wonderful, efficient country, an insight into what the natives really think, and by the way, talking of efficiency, why did your rotten reservations department never reply to me?

This rather stopped her flow. She looked evasive. Oh terrible, terrible, can't apologise enough. I've looked into it, and they were just checking things, I gather. Someone will be for it, no excuses. I'd been put in a suite, not a single, at no extra expense, to make up for it. She hoped I liked it.

Had I noticed the curtains? Noticed them? I had practically got lost in them. Walk into one of those folds and you might not reappear for days.

'All made in England,' she boasted. 'Not only made in England, the men come all the way from Mayfair, London, to actually hang them. No German could do that. No German could make curtains like you do in England.'

She beamed and I felt I had to beam as well, realising some terrific compliment was being made. Oh, we might be lazy, have no work ethic, skive on the National Health, but by golly, when it comes to running up a few velvet drapes, we're world beaters.

After lunch, I was given a conducted tour of the hotel. I had requested it, thinking it was the obvious place to start. Brenner's itself is one of the sights of

Baden Baden. I had hoped to see the manager, Richard Schmitz, but he was in New York. She spelled his name out carefully, just in case I got it wrong. Germans called Schmitz originate from Cologne and are very proud of it, whereas your common or garden Schmidt comes from, well practically anywhere. So get it right.

The hotel is divided, like Gaul, into three. There's the hotel proper with all its stately bedrooms, public rooms and gourmet restaurants. The staff number 230, the guests when full 160, so the ratio is rather generous. Then there's the Lancaster Beauty Farm, which is apparently a trade name, like Elizabeth Arden, and not named after the English town. The third element is the Schwarzwald Clinic which is in effect a little hospital, a private Harley Street style clinic with all the latest medical equipment and eight different specialists on hand. You can have plastic surgery, and many famous beauties, or passing beauties, come here, taking the treatment, keeping very very quiet till it is all over. Or there's the gland treatment, a form of injection to help the ageing hide their age, which I had always thought was partly legend, and millionaires were only ever *supposed* to do such things. All it costs is money. Most of the specialist treatments start at around 1,000 marks.

In Baden Baden, especially in the best hotel, one expects such extra medical facilities, in a town which has always been known for its health. But you don't have to lash out to that extent. You can simply take the waters, as millions have done for centuries.

*       *       *

The first people to partake of the waters in Baden Baden were the Romans in 80 AD. They named it Acuae Aureleae, after the Emperor, Marcus Aurelius, the last of the so called good Emperors. (After him, according to Gibbon, it was downhill all the way.) The Emperor Caracalla, in the 3rd century, was not such a goody, but he was brought here after he was wounded in battle and built a thanksgiving temple – the remains of which were discovered in the late nineteenth century. He swore that the thermal springs had cured him, which has endeared him to the locals ever since. Elsewhere, his fame is for rather different activities. He was the one who had his father in law executed, killed his own wife and then went on to kill his younger brother.

It was not until the end of the eighteenth century that Baden Baden became famous once again for its natural springs. (Its modern name, by the way, comes from a local family called Baden, not from its bathing qualities.) After the French Revolution, aristocracy flocked to Baden Baden, taking up permanent residence, and many fine buildings and gardens were built. By the 1830s, it was attracting about 15,000 visitors a year. One visitor called Dr Granville, who inspected the town in 1837 (and later published a book about German Spas), praised the waters but was rather critical of the behaviour. 'The morality of the temporary inhabitants of this watering place must be of a very low standard and licentiousness would seem to be tolerated.'

Thackeray came in 1851 with his two daughters, by then a very respectable married man, but didn't stay too long as he also thought the place was rather wicked. His wife, who suffered from mental problems, went for a spell to a spa town not far away on the Rhine (at Boppard), where she was subjected to the most fiendish sounding water cures. Buckets of ice cold water were poured over her head, followed by hot blankets, until the sweat streamed off her. After a month of this daily treatment, Thackeray considered she was 'extraordinarily better'. (But it didn't last long when they got home, and she spent the rest of her days in various institutions as an invalid.)

In the middle of the nineteenth century, it was the turn of the Russian aristocracy and writers, amongst them Turgenev and Dostoyevsky. Dostoyevsky lost money gambling, while Turgenev was infatuated by a lady called Pauline Viardot. He took up residence in Baden Baden for many years and set one of his novels in the town, *Smoke*, which was published in 1867. It gives a vivid picture of life amongst the emigré community in Baden Baden in the 1860s. According to Turgenev, the Russian aristocrats had their own tree in the Lichtentaler Allee where they used to meet, but they were so busy putting on airs and graces, being as haughty and superior as possible, that when they actually sat down and talked, they had nothing to say to each other. He described other residents as being 'effeminate looking Germans, American spiritualists, hot blooded devotees of the local *dames aux camélias*, card sharpers, people who thought the English poor tax was a tax on the poor, and the many women in whose arms Chopin had died.'

*       *       *

I set off to explore the town, looking first for the Lichtentaler Allee, whatever that might be. I'd read stories about it everywhere. A Duke of Hamilton had once led a calf along it on a blue riband to win a bet. The Prince of Wales ran along it in a white sheet, hurrying to a ghost party. Queen Victoria, Bismarck, Napoleon III, Kaiser Wilhelm all rode along it rather sedately. The King of Prussia nearly met his end amongst its trees when someone tried to assassinate him there in 1861. Then of course all those other famous people who took Baden Baden in on their Grand Tour had a stroll along it, such as Victor Hugo, Schiller, Liszt, Wagner, Brahms, Berlioz. But what was it? Some sort of narrow, cobbled, medieval alleyway. Or perhaps a grand boulevard.

It turned out to be a simple tree lined path, modest but pretty enough, running along the banks of the little river Oos. Brenner's Hotel leads directly on to it. The main street of Baden Baden is fairly ordinary, typical of many German towns. It's the park land hidden behind which is so attractive. It reminded me of strolling along the backs in Cambridge.

I turned left at the end of the Lichtentaler Allee, clutching my guide map to the town. It was one of those beautifully ornate maps, in full colour on sort of vellum paper, with all the main buildings done as paintings, like a posh architect's plan, lovely to look at, but hell to use as the scale is all to pot.

I eventually came to the vast Kurhaus, built like a Palace, which is not in fact a Kur house these days, unless it can be considered as the perfect cure for those burdened by too much money. It's the town's Casino, the oldest in Germany, which dates back to the 1820s, preceding the Casino at Monte Carlo by about forty years. There was gambling in Baden Baden from around 1801, as various hotels set up tables for the amusement of guests, even though the government and the church, as in almost every country in Europe, banned all games of chance. But somehow, in bathing establishments, the authorities usually looked the other way.

Why should gambling and bathing traditionally be connected? The Romans did both, in the same building, as anyone can see who visits the bath houses on Hadrian's Wall. At Chester, they've found a gaming board and little figures carved out of stone which could have been counters. Seneca in one of his essays describes what it was like if you were unlucky enough to live near a Roman bath house, with the groans of weightlifters, the slapping of the masseurs, the splashings of the swimmers, the cries of the sausage sellers, referees calling out scores in some game and the howls of people having surplus hair removed.

It was quite a palaver to get in. Luckily, I had brought my passport, in fact in Europe I had grown accustomed to carrying it everywhere, especially in Germany. The reason for the close scrutiny, however, before you can get into the Casino, is that no locals are allowed. You have to live at least twenty kilometres outside Baden Baden, or have a special letter from the Mayor, before you have a chance. You must also be over twenty-one. What are they frightened of? That the locals will go mad and bankrupt themselves? Or are they saying that gambling is a stupid pastime, fit only for half witted visitors.

It was mid afternoon, and not very full, but I had no eyes at first for the gamblers. I don't think I have ever been in such a splendid public building. The enormous rooms were like theatrical sets, created and decorated by some mad millionaire as a showplace for the Second Empire. It reminded me of the interior of Queen Victoria's private railway carriage, the one you can see at York Railway Museum, but only a thousand times larger, with equally preposterous furnishings for a mundane activity. Vast rooms fitted with white marble, gold leafed woodwork, fountains, chandeliers, sculpture, paintings, murals, frescoes, ornate fireplaces, Aubusson carpets. I had to shield my eyes from the glare.

As for the gamblers, they were something of a disappointment. How anyway could mere 20th century humans compete with all that glitter. They were mainly youngish men, in their thirties, wearing jackets and ties, as demanded, but quite a few looked rather, shall we say, ungentlemanly, in fact rather grubby as if they might have come off the night shift and hurriedly shoved on a tie. Several looked Turkish, perhaps immigrant workers from elsewhere in the state of Baden Württemberg.

It was such a contradiction. Old Father Rhine, watching from his fresco, surrounded by priceless treasures of high Victorian art and good taste, must these days be rather appalled by some of the sights below. The gamblers themselves seemed aware of their surroundings, miniature men, slumped round the little green tables, as if they had accidentally all walked into the wrong place and the wrong century.

I asked to see the Manager, Baron Hartmut von Richthofen, a nephew of the famous wartime German ace pilot, but he was not in. I talked to an under manager who said the afternoon guests were yes, perhaps not quite the same as the evening guests. When full, the Casino can accommodate 2,500 gamblers at its 35 tables, which it usually does in August and September, their busiest months of the year which is when the races are on.

I can't understand gambling, either the desire or the rules, but I saw a roulette table in the Red Hall which had a notice saying Minimum ten marks. I thought what the hell. Let's have a little flutter. I wasn't quite sure what to do with my precious ten marks, so I watched for a few minutes as the croupiers in evening dress raked in the counters, and I realised I had to change my real money for their pretend money. I stuck my counter on number 13, just because it was empty and seemed rather lonely. The wheel was spun, the rake came out again, life went on, the world kept turning, and I had lost. Well, he paid me nothing. So I suppose that was a clue.

Mark Twain visited Baden Baden in 1879, when he was on his grand tour, but really for the purposes of writing a book, oh it's all been done before, which the world still knows and loves as *A Tramp Abroad*. He was pretty unpleasant about the tradesmen of Baden Baden, finding them rude and trying to be superior, hating Americans, disliking the English, and only being polite when they were serving Russian or German aristocracy. He said they swindled poor visitors and in the case of some Americans, chucked back their money with disdain, refusing to take foreign money. 'If you wish to see what abyss servility can descend, present yourself before a Baden Baden shop keeper in the character of a Russian Prince.'

He visited the Trinkhalle, which I realised was almost next door to the Casino, just as all good visitors have done for the last 200 years, to have a glass

**THE SEASON AT BADEN.**

MR. ROBINSON TAKES A SEAT AT THE ROULETTE TABLE.

MR. ROBINSON IN THE COURSE OF AN HOUR.

MR. ROBINSON HAVING LOST THE WHOLE OF HIS MONEY "À LA ROULETTE," WORKS OUT HIS HOTEL BILL.

of the water which has made Baden Baden famous. It looked more like a Palace than a Pumphouse, grand enough to be an opera house, though all they do inside is dispense glasses of hot water. Should I try it? Spa water often tastes like rotten eggs, and smells worse, but of course the whole psychology of the Cure is that if it tastes bad – it *must* be good for you.

'They don't *sell* this hot water,' so Mark Twain wrote. 'No, you go into the great Trinkhalle and stand around, first on one foot and then on the other, while two or three young girls sit pottering at some sort of ladylike sewing work and can't seem to see you, polite as three dollars clerks in a government offices.'

Eventually, one lady, rather contemptuously, did draw a glass of hot water and set it down before Twain. He asked how much, and she replied, with elaborate indifference, 'Nach Belieben.' (What you please.)

This interchange is repeated over and over again, in fact Twain devotes a whole page to it, well I suppose it's one way to fill up your book, till at last Twain gives in and slides a silver twenty-five cent piece in her direction, hoping to wither her with his sarcastic smile. She pockets the coin, but not before biting it, to make sure it was real. Poor old Mark Twain. Would anyone treat Americans like that today, especially one shoving silver around?

I must admit that the two ladies in white coats who seemed to be in charge were preoccupied with other things when I approached, arranging some flowers, and I had to hang around to get their attention. I noticed that the price of a glass was three marks, so at least it is made clear today, but I found I had no change. I explained this to one of the ladies, in faulting German, and she replied in faulting English, but very pleasantly, that I could have a glass for free.

She picked up a tea towel which was covering a tray of clean glasses, ready for visitors, and two large flies immediately buzzed out from underneath. She and her companion immediately started yattering away in German, blaming each other, chasing the flies, trying to swat them with their tea towels. When they had finished, satisfied that the pump room was now fly free, one of them poured me out a glass of spa water.

Mark Twain does not describe the taste of the famous water, as he was presumably too occupied by the behaviour of the attendants, but I have to report that it was remarkably pleasant. There was no smell and it was clean and clear, rather warm and tasting ever so slightly salty. I drained my whole glass and stood still, trying to work out if I felt better already, or was it just the delightful surroundings and the nice German ladies.

# ~ *Chapter Eighteen* ~

# Taking the Waters

*The remarkable Dr Lang;*
*an encounter with some Americans in the*
*Roman–Irish Bathing establishment,*
*and a slap on the posterior.*

Taking the waters means not just taking them in, by having some quick gulps of the local thermal stuff, straight out of the ground, but also taking oneself *into* the waters, immersing all over, splashing around, perhaps even having them poured all over you. Oh no, not that cold water treatment Mrs Thackeray had. Then I remembered. The natural water in Baden Baden is hot.

I went first of all to see the person who looks after the spa things in Baden Baden, in fact the lady said to be the most important in the whole town. I had mentioned her name in passing the previous day at the Casino, saying I hoped for an appointment with her, and they were all most impressed, do pass on regards, if you manage to see her, mention our name.

I'd presumed she must be the town's information officer or tourist officer, when I'd first been given her name by the German Tourist Office, back in London, and expected to turn up and find a harassed elderly person, stuck in some corner of an office, giving out ancient hand-outs with very little knowledge of what was really going on in the town. In my experience, that's usually what small town tourist information officers are like.

Dr Sigrun Lang was a surprise. Her office was enormous and she was very elegant and chic, a clever looking lady in her forties, with a first degree in architecture, and another in engineering. On her card it said she was managing director of '*Der Bader-Und Kurverwaltung*'. Hmm. But what exactly is that?

Well she does give out tourist literature, at least her staff on the ground floor do that, but it's just a minor occupation. Dr Lang in fact controls a company employing 450 people and her annual budget is around 50 million marks, or £12 million. Everything in the town seems to revolve round her office.

For a start, there is the theatre and the Baden Baden symphony orchestra, then the Baths, all the various Spa amenities, the Casino, park facilities, conventions, advertising, plus building and engineering departments, all of which she controls. Her company does not necessarily own any of the buildings, as they are the property of the local council. She is simply responsible for their efficient running.

I had not to think all German resorts ran their tourism on these lines. Her company, which is semi-private, is unique. Elsewhere, the local council usually does what she does. One third of her income comes from the various Spa enterprises, while the rest comes from the Casino. A different company actually operates the Casino, but they own the gambling licence, and for this her company takes about 60% of the Casino's takings.

Her job is to run Baden Baden's amenities efficiently, think of new ones, and market and promote Baden Baden to the world at large. She is obviously proud that they are doing it so successfully. The town itself is very small, with only 35,000 residents, plus another 15,000 in the immediate villages, yet they attract 250,000 visitors a year, or a total of 800,000 bed nights.

Dr Lang's fame as a Health Spa Promoter and Exploiter is known internationally and she is in demand for her advice overseas. She was recently in Britain, where our many ancient spas would love to have the success of Baden Baden. She even gave a talk in Bath.

'I was asked the secret of our success,' she said with a smile. 'It's very simple. To have a successful spa town you just need one vital factor – a Casino.'

About one third of the visitors come for Health reasons, mostly German, taking the cure in some form, often *before* they feel sick, which is of course the sensible thing to do. One third come for the Conventions, again almost all German, and the final third come purely for their Holidays. About 44% of these holidaymakers come from abroad, with Americans being the most prominent, followed by French and Swiss. The Brits hardly seem to make the rankings, poor things, they just have not got the money perhaps, or are not aware of the wonders of Baden Baden. There was a permanent English community at one time, before the war, but not now. The town's tennis club, which claims to be the oldest in Germany, was founded by the English. Now, even the English Church has become Lutheran.

On the health side, the main cure they are offering is for rheumatics, and for centuries German doctors have sworn that the Baden Baden waters are frightfully efficacious, but alas, when you are in the Spa business, you always run the risk of fashions and theories changing, hence the need for a smart marketing lady like Dr Lang to be at the helm and see the way ahead.

Yes, it was true about getting the cure on the National Health, but the German federal authorities recently decided that doctors had become far too free with their prescriptions, and made them cut down. Many spas had no advertising, no marketing strategies, no diversification into different attractions, and some, alas, have had a drop in visitors of up to 60%. 'We only lost 3%,' she said, 'but that was worrying enough. Now I think we have them back.'

Baden Baden, being right at the top end of the market, hardly relied anyway on National Health custom. (When a doctor sends you for the cure, it may be free, or part free, but you have to take it at certain places and stay in state aided accommodation.) However, there is a much more worrying development. German doctors, can this be true, after centuries of slavish devotion to the

wonders of thermal waters, are now not as convinced.

'Until very recently, all German doctors, when they were at university, had to pass an exam in Balneologie, the science of taking the waters, but this is not compulsory any more.

'In the last twenty years, there has also been a tendency for more chemical treatment of disease, using drugs which are said to be much faster, and of course there is great pressure from the chemical and pharmaceutical industry. Their lobby is very strong.

'But now there's a return to more natural treatments in the Western world. We're back to health foods and homeopathic medicines. So I think the future is very good for us. But we have to work very hard all the time, to think of new things. In this job, I have to have a new idea every day.'

I said that Mark Twain must have done a lot of harm to the town, and given the Tourist Officers of the 1870s a few heart attacks. Yes, she knew his writing well. She would not deny his complaints, but pointed out that perhaps the local people were not used to Americans in those days. 'Today, our shop keepers try very hard with everyone. After all, it is their living.'

The latest big idea, which was obviously taking up a great deal of her attention, was a brand new Spa Bath due to open in a few weeks' time (in August, 1985) with an outdoor and indoor hot thermal pool. It was going to have a lavish opening ceremony for VIP and media guests with a huge Roman banquet and over 150 people in full Roman uniform.

She handed me some literature, which boasted that 'malfunctions of the body and paralysis following illnesses and accidents will be treated.' So the cure element is still being pushed, despite the jaunty Disney-like cartoon figure in a Roman toga who is featured in all the brochures for the new spa. I turned over and saw it was called the Caracalla Spa. You've called it what?

'Yes, that is a sore point,' she said. 'I did do Latin for nine years at school. I do know all about Caracalla. I know it would have been much better to have called it after Marcus Aurelius, but that name just does not sound right in the German language. Caracalla sounds very good, and in most other languages. That was the most vital thing.

'Only today I've had a letter from a local school teacher, complaining about the name, saying he was the worst Roman Emperor ever. You can't please everyone.'

*    *    *

It was Tuesday morning. Curses. Mixed bathing only takes place at the Roman–Irish Baths on Wednesday and Friday, according to the brochure which shows naked ladies prancing around with naked gentlemen. Another day, another year perhaps.

These are the best known baths in Baden Baden, the highlight of every tourist's visit, and will remain so no doubt, even with the new Caracalla. But where did the Irish come from? I'd asked Dr Lang this and for once she was stumped. She could only suggest that it was a visiting Irish doctor who had recommended them.

I went up the grand steps of the Friedrichsbad, built in 1877 and named after the Grand Duke Frederick, and paid my twenty-five marks entrance fee. It is heavily subsidised, so Dr Lang had told me, and they keep the price down to help visitors as the cost of the amenities far outweigh the income. It did look more like a grand hotel, another version of the Brenner's than a public bath house.

In the changing room, I met up with two Americans, a short jolly moustached man from New York who looked like an Italian waiter and a tall gangling man from Hot Springs, Arkansas, who looked like a cowboy. They were in Germany to sell aeroplanes and spare parts to the Germans, or it could have been the other way round. Anyway, they were on expenses in Baden Baden, doing aero-space business.

'In Hot Springs,' said the Cowboy, 'you can boil an egg in our baths, it's so goddam hot.'

Must be a bit messy, I said, if you make a mistake.

The Cowboy paused and looked at me, but the Waiter laughed and slapped my back. As we were all naked by then, it was rather painful, but we all set off together, making feeble jokes, wondering which room to go into first.

We entered a large bathroom, with tiles and mosaics, and a series of marble slabs in the middle for lying on. You slowly climb up higher, if you can bear it. Hot air rises, as even the Romans and Irish well knew. Eventually we got used to that and moved next door into an even hotter air bath.

In all, there are fifteen stages in the Roman–Irish Baths, a complicated combination of hot air, water or thermal steam, alternated with various cold dips and showers and sprays. It's a sort of multi-scale version of a Turkish bath, though I'm sure Dr Lang would deny that, listing the unique treatment rooms and pointing out all the wonderful properties of their sodium chloride thermal waters. Why, some of the waters from Baden Baden's twenty-eight natural hot springs are radio active. So that must be good for you.

The Roman connections were obvious. The plan of the baths is very similar to the original Roman military baths, with interconnecting rooms and chambers, only today they have hidden behind the tiled walls all their modern heating technology. (The Baths were carefully restored in 1981.)

'Look at me, you guys,' shouted the Waiter.

I failed to find him at first. He was in a semi-crouching position, naked of course, flexing his muscles like Mr Universe, leaning on one hand and standing in an empty niche, just like a Greek statue. Oh, what a joker. There are statues and columns and arches and mosaics and decorated ceilings all over the building. Terribly classical.

You are supposed to spend about two hours, doing the whole sequence of rooms, and at every stage an attendant told us roughly how long we should stay in each room. About half way through the process we all trooped in for a

massage. I was a bit worried at first when the masseur took up a large scrubbing brush, the sort my mother used for the kitchen floor, and started bashing away at my bare flesh, starting on the toes, doing each meticulously, then working his way up the body. The pain was minimised by the fact that he was using lashings of thick, rather oily soapy water.

'Do you speak English?' I asked.

'This is Germany,' he replied, rather tartly. Hmm, had I come across one of the superior types Mark Twain had encountered. He was bashing away silently, working his hands into all my muscles. It felt terrific, but I would like to have talked to him.

I suddenly started giggling. Well, I am rather ticklish. It was the combination of his hands and the soapy water, plus the sight of my two American friends beside me, each being walloped and soaped, but both looking distinctly nervous.

My masseur finished with a resounding slap on my bum, signalling he had finished with me. This too is in the brochure: 'The ceremony ends with the traditional "slap on the bottom" and we are already looking forward to the next time . . .'

In the next room, we all compared notes. The Cowboy had not been at all happy about his massage.

'It was turning on my front that worried me. I've been in the Marines. I know what can happen if you turn your back on certain sorts of guys . . .'

We all enjoyed the main plunge pool, a vast circular pool in a high domed, highly decorated building, which is where the ladies and men meet up in the mixed hours, judging by the photographs. They both mourned the lack of ladies. It was just what they wanted. Their own wives had gone back that very day. Sounded a good business trip, if they had had their wives as well.

'Ronnie Reagan, where are you,' shouted out the Waiter.

He was now lying on his back, looking up at the high domed ceiling. It did look a bit like the Capitol building in Washington.

The last stage of all is Rest and Repose which takes place in a large circular room like a hospital ward. There were about twenty beds laid out, each with a dark green blanket and a crisp white sheet. An attendant tucked each of us in, wrapping the blanket and sheet round us like babies in a cot. It felt marvellous to be cocooned, so cool and comfortable, after the exertions of the thermal baths. It was so silent and relaxing that I became drowsy and soon fell asleep, only to be wakened by the Cowboy in the next bed who was snoring loudly. Then I dozed off again.

Mark Twain, for all his complaints about the local tradesmen, was very impressed by the *Friedrichsbad*. It had recently opened, when he arrived in 1878, and was considered one of the wonders of Europe.

He spent two weeks going to the Baths every day because he was suffering from rheumatism. 'People say that Germany with her damp stone houses is the home of rheumatism. If that is so, Providence must have forseen that it would be so and therefore filled the land with these healing baths.'

# ~ *Chapter Nineteen* ~

# Spa

*A quite interesting journey
to the end of the line;
a rather modest hotel but a most exciting
meeting in the Casino.*

I last visited Belgium almost thirty years ago, when I was a student, hitch hiking round Europe. Everyone tried to hitch hike in those days. I never once thought of taking the train. Have the Motorways killed off hitching, or is it the fault of the cheapo student rail cards? Discuss. We stayed in youth hostels, if we could find any. Today, when my own teenage children have done Europe, they've either slept with friends of friends, or taken a sleeping bag and slept rough. Are hostels now only for oldies?

I caught the Brussels train from Cologne, managing once again to escape the rucksacks, and got out my maps and tried to find Spa, which was pretty hard. I never knew it existed, till I'd started thinking about Taking the Waters and discovered that there really was a place called Spa, from whence the term has come. *Is* a place called Spa. I eventually found it, at the end of a little branch line, but almost on my route home. Change trains at Verviers. If you get to Liège, you've gone too far.

I was all ready when we arrived at Verviers and I crossed the platform where the local train to Spa was waiting, just two coaches, rather worn and faded. I went to the driver's cabin, to check it was the Spa train, as I always like to reassure myself twice, if not thrice. I had not once got on the wrong train throughout Europe. So far. The driver and his mate were sitting with their feet up, eating chips out of a paper. It seemed such a British thing to do, which was a daft thought. The whole world eats French Fries.

I sat myself down in a near empty train, and put my feet up, only to be reprimanded by the driver's mate, who turned out to be the guard. Was he getting his own back for me catching him with his chips? No, I think it was typical of European trains. The guards are very bossy. On English trains they just ignore bad behaviour these days, unwilling to get a load of old abuse, or a thump on the nose.

We set off along a valley, following a little river, passing through deserted industrial villages, with brick terrace houses, very like the North East of England, rather deprived, rather poor looking. Pepinster sounded English, and

I rolled the name easily round my tongue, but Theux defeated me. The valley grew more wooded, more lush and attractive, and I began to think that Spa after all might be a pretty place, though I had no idea what business might be like today, either booming and high class like Baden Baden, or forgotten and decaying like so many local English spas.

It was the English who made Spa. They came first in the 15th Century and Henry VIII's physician, Agostino, is one of the earliest recorded visitors. Spenser mentions it in his *Faerie Queen*, but it was not until the early 1600s that it entered the English language. Two doctors, William Paddy and Richard Andrew, came to Spa to study the mineral content of the waters and when they returned to England they spread the idea of ferruginous waters from Spa being medically very good for you. After their endeavours, almost all English places with natural springs started adding Spa to their name, such as Leamington Spa and Buxton Spa.

Meanwhile in Spa itself, the English arrived in hordes and an English church was erected in 1626. The bottling of Spa water, and exporting it overseas, was also partly an English development. By 1776, the English were so established in the town that an English Club was formed, under the presidency of Lord Fortrose. The Duke of Northumberland, Lord Palmerston, Lord Stewart were all members. They used to meet in an establishment called Waux-Hall, a derivation of the London pleasure house.

But the distinguished visitor who really put Spa on the European map was Peter the Great, Tsar of Russia, who stayed in the town in 1717, along with forty of his companions. A mansion was offered to him, but he chose to live in a tent, mingling with the water drinkers on equal terms. He thought so much of the waters that he consumed twenty-one glasses of it between dawn and dusk. After a month, he was so delighted by his recovery from his various illnesses, that he gave the town a certificate.

It was the custom, apparently, to consume enormous numbers of glasses of the local waters and coach loads of visitors would career round the town, going from well to well, filling themselves up. According to a Baron von Pollnitz, who wrote an account of taking the Spa waters in 1734, this led to some embarrassments.

'The natural effect of the waters causes no little perplexity, particularly amongst the ladies. None will alight first, but each pays the compliment of precedence to the rest, till at the length the most pressing necessity decides it. But as soon as one coach halts, all form themselves into parties and screen themselves under bushes or great stones. At length we get up again and everyone is then in a laughing vein.'

\* \* \*

What would I find today in Spa? I knew it was quite small, just under 10,000, but that was all. I had phoned in advance from Baden Baden to the local tourist information office, asking them to book me a single room. An old hotel or a new hotel? I said an old one, of course. Let's have the atmosphere.

I got out of the station and took a cab to the Hotel, as directed. It was almost ten o'clock at night, so the town was very quiet. From the outside, it looked modest but interesting enough, a flat fronted building, right in the middle of the town, near the Baths and the Casino. Very handy. After Brenner's Hotel in Baden Baden, it might be nice to have something smaller and less pretentious for a change.

Inside, it was not just unpretentious but verging on the run down, as if the toffs had all left a century ago, and nothing much had happened since. I stood alone in a little empty foyer, looking for a bell or button to press. There seemed no sign of life at all. Eventually a tired looking man of about fifty-five arrived, in a suit, but a rather faded one, with dandruff on his shoulders. He looked like Denholm Elliott, and not at all happy with the poor part he'd been given in this minor French movie.

He led me upstairs, along a dark and rather dank corridor, covered in plastic wooden panels, and into my bedroom. It was small and badly furnished. The carpet had a violent blue pattern, the wallpaper was a shocking yellow flock and the curtains were a nightmare of reds. My eyes hurt with the dazzling power of the bad taste. The bathroom turned out to be only a shower and WC, though there was a sort of hip bath, about two feet long.

I couldn't face trying to sleep straight away, as my mind was still full of the day's journey, so I went downstairs again and into the street, wondering if there might be a late night chemist, which would sell me some baby cream, as my face felt dry and flakey, or just anywhere for a cup of coffee or late night drink. The whole town seemed dead.

I crossed the road and climbed up the stone steps of the Thermal Baths, pressing my nose against the glass doors, not knowing what I hoped to see inside. It was hard to read the opening hours, but it appeared to be from eight-thirty in the morning. Perhaps I would give it a try, if I survived the night.

To the left of the building, I noticed the lights of the Casino, an illuminated sign at the top of a rather swish building which announced 'Casino'. There was a nice garden in front and lots of pillars and domes. I went through the main entrance and found myself in a long curved hall, like a theatre foyer, with a sweeping counter, behind which two girls in uniform were standing, staring into space. There were no other customers as far as I could see.

I coughed and asked if it would be possible just to see into the Casino, not to gamble, just a quick visit, sorry to bother them. One of the girls asked for my passport, as ever, and then which hotel I was staying at. She said I was lucky, it was one of the ones on her list, so it meant I could get in for free. She gave me a *Carte d'Invitation* made out in the name of Edward Davies. I had to think twice to realise that was me. I never use my first christian name. Even at school it confused me when health visitors came to inspect teeth or nits and would call out Edward Davies, come here, and I would look around, wondering who it was.

The girl was very charming and friendly and spoke good English, except she asked me, when making out my card, whether it was Tuesday or Thursday. She could never remember which was which. I said in French I always got soldiers and slippers mixed up, which could be much more confusing. I remember once translating a French unseen in which I said a lady put a pair of soldiers under her bed before going to sleep. Oh how the clever clogs teacher laughed.

I went upstairs, as directed, thinking the whole place was empty, then I heard a noise of people talking and followed it to a door which I opened gently. And there was the Casino proper, a large room, very ornate, though nowhere as large or as rich as the Baden Baden Casino. About a hundred people were gathered round five or six tables. It was a surprise to suddenly come across so many people. I didn't have a tie on, which would never have been allowed at Baden Baden, but then neither did many of the people at the tables. They were all ages, men and women, but perhaps with more elderly than young.

I went to the bar and asked for a capuccino, but stopped myself just in time. Ever since entering Germany and Belgium I had been fooled by the capuccino, seeing it on a menu, or hearing people ordering it, only to be given a revolting huge dollop of nasty, synthetic cream on top of perfectly ordinary espresso coffee. Instead, I ordered a beer, although it was a bit late at night to start drinking, either alcohol or coffee, as I was planning to go to bed very soon. I would really have preferred a nice cup of cocoa, but I thought that might sound a bit soppy. I don't think real men drink cocoa.

'Skinhead!'

I had sat beside an elderly man, very merry and affable looking, wearing a smart but old fashioned suit, with a pullover underneath. Was he accusing me? Was this a new sneer for all English people, to make up for the years we have called foreigners Frogs or Krauts?

'Skinhead!'

He pointed across the room to a far table and then gabbled something to me in German. All I could make out, once again, was the word Skinhead.

I looked across and eventually noticed that there was a boy, sitting at a roulette table, who did have very close cropped hair. Nothing remarkable about that. In fact on closer inspection, as much as my eyes could manage at that distance, he might even have had a skin complaint. But I smiled at my friend and nodded.

You call him Skinhead in German? I spoke English without realising, and the man laughed and responded in English. He spoke it pretty well. Yes, Skinhead has passed into every European language now, we all know what it means, same as Punk.

He had come in a bus party from Aachen, along with thirty or so other Germans, mostly senior citizens. There were casinos at home, but it made a nice weekly outing, coming across the border to Spa. The Casino organised the buses. 'I always think it will improve my luck, coming here, and it usually does. Spa is a very nice place.'

'Don't listen to him,' said another old man, turning suddenly from a table, looking rather disgruntled. 'This is a dump. All Belgium is a dump. And there aren't even any hookers.'

His English was so good, and so colloquial, and he had spat out the words quickly, that I didn't at first know whether he was serious or not. He looked so fierce, the way old men often do when trying a joke, hoping to catch you out, then they go away, laughing to themselves for hours at their own wit.

'He's just lost his money,' said my friend. 'That's why he's so upset. Take no notice of him. Will you have another beer?'

He'd been a widower for twenty years, a retired soldier, just an ordinary soldier he said, nothing important. I asked if he had fought the Brits but he said no, he fought the Russians, at least he was sent to Russia, but he didn't do any fighting. 'All I did was a lot of writing.' He then told me a long story about a consignment of vodka which they captured, or pinched, but when they retreated, they had to leave it all behind. He laughed all the way through the story. In fact he laughed a lot, slapping me on the back. Then he asked me what I was doing and why I was alone. I explained my Grand Tour project.

'Over there,' he said, taking my arm. 'Don't stare. That woman. Wait till she turns round. Sitting on that high stool. She's the chief croupier. Very nice, huh?'

I agreed, though I wasn't sure which one he was pointing out. There seemed to be three girl croupiers, all blonde and smart looking, terribly cool and superior.

'Now, look, she's turned. That one. She's English! She could do very well for you, no.'

There was then a lot of winking and nodding, just as he had been winking and nodding when he'd first tried to get me interested in the skinhead. I asked him if he was sure. Certainly, he said. Caroline or Carole, one or the other. He had talked to her in English. No question.

I bought him a beer and eventually got my tired eyes trained on the so called English croupier. I only wished I'd brought my specs. Seeing across any large room these days, or watching a football match, or sitting in the cinema, is hell.

There seemed to be a lull around her table, so I carefully went over, nudged on my way by my German friend, with a few leers and sniggers. There were two heavies in evening dress, watching me carefully. I waited for a while behind a little red rope, which I'd stumbled into, trying to catch her attention. I suppose all night long, every day of the year, there are strange blokes trying to catch her attention, coming out with the same sort of inane chat. But an English girl, in this back of beyond small town in the Ardennes, how had she come here?

'Excuse me,' I said at last, when she obviously must have realised I was trying to attract her attention, though she had steadfastly ignored me. 'Scuse me. I gather you're English. Where from?'

She went on instructing another croupier in French who was working the table. I asked my question again, adding that I was an English writer, just passing through, so I'd be grateful if she could spare me a few minutes for a chat. I had to shout quite loud, as she was several yards away, behind several hefty bodies, but at length she turned in my direction.

'You what?' Her gaze was cold and completely lacking in interest.

'Where you from? You are English then?'

'Barrow in Furness,' she said, then returned to her work.

I had to stay now. How amazing. I happen to know Barrow rather well, and can understand anyone wanting to leave that dump, I mean lovely industrial town in Cumbria.

'I can't talk now,' she suddenly whispered. 'I'll come across to the bar later. If I can. All right.'

I nodded and quickly went back to my German friend. He was delighted with my news, and insisted on having another round of beers. We discussed football and Germany's chances in the next world cup and the awful tragedy which had happened at Brussels just a week previously.

She came across, in ten minutes, just as she had said. I moved my stool to give her room, very pleased, looking for a place she could sit down.

'Sorry. I can't stop. We're very busy and the manager's here. I'm not allowed.'

'Tomorrow then, what time do you finish tomorrow?'

She stared around, thought, looked at me carefully, started to shake her head, saying she slept all day really, she didn't really have time.

A coffee in the afternoon, I said quickly, what about that? She nodded her head. Two o'clock at the Louvre Café. Anyone would tell me where it was, then she dashed back to her table.

My friend was very pleased. And so was I. I bought him a final drink, and then immediately left. Spa might have some interest after all. I had tried in Baden Baden to find any English residents, either retired folk or workers, but with no success.

The hotel bedroom did not seem as barren and miserable when I returned. I slept soundly, without waking once. In the majesty of the incredible Brenner's Hotel I had slept badly, kept awake by the Versailles fountain out in the grounds.

# Chapter Twenty

# The Belgian Croupier

*Bubbles in a very strange copper bath;*
*going to the Tourist Office;*
*a walk with Monsieur Marquet*
*and the extremely engaging young*
*Lady from Barrow.*

*I*went downstairs for breakfast, as I always do in hotels. I hate eating in a bedroom. Even in the nicest places, it always seems either decadent or furtive. Denholm Elliott was this time playing the part of the head waiter. His suit was exactly the same, and his shirt, but his collar looked new and he seemed to be enjoying this role a great deal more.

The dining room contained about four other single men, all in their sixties, sitting and coughing and spluttering. I noticed two of them had sticks beside their chairs, presumably invalids, come to take the Spa waters. Denholm Elliott spoke to them in French, so I assumed they must be Belgians.

I arrived at the Baths not long after opening time. In the entrance hall were two fountains, one on either side. One was marked Source de la Reine, so I had a glass of that. It was cold, clear, fairly tasteless, not unpleasant, but I would not like to have swallowed twenty-one a day like Peter the Great. The other was marked Pouhons, a local name for another spring water. There was a very tired looking young man sitting beside it, slowly drinking a beaker full. I studied some literature and learned that Pouhons is rich in iron while the Reine contains little mineral. In each case, the specific mineral contents, all in great technical detail, went on for pages. Drinking a glass of natural water is not enough. They like to impress or baffle you with their science. Baden Baden was the same, only the printing was better and the words, being German, were much longer.

I went to the reception counter and asked two ladies in white, sitting behind an enclosed till, like a cinema, what I could have. Not a lot, was the answer, unless I was under medical supervision. That could take for ever, and I had my mysterious croupier to see at two o'clock. I had a sore jaw, which I'd had for a year, but I couldn't see anything in their brochure for sore jaws.

After some discussions, I opted for a copper bath and a massage. The leaflet assured me that the bath would be very good. 'The ferruginous carbo-gas water gives off carbonic anhydride which is absorbed by the skin within which this gas brings about vasodilatation of the dermic vessels.' Actually, I chose it for aesthetic reasons. In the photograph, the copper bath looked so colourful.

The copper bath itself was absolutely splendid, rich and gleaming, raised high on a floor so I had to step up into it, with a brass rail over the top, bang in the middle of a large, green tiled bathroom. It was completely Victorian, especially when a maid figure in white uniform appeared and ran it for me. I watched in fascination as she turned some large taps on the floor, using both hands to work them, then very slowly water started bubbling upwards from the bottom of the large copper bath. It looked just like fizzy lemonade.

She pointed to some pegs in the corner of the bathroom and told me to get undressed, then left the room while the bath was being filled. When it was full, I got in, sinking gingerly into the lemonade. I tried a taste, and it was a bit like lemonade, sort of fizzy, but very minerally. This is the natural water, which comes out of the earth at 9.6 degrees centigrade, then is heated up a bit more, to 33 degrees, for the bath.

I could hear a slight tick tock sound. I wondered if there was some gremlin below, some water spirit living in the gassy water, then I realised it was a large egg timer on the wall. The lady had set it for a certain time and would no doubt come back when I had my allotted time.

I lay back and luxuriated. It did feel very good. Pouring Sainsbury's bath foam from a plastic bottle into your domestic bath might make it smell good, but the fizziness was an extra element I had never experienced before. I wondered what ass's milk might feel like.

My body began to look funny as the gas slowly started to subside and the bubbles settle. Millions of little gassy bubbles had attached themselves to the hairs of my skin, like underwater frost. Very strange. A complete pubic forest of frost had established itself, but if I moved slightly or even breathed quickly, the forest shattered, the frost scattered like mercury, only to reform and re-frost when I lay still again.

When I'd exhausted all the possible games, I looked round the bathroom, noticing where new tiles had been replaced, where joins were badly done, where pipes needed cleaning, the way you do when you're ill in bed and have only the wallpaper to analyse. There was a little metal box on the wall, with pipes leading to it. Perhaps this was where the water was heated.

I was dozing off when the egg timer suddenly screamed and the maid dashed in and told me it was time to get out. She opened the metal box and produced from it a white dressing gown and gave it to me. It was beautifully hot. Inside the box, were little hot water pipes. They had been heating up the dressing gown for me, while I had been soaking. They think of everything, these thermal people.

The masseur was brisk and uncommunicative. Hairdressers will talk non stop, once given a chance, and so do most taxi drivers, but in my very limited experience of masseurs they seem very short on conversation. A body is a body and their own minds are miles away. It was not a very pleasant massage anyway. All he used was talcum powder and his hands felt rough and dry and I was exhausted afterwards, not invigorated as at Baden Baden.

After it was all over, I asked to see the Director, Louis Donjean, who took me on a tour. I very much wanted to see the peat baths, for which Spa is famous, though you need a medical prescription to use them. We went down into the basement and I saw trolleys of real peat being carried along, very thick and rich and dirty. Some of the bathroom doors were half open and I glimpsed several ladies being covered from their neck downwards in handfuls of peat. 'It is put on very warm and can be very dangerous. It could be bad for the heart, so we don't let the general public use it.'

The public side of their work is the smaller part, catering for chance visitors like me. They are mainly concerned with strictly medical treatment, mostly on the National Health. The majority of their patients come for two weeks of treatment, staying in guest houses and special homes nearby, almost all of them Belgian, sent by their home doctors, getting at least 60% of their bills paid by the state.

The building is owned by the town, but the company is run by Spa Monopole. I had seen this in the town's brochure, but wasn't sure what it was. By the sound of it, they are the centre of local power, as the Tourist Office was in Baden Baden. Spa Monopole manages all the springs in the Spa area, and there are several, plus a large factory which is by far the biggest employer in Spa, with 700 workers. It turns out 2½ million bottles of Spa water every day and is the biggest company of its type in the Common Market. It is open for inspection, but I thought no, a bottle factory did not sound all that fascinating. I can visit them at home, or I can get Beryl Bainbridge to tell me about them.

\*       \*       \*

I headed down the main street to the Tourist Office, wondering if they would be more typical of their breed than the super modern company at Baden Baden. Their advice on a hotel had not been all that marvellous.

The building was very attractive, like a Victorian summer house, but inside it was all open plan, so I could see the man in charge, M. Houyon, talking on the phone, long before he was free to talk to me. There were two girls at the desk, none with very good English, judging by the struggles they were having to explain something to an American who just wanted a simple book on Spa, in English, to buy and take home, as he was only passing through.

All the leaflets looked old, even the obviously up to date ones, printed on cheap lavatory type paper, with little colour, poor printing, awful English. It did add to the impression of Spa as a faded resort, so I was surprised when I eventually talked to M. Houyon and he dug out some facts about how many people visited Spa each year. In 1983, his latest year for figures, 120,334 hotel bed nights were spent by visitors to the town, the vast majority coming from Belgium, 85,295. Then came the Dutch (16,083), West German (10,000), British (2,695), French (1,613), Japanese (860) and Italian (827). Down at the bottom of the list came Russians (17), Portuguese (12) and Mexicans (11).

Business must be quite good after all, though from his figures it was clear that the vast majority of visitors are ill or elderly Belgians, sent by the state for their health reasons, probably not spending much money on fripperies. What a change from the days in which Spa was an affluent, international town, with the cream of the aristocracy from Britain and elsewhere, living it up in the smart hotels and entertainment establishments.

I asked M. Houyon if the Hotel des Pays-Bas still existed, as I knew that in 1848 Thackeray had stayed there, in room 32, and had written the first few chapters of his novel *Pendennis*. He was not a famous author by then, as *Vanity Fair*, though completed, had not yet hit the headlines, but he was nonetheless a bit peeved when the posh hotels of Spa had not considered him to be a real gentleman. In one hotel, he was offered a servant's room, because he was carrying only one portmanteau. 'These miserable miscreants,' he wrote in a letter home, 'did not see from my appearance that I was not a flunkey but on the contrary a great and popular author.'

M. Houyon picked up the phone and I could hear him dialling the local library. Oh no, no, I said, it's not all that important. I could see myself sitting around waiting for hours as I know what libraries can be like. He hung up, saying they were going to ring him back. Now, what else could he tell me. And anyway, what was I doing in Spa?

I explained about my Grand Tour book, and mentioned that I'd met a few well known writers on my travels, such as Muriel Spark. This greatly interested him and before I could stop him, he was on the phone again, saying they had a writer living in Spa and would try to arrange a meeting. Could it be Simenon, about the only Belgian writer I could think of? Had they got a Nobel prize winner I had missed?

It was arranged that a M. Leon Marquet would come to my hotel at one o'clock. I thanked him profusely, how kind to organise it for me, terribly helpful. What exactly had M. Marquet published? He wasn't sure, but he knew he was working on a booklet about the history of Spa. He was a retired school teacher and would be very pleased to meet me.

As I left the tourist office, I picked up a leaflet for a forthcoming summer festival of plays, given by the Belgium National Theatre, and organised by the inevitable Spa Monopole. They were coming for two weeks in August to put on Molière's *Le Misanthrope* and Hugo's *Les Misérables*, good solid French classics, but all the others, to my surprise, were British, modern plays at that, by people like Caryl Churchill and Christopher Hampton. There was even a production of *Trafford Tanzi*, the women's wrestling play set in Manchester. What on earth would the invalids of Spa, full of their ferruginous fluids, make of that?

*       *       *

M. Marquet did look like a retired school teacher, which is not meant to be rude, just that his faded sports jacket and very serious expression made him very recognisable. He had not had a very good shave that morning, though I suppose my face, still peeling, was not all that impressive.

He arrived at my hotel with masses of little books and leaflets and was exceedingly helpful. He had taught English and German at the local lycée and now spent his time researching local history. His main project at present was into the life of a Scotsman called James Skene who was a friend of Walter Scott. Skene had kept a diary of a visit to the Spa area, in which he had recorded a local legend. Scott had used the story in his novel *Marmion*, either the fifth or sixth canto, he wasn't sure, but he could go to the library and look it up. No no, I said, the library is already being overworked this morning.

Did I realise that in 1780, when Spa was filled with the British aristocracy every year, that there had been fifteen hotels in Spa with English names? This did strike me as very interesting, so I asked if he could list them. He got to four, but said he would really, after all, have to check his sources. Perhaps we should take a little walk.

As we walked, he stopped at every building and gave me its history, pointing out fountains and statues. He indicated a plaque put up to American soldiers killed during the war and said the Americans were not very pleased with it. Look what symbol of America the sculptor had used. It was the face of a Red Indian, out of whose mouth a little fountain was spurting. 'Americans don't like to think they are Red Indians.'

I realised we were standing outside a café called the Louvre. I'd forgotten this was where I was going to meet my friend from Barrow, if she ever turned up. I didn't think they would exactly mix, my retired school teacher and the young blonde girl croupier.

I looked at the café – and saw that it was closed. Most of Spa anyway was closed for the lunch hour and was very dead. More complications. Had I made a mistake? Had she just said anything to get rid of me? There were still ten minutes to go, so she might still appear, but would she stand outside and wait for me? What should I do?

While I dithered, M. Marquet was steering me round the corner to the old Town Hall, pointing out some fascinating brickwork, ushering me inside to look at a remarkable staircase, and certainly do not miss those wrought iron banisters, Mister Davieez. I admired everything, at least I hope I did, then I said really, I had to get back to that café, trific though the Town Hall is, yes, the café that's closed, the same one, because you see I've planned to meet someone there. We both went back. Me and Monsieur Marquet.

The croupier was standing there, right outside the Louvre Café, bang on two o'clock. So I introduced them.

*     *     *

Carol was wearing a little black trilby and a long skirt and looked very dashing and glamorous, especially for early afternoon in a very dead Spa.

M. Marquet suggested we all had a look in the Pouhon, a vast hall like a market hall, containing the Spa where Peter the Great had taken the waters. Carol said yeh, she wouldn't mind seeing it. In fact her flat was in the same street, almost opposite, just over there, yet in four years of living in Spa, she had never once been inside that building. Funny how you missed places on your doorstep. Always wondered what went on there.

There was a marble table in the entrance, where Peter had carved his initials in 1717, and the Russian coat of arms in alabaster. Carol and I had a glass of the famous ferruginous water from the spa, Pouhon Pierre le Grand, which was quite pleasant. Then we went into a large hall at the rear, like an empty drill hall, marked on the floor for basketball. We all got something of a fright when the heavens opened and the rain came pelting down on the overhead skylights. The noise was so loud we could hardly speak to each other.

I noticed at one end a vast painting and went over to inspect it and realised it was the original of various reproductions I'd seen for sale in the Tourist office. Yes, this is the famous *Golden Book* painting, said M. Marquet, done in 1894. It was about twenty feet long and contained full size portraits of ninety-six famous Europeans who had visited Spa. M. Marquet smiled and said of course it was a bit of a cheat, all those people had not been in Spa at the same time, not even in the same century. Peter the Great, for example, here in 1717, could never have met the Duke of Wellington, as he arrived 100 years later. But the group was most impressive and I spotted lots of kings such as King Leopold I, Louis Philippe of France, Joseph II of Austria, Gustaf II of Sweden, Tsar Nicholas of Russia, William II of Holland, Empress Eugénie, Charles II of England and Henry III of France, plus Descartes, Dumas, Montaigne, Gounod, Offenbach. Not many British, in the vast line-up, apart from Wellington and Disraeli, but a hell of a lot of impressive foreign titles.

M. Marquet suspects that most of the portraits were copied from the Larousse Encyclopaedia, which is why there were so many European Royalties included. As I examined the splendid painting, working my way down its whole length, almost falling off the stage at one time, I came to a large rip in the canvas, about six inches long, over which someone had crudely stuck a bit of Sellotape. I exclaimed in horror. What a way to treat a national treasure. M. Marquet shrugged his shoulders. That was today's Spa. The past was being forgotten all the time, which was why it was important for him to finish his researches and get it published.

I said that *if* he had to rush off now, back to his researches, that would be fine, if not, well, he was welcome to join us for some coffee. I was just going to have a little chat with Carol. If we could find a place.

The café was still closed when we returned to it, so all three of us came back to my hotel and I ordered three coffees from Denholm Elliott, who had obviously been hoping to have a quiet afternoon. I also ordered a brandy for me and M. Marquet. Carol refused. She would have to start work later that afternoon.

When M. Marquet had finished his drink, he said he would have to rush to the photocopying place. But wouldn't be long. He wanted to give me a copy of an official list of Lords and Ladies which used to be published in Spa every week, back in the grand old days. It meant that when you arrived in the town, you could look up and see which of your friends was in residence. He knew I would be intrigued by all the English names. The list had started about 1751 and had gone on till 1900. I said it did sound fascinating.

He bustled away, so at last I said to Carol, come on then, tell me how on earth you've come from Barrow in Furness to Spa in Belgium. Oh, it's a long story, she said. It's taken me round the world, but I'll tell you briefly.

*　　*　　*

She was a hairdresser in Barrow, clipping away, when one day when she was about twenty she thought what am I doing, where am I going, if I stay here any longer I know I'll end up with two kids on a new estate when what I really want to do is see the world.

So she got a job in Jersey, as a hairdresser. In Jersey she had a friend who was a croupier and who suggested she had a go, telling her there was a lot of money in it, and they always liked young girls. She did it for a bit, liked it, but realised she had to be properly trained. Trained? Oh yes, England is the only country in the world where croupiers are not just officially trained, but they have to be registered and licensed by the Government authorities. No other country does this, that she knows of, which is why English croupiers are wanted everywhere. There's a sort of international circuit of English croupiers, passing on jobs to each other.

She trained in Birmingham and worked at the Rainbow Casino in Edgbaston, then she started her wanderings, round Europe and America. The dodgiest was a Turkish-run casino in Cyprus, just after the troubles. The most glamorous was on the Atlantic cruise liners.

Spa must be rather small beer, after all that. What brought her here?

M. Marquet returned at that moment, bearing handfuls of inky photostats. He'd run me off a few lists and had also copied out the names of those fifteen English hotels he had mentioned from the 1780s. They were La Botte Anglaise, La Belle Anglaise, Duc de Cumberland, Vaisseau Anglais, Cour de Londres, Duc de Bedford, Prince des Galles, Duc de York, Armes d'Angleterre, Prince Charles, Roi d'Angleterre, Voiture Anglaise, Château de Douvres, Hôtel d'Irlande and Château Anglais.

How fascinating, I said. I had noticed few British connections today, apart from a large state looking guest house called Balmoral. But what about the Hotel Pays des Bas, where Thackeray had stayed, what had happened to that? Ah, yes, he would now go to the library and find out.

Carol had come to Spa through friends. Someone had worked here and told her they were looking for English girls. This was four years ago. Now she had risen to be Pit Boss, in charge of Black Jack and American Roulette, with eleven croupiers and five tables to look after. If she was looking after the French Roulette, she would be called Chef de Table. With Black Jack, all Casinos use the American term, Pit Boss.

Her take home money each week, after tax, was usually about £200, but it had gone down recently because the union had insisted on a different distribution of the PB. PB? Pour Boire. Tips. They didn't get a salary. All they got was a percentage of the tips. That was normal in Europe, she said, though illegal in England. In England, it is not allowed to give a croupier any tip, even if you have just won a fortune.

The Spa Casino was thought to be about the poorest in Belgium, in fact out of the eight she knew of, its tips were the lowest, only about £2,500 a night on average. The Directors got most, around 85%, then it was on a points system, depending on how senior a croupier you were. It was all above board. Everyone knew how it was done, both the union and the tax man. There was no fiddling. In English casinos, there were, yes, quite a few crooks around, that was why the British Government was so strict, because they feared the Mafia would move in. 'I've met people with criminal records. They're quite nice people, really, okay to work with.'

The Spa Casino is German-controlled, under licence, and it was run very tightly and efficiently. She felt under pressure most of the time. In England, most casinos are in large centres of population, London, Manchester, or Birmingham, so you have a lot of regular local gamblers you can depend on. 'We're stuck right out in the wilds here, just a little town, plonked down in the middle of nowhere, so we depend on all the coach loads from Germany to keep coming. I suppose fifty years ago Spa was a fairly exciting place to live in. Now it's pretty deadly.'

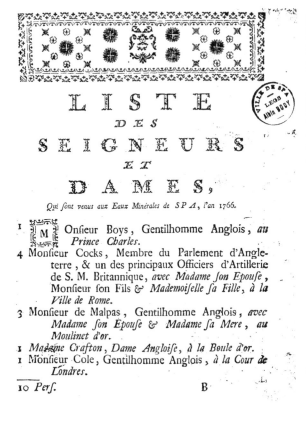

## LISTE
### DES
## SEIGNEURS
### ET
## DAMES,

Qui font venus aux Eaux Minérales de SPA, l'an 1766.

1 Monfieur Boys, Gentilhomme Anglois, au Prince Charles.

4 Monfieur Cocks, Membre du Parlement d'Angleterre, & un des principaux Officiers d'Artillerie de S. M. Britannique, avec Madame fon Epoufe, Monfieur fon Fils & Mademoifelle fa Fille, à la Ville de Rome.

3 Monfieur de Malpas, Gentilhomme Anglois, avec Madame fon Epoufe & Madame fa Mere, au Moulinet d'or.

1 Madame Crafton, Dame Angloife, à la Boule d'or.

1 Monfieur Cole, Gentilhomme Anglois, à la Cour de Londres.

10 Perf.                    B

N°. 3.

Spa, le 26, Prairial, an X (15 Juin 1802, v. ft.)

37 Tranfport.

5 Monfieur J. L. Kien, avec Mde. fon Epoufe, les Demoifelles fes Filles, & Mademoifelle Meerman Vander Goes, d'Utrecht, à la Couronne d'épines, rue de l'Affemblée.

1 Monfieur Skenes, de Rubislau, d'Ecoffe, à l'Hôtel d'Yorck, rue de la Sauveniere.

1 Monfieur Bergallant, à l'Hotel d'Yorck, rue de la Sauveniere.

1 Monfieur Peyrene, de Metz, à l'Hotel d'Yorck, rue de la Sauveniere.

2 { Mr. Henri Barbier, Négociant de Paris. Mr. Florent Damecourt, à l'Hotel de la Pomme, rue de l'Entrepot.

2 Les Demoifelles Haeksolte, au Dragon d'or, Grand'Place.

1 Monfieur Beamish, Gentilhomme Anglais, à l'Hotel du Loup, Grand'Place.

3 Monfieur A. L. Deprez, de Liege, Agent de Meffieurs Dl. Danoot, fils & compagnie, Banquiers de Bruxelles, avec Monfieur fon Fils & Mademoifelle fa Fille, au grand Monarque, Grand'Place.

53 Perfonnes.

So why did she stay? Judging by her various other foreign tours, she had stayed no more than two years. Four years was a long time in a small, out of the way town?

M. Marquet came back with the exciting news that he had found out the address of Thackeray's hotel, but the bad news was that it had been knocked down one hundred years ago. It was now a garage. He could take me to it, though, both of us in fact, he knew the garage very well, it would be most interesting to see. I ordered him another coffee and said no thanks, I'll be catching the train to Brussels this afternoon. Got to move on. We Grand Tourists.

Carol said that technically, casinos in Belgium were illegal, wasn't that strange?

Perfectly true, said M. Marquet. The Spa Casino was built in 1762, said to be the oldest in Belgium, and probably has never been legal, so Leon said. 'They get so much tax from it, they turn a blind eye. In 1762, both the Church and the State said gambling was illegal, but the Bishop of Liège allowed the Spa Casino to operate – and he took one third of the takings. He needed all that money for his mistresses.'

Carol laughed at this. Yes, she said, they were still very keen on mistresses in Belgium.

I waited for her to expand, but I did not wish to be forward, especially as M. Marquet, a local resident was listening. As a passing visitor, going out of her life for ever in half an hour's time, she might tell me, but any name she gave me would be meaningless. Oh no, it couldn't be him, could it? Had it all been a charade, walking round the town in a threesome? I dismissed the thought instantly.

About 75 per cent of the customers were German, she said. They could be a bit brash and pushy, laughing at you and trying to make you look an idiot if they didn't like you. 'Then the next moment they are all over you, loving you.' The Belgians in the Casino, so she found, were calmer and more relaxed. 'I suppose in a way they are quietly arrogant, looking on at the noisy Germans, thinking what fools they are. Belgians don't show emotions very much. They get nervous if they give emotions away. The English tend to be reserved and quiet. The Dutch are noisy. The Americans are the noisiest of all. And they expect everyone to speak English. I met one yesterday in the Casino wandering round lost, and he just grabbed me and demanded very rudely "Where's the washroom?" Now he didn't know I was English, but he just expected to be understood. You would have thought he would have worked out the French for washroom, or even used a word like toilet, which everyone can understand.'

M. Marquet nodded in agreement with these generalisations. He had been so friendly that I decided I could call him Léon from now on. I asked what he thought of the British. 'From my experience they behave differently when they are abroad. At home they are very friendly.'

'I was so ashamed about the Brussels football disaster,' said Carol. 'It was my nephew's fourteenth birthday that day, May 29, and he's an ardent Liverpool supporter. It was going to be his sort of birthday present. I rang him in England – and he'd been crying all day.

'I was off that day, and I didn't go into work for the next two days. I'd never realised till then that I was proud to be British. Now I felt ashamed to be British. I worried what people would say when I went back to work, being the only British person around. They were all very nice, except one Belgian who was a bit shitty. My Mum rang me to ask if I was okay. It will take a long time before it's forgotten in Belgium.'

I asked if she felt homesick, living in such a remote town, with no other English around. She does miss the TV news, but listens to the British Forces Radio every morning in her flat. 'I miss my Mum and Dad and I miss British bacon. They go on about French cooking, but I prefer British.

'I think now, after ten years of wandering, I will go home, settle down somewhere in a little community.'

Go back to Barrow and have those two children and save for the semi on the new estate?

'No way. I didn't say I was getting *married*, although I might one day. I want to start my own little business. Perhaps a hairdressers. I dunno. I've saved all my money, I've been very careful.'

It seemed a long time, four years. Was there something else perhaps keeping her in Spa?

'Oh I quite like it here. There's no social life, no social clubs I can go and meet people my age, but they're all very nice. It's an unviolent country, Belgium, that's one big thing, if you're a single woman. I can walk round Spa at night time and feel no fear at all.

'But I do feel it's time to move on. If only . . .'

I looked at Léon, wondering if an interesting confession was finally coming out.

Yes, she said, there is a local bloke. Makes things very difficult. Older? She smiled.

On the train to Brussels I wondered what would happen to her in the future. Was it a tangle which could be unravelled, or would she be in Spa for ever? Working all night at the tables. Sleeping most of the day. Meeting her bloke secretly. I'd got the impression he was somebody rather important.

When Wordsworth became involved in his European romance, during which his French girl friend became pregnant and he had to leave her, he was only twenty-one. In the end, it did not affect the rest of his life. Carol, from what she said, must be now aged thirty. She would have to be finishing the affair soon, if she wanted to end up with her own business, back in Blighty.

That's the worst of grand touring. You move on, and never know what happened next to the people you meet. I made a note to myself to keep an eye on the *Bookseller*, to see if the definitive history of Spa ever comes to be published.

# ~ Chapter Twenty-One ~

# Euro-Man

*An anthropological expedition;*
*it ends in a German party;*
*surprise pictures on the little box in the corner;*
*the gentlemen of NATO who are looking after*
*us so well.*

There is a new creature at large in Europe these days and I was hoping in Brussels to track him down, to discover him at home in his lair and to observe his working environment, perhaps even roll him over and count his spots and see what makes him function. They never had such animals, in the days of the old Grand Tour, and I personally had never come across one in the flesh, not in his natural habitat. I felt almost on an anthropological safari as I approached Brussels. In search of Euro-Man.

If you read the old Grand Tour diaries and books they were always coming across, much to their surprise, an Englishman who was now running a hotel in a remote Tuscan village, or a Scotsman who had somehow or other become a musician for a Grand Duke in the Rhine Valley, or a Welshman now living in the Low Countries and bottling spa water. There always have been such wanderers, people who have deliberately changed countries, or been dropped accidentally in strange place, flotsam from an army, or jetsam from a life that had possibly gone wrong at home. My croupier friend in Spa is part of this long tradition, an exile working abroad, but considering herself still English, planning one day to return to her native land.

But in the last twenty years there has arisen a new breed of wanderers who will never go home to their birthplace, because that is no longer their home. They have given up their native lands, quite willingly, and have long since ceased to look upon themselves as belonging to any one place. They still, on paper, have their original passports, and can claim citizenship of the land of their fathers, but in their minds, in their day to day work, in their plans for the future, they consider themelves without a home country. They have now, for better or worse, become European.

They expect, in their working lives, to move around, and will go willingly, with no regrets, knowing that wherever they go they will meet up with others like themselves, fellow Euro-men and Euro-women, stateless people, having long floated free from all those boring emotional and family and national ties which for centuries and centuries have kept citizens at home. Euro-man has no real idea where he might end up. Somewhere in Europe. That's about all he can see ahead.

Brussels is the capital city of Euro-man and I estimate that there are at least 20,000 of these new creatures presently residing there. For a start, the European Economic Community requires around 7,000 such animals to run their headquarter organisations in Brussels. Then there's NATO, with a staff of 2,200. As for all the multi-national commercial firms, like Rank Xerox, Esso, IBM, Philips, which have headquarters or departments in Brussels, they too require armies of executives who are able to move on demand from Rome to Paris, London to Brussels, different cities in different countries, but in each case they carry the same baggage and are for ever the same people: Euro-men.

I had the address of what sounded like a perfect specimen, in the Woluwe St Lambert district of Brussels. I had rung him in advance to ask if he could put me up for the night.

Wing Commander Terence Maddern, to give him his pre-1983 title, was a fellow student when I was at Durham University in the late 1950s. I have met his children in London, during their time at English boarding schools, and now at English universities, but I have never in all this time been to visit his home. It would have been a pretty hard thing to do anyway. In the last twenty-three years, he and his wife have had eleven different homes in five different countries.

At Durham, I remember him as being a keen sportsman, excellent at pole vaulting, rather reticent, even clipped, full of English restraint, but considered a good chap. He read Geography, I remember, so it was a bit of a surprise when I went to his wedding in 1961 to find him in RAF uniform. Since then, I think I have only seen him two or three times, and the last time must have been eight years ago.

I got a taxi to his address, wondering if Woluwe meant it was a Walloon district. When the taxi driver learned I was British, I was given a lecture on the awfulness of English football fans. He had been saving up his fury because since the Heysel stadium tragedy, he had had surprisingly few English people in his cab. 'Usually I have half a dozen a day, but since that match, people say they're Canadian, South African or Australian.'

I arrived at the flat before Terry and so I stood outside, wondering if I had got the right address. It was a modern block in a broad, suburban street, full of residential buildings, with an entry phone at the front door. I only had to wait five minutes before Terry arrived in his own car, straight from work. It was six-thirty in the evening.

His hair had gone grey since I'd last seen him, but lush and thick and distinguished, and he still looked the same weight, fit and healthy. His wife Margaret was abroad, visiting her parents, while the two children were still in England, due home the next week for the holidays. So he was on his own in the three bedroom, well appointed ground floor flat with its own back garden, a rented flat, but filled with their own furniture and possessions.

At Durham, he had been in the university Air Squadron and had joined the RAF straight afterwards as a pilot officer. At twenty-nine he was a squadron leader, very quick promotion for peace time. At the age of thirty-one he was sent to France as a liaison officer and attended the French War College. Then he became a staff officer for an Air Marshal and had a spell in London, at the Ministry of Defence.

The first ten years of his RAF career had been by far the most exciting, as he was then flying full time, in all the latest super jet fighters. The second ten years had been more administrative, but that is the nature of the beast, as you get older, though he had gone back to a spell of flying in his late thirties. He had fully expected to stay on until the age of fifty-five, hoping to manage further promotion, and then retire in the normal way.

By 1983, he was a Wing Commander in Germany. While looking through a list one day for a possible teaching job for his wife, he saw the NATO advert. It was to work in the Air Defences Systems Directorate in Brussels, a sort of senior civil service job, helping to plan the air defences for the sixteen member nations of Europe. It seemed tailor made for him. He had spent many years in defence. His RAF career had taken him to France and Germany, and he is fluent in both languages, and of course he had had Whitehall experience. Such an obvious job for him might never come his way again. So he applied and got it and took early retirement from the RAF.

But if his best fun had been flying, why did he not then wait and change to

some sort of flying job, rather than a civil service position, however important?

'Yes, I could have become a commercial airline pilot, but I never seriously contemplated it. When you've been trained all your life on Formula One racing cars, you can't suddenly change to driving a bus.'

It must have been strange, all the same, spending his whole career, which came to twenty-three years, being trained as a fighter pilot, without ever fighting.

'There is part of you that would like to have fought just once, because that's what every serving officer is preparing for, but I'm glad I did not have to experience it. Wars are always stupid. No one wants them, whoever wins.'

So I'd now got the story so far, and caught up with his life till he came to Brussels, and also put away quite a few beers. That's something I'd forgotten. He was always a keen beer drinker.

His new job has gone well and both he and his wife, who'd got a teaching job at the International School of Brussels, liked Brussels, the theatres and cinemas, the restaurants and amenities. The town was a good size, just one million, not too big. He felt he was at the heart of Europe.

'I'll be quite happy to stay here for ever, if that's the way it works out. Otherwise, I'll move somewhere else on the Continent. No, I have no desire to go back to living in England. I like it in Europe. I like Belgium. I liked Germany. I hardly miss anything about England, at all.'

He did not then go on to rubbish Britain, which is what so many exiles and colonials do, saying we've all gone to the dogs back home, the unions have taken over, no one works any more, we're now a backwater, etc. That might have been the implication, but he never said it. Instead, he stressed the many advantages of life in Brussels.

I found it so hard to put myself in his shoes. During his endless European changes, I have been a real stay at home, twenty-three years in the same house, with my children going to the same schools, never changing once, growing up in a community which I feel part of and have no intention of leaving. His children must be partly strangers to him, going off all those years to boarding school. I have had supper with mine almost every day of their lives. I have acquired so many roots it would now take a machete to hack me out of my various roots. Terry and his wife Margaret are now citizens of the world. I'm little more than an urban yokel.

'Another beer?' said Terry. 'Or would you like to go to a party?'

*     *     *

We drove a few streets away and came to a series of high, exclusive looking residential blocks, very popular with the international community.

As we walked down the silent, well carpeted corridors, trying to find the flat he was looking for, I examined several mail boxes, noting the spread of nationalities from their names, the copies of various foreign newspapers waiting to be picked up, the post from official organisations round the world.

The party was being given by one of Terry's colleagues at NATO, a German colonel and his wife, and it would be very much a NATO party. What a chance to see these exotic creatures at play. I wished I'd had Desmond Morris with me.

At first sight, all the men looked the same. It was impossible to tell anyone's nationality by his appearance. If anything, I would have said *all* of them were English, because there seemed so many short back and sides hair cuts, neat school boy partings, nice grey suits and sparkling white collars and club ties, often with an aeroplane symbol. They were giving those charming English smiles and nods, their heads slightly to one side, professionally interested, professional cocktail party goers and givers, Foreign Office types perhaps. I had not realised that every country's standard diplomatic type now looks and dresses like Major Thompson, the archetypal English gent, or what they would think of as the English gent. Even a Turkish officer I met had his club tie and Savile Row suit.

Listening to their conversations, as I moved round the various little groups, it was also impossible to tell their nationalities. I went past a group of four, all speaking English, but as I moved on, trying to decide on the next group, the first group had changed to speaking German, much to my surprise, all sounding very fluent and with hardly an accent. I looked back and saw that someone had joined their group, and like chameleons change colour, they had all changed their voices, automatically, without anything being said, moving effortlessly to whatever was now the new common denominator language.

I remarked on this to Terry and he said yes, there were actually very few English people present, perhaps only a couple, plus an American, but he reckoned that during the evening English would be the most spoken language, as it was at work. But if three Germans or three Italians found themselves all together, then naturally they would talk their own language, till someone else joined, then they would probably talk English.

**BRUSSELS** centremap
**BRUSSEL** centrum plattegrond
**BRÜSSEL** Stadtmitteplan
**BRUXELLES** plan du centre

I met an English woman from Yorkshire, married to a Frenchman, and she said she was definitely never going back to England. What on earth for? I met an American from Boston who said he was European and would never ever leave. Then I met a Belgian, born in Brussels, and I asked him what it was like, now that Euro-men had taken over his native city.

'It all started in 1958 when we had the World Exhibition. Then the EEC came here, and it never stopped. Building work has gone on full time since then. It's obviously very good for local business, but a lot of Belgians feel they have given up their own capital city. I live well out into the country now, so it doesn't matter to me.'

I caught his wife looking at her watch, very rude for diplomatic circles, and I realised, apart from me, she was the only person present not multi-lingual.

Beer was being served, by two young men filling glasses from a large barrel. Terry said they would be German soldiers, hired for the night by the Colonel. Almost everyone was drinking beer, though there was also whisky available. I'd requested wine when I'd arrived, not thinking for one moment this would be a beer party, but there was no wine. I don't think I've been to a beer party since I was a student. Every NW5 person, in every British town, serves wine today when they have company. Never beer. Very low class. Yet this party was full of high class European achievers, on handsome salaries, with tax free drinks available, all of them of Colonel level. Terry explained that the beer was special German beer.

I had a look round the German Colonel's flat, which was much the same as Terry's, with similar rooms and furniture, but with far fewer books on show. I found a set of Shakespeare in German, Henry Kissinger's Memoirs in French and John Kennedy's life story in English. In the lavatory, there was a little notice board with some cartoons pinned up, cut out from German newspapers. The style was just like Posy in the *Guardian*, or Feiffer in America.

I got talking to another Belgian who said that in fact all the people at the party were not the same, even though they were all NATO people. If I looked closely, I might with practise spot the difference. Firstly, there were the diplomats. These were members of official delegations, professional diplomats, doing a spell in Brussels, and no matter which country they were from, so he said, all diplomats were all the same and all boring. Then there were the military people. Naturally, they were not wearing uniform this evening, and usually did not, even at the office, but there were a lot of serving officers seconded to NATO, and as a rule these were the most aggressive people. They would eventually be going back to their commands at home, sure of their pension, very sure of their opinions, and they could get very stroppy. But now and again though, an aggressive military type would decide he was going to try to be diplomatic. Then that could be very funny. Thirdly, there were the International Civil Service types, people like Terry, hired directly by NATO, who might well have identical backgrounds to the other two types, be similar sorts of people, but they were the ones most under pressure. They were the most interesting to watch, to see if they would crack. It is, you see, very worrying, only being on a three year contract.

Goodness, what a lot I'd missed.

∗      ∗      ∗

We left about ten thirty, having had a smattering of cocktail food, the usual stuff, things on sticks, cheese biscuits with bits on, slices of quiche, all the normal middle class stand up party fare. We had intended to have a meal, but we were a bit late. We tried a Yugoslavian restaurant he often went to, but it was closed for the day, and then a Pizza place, but it closed just as we got there. Brussels is an excellent place for food and claims to have more Michelin awards for its size than Paris, but we were rather out in the suburbs.

We went back to his flat, for late night whiskeys, and I asked him about the three year contract business. Yes, it was true, but having your salary completely tax free was meant to make up for not having full security. Other NATO personnel, still employed by their home governments, paid their own country's tax, though they got generous allowances which were tax free. He expected to have his contract renewed for a second three years, and hoped for a third. Then he would have to wait and see. There is a NATO rule, apparently, that you have to complete ten or more years of service to become entitled to a retirement pension. At nine years, there was often a big fall out, when contracts were terminated, not necessarily because you were doing badly, but because the organisation claimed it needed new blood. It also meant they could get a younger person for the same job, at a lower salary, and save on the pension schemes. That could be a worrying time. To make up for this, you were offered a golden handshake. Terry was willing to take this chance and no, he didn't personally feel under any special pressure. All jobs of this level had certain pressures to them.

He poured me out another drink and then went off into a corner and started looking through masses of papers. He came back with what looked like a set of architect's plans – which indeed they were. The lease on his flat would be up in six months' time, so he had decided to build his own house, a four bedroomed, detached villa on the outskirts of Brussels, in a Flemish speaking area. It was costing him in all around £85,000, for the land and the building.

I suppose that showed how confident he was, and not under too much pressure, if he was taking this major step, putting down some roots in Brussels, despite being on a contract job. If he then had to move again in the future, then so be it. It wouldn't matter too much. They had moved around enough times in the past. But at present they both liked Brussels very much, the people, the work, and would be happy to stay, if that's the way things worked out.

Oh yes, except that Brussels did have a lot of dogs around. I was a bit lost by this remark. He said Brussels, I had been asking what he liked and didn't like about Brussels. The amount of dogs, that was about the only thing he had noticed which was not so good. And the locals did drive a bit wildly. But, apart from that, he liked everything.

I noticed he had several English language newspapers around. I picked up one called the *Bulletin*, a rather glossy news magazine. That's the local English language rag, quite good actually, everyone read it, even the French and Germans. Jolly good for adverts. I flicked through it and was quite impressed, making a note to try and find out more about it tomorrow.

There was also last week's *Sunday Times*. I said that must be a bore, at least it would be for me, getting the English Sunday papers so late, and of course without any of the colour magazines. I know when we're on holiday in Portugal every year that it's a drag to have to hang around till Monday lunch time, waiting for the Sunday papers. Then they cost a fortune, and have no mags.

This time Terry was a bit confused. He got the *Sunday Times*, delivered to his flat, with the magazine, every Sunday morning at nine o'clock. The service was better than when he had been stationed in Leuchars in Scotland or in Norfolk. I had to realise that Brussels was the international capital of Europe. Things were organised here.

Oh come on, I said. It must be some of your RAF chaps, flying them in by Lightning. No, a chappie comes to the door first thing on Sunday and shoves it through the letter box, just as they do in London. But Brussels isn't even on the coast, I said, it's deep in the middle of Belgium, about 100 miles from the Channel ports. No problem. Private enterprise, you see.

Someone had realised that, because of the enormous number of English speaking residents in Brussels, it was worth his while taking the night ferry to Dover, picking up several thousand copies of the first edition of the *Sunday Times*, then coming back to Brussels and hiring people to deliver them. He still made a profit, selling them at around £1.50 a copy, *with* the magazine. So much so, that the normal wholesalers and newsagents, selling the *Sunday Times* later on Sundays, without the mag, but at the same price, had been forced to supply it.

I went to bed thinking that perhaps life in Brussels was not so foreign after all. Euro-men can still carry their native habits around with them, that's if they're lucky enough to be English. I bet the Turkish delegates and the Greeks don't get their own Sunday newspaper with their Sunday breakfast.

Perhaps their working life was much more foreign. Terry had promised to take me to NATO next day. I'd seen them at home and at play. Now for the serious stuff.

*       *       *

We had Weetabix for breakfast, then he switched on the television. Oh, I thought, they have breakfast time tele in Belgium, how advanced. Then I recognised Selina Scott and Frank Bough. Some mistake surely here. My eyes are usually very poor in the morning. Come on, Tel, it's a video, flown in by the boys in blue, own up.

He picked up the remote control switch and in turn tried out sixteen different channels. It had never struck him before to see if other European stations did a breakfast show. If he watches TV in the morning, he tunes in to the BBC. I was amazed. Sixteen channels. It included all the major channels from Belgium, France and Germany, some cable companies, plus BBC TV, direct from London. He and Margaret watched BBC 1, or BBC 2, most of the time. Or listened to Radio 4. No luck with ITV, though. Well, you can't have everything.

We drove to the NATO HQ, which took about twenty minutes in his car, along several broad boulevards. There is a rush hour in Brussels, but it never lasts more than an hour.

'Look out for signs of crashes. It's an unusual morning when I don't see someone who's just had an accident.'

Was this a threat, or a promise? I didn't fancy seeing one, but I felt confident enough with Terry's driving. Twenty years as a fighter pilot, driving 1,000 miles an hour stuff, he must know how to handle machines. That morning, we didn't come across any bangs or bumps.

The NATO complex is on the north side of the city, not far from the airport, a series of low lying buildings in a large, landscaped park, surrounded by high wire fences. There was security at the front gate, and Terry showed his identity card, and then drove to his allotted car park space.

There were streams of men like Terry walking down all the corridors, neat grey suits, short hair, carrying brief cases, looking trim and important. There were also quite a few women, secretary figures, talking to each other while they walked. The men seemed to walk alone, in silence, only throwing off Hellos, in various languages, when they passed a colleague.

We came to another security desk where Terry signed me in and I got a special pass for the day. As I waited, I read a poster on the wall. *Gardez Contre les Indiscrétions*. Underneath was a cartoon of a worried-looking civil service figure being tempted by a big busty blonde, a man waving wads of bank notes and another offering a drink. All pretty simplistic, like a wartime *Beano*. It had never really struck me that Terry must be doing secret work and had signed the Official Secrets Act. The point of NATO is to counter any threat to the Alliance, such as from the Warsaw Pact countries, so there must be a lot of spying, on either side.

Terry shrugged it off. He had been under the Official Secrets Act since he first became an RAF pilot. It was second nature to him. He would never for one moment discuss anything at all confidential with me, or anyone else. I looked around at all the faces, searching for eyes that might hide spies. Later that day, I met someone who told me that the Security people reckon that at any one time, there are two spies working amongst NATO's 2,000 employees. Stands to reason. Law of averages.

'I wonder who the other is,' he added, with a smile. V. English joke. At least that was how I took it.

On the way in, we had passed a shopping complex, with a restaurant, café, barber's shop, travel agency, a bank, post office, dry cleaner's, and a news-agent. Terry queued up and bought his morning copy of *The Times*, as he does every day. All around him, his counterparts were buying *Figaro* and the *Frankfurter Allgemeine Zeitung*.

We went into the travel agency, where I checked the boat trains from Ostend. The assistant asked if Terry's wife had arrived safely in South Africa. That was where she had gone, to visit her parents. Terry had booked her tickets from here. Like all large Euro-institutions, life is arranged so you need hardly ever venture out beyond the perimeter fence.

We came at last to his office, which was regulation size for his rank, quite big, so it seemed to me. I admired his decorations on the wall, framed certificate or awards for his exploits in foreign parts, in the USA, Germany, France, and Great Britain. His French War College graduation certificate looked particularly impressive.

Now, Terry, take this carefully, what exactly do you do? I don't want any secrets. Just a simple outline. Don't confuse me with science.

I suppose I have been lucky in my life in that I have always been able to come home and tell my wife and family not just what I've done that day, whether interviewing someone, witnessing some event, but I've always been able to point to some proof that I have in fact *been* working, whether it was an article, a book or a programme. My children, naturally, have been totally unimpressed, but that is the way with offspring. But at least they *understand* how I put in each day, yawn, yawn.

Very slowly he explained the NATO Air Defence system, and all the various sub committees, the different geographical regions, and the philosophy behind it all, but I wasn't much wiser.

I noticed a huge pile of folders, documents and letters stacked neatly on his desk, to be ploughed through that day. So essentially it's just a clerical job, old son, pushing papers around? No, not really. As NATO staff, he and his colleagues act as the official secretaries, setting up meetings, writing up what happened, then getting out reports. I see. So it's secretarial? No, not so. An awful lot of work is put into getting a consensus, producing original papers and ideas, then trying to get agreements from all the other nation members and their delegates.

'Every nation has its own national interests. We hope they'll subjugate them, or temper them, for the common good, but this is hard for them. Every military decision causes some problems. If they were to agree for example to come in on a common European fighter, which is something we all hope will happen, then there will be industrial, political and economic interests to be considered at home. An idea has to be massaged towards common agreement. That's what *we* do.

'We can have our own private opinions, but they don't matter. It is our job as international civil servants to help bring about cohesion, to improve international communication, so that everyone understands each other and what is happening. Then if and when the Nations arrive at a common decision, we have to make it work.'

He is not aware of being British in any of this. His outlook is international, that's what he feels himself to be. But he suggested I should see an official NATO spokesperson, then I would get the overall view. He only knew the Air Defence part of it really well.

I eventually had an audience with NATO's chief spokesman, Robin Stafford, a by-line I recognised, back in the Sixties when he was a *Daily Express* foreign correspondent. He'd recently arrived at NATO after a similar job at SHAPE, running the Press Services. It seemed a bit unfair to ask him leading questions, when he'd hardly got into the saddle.

'Oh no, it's very easy to tell you what I do. My speciality is giving out statements which say nothing. When you have to have the agreement of sixteen nations, all you can normally agree on is the full stops and commas, if you're lucky. When a new policy is being discussed, I really can say nothing at all. It's all done by concensus. They talk in NATO about the Rule of Silence, which is exactly right. When a policy is being discussed, it is only said to be agreed when there is no objection – when there is silence. So what we are all listening for in life is silence.'

He saw the job as a great challenge and gets very upset when people, especially young people, criticise the work of NATO.

'They ask why we have to spend all these millions on defence, and why can't we get rid of nuclear weapons. I have to explain that there has been no war in Europe for forty years, the longest time ever in Europe, and that's because of NATO. Young people just don't appreciate this.

'NATO will never fire the first shot. All we are doing is building up deterrence. We have to be strong enough so that anyone who might think of attacking us, will think twice. They will realise there will be no profit in attacking us. So far, this strategy has worked.

'There are two sorts of deterrence – using conventional weapons and nuclear. At the moment, the Warsaw Pact countries are far superior in conventional weapons. We're ahead in nuclear. That means they will always think twice about starting a nuclear attack. What we have to do now is build up our conventional side. If they did attack us now with conventional weapons, we might be obliged to consider our nuclear weapons at an early stage. So we have to improve conventional, to put the threat of nuclear further away.'

*     *     *

I thanked him for his time, and went back to Terry's office to thank him, for his hospitality as well as his time.

I then caught a taxi into the centre of Brussels, clutching a huge wad of NATO literature which I'd been given. There were so many detailed graphs and lists, comparing the NATO forces with the Warsaw Pact forces, rifle for rifle, that I wondered if there was any point in spying. Why bother winkling out secrets when so much is published.

I was of course completely confused by most of the language, although at the back of the NATO Handbook there was a handy list of 200 'Abbreviations in Common Use'. Did you know Nammo meant Nato Multi Role Combat Aircraft Development and Production Management Organisation? I was interested to see that all the nastiest sounding nuclear missile things have terribly simple, wholesome names, such as Honest John, Lance, Buccaneer. That's just on the NATO side. On the Warsaw Pact side, they have Fishbed, Foxbat, Bear, Badger. It's as if they have both gone back to the nursery and searched Beatrix Potter for harmless titles.

I'd chatted with Terry's secretary, a girl from Edinburgh who had worked in similar big organisations around the world, and she said there was a Natoese which was very difficult for newcomers to pick up. The acronyms are used as real words, which makes them very hard to crack. But they also have their own way with grammar. She was typing a document with the words 'iterative process' that morning, a very common NATO phrase, but even after eight years, she had no idea what it meant.

The language is I suppose the most foreign thing about Euro-life. You really need to be a Euro-man to understand it, though in private life, just to show they're human, many of the officials make jokes about the names, referring to NATO as the North Atlantic Travel Organisation. SHAPE, which properly stands for Supreme Headquarters Allied Powers Europe, is often known as Super Holidays At Public Expense . . .

# ~ *Chapter Twenty-Two* ~

# Brussels and Home

*Railway ramblings on the Central Station;*
*a visit to the Bulletin;*
*our hero talks to some Young Americans*
*and postulates a theory; a truly modern boat;*
*the peculiar odour of arriving home in the*
*Great Wen.*

I got to Brussels Central Station and dumped my bags in the left luggage. I had a few hours to put in before it was time to catch the boat train home. Should I do a few sites. Brussels did look much more splendid than I remembered it from thirty years earlier, when I'd been hitch hiking round Europe and spent the night at a very dirty, very crowded youth hostel. No, I felt like a rest from sites or Sights. When in doubt, have a coffee.

I bought a magazine and sat in a station bar called the Taverne Stephenson. And I felt quite proud. How apt to be leaving Europe thinking of my old friend George. All the way by train across Germany and Belgium I'd been looking for a chance to talk railways with chance passengers, but had found no one with any interest in the subject, yet in all their coaches, both countries were proudly boasting that the year 1985 was the 150th anniversary of their national railways, listing the big celebrations and processions that were taking place. In each case, George and Robert Stephenson had been responsible for their first locomotives. King Leopold of the Belgiums even gave George a Knighthood. Such a pity that the world does not realise that it was a rough Geordie, who never went to school, who gave the world railways. Each country thinks it invented railways by itself. In fact the Russians and Americans are absolutely convinced.

I flicked over the pages of the magazine, which were in English and quite easy to read, and understand. 'Caroline, high class massage and escort, at your place or mine. I also can visit Antwerp.' 'Sybil, charming and attractive escort, Rue Edith Cavell. Easy parking.' 'Lore – High class hostess, any time, at your place or mine.'

Should I investigate the Euro-call girls? Young gentlemen on Grand Tours very often did, especially in Italy. Very reassuring about the easy parking, and jolly kind to offer her place or mine. It could be sociologically quite interesting to see how the oldest profession was getting on in Europe these days. No, I was too tired for such excitements.

I contemplated a flea market being held by the First Brussels British Scout Association, that sounded fun, or a charity jog organised by the Irish Club. Or I could audition for the American Theatre Company, they're terribly in need of new men, or watch the Royal Brussels Cricket Club play the Antwerp Cricket Club. Even more exciting.

I realised I was reading the *Bulletin*, the English language magazine which Terry had recommended. It was clearly a very serious, well produced news magazine, judging by the editorial pages, but as ever, it's the small ads in any mag which give away the flavour of its readers, the quick sales that have to be made as Euro-men and women rush to their next posting, having to get rid of their German beds, Italian chairs, American pine dressers, their Japanese videos. And all the flats being advertised as 'very handy for EEC'.

There was one announcement which puzzled me at first. 'Century House Old Boys, meet in the Drum, 25 Avenue d'Auderghem at 6 pm on last Monday of each month.' It could have been some prep school get together, then I remembered that Century House, in South London, is the HQ of MI6, Britain's counter espionage agency. Spies like get-togethers and reunions just like any other group. And there must be lots of them in Brussels, hidden under the woodwork.

*    *    *

I finished my coffee and went to find a phone, having decided what I would most like to do for my last couple of hours in Brussels. I dialled the *Bulletin* and asked for the editor, Aislinn Dulanty, reading it off the masthead, and probably getting the pronunciation wrong. He or she could be Indian, French, Celtic.

A gentle, refined female voice eventually answered, English with traces of Irish. She was polite, but obviously very wary. I always feel sorry for people when I do this to them, ringing out of the blue and trying to pinch some of their precious time. If people do it to me, passing through London, I'm usually very inhospitable. I chuntered on about my project, who I was, what I'd been doing, and finally talked her into a quick bite over lunch. I'd caught her on press day, and everything had now gone to bed, so she was waiting for the first copies.

It took me over an hour to walk there, as it was miles down an enormous street called the Avenue Louise, and I got caught in a downpour. Luckily, I had my neat little fold-up umbrella, very European, which I'd carried everywhere. No hand-bag, though. Still not got round to one of those.

The *Bulletin* office was very smart and modern looking with a receptionist working away at a word processor. Aislinn Dulanty looked a bit exhausted when she appeared, but interesting in a Diane Keaton tweedy clothes sort of way. She led me round the corner to a little café where we ordered toasted sandwiches and coffee. She doesn't drink at lunch time. I had my coffee, then I had wine. It was my last Euro-meal. I had to catch the boat train at three o'clock. A time for celebration.

Aislinn had gone to school in England, despite her Irish ancestry, because her father, John Dulanty, a poor Irish boy, who had risen from the gutter, was appointed the first ever Irish Ambassador to the Court of St James. She's always wished she had written down his life story. His career was remarkable.

She married an Austrian, had two daughters, moved to Israel, but things didn't work out. It was chance that someone said come and stay in Brussels for a few months, I'll put you up. So she went, with her two young daughters. That was twenty years ago. After radio work and freelance writing, she joined the *Bulletin* in 1968 as editor.

When she arrived, it still had a pre-war look to it, covering cricket matches and English flower shows. Now she feels its base is more mid-Atlantic, catering for the whole English speaking community in Belgium, not just Brussels. Its circulation is 12,000, while the readership is estimated at 60,000.

People still think it is an *English* magazine, which upsets her, and at cocktail parties her more liberal friends, of which she has many, complain about the right wing attitudes of one of her columnists, Eric Kennedy, who is always lashing out at modern youth.

'There still is a very large English community here. There's a Shakespeare Society, Comedy Club, Choral Society, Madrigal Society. The time to see the English coming out en masse is the first night of a Gilbert and Sullivan Society production. It's always packed. You see these terribly old-fashioned Brits in their clothes and hair styles, who talk like actors from a 1950s' British movie. They toast the Queen on almost all possible occasions. But their own children are quite normal, that's the interesting thing. Just like 1980s' teenagers anywhere.'

She's active in an English-speaking feminist group, though she was a bit reluctant to give me its name, as it's so awful. 'Okay then, we're called WOE. It stands for Women's Organisation for Equality. But it's a thriving group and we have a lot to do because abortion is still illegal in Belgium.'

She sees herself staying. Her daughters are now grown up, one working as a professional singer in Brussels, the other as a journalist in Rome. She feels European, neither Irish nor English any more, but like all other local Brits, she was shocked when the Brussels football disaster took place.

'For weeks people have been ringing or writing to the *Bulletin* saying they were ashamed to be British. I've even had readers telling me that they have removed their GB plates from the cars. That shows you how bad it was.'

This time, on my way back to the station, I kept very quiet and so avoided any trouble with the taxi driver.

\* \* \*

There was a very thin, rather scruffy looking young man watching me as I was waiting on the platform. He came and sat down beside me, wearing a dirty flat cap and carrying a very worn canvas sports bag. He kept on looking at me, studying my bag, trying to read my label. I decided to be English and reserved for once, something I find very hard to do.

'You from London?' he asked.

'As a matter of fact, yes, actually,' I said, carrying on reading my mint copy of the *Bulletin*, fresh from the presses.

'You're so lucky, living in London.'

I turned over a few more pages, thinking perhaps he was a bit potty.

'London is full of stars.'

What kind of stars could he mean? His English did seem remarkably good, for someone who could be potty.

'Do you know Laurence Olivier?'

'Not personally.'

'I've got Alec Guinness, but I dream about getting Laurence Olivier. Can you help me?'

'Well, not really, why don't you look up his agent, write to him . . .'

'I've done all that, and the BBC, and three film studios, but he hasn't answered. That's how I got Charlton Heston. He replied by return. I read somewhere he was filming in London, so I wrote off. I've also got Ingrid Bergman. I went to London in 1976 to try and meet her. I got her autobiography and a photograph of me with her. I did the same in 1972. I was trying to photograph Jerry Lee Lewis, but he broke my camera. How about Elizabeth Taylor? Have you an address for her? I write letters and letters every week. It would be my dream come true to get her autograph. I love all stars. I dream about all stars.'

Now it so happens that I collect autographs. I've got every British Prime Minister since Walpole, all forty-nine, plus a terribly good collection of Poet Laureates. I also have some interesting Suffragettes. I might not have met any railway fans on my travels, or stamp enthusiasts, which are my other hobbies, but here was a fellow autograph hunter, just dying to be friendly.

He was a postman, living in Liège, and on night shifts he spent his spare time writing requests to film stars all over the world. He wrote down his name, Jean-Claude Jamar, and his address, and I promised faithfully to let him know if I heard of a good Olivier going cheap, or an Elizabeth Taylor. Then we shook hands and I caught my train.

*      *      *

I dozed off soon after I got on the Boat Train, and slept the first hour or so after Brussels, then I woke up and looked out and found we were going through Ghent. Only a few days previously I had gone through Aix, or Aix-la-Chapelle, or Aachen as it's now called. I tried to remember what the Good News was that Robert Browning wrote about in his famous poem. I don't suppose it is famous any more. My own children never learned it at school.

Browning did the route by coach, when he first travelled this way in 1834, as George Stephenson had still not launched himself onto the Continent. He was actually heading for Russia, a 1,500-mile journey from Ostend to St Petersburg, which he had to do all the way by coach and horses, night and day, for week after week. What a journey. No wonder the rhythm of the route still haunted him, when he came to write the poem, many years later.

At Ghent, two rucksacks got in, followed by two young Americans, both from San Jose, California, both newly graduated from University. They had done almost the precise European route I had taken, so naturally we compared notes. In Naples they had had their pockets picked, just as I nearly had my things stolen in Milan. It always seems to be in Italy that nasty things happen to tourists. Or is it because we tend to spend a longer time there?

'We decided in Europe not to advertise that we were Americans,' said the girl. 'We had been told in Germany there was a lot of anti-US missile feeling. The Canadians we've met always have a maple leaf on their packs. So they're not mistaken for Americans, I s'pose. Yet the funny thing is that wherever we've been in Europe, and sat down in a restaurant, we've been given the English menu. How do they know? I think it must be our blue jeans.'

They had been travelling for two months on an average budget of thirty-five dollars a day. Half way through, though, they had begun to cheat, as they realised they were not eating very well. 'So in every big city we had one big meal, and I put it on my Visa charge card. We'll have two months to pay it off when we get back to the States.'

They were carrying a small tent, and hoped to get a camp site most nights, or a cheap pension. The trouble with camp sites was that they were often miles out of town and it took hours finding the right buses and getting there, often ending up lost. 'But the camp sites are very good, far better than in America. You get rows of sinks in Europe and proper showers. In the places we've used in the States you're lucky to get one tap.'

The currency had confused them most of the time, going from country to country, so in the end they split it. She was in charge of paper money. He worked out the coins. But they still got confused.

'We were a bit disappointed by Venice,' she said, 'but it was raining all the time. Then in Naples we went all the way to see Pompeii – and it was closed. We had to choose that one day. So we went out to the island of Ischia instead and that was wonderful.'

'We were glad to leave France,' he said. 'That was the only place we felt people were a bit cool, though on the Metro, which everyone had warned us about, people were so friendly.'

'I didn't like Rome or Paris. They just reminded us of LA. Big and noisy with traffic. London was a bit better, thanks to Hyde Park. That was marvellous, having such an enormous park right in the middle of the city. On the whole, we enjoyed the countryside most of all.

'I think we'd have to say that the best places of all the places we went to were Bavaria and Switzerland, that was so clean. Then after that the Cotswolds. And the ice cream from Vivoli's in Florence. Gee, that's the best in the whole world. . . .'

*   *   *

What had been my best? It's the game most travellers play, when they're on their way home, going over the mental tracks, flicking through the images. The French section of the Orient-Express had been magnificent, especially the first sight of it at Boulogne. Then dancing on the train with those matronly ladies. In Brussels, while walking through the town, I'd noticed a branch of the Nagelmackers Banks. I'd meant to stop and go in, but it was raining and I was late. It was strange to see again the name of the family which had created the Orient-Express, right at the very end of my journey.

Harold Acton's garden and the preparations for the Palio in Siena, they would both be in my mind for many years, and the long lunch in the village that turned out not to be Jimmy Jimmy. And, from now on, I'll always turn first to the Italian league in the *Guardian* on a Monday morning, just to see how Sampdoria got on. Those West Indian ladies, fresh from the Pope. I can see them now. Not much from the Rhine cruise, which is strange. All those castles have rolled into one, but I can remember waking in my suite in Baden Baden and thinking there's a five minute walk ahead, just to get up and open those curtains. When I get back to London, I must ring Carol the Croupier. I do want to know what she did next.

Just another European journey, one that has been made by millions over the last four hundred years, following very much a Grand Tour route. Was it fair to call it a Grand Tour? Strictly speaking, that belongs to the 17th and 18th century, but I have stretched it well into the 19th century to include the glorious age of the train. You certainly can't count aeroplane travelling as Grand in any way.

I think there are still grand tourists today, with small letters of course. In fact

I'd just recently been talking to two of them. You can't call them Grand as they travel without servants, nor do they stay at the best hotels, or look up the local princelings, which was what I'd tried to do, at least their modern equivalents.

But these modern day grand tourists do have lots in common with the original versions. They have time and leisure on their side and are willing and able to stop and stare for a few weeks at a time. They are heading for Italy, as ever, and are always on the look out for cultural, educational, natural and pleasurable experiences.

They tend to be young, which most of them were in the olden days, either pre or post university. Charles James Fox was only fourteen when he went on his tour. The Earl of Carlisle was a boy of seventeen. But in those days they had tutors or companions to accompany them. Today, they are more likely to be around 18–24-year-old young men. And also young women. As in the old days, most of them know they are not likely to go that way again. It's a once and only trip, as they are unlikely to have so much time ever again.

Today's rucksackers are the modern equivalent of the Grand Tourist, setting out with eyes wide open to behold strange lands, to see for themselves what each country considers its best paintings, best architecture, finest landmarks. You can't call the package tourist to the Costa Brava a grand tourist, even if the package does take in five centres in fourteen days. They never leave themselves.

The rucksackers might not have the means of the lordlings, but then not all those gentlemen had money. Think of the young Wordsworth with his bundle on his back, the young Thackeray sleeping on the coals.

They did in the past have much more time, but there are British and American students these days who take a whole year off, to ease their way round Europe. And the Australians, they often spin Europe out for up to two years.

I suppose, as long as Europe is there, tourists will grandly decide to tour it. Leisurely.

*     *     *

The boat train arrived at Ostend on time and I joined the queue for the Jet Foil. I found myself standing beside another single bloke and we got talking in the Jet Foil lounge. I'd been calling it Tin Foil in my mind, making mock, but he said no, it really was a great piece of engineering. He had come over on it the previous day and had loved it.

He was called Peter and was in the Civil Service, about to be moved to Brussels. Yet another Euro-man in the making. He was joining the British delegation to work on Infrastructure. I resisted the temptation to ask him what that meant. I still hadn't got Air Defence Supports Systems straight.

He loved the Civil Service. Oh yes, always had done. He knows that British people make jokes about it, how boring, how can you stand it, but personally he can't think of a better life. He started as a basic, lowest grade clerk doing the wages at Portsmouth Dockyard. Now, twenty years later, after exciting postings from Scotland to Whitehall, he was a higher executive officer, with the prospect of this plum job in Brussels, the heart of Europe, to look forward to. As we talked, I enjoyed his enjoyment. He also turned out to be a stamp and postcard collector. Oh joy.

The boat was very comfortable, if boat is the correct term. It looked like a boat, a sort of large speed boat, but it rode through the water on two horizontal steel foils, like water skis. It is computer steered, so I read on the back of my duty free leaflet, propelled by two water jets. Its cruising speed is forty-five knots, which I take to be about fifty miles an hour.

We were across in just over 1½ hours in complete comfort, no more unsteady than travelling by train. It was a very calm day, which helped.

The white cliffs of Dover looked so dramatic, one famous view which never disappoints. They are white, and they are definitely cliffs, and they do grab hold of the eye, whatever the weather, whereas the opposite French coast is so dreary and unmemorable.

As I stepped ashore, I remarked to Peter that it didn't smell different. England had no English smell. Then I realised I had got things the wrong way round. Today there is no European smell. Since leaving the South of Germany, I was not aware of any funny foreign smells. With my eyes closed, I could have been anywhere. Yet as a boy, on my first trip to Europe, to that little north French town of Abbeville, smells of every sort were overpowering. Have we changed? Have they changed? I suppose we are all eating the same funny foreign foods these days, smoking the same sort of cigarettes, shoving on the garlic and herbs like our Euro-brothers.

The Mediterranean still smells quite different to English nostrils, but that's because of the sun and the heat and the vegetation which even the marvels of modern science are not going to be able to import to Britain. But in Northern Europe, so much of our life, the sights and sounds, are becoming standardised, even if our NATO fighter jets are not.

There could be worse to come. As I write, plans for a Channel Tunnel have at long last been officially agreed upon, after discussions and arguments, fantasies and plots, which have gone on since 1802. In the future, we'll be tied even more to Europe, not just by smells and life styles, but by a physical cord. Sailing across the Channel was a huge event for all Grand Tourists in the past, a spiritual experience, and countless poets and novelists, pilgrims and adventurers as well as ordinary travellers wrote endlessly about it. Will a short train ride in a boring tunnel be ever worth recording? And will the White Cliffs of Dover lose their point completely, if on returning home we can't actually see them? When the Channel Tunnel is eventually completed, the sense of setting out on a Grand Tour might, after all these centuries, finally come to an end.

ENGLAND

*NORTH SEA*

HOLLAND

**London**   **Dover**   Bruges
**Folkestone**   Ghent   Antwerp
Brighton   **Ostende**   **Brussels**
   Calais   Liège   **Cologne**
*ENGLISH*   **Boulogne**   BELGIUM   Spa   **Aachen**
*CHANNEL*   **Verviers**   **Koblenz**
   **Abbeville**   Frankfurt
Le Havre   Dieppe   Amiens   LUXEMBOURG   Würzburg
   Rouen   **Mainz**   Nuremberg
   Reims   **Heidelberg**
   *R. Seine*   **Paris**   Stuttgart   *R. Danube*
   **Baden-**   Augsburg
   **Baden**   Ulm   Salzburg
Orléans   Munich
*R. Loire*   Dijon   **Basel**   Zurich   Innsbruck   **AUSTRIA**
   *R. Saône*   Bern   **Lucerne**   Trento   Trieste
F R A N C E   Lausanne   **SWITZERLAND**   **St Gotthard**
   Geneva   **Simplon**   **Chiasso**   Padua   **Venice**
   Lyon   **Domodossola**   *ADRIATIC*
   *R. Rhône*   **Milan**   Verona   *SEA*
   Turin   **ITALY**
   Bologna   Ravenna
   **Genoa**   San Marino
   La Spezia   **Florence**
Monaco   *LIGURIAN*   **Pisa**
   Nice   *SEA*   **Sienna**
   Cannes

EAST GERMANY
(D.D.R.)

CZECHO-
SLOVAKIA

G E R M A N Y

*R. Rhine*

*R. Mosel*

*R. Rhine*

*PISA*

*FLORENCE*

ELBA

**CORSICA**

Rome

**SARDINIA**

Miles
0      60

0      100
Kilometres

*MEDITERRANEAN SEA*

DJC